THE MASTERLESS MEN

'An action-packed story, with
lots of thrills and excitement'
Publishing News

THE
MASTERLESS
MEN

J. K. Mayo

PAN BOOKS

First published 1995 by Macmillan

This edition published 1995 by Pan Books
an imprint of Macmillan General Books
25 Eccleston Place, London SW1W 9NF
and Basingstoke

Associated companies throughout the world

ISBN 0 330 33782 3

1 3 5 7 9 8 6 4 2

A CIP catalogue record for this book is available from
the British Library

Photytypeset by Intype, London
Printed and bound in Great Britain

THE MASTERLESS MEN

Chapter One

John Hynd came off the hills late in the afternoon. It was one of those spring days when squalls of rain came dense and heavy off the sea. In the intervals between the squalls it might have been a different land, another climate. The sky was a brilliant blue and the clouds flying over his head shone white in the sun.

It would have been a perfect day for him if he had not known there was a watcher up there. He had sensed it a week ago, and tried at first to shrug it off, but the feeling had been with him too long to be ignored. Now it was no longer a sense, an intuition: now it was knowledge.

Whoever it was was good at it. Hynd had seen nothing, not the flash of light on a lens or an alien shape on the skyline. Up high he had seen no movement of nervous deer, and lower down no run of startled sheep. He had heard no cry of disturbed pheasant breaking from the bracken, no alarm call from curlew fearful for its nest.

No one had approached his house. If Hynd had been within it he would have known, and if he had been away he would have known on his return. Day or night, he would have known. He would have known it as surely as a fox in his lair would have known.

As he came up the knoll to the house the sunlight went again and the stormclouds came in from the west. He went inside and hung the ancient nine-foot greenheart trout rod on a hook in the hall. He laid the three small trout, which he had gutted and washed in the loch, on the stainless steel draining board beside the sink.

He threw off his wet clothes, stirred and fed the wood stove at the living-room end of the big L-shaped space which had a dining-table further down the stem, hung the wet garments on a clothes-horse beside the stove, and went down to the kitchen which formed the foot of the L. He put the trout to fry in butter, and spring greens in cold water ready to cook, and went to the bathroom to shower.

He was out again in five minutes, towelling himself as he walked back to the stove to switch on the heat under the cabbage.

In his bedroom he pulled on thick cords, a woollen shirt, and an Orkney sweater, and then he went outside. He climbed to the top of the knoll behind the house, and looked west. The peninsula stretched away from him in a wild landscape of rock and bracken and heather towards its tip a few miles away. Beyond that a path of fire streamed across the sea to where the sun lay at the foot of the sky.

In the birch copse to his left a blackbird celebrated the refulgence with which the day was ending, but on his right, where rough grazing land fell to the seashore, gulls debated with melancholy cries the prospect of worsening weather and the wisdom of a shift inland. Down on the shore bullocks on the rough pasture hung together before the onset of the dark, and watched one of their fellows, still out there on the rocks, working his way back to join them.

They were clumsy beasts to look at, but they were as accustomed to these rocks as wild goats to mountain crags, and Hynd had one day seen a bullock out there exchanging looks with a seal bobbing on the swell.

For him this was an edge of the world. It was why he had come here.

With the purity of the evening light before him, the curlew wheeping sadly on the moors, and the sheep calling in their lambs for the night; with the sun descending now – in this its last moment of the day the very shield, the blinding golden shield of Apollo – below the rim of the ocean; with fresh-caught trout cooking for his supper; with Boyle's extraordinary biography of Goethe, and whatever choice of music he might make, waiting to fill his evening; and not another human being in sight: with the wealth of these miracles of myth and nature the blood of his life was filled.

He turned and went down to the house. It was as plain a house as you could find, a loghouse imported from Norway, a house close to nature. Inside as out the walls were the round trunks of pine, unvarnished with any kind of decoration: the one big L-shaped room, the bedroom and the bathroom, it was simplicity itself.

The last of the clouds that had come off the sea had settled on the hills, black in the day's afterlight. Where was the watcher now? For a man as instinctual as Hynd, as given to accept the symbolisms of the day as others to trust their horoscopes, to face now that black sky with the last image of the blazing sun still on his eye was to confront the foreboding that the past was return- ing to force itself upon him.

When he had eaten, he stretched out on the couch with Boyle's Goethe, but after he had read three pages and found he had absorbed none of it, he laid the book aside.

He went to a window. It was that time of half-dark when he could see through his reflection to the young and waxing moon. The reflection showed a face lean and honed that had a hard look to it, with black hair cut short like a brush, and a body wiry with energy. That was what the reflection showed. What the moon saw was a man in the equipoise between peace and action; and it saw that the force driving him towards action was anger.

He went into the passage that ran to the front door. It was a passage without windows, private from the outside world. He opened the cupboard where his coats hung and shoved them to either end of the rail. He put a hand up to the wall and released a bolt, and then knelt on the floor and pressed down, and a section of the wooden planking revolved on a central shaft and became vertical.

From the cavity below came a smell of gun oil. Hynd was looking down at a small arsenal: two rifles, a sub-machine gun, and four pistols. He took out one of the pistols and hefted it in his hand and laid it beside him; and then with more care, with the appearance almost of tenderness, though this may have been due to its weight for it was a heavy weapon, lifted out a rifle.

This was the Belgian FN 7.62mm. He rested it on his thighs and from the arsenal lifted an image-intensifier. He was about to fit it to the mount when his jaw stiffened, and he looked off to one side and nodded a few times, as if he had decided something. He waited in whatever abstraction it was that had come to him a while longer, and then as if he had thought a thing through smiled a little: not a pleasant smile.

He put the nightsight back in the cavity, replaced

also the rifle and pistol, and took out a narrow dagger. He drew it from its sheath and tried point and edge. The knife had a black handle and a black blade, the blade nine inches long. He pushed the section of floor back as it had been, stood up with the knife in his hand, and replaced the bolt that secured the trap in the floor.

After that he resumed, more or less, the evening that he had begun after his supper. The only difference was that he drew the shutters and read at the table, so that he might whet the knife as he went.

For music he had Mozart's divertimento in E flat for string trio. This was not fortuitous: it was apt to Goethe, and it was apt to what was in his mind, the nature of the English. Earlier in the week he had listened to a man, English but Austrian by birth, on *Desert Island Discs*, and one of the records he had chosen had been the E flat divertimento, and chosen it also as the record he would have had had he been allowed only one.

As to the nature of the English: the man had been asked if he felt himself to be British, and his answer was no, you can hear my Austrian accent, I feel myself to be a Middle-European intellectual who lives in England. Asked thereafter (according to the format of the programme) what book he would want to have with him in addition to the Bible and Shakespeare's works, he said the collected Goethe. This was forbidden him, on the ground that he would already have thrust upon him the collected works of the Bard, so Gombrich contented himself with Goethe's poems.

How very English, Hynd had thought, to be so inflexible as not to see that for a native German-speaker, no matter how used he was to English, the collected

Goethe would be as the Shakespeare was for an English castaway.

He bent close over the knife, and the bright silver edge of the blackened steel gleamed at him, and lit an answering gleam in his eye. Economy of means was one of the merits that had commended this piece by Mozart to the Austrian.

Economy of means: Hynd slid the knife back in its sheath, and went to bed.

This was at ten o'clock. The alarm roused him at one. He dressed, in the dark, in the clothes he had put off three hours earlier, with the difference that he pulled dark socks up over the ends of the trousers and wore a second sweater, a navy blue fisherman's jersey. He put blacking on his face and hands, put on black leather gloves, and slotted the sheathed knife onto his belt.

There was no way to know where the watcher, or watchers, might be. He left the house by the front door, as the lesser of two evils. The door at the back of the house, which opened onto the garden, was glass, and its movement might have caught the moon.

He slipped out and closed the door soundlessly. Crouched low, he ran for fifty yards along the sheep-cropped grass and then went to the ground, and waited there until he felt himself one with the night.

The quarter moon, now well along the sky, shone palely, masked by the rising mist, and Hynd welcomed the richness of the dark about him as a gift. He had walked this peninsula by day and night, and knew it like the back of his hand.

When he had chosen the way he would go, he set off eastward, moving at a fair pace but without haste, for he had time enough for what he wanted to do. Every so often he stopped to listen into the wind and look about him into the dark, and, as he gained higher ground, into the mist. On all the ten miles or so he covered he heard nothing that spoke of another human being abroad. He would hear a sheep cough, the squeal of a rabbit falling to a weasel, the bark of a fox, an oyster-catcher's piping; and later, as he walked up a small glen, with not far to go to reach the place he had chosen, an outburst of birdsong came from a thrush anticipating the dawn in a fir plantation on the right. The trees were hidden in the mist, but he knew they were there.

You could not walk at night in this country unless you knew it. These were hills he was walking on, not mountains, but to slip over a twenty-foot drop could do you as much harm as a fall off a mountain precipice.

When he came to the ridge he wanted, it was not yet five o'clock. He advanced warily to the lair in which he intended to lie up, in case the watcher had found it and made it his own; although he did not seriously believe that whoever it was was sleeping rough, rather than harbouring by night in some hotel a good distance away.

The lair was empty. It was a deep recess under an overhang of rock, which gave four feet of headroom at its extremity and sloped to two feet at the back; a dry place where a man could lie full-length and be out of the weather.

He stood there for a minute or two with his back to the stony ridge, staring into the mist, listening, sensing, opening himself to the night. For Hynd, to travel on foot across this wilderness in the mist under the invisible stars, to hole up in that cleft in the rock behind him and wait for dawn, wait alone in the dark until it was time to stalk his prey, gave fulfilment to the atavistic spirit in him. Who might not have stood here four, five thousand years ago, lain in the same den, waiting for what the day might deliver up to him?

'Perhaps me, myself,' Hynd said aloud, and meant it.

He took off the top sweater, the oiled fisherman's jersey, and shook the damp from it as best he could, then he folded it twice and crawled in under the rock and put it there for a pillow, and stretched out. It was hard-lying and it was cold; but this was no more than discomfort, and would last for only a few hours.

He made a fist and put the flat of it against the rock over his head. In his bones he felt the weight of the rock above him, and the depth of it under his back.

Voices woke him.

Looking out from his lair he saw two men standing in sunshine with their backs to him, and far beyond them the sea. They were no more than thirty feet away and he heard clearly what they were saying.

' . . . not a thing else. Nobody has come to the house, he walks his fifteen or so miles every day, sometimes with a rod, once with a gun, never goes home empty-handed. Living off the land, so far as he can. Very like the man.'

'What did he shoot?'

'That day? Two rabbits and a barnacle.'

'A barnacle?'

'A goose. Illegal, of course.'

'Much that would worry Hynd.'

'He has his own game laws. The day he was out with the gun there were a parcel of hares being mad, the time of year, you know. A shot like Hynd, he could have got two of them before the others knew it. He just lay there and watched them. Watched them a long time.'

The other man was playing with a pipe. He turned out of the wind to get it going, and Hynd saw his profile, saw both their profiles when the other turned to him, the tobacco smoke between them being whipped off the pipe by the breeze. He knew the man with the pipe, he had known the voice.

'What's so special about hares?'

'For Hynd? It's not for me to say. But the hare is a special creature. Myth and magic, the hare.'

'Myth? Magic? Do we know this about Hynd?' the man with the pipe said. 'I thought Hynd was as steady a man as you would find.'

Even at thirty feet, even as the other man's face turned away from him again to face the sea, Hynd believed he saw amusement on it.

'It is possible,' the amused and younger man said, 'to apprehend the mythic quality of the hare and still be a steady man.'

'Not in my book,' the other said.

'A thin volume,' the amused man said.

Their proximity was more than Hynd had bargained for. He had expected to be able to turn the tables on the watcher, to lie low on top of the ridge behind him and wait for the man to show himself; and now there were two of them, and on his very doorstep. He decided to turn this to his own advantage, and make a demonstration.

Hynd crept out of his lair and came upright. He grimaced as he felt the stiffness in him, and made a full body stretch, keeping an eye on the men standing with their backs to him, surveying the landscape on which they hoped, doubtless, he would appear.

He jounced on his toes, for a moment held himself still, tensed like a runner at the start of a race, and then simultaneously pulled the knife from its sheath and walked forward, fast and light on his feet.

He came up behind them, knocked the man on his left to the ground with a punch to the back of the neck, and seized the other in a throttling armlock and stuck the knife through coat, jacket, shirt and skin, being assured of the last when his victim stopped struggling, for the point of the blade was within an inch of his kidneys.

Hynd eased the pressure on the throat. 'Spit the pipe out, Halkett,' he said, 'and tell your young friend to lie quietly on the ground.'

'That's a damn dangerous punch, Hynd,' the man on the ground said. 'You might have killed me.'

'I might indeed,' Hynd said, 'but I didn't, so now we can sit around and talk. Nice morning for it.'

He let go of Halkett, who gagged and shook his head and stooped to pick his pipe off the grass. He straightened up, feeling for the damage the knife had done.

'You are such a bastard, Hynd,' he said. 'You know perfectly well this is a good coat. There was absolutely no need for any of this. Now how will it look? And my suit?'

'They'll look very neatly patched,' Hynd said, 'or they would if you weren't such a bourgeois kind of snob. As it is you can give them to Oxfam. It's called making a virtue of necessity. Now, kindly sit yourself on the grass where I can see you. And do tell that lad not to draw his pistol.'

'Raleigh,' Halkett said. 'Leave it alone.'

Hynd sat on a boulder and looked about him. A shining breezy spring day, lambs gambolling down on the hillside, the sea far off, five miles or so, your true caerulean sea-colour, a fine greeny-blue with the wavetops turning whitely: wavetops turning, Hynd registered automatically, wind force five. How he looked forward to breakfast.

Meanwhile, he contemplated Halkett and Raleigh. Halkett was a black-a-vised man with dark hair, and a thick moustache with a flavour of ginger to it under a strongly hooked nose. Hynd knew him for an unpredictable mixture of the hot-head and the phlegmatic, and a man with some power in him, and on the same scale some intelligence and some capacity. He was sitting on the damp grass with his knees up, rummaging with the pipe in his tobacco pouch. Other men in his situation might have lost face, but not Halkett.

Raleigh was tall, thin, pink, and white, with short fair hair, probably quite tough. He looked like a man for cities, but he had done well enough out here, watching Hynd for a week without being sighted. And he knew about hares.

He wanted to go for that gun, though. Young – well, youngish, not so young as he had seemed at first sight – and foolish.

'I think I'd better have his pistol,' Hynd said.

'Give it here,' Halkett said. 'Bring it out with just two fingers on the butt, that's what Hynd would like you to do.'

'He's only got a knife,' Raleigh said.

'You are an ignorant, stupid, vainglorious little shit,' Halkett said nicely. 'He'd have that knife in your gizzard

11

before you had time to shoot yourself in the foot, never mind get a bullet into him.'

He held out a hand with the tobacco pouch dangling from it, pinched between his fingers. Raleigh, the pink patches on his face pinker and the white areas whiter, got up and went to him. He pulled the pistol out from his anorak and laid it on the flat of Halkett's hand.

Halkett extended the arm towards Hynd, who reached for the pistol and looked at it and dropped it on the grass beside him.

'What's it all about, Halkett?' he said. 'Why has Raleigh been watching me all week? Why are you here?'

Halkett, his pipe drawing and clenched between his teeth, sitting there on the ground in his city clothes with his arms round his knees, showed no sign that this conversation was taking place in odd circumstances, or that he hadn't wanted it. He was as comfortable as if his diary had him down for an early conference, and this was it.

'Some of our redundos have disappeared,' he said. 'We think now that they've been approached. Hired, you understand.'

'When people are sacked,' Hynd said, 'don't you expect that? Quite apart from the wish to earn money, people like to do things with their lives.'

'You're not doing anything with yours,' Halkett said.

'Long may you think so,' Hynd said. 'It would confuse too many of those who know you if you became perceptive.'

Halkett nodded once, indifferent as he always had been to remarks, about himself or anyone else, that made no sense to him.

'Also,' Hynd said, 'I wasn't made redundant. I was constructively dismissed.'

'What's that mean?'

'It means,' said Raleigh unexpectedly, 'that when a man gets tired of being called an ignorant, stupid, vainglorious little shit by one who is, formally speaking, his superior, and quits because of it, he may have recourse to an industrial tribunal and claim that the behaviour of the said superior has been such as to make it impossible for the claimant to continue working in that firm, and was intended to drive him out.'

'How on earth do you know all that?' Halkett said.

'Been reading up on it.'

'Much good may it do you,' Halkett said. 'You can't go to an industrial tribunal from the Secret Intelligence Service.'

'It's not usual,' Raleigh said, 'but I could certainly start the process, make the formal application. Which failing, the new complaints procedure will be up and running soon.'

'Bloody bolshies,' Halkett said. 'You and Hynd should get together and plan the rebirth of Communism.'

'Communism as such,' Hynd said, 'had something worth thinking about.'

Halkett looked out to sea. 'This is getting us nowhere,' he said, 'and if that's not a rain squall coming in I'm a Dutchman. Raleigh, I wonder if I could impose on your kindness to the extent of asking you to toddle down the hill and bring the car up. I do realize it's a lot to ask, but . . .'

'Good Lord,' Raleigh said, meeting irony with irony.

'I won't hear another word. Glad to be able to do something useful.'

He set off up and over the crest of the hill with a long fast stride.

'That lad's better than you think he is,' Hynd said.

'They always are.'

'I have not been approached,' Hynd said.

'That's what we thought,' Halkett said.

'I haven't even been sussed out,' Hynd said. 'No one's been near. No one except Raleigh, and I knew he was there. Never saw him, he's good at it, but I knew he was there. If there'd been anyone else about I'd have known.'

'There are other ways of sussing someone out than sniffing over their home ground,' Halkett said. The next words burst from him as if he could not contain himself: 'What do you find to do all day, up here in the back of beyond? No one to talk with, no theatres, cinemas, no decent restaurants.'

Instantly Hynd's face concealed him. 'It's what I'm doing just now,' he said. 'It's what I want to do just now.'

'A whole year of it? More than a year of it?'

'Life is long,' Hynd said. 'I'm only forty-seven.'

'And women, what about women?'

'A man can do without a woman,' Hynd said. 'You're older than me. I've noticed that at your age men can get really screwed up about women, as if there was no tomorrow, and having been quite sensible for thirty years or so, all of a sudden they seem to feel the need to behave as if they were twenty again.'

'Men of my age,' Halkett said in a flat voice. 'There's not ten years between us.'

Hynd heard an engine in low gear on the far side of the hill.

'Yes,' he said. 'It's a classic security risk.'

'My word,' Halkett said sarcastically. 'I don't know how we get along without you.'

'Anyway,' Hynd said. 'This may be remote, but there are women here just as there are in Amazonia, or the Bight of Benin. And it's a very sexual culture, the Celtic culture. Did you know that?'

'No,' Halkett said. 'I'm not a bloody anthropologist.'

'You could always read a book,' Hynd said, 'now and then.'

Halkett said, 'Talking of books, the woman you're sleeping with, the writer who moved into the cottage outside that Godforsaken hamlet . . .'

Hynd stood up and stepped forward with terrible speed. He saw fear change the other man's eyes, and let his anger leave him. 'If you talk about her like that again,' he said, 'I'll do something bad, Halkett.'

He saw the four-wheel drive come over the hill behind Halkett. Halkett heard it and stood up too, and turned, to hold up a hand to stop Raleigh where he was.

He faced Hynd again. 'She was with the National Security Agency until last summer,' he said.

'If you smelled as putrid as you are,' Hynd said, 'the stink would kill you.'

'Yes,' Halkett said. 'I'm getting uncouth in my late middle-age. Well, we think someone's going to make you an offer, Hynd, and it may come from Miss Thingie. If such an offer is made, we'll invoke the Act and put you back on the payroll.'

'You want me to double? To take the offer and double for SIS?'

'I don't just want you to, I'm telling you to,' Halkett said, 'and this comes from the very top.'

Hynd laughed, a young laugh for a man his age. 'What's the top, Halkett?'

'Downing Street,' Halkett said.

Hynd said, 'That's not very high up, in my scheme of things. The answer's no.'

'You can't say no. If we have to we'll fit you up. There are three killings in your file that we can make stand up as murder in court.'

Hynd became very still. 'Nothing,' he said, 'that was not ordered.'

Halkett's pipe had burned out. He held it and studied it for a moment. 'That's not how it will seem,' he said.

'The answer's no.'

'They'll do it,' Halkett said.

'No, they won't,' Hynd said. 'Do you think I have nothing salted away to protect myself? After working for you lot for twelve years? Do you want me to name names?'

'Shite,' Halkett said, 'and damnation.' He knocked the pipe out on the heel of his shoe. 'We can burn your house down. Invalidate your pension. Anything. Ruin your life.'

'The house and the pension, yes,' Hynd said. 'You can't ruin my life. You don't know where my life is. And I might sit still for it, while you did these things, but I might not, and if I decided not, you'd be the first to know.'

Halkett stood up. 'Oh, bugger it,' he said. 'I told

them this wouldn't work.' He lifted an arm and waved Raleigh in.

The Range Rover pulled up beside them and sat there, the engine sizzling gently. Halkett made an attempt at humour. 'You are bound by the Act,' he said, 'never mind your responsibility to your country. And if these solemn matters are not sufficiently persuasive, I can always let Raleigh loose on you.'

Hynd looked up at Raleigh in the driver's seat of the Rover. Raleigh made a deprecating face.

'I take it everything failed,' Raleigh said. 'Threats, blackmail, bribery, all that sort of thing?'

'That's right,' Hynd said.

'I didn't try to buy him,' Halkett said. 'At least I knew enough not to do that.'

'Then what did you offer him?' said Raleigh.

Something relaxed in Hynd. He had been standing taut with irritation, waiting for them to go, to get off his territory. Now he leaned a shoulder on the Range Rover and watched the rain that had come off the sea darken the sky to the west. It would be here soon.

'Offer?' Halkett said, with something like a wondering doubt in his voice. 'What do you mean? I told you, you can't bribe Hynd.'

'Indeed,' Raleigh said, 'but you want a favour from him.'

'It will be a cold day in Hell before I ask Hynd for favours,' Halkett said.

'Yes. Sure. Absolutely,' Raleigh said. 'All the same, it will be a tolerably chilly day or so in London if you go back without securing Hynd for them.'

So far as he could do it, sitting in the car, Halkett had come over all dominant and sulky, misunderstood by these lesser folk. 'If you have a proposal, what is it?'

'Offer him a gift,' Raleigh said.

'A present!' Halkett said. 'What is this, a kiddies' party? This is business we're talking here. Rough and dirty and sophisticated and excruciatingly important business. Prezzies. Christ, boy! Do you know who Hynd is? Do you know how much blood has followed that man? I despair of you, Raleigh.'

'Do that all you want,' Raleigh said equably, 'but don't be so fucking pompous about it.'

'Don't talk to me like that,' Halkett said.

'Hush,' Raleigh said. 'Hynd,' he said. 'If you were offered a present, anything, the thing you would most like to have, what would it be?'

'A Steinway,' said Hynd, who had seen this coming. 'A concert grand, a real old vintage Steinway, maintained and reconditioned by Steinway, and Steinway maintenance of it for my lifetime.'

Raleigh said, 'And of course, if you moved house now and then, you'd want insurance and safe transport for it wherever you might choose to go.'

Hynd met Raleigh's eye. 'Wherever,' he agreed. 'Chad. Southern Patagonia. Ekaterinburg. Who knows?'

'You're not a piano-player,' Halkett said. 'It would be on your file. Stop playing the fool, Raleigh. Get us on the road.'

'Would you accept a Steinway from us, Hynd?' Raleigh asked.

'A Steinway like that, which had lived its own life for a long time already, so to speak, would hardly seem to be touched by SIS. If you were to seek it out, Raleigh, and make the arrangements,' Hynd said, 'yes. I would.'

'I'm to take this seriously?' Halkett said. 'You mean you'll do it?'

'No,' Hynd said. 'Don't get carried away. I have become a reflective man. I shall go and reflect.'

'*Allegro ma non troppo*,' Raleigh said.

'That's the thing,' Hynd said.

Without consulting Halkett, Raleigh let the car go gently away, up the hill and over the ridge.

Hynd picked Raleigh's pistol from the grass and set off for home at a steady pace, running to meet the rain as it came in off the sea, running through it with his head up, letting his mind be empty, his skull washed first by the teeming rain and when that had passed, by the sun.

He let his mind be empty, because what Halkett had said about the woman in the cottage was tearing at his heart.

Chapter Two

He went straight to bed and slept the day through, and in the evening, unshaved and unbathed, he got into his car and drove the winding, hilly, single-track ten miles of road to the end of the peninsula.

She had laid the kitchen table, and she was at the stove with a fork to her mouth, in the act of testing a piece of meat from the stewpot.

She was tall and strongly made, the legs long and lithe, the shoulders broad, the breasts firm and of the perfect size for Diana the Huntress. Her body was athletic, not luscious, and it had come to be, for him, the most erotic body that ever was.

Now her eyes went wide with the pleasure of being surprised. She gulped the piece of meat and made a waving movement with a hand to show this surprise; to show that the meat was burning her mouth; that she had been off somewhere else in her mind and this was all a bit much to deal with, but it was good to see him.

'I thought we'd agreed,' she said. 'You're at least a day too early. I'm still sodden with love-making.'

'Hardly,' he said. 'It was noon yesterday. In any case, I'm not here for love.'

At this curtness her face changed, and became solemn. She licked gravy from her lips and tossed the fork into the sink.

'You're angry,' she said. She slid the stewpot off the heat to the back of the stove, where it could simmer.

'You wouldn't be angry if there weren't love.'

She walked past the kitchen table, collecting a pack of cigarettes from it on the way, and installed herself in a battered armchair with its back to the wall.

'So what's up?' she said.

Her hair was ash blonde with grey in it, for she was almost fifty. The forehead was broad, the eyes wideset, the nose straight and sweetly shaped, the mouth generous and firm, the jaw a long curve, and the chin firm but of perfect roundness. She was not merely beautiful, she was a beauty. Her name was Caroline Swift.

'Tell me,' she said.

'No,' he said. 'You tell me. Tell me about the National Security Agency. Tell me why you came here in the first place. Tell me who planted you here. Tell me if you've been working up to making me an offer, and, if you have, on whose behalf. Tell me those things.'

He supposed he must look pretty bad. In the past twenty-four hours he had reverted to type, or gone from one type to another, from one personality to another. Yesterday he had been the man who caught fish in the burn, who read about Goethe and listened to Mozart. He had been the man who lived with nature and with himself, who lived with thought and in his own thought. He had been learning to be his own man, and to be at peace with himself.

Since she had come into his life, all his knowing of her had enhanced this. Her whole being had laid its hold on him: the ardent and eager spirit, which expressed itself in an intimacy that had been extraordinarily immediate, and in her passionate gift for sexual joy; her strong will and the awareness of herself that went with it; the lucid intelligence and the way it ran

21

in harness with the vivacity of her imagination. And in all of this, the mixture of daring and vulnerability that flashed in her eyes.

And the dark side, when she became inaccessible, when she turned to herself and away from him: he valued that too. She would send him off, sometimes for days, until she came swinging up to his house and threw an arm round his neck as if she had never been away, or as if she had been away for years, but here she was back as though it had been only yesterday that they parted.

Well, yesterday, indeed, it had been. Now all that had been taken from him. She had come to him under contract. She had been sent to captivate him, and he had fallen for it. Now he was back in the old mode and he hated her for it.

But with all the anger and hate in him, he had never admired her more. She had the nerve of the damned. She sat there looking at Hynd, who had turned into this creature she had never met before, with her eyes wide and steady.

'Pour yourself a drink, if you want one,' she said, and gestured at the bottles on the dresser at the far end of the room. 'I'd like some whisky.'

He ignored this.

'Tell me,' he said, 'that everything that passed between us was a lie, and how you were laughing inside yourself when you were making love to me.'

'I did laugh inside myself,' she said. 'I laughed for joy. It has not been a lie.'

She stood up and walked past him and poured whisky into two glasses. She put one on the table for him and sat down again. Her ashtray was at her right hand on the hearth; at her left hand, on a stool, she put her glass.

She reminded him of Wellington preparing to meet the enemy. 'I suppose your cavalry is waiting out of sight over the ridge,' he said.

She shook her head impatiently and brushed the hair out of her eyes. 'Johnny,' she said, 'for God's sake, sit down and don't stand there looming over me like the Avenging Angel. You'll want that drink. It's not a happy story. I'll tell it you fast, because I hate it, and fill it out for you later.'

Since he came into the room he had been standing as taut as a strung bow, the energy of his emotions discharging a barrage of hostility at her that made her feel weak in the gut. Now he rubbed his hands all over his face and head, and shuddered. His body eased, and when he brought his hands from his face she saw that the brilliance had gone from those black eyes of his. He sat on the end of the table as if he was suddenly exhausted, pulled round a chair, planted a foot on it, and sat there with one leg swinging loose.

He picked up the glass beside him and took a swallow from it, stared into the fire burning behind the bars of the stove, and gave a great sigh.

'All right, Caro,' he said. 'Tell me.'

'When I was nineteen my father was murdered by the KGB,' she said.

Hynd's head came round abruptly. 'He was in the intelligence business?'

'Johnny, let me just tell it, will you? No, he was not in the intelligence business. He was US Army, in Europe working with NATO: defence planning. He was on a sailing holiday in the Baltic and the KGB kidnapped him and tortured him to death.'

'Dear God,' Hynd said.

'Yes,' she said. 'I was in Nepal. It was the end of the sixties, everybody was in Nepal. Look at me when I'm talking to you.'

He was staring into the fire again and he turned to look at her. Her eyes on his were wide and stern.

'I wanted to fight the KGB,' she said. 'I got my degree and joined the CIA. I was a looker, I was sexy, young.' Her eyes were inflexible. 'They said they'd take me on if I'd be a honey-pot for them. You'll know the expression. I seduced the men they targeted for me and became their lover and wormed their secrets out of them. I was a patriotic callgirl. I was fresh meat. I fucked for the Flag. Do you feel sick?'

'I feel sick anyway,' he said. 'This doesn't make me feel any sicker.'

'For eight years,' she said. 'Till I was thirty-one. I was a real pro. Then I fell in love and wanted to stop, move to a desk job, anything. But the CIA said no, I was too good at what I was doing. Hell, they had the film to prove it. On some of the cases they used film of me and the target to blackmail him.'

She lit a fresh cigarette. 'But I had friends in high places by then. I quit the CIA and got a job with the National Security Agency. I was good at that, too. I made a career of it, for twenty years, and resigned three years ago.'

'The man you fell in love with, who was he?'

'Which man? Oh, Archie. Archie Teller. He was a lawyer,' she said, 'in Washington. Washington's full of them. Special interest groups need them, lobbyists need them, government contractors need them. They get rich. We were going to get married, I wanted to marry him. It had been two years and I thought he was the man for me.'

She stopped and went back in time.

'You didn't marry him?' Hynd said.

'No. He was working on a bid for a defence contract and a rival bidder was preferred for the contract by the CIA, so the CIA made one of my films available to the rival bidder and he passed it to the Pentagon. It showed me in the sack being busy with a man identified as an East German agent. It made Archie a security risk, since I was about to marry him.'

She shook her head. 'Wow,' she said. 'That was a storm. Archie wanted to know what the hell had happened to his contract, he'd thought he had it sewn up. So the Pentagon let him see the film. He called me a filthy Commie whore and was working up to call me a thousand other things, so I left him standing and shouting in his nice big drawing-room in Georgetown and went away from there.'

She shrugged. 'He was right, except for the Communist bit: I was a whore and it was recorded. After that, I made a point of avoiding the big relationship deal. I made my life for me, bought a little house on the Maryland Shore and filled it with books and music, made it mine and made a garden, went swimming and walking. I fell in love, or more or less in love, a few times and would take my lovers there, but mainly it was for me, that cottage. I've told you about that.'

'You've told me you'd like to take me there,' Hynd said.

'Have I?' But Hynd was used to this, that she would

say things that meant a good deal to him which turned out to have meant so little to her that she forgot them.

They sat for a little in silence while she thought whatever she was thinking, and he let what she had told him settle into him. He fetched the whisky bottle and refilled the two glasses and sat on the table again.

She looked tired out and sad, and beautiful. Caro Swift, he thought, beautiful and tired out and sad. And John Hynd, he was full of sorrow.

'So,' he said. 'Finally?'

'Finally?' she said. 'Yes, I guess we've reached that. Finally, there I was in my cottage, coming up to three years retired from the NSA, nearly fifty, living in the peace of my being, when one bright morning these men came to the door. There were two of them, a smoothy and a plug-ugly. The smoothy was English and the other one looked East European to me, I mean like an East European from East Europe, not the US. They never gave me a name. Either of them. I still don't know who they were or who they worked for. They just came in and went straight at it.

'Jesus,' she said, remembering that morning. 'I had a dog, a German shepherd called Duke. He didn't like them. When I opened the door they came straight in and Duke got his dander up and snarled at them, and the smoothy said to the heavy, "Shut that thing up," and the heavy pulled out a pistol and shot Duke dead on the carpet. One shot through the heart, and Duke was dead on the carpet.'

Well, it was the professional way to do it, Hynd thought, the quickest way to put fear into the subject.

She echoed his thought. 'Classic routine, to terrorize me. I knew that. And I was terrorized. The smoothy said he had a job for me. He wanted me to be a honey-pot again, one more time. I asked him how he knew about me. He said that the business he was in, he saw films that were not on general release.'

'Those words?'

'Yes, those words. Why do you ask?'

'His style of speech,' Hynd said. 'It might help in identifying them.'

She frowned at him and then went on. 'So,' she said. 'These damn films again, thirty years on. I said to him, I told him I was hitting fifty, for God's sake. And he said, twenty or fifty, I still had it. He told me I was to come here, get next to you, and persuade you to join his organization. He wouldn't tell me what organization that was. He said I'd hear from him when he was ready, but I had three months, maybe four.'

'It's been nearly three,' Hynd said.

'Yes,' she said, 'it has.'

'What did you say to him?'

'I said,' and she took a deep breath, 'Jesus, I said no, I didn't want to do it, and he said to the other man, "Show it to her," and this guy came out with a knife and flicked open the blade and grabbed me by the hair and laid the blade on my neck. "You'll do it," the Englishman said, "or he'll cut your throat now, this minute, and leave you down there beside your dog." '

'Ah,' Hynd said.

'What do you mean, "Ah"?'

'A private thought,' Hynd said, and even as he sat there on the table she could see his body become limber and relaxed and his face open as if he was listening for some sound out of the night. 'What happened then?'

'With the knife at my throat? I said right, OK, I'll

do it. The top man, the Englishman, told the other guy to let me go, and became as nice as pie, just like that. He put an envelope on the bureau, and said it had money in it and airline tickets and the address of this house and the name of the lawyer here who had handled the let who would tell me how to get the keys. He even asked me if I wanted the thug to bury Duke for me.'

She paused and shook her head. 'Poor Duke. I said no, I'd bury him myself. Well, of course I would, and did. But most of all I wanted them out of there.'

She got up and threw her cigarette into the grate and stood facing him with her back to the stove. 'That's it. I came here and went out walking and came to your house and you were outside there, chopping wood, and I stopped and said, "Hi," and so we met. That was all according to plan. The rest of it, what happened between us, none of that was a lie.'

She stood there, poised and staunch, ready to be his adversary or to be at peace, depending on how it went. And he sat there on the table, swinging that one leg, his face dark with stubble but its expression light and clear and alert to something that was not in this room. There was a newness to him, something about him that she had not known, and in his eyes was a look she had never seen there before: cold and hard, even vicious, yes, but an unexcited viciousness, a sure and deadly look.

'Well,' she said, 'so where are we now?'

His eyes became aware of her. 'In a mess.'

'Are we, Johnny? What shall we do about it?'

'I know what I'm going to do about it,' he said. 'I'm going to find him and kill him, kill them both.'

'Oh, shit,' she said, 'then we are in a mess.'

And her temper broke. 'What a fucking cop-out,' she said, and heard it come out almost in a shout. 'I tell you all that wretched stuff about me, I tell it you absolutely straight from right inside myself and instead of hearing it and facing it' – she was yelling like a fishwife now and didn't give a damn, either – 'instead of telling me what it does to you, instead of having the guts to look at what it means to you and what it means to me, instead of telling me I'm still me, still the same Caroline that you love, or hitting me on the face, even, goddam you, Johnny, I'd rather you hit me and told me I'm a slut and a whore and a liar and a piece of shit than just run away and hide from it into some other world like . . . like . . .'

He came off the table and stood in front of her. 'Like what?'

She was just about used up, but she kept the last of her temper going to yell into his face: 'Like some English asshole of a hundred years ago shrugging his shoulders at the faithlessness of women and going off big-game hunting to get over it.'

'Or joining the Foreign Legion.'

He saw a flicker of the old mischief flash in her eye. 'Jesus Christ! Can't a girl have a row with you about one of the most hellish things in her whole life?'

'Not today. You're still you,' he said. 'You're still the woman I love.'

'No,' she said. 'You don't know that. That would take time to find out, to find out if that's what you felt. And you're not going to take the time, you're going to go off and work for that mob so that you can find these guys and kill them. Give me a hug.'

He held her close and tight, a grip like iron round

her ribcage as if he would crush her. 'I could do both these things at the same time,' he said, 'if I thought I needed to. But I don't. I love you, I love who you are.'

'Kiss me,' she said.

But then she came out of it and away from him. 'No,' she said. 'You're out there on the prairie already, hunting them down.'

She picked up her cigarettes and sat on the table where he had sat and lit one and tossed the hair back off her face. 'I'm not the woman you knew yesterday, and you're not the man I knew yesterday, either. It won't be good between us if you go off on this manhunt.'

'For God's sake, Caro,' he said, 'use your head. You won't be safe till these men are dead.'

'I don't need to be safe.'

'You need to be safer than this.'

'That's for me to decide.'

'I see that,' he said, 'but I've decided on my own account, and you can't control me.'

'I don't want to control you, but it's us we're talking about. We're talking about what to do about us. We should share that.'

'No,' he said. 'If I don't join them, they'll kill you as casually as they killed Duke.'

'They might kill you.' She was looking at him as she said it, and the expression in his black eyes made her blink. It was like looking at a wolf laughing at some secret joke.

'I don't think so,' he said. 'It's always possible, but I don't think so.'

'I knew you were with intelligence,' she said, 'but I don't think I quite know what you did. Is this the sort of thing you did?'

'Sometimes.'

'And nobody's killed you yet.'

'No, not yet.'

'And the ones that tried,' she said. 'What happened to them?'

'I killed them.'

'You're two people,' she said, 'and this one I don't know. Is that it?'

'Yes,' he said. 'That's it.'

The brown eyes and the black stared into each other as if the two of them had met on a desert and neither of them had ever seen another human being before.

'I might not be here when you get back,' she said.

'I know that. I'd rather have you alive somewhere else than here and dead.'

She went on looking into his eyes, seeing in them the deaths of other men, past and to come. 'There's no rubbish like chivalry in this mission of yours, is there?'

'No,' he said. 'None. I'm doing it for me, I'm not doing it for you. I'm doing it because of you, but I'm doing it because I need to. It's what I'm best at, so I can't avoid doing it.'

Still she looked into him. Her eyes were dark with loss, but they were inflexible against him.

She got up off the table and looked into his face as if she was trying to see him through a gauze curtain.

'Living is what you're best at,' she said. 'Being yourself is what you're best at. You're one of the most real men I've ever met. Knowing yourself is what you're best at. This man who kills people because it's what he does best, this man you say you once were and have become: being him is a way of killing yourself.'

31

She brushed past him, driven by an urge to move about the room.

'I've fallen in love with you,' she said. 'You know that. And now you say you've thrown away the man I love and reverted to being, to being a . . . a fucking werewolf or something.'

'I'll be back when it's over and done with,' he said. 'I'll come back . . .'

'And you're doing it to me too,' she went on heedlessly. 'You're turning me into something else. You're turning me into a cause, as if I was Joan of Arc or the Emancipation of Slaves or whatever.'

'For Christ's sake, Caro,' he said, 'who brought this on us? It was you, not me.' Despite what he was saying, he felt oddly remote from the argument, reeling out this logic as if he was already somewhere else. 'Whatever's happened between us since, it was you who brought this with you at the start. You came to me absolutely planning to make me fall in love with you to save your own neck. When you came to me you didn't give a damn about what was going to happen to me, so long as you came out of it in one piece. You can't simply forget that, you can't lay it all off on me just because you don't like the effect it's having on me now.'

The controlled vexation in his voice, emotionless and withheld, was filling her with frustrated anger. 'It's not "having an effect" on you,' she said. 'You're not letting it have an effect on you, you're just walking away from that. I came to you as a cheat and a liar, and I'd like it a lot more if you had the guts to take it out on me, instead of getting on your horse and running off to fight somebody else.'

'I know you can't stand it,' he said, rubbing his hands

up and down the back of his scalp in a kind of despair, 'but these people threatened to kill you, and for that I'm going to kill them, for that I *have* to kill them, and make you safe in the by-going: I'm afraid that's me being honest about the order of my priorities. Who do you think told me about you and the NSA? It was the people I used to work for, it was MI6, and they want me to put the skids under these bastards and that's what I'm going to do. I can't do anything else. It's what I am. Can't you see that?'

She was standing with her back to the window now, her arms folded, hugging herself. It should have been him hugging her, but there was a wall between them now. 'I'll hate you for it,' she said. 'It's nothing to do with human beings. It's a fucking cop-out.'

'I know you'll hate me,' he said. 'I feel it off you. But I can't not do it. I must be out of my head, I must be seriously off my head.'

'You don't believe that,' she said. 'You know exactly what you're doing. You can't wait to get at it.'

She let her arms fall and came away from the window. It was such a good room, this, such a good simple room, with its plain board floor, the wooden table and kitchen chairs, and the stove that gave it life, gave life to the house. She touched the back of the battered old armchair, where she would sit and read and think, think sometimes of him, talk to him when she was alone. It was her chair, it was her place, even though it was rented. What would it be like for her here when he was off playing spies, going through doors with a gun in his hand or whatever it was he did?

'No,' she said, quiet and sad now. 'You don't think you're off your head. You think you're going back into the real world. You think you've become what you would call sane.'

'You'll destroy us with this,' he said. 'I've gone away from you, it's true, I admit it. But it will come back, Caro, when it's over, when I've done this job. We'll come back too.'

Her face flared red and suddenly she leaped up and shouted at him. 'Damn you!' she yelled. 'If you do this we'll never come back. Don't you care? No, you don't care. It's all gone for you, hasn't it? It's safer for you, isn't it? Going out and risking your life and killing people is safer than knowing someone else, than loving me. You're a coward, Johnny Hynd. I wish I'd never met you.'

Her whole body was alive with the emotion trying to burst out of her. Her face blazed at him through tears, and her hands were working, opening and shutting as her arms pumped up and down, until he thought she was going to tear at his eyes when she reached him.

Suddenly she went at him with her fists, punching him three times in the face, driving him back across the room till his back met the wall before he knew where he was. He got his arms up to block the punches and caught hold of one of her wrists, but she pulled it free and stood away from him.

She was a fit and athletic woman and the blows she had landed had been powerful, and he braced himself for the next assault, but she had finished with that.

The colour had left her. Her skin was lifeless now, as if she was exhausted. She wiped the hair off her face with a sweep of her hand, and turned her back and walked away from him and threw herself into the armchair. She fished her cigarettes off the floor beside her and lit one.

'You've got a bloody nose,' she said. The eyes were cool, the voice was hard, the tears were over.

He got out his handkerchief and staunched the bleeding. 'You pack quite a punch,' he said.

'I suppose you could have killed me,' she said, 'now that you're the old John Hynd. One kick or one of those cunning blows with the edge of the hand.'

'Either, but not till you'd got those punches in. I'm not that much the old John Hynd yet, I let you take me by surprise.'

Her eyes closed and opened again. She drew on the cigarette and let the smoke out of her mouth. 'I thought I was going to tell you to get out. But I think I want to meet this other John Hynd. I need some space, though. Why don't you go outside for a bit, and I'll get the food ready.'

Her mouth twitched, an ironic spasm of a smile that was gone as soon as it came.

'What is it?' he said.

'It would have been like a line in an old B movie,' she said.

He blew his nose lightly, an experiment: it was still bleeding. 'What would?'

'If I'd kicked you out,' she said. ' "So long, Johnny." It's the kind of thing the torch singer used to say.'

'Why didn't you say it?'

'Not my movie. Too like the one you're bent on making.'

He left her sitting there and closed the door behind him, and went out under the stars.

Chapter Three

Harry Seddall stood on the steps of the Tate Gallery
and said under his breath, 'Christ, I'm tired.' He was
tired not so much from overwork as from boredom.
Boredom came to him from too many committees. He
was being turned, or he was allowing himself to turn,
into a civil servant. This, doubtless, was life among the
adult majority, though to Seddall it did not always seem
that people on committees behaved very much like
adults. Underneath those rectitudinous suits that were
the habiliments of power beat the hearts of a great
many overgrown schoolboys, and girls.

Just like yourself, old son, he said, with an inward
smile. Then the smile went away, and that elusive sense
of premonition came back.

He was not sure how much to make of it. Usually
when he had that whisper of warning from within he
was on the job, breaking into a strange house with a
pistol in his teeth, that sort of thing. He felt with his
tongue at the loose crown that was going to break off
the next time he forgot about it and bit into a steak; it
would have to be a very small and lightweight pistol.
Back to the dentist.

Premonition: was it real or was it not? He had slept
badly last night, waking at three in the morning from
foul dreams and walking the floor and smoking cigarettes for two hours, growling at this long absence of
Olivia. He had risen crossly at something after nine and

reacted against the administrative life, gone out for a long and idle breakfast. He should have been at the Office three hours ago, not looking at paintings in the Tate. He stared across the river at the new Secret Intelligence Service building, the kind of thing you would hope they had now stopped building in Russia. At least he didn't have to work there.

It was in the Tate that he had experienced the premonition, standing in front of a painting by Francis Bacon: the haunted figure of Van Gogh which was not so much a human being, an entire human being, as a soul in torment which had passed through the Gates of Despair and heard them clang shut behind him.

Seddall had become absorbed and had lost account of time. He had inhabited the painting and the painting had inhabited him. And then, elsewhere in his vision he saw another painting, equally black but instead of passive raging with violence, the wild painting by Cezanne of a man and a woman holding down their victim while the man hacked him to death.

He had come out of his spellbound state when someone brushed against him and apologized. Seddall had said, seeing only Van Gogh before him now, 'Not at all,' and felt the incongruity of that image and the empty social phrase. He had felt for his cigarettes and remembered where he was, and made his way out, here, to the top of the steps, and lit a cigarette and watched the first exhalation of smoke drift away into the sky. He had experienced a striking sense of relief as the smoke dispersed with the natural freedom afforded it by the laws of physics, in contrast to the fixed and implacable images that he had just encountered.

Where was that Cezanne? It was not in a London

gallery. It was up north somewhere, and he had not seen it for years. Why should it come to him now?

He ground the cigarette out under his heel and kicked it away. He was left with the taste of tobacco in his mouth and of premonition in his blood.

He made a sound like a dog snarling and startled the firstcomers of a group of schoolchildren coming up the steps. They looked at him and he gave them a lazy smile, like a wolf. The looks became stares. What they saw was a pair of yellowish eyes blinking against the sun, a face that had a perpetual but worn tan as if it had spent its early years in the Tropics, a round and stubborn chin, and a body of middle size whose suit, despite its excellent grey cloth and cut, suggested that it was stored overnight in a peatbog, topped by a brown trilby from the same bog that sat tipped back on his head.

'Premonitions,' this apparition said to them, and raised the hat from an inadequately covered scalp, not, as it transpired, from courtesy, but simply so that he could scratch his head.

'Silly old moo,' he heard, and went down the steps and took a taxi to Whitehall. It was a glorious day, on the bridge between spring and summer, and the pavements were decorated with women living up to it, wearing in these eclectic times variously short skirts, miniskirts, shorts, leggings patterned or plain: plenty of them with their men.

He felt hellishly left out of it. His Olivia was off riding camels in Mongolia, drinking tea with butterfat in it and living, presumably, in yurts. Yurts? Yes, he was sure of it, that was what the nomadic descendants of Genghis Khan called their benders.

This way of life that Olivia insisted on, in which she behaved like some modern version of Lady Hester Stanhope, shooting off to whatever far reach of the earth she felt like, was not his thing. He had ridden enough camels and slept in enough deserts in the way of business not to want to start doing it for fun. Certainly it was her right to do what she chose, but it left him Olivialess, and being Olivialess, for months at a time, made an absence which irked.

Damn you, Harry, he said to himself as he paid off the taxi, you're feeling sorry for yourself. Don't do it. If you don't like the way things are, change them, do something about it.

He trotted up the wide staircase of the old Office – all this swimming was really doing its stuff – and nodded or What-hoed at those he met. He unlocked the door and went into his room. There was a note from young Deborah saying she'd gone to lunch, which was perhaps rather a pity, since on the way upstairs he had thought of skimming through the paper on his desk and whisking her off to swim and a late lunch at the club: Harry Seddall's answer to the yurts.

He took off the coat of his suit and emptied his pockets onto the desk, a habit of his: wallet, glasses, pack of Gauloises, pens, keys, diary, cards with scribbled notes on them. He put on a tape of Mozart's 40th and turned the volume up. He went over to the coffee machine and poured himself a cup – Deborah's Java again, wonderfully strong but bad for the liver, and then sat on the edge of his desk and considered the blueness of the sky.

A cigarette was called for. Where were the bloody Gauloises? He went round the desk and saw they'd fallen to the floor, under his chair. He got down on his knees and reached for them.

A tremendous sound whacked into his head and he was on his back on the floor, looking up at the ceiling which had broken open, was breaking open even as he looked, dark fissures running over it and letting loose lumps of white plaster, collapsing onto him right now, but he knew a trick worth two of that – was instantly agile and alert and clever – and hurled himself under the desk.

Where he crouched while the great bursting noise rang on and on in his head and the world thumped and clattered about him, and then fell in bits in a residual sort of way, tailing off with a dribbling sound, until finally there was only dust falling out there, falling and rising again and drifting in around him.

Then the noise was over, and there was nothing but the dust choking him, huddled there under the desk. He crawled out of his shelter and picked himself off the floor and looked down at it warily, as if it were the floor of the world and no longer, suddenly no longer, to be trusted; as the floor above had, plainly, proved untrustable. The floor above.

'Kenyon's office, by God,' he said, and sprang for the door.

As he opened it the alarm siren whooped, an earsplitting and unhelpful racket. In the outer office Deborah was coming towards him with a pistol in her hand.

'No, no,' he said. 'Nothing like that. Put it away. It's above us, the general's room. Let's get there.'

All hell had broken loose in the building. Security staff and fire teams were tearing about in all directions, not with the soundless efficiency one would have wished but with orders being shouted by voices that seemed to have acquired inbuilt megaphones.

He did not have time to make his way among that mob. He went to the lift and found it waiting. He and Deborah stepped in, against all emergency regulations. On the floor above he stopped for a moment to take in the situation there.

In the stairwell a cloud of dust had billowed and hung now at its apogee, active and beautiful in the sun that shone through the great skylight.

There was less racket here, a sense of more orderly procedures at work, and when he had made his way over and past rubble and debris towards General Kenyon's room he saw why.

A Ministry of Defence Police captain had identified the area to be kept clear of superfluous personnel and a squad of his men held it against all comers. Held it was not too strong a word, since all comers included fire, bomb and medical staff as well as a pack of what amounted to irregulars, since they had no assigned function particular to such emergencies. The captain's men stood against chaos with weapons drawn.

'Colonel Whithorn's in there, sir,' the captain said, 'and an RAMC major with him. Colonel Whithorn told me to hold the line.'

In the language Seddall heard bugles on the breeze, but the words made good sense.

A lieutenant-colonel in uniform appeared out of the dust. 'Whithorn,' Seddall said, 'get out there and impose some discipline on that rabble. I've never seen anything like it in my life.'

'Bloody right,' Whithorn said, and went.

'I'm going in,' Seddall said. 'Kenyon's mine.'

41

He made his way over the mess of stuff in the room, which had been destroyed. The windows were gone, and smoke and dust flowed out of the spaces where they had been. The only stick of furniture left that looked like anything was the heavy desk, charred and doused in extinguisher foam, beside which the doctor was working on the general. Twisted scraps of scorched metal bespoke the wreckage of filing cabinets, and an MoD sergeant and one of his men were playing fire extinguishers on the flames, which would die out and flicker up again in new places.

Seddall knelt beside the medical major but at a respectful distance. The doctor, who flicked him an irritated glance, had cut Kenyon's charred and bloody shirt from him and had been swabbing off some of the chest and abdomen. On the left side the bones of the ribcage showed through torn flesh. The torso was lacerated with other wounds, and the rest of the body was a mass of burnt cloth with skin burns showing through.

The doctor made a gesture and at the invitation Seddall went close and knelt over Kenyon. In the wounded man's eyes he met no recognition.

Kenyon's head rolled to the side and he gave a kind of sigh.

The doctor made sure and then sat back on his haunches. 'Yes,' he said. 'He's dead.'

Deborah was waiting for him at the MoD Police line out on the corridor.

'Kenyon's dead,' he said.

They went back to the lift and down to his office.

The coffee machine had bought it but the Berlin Philharmonic had survived, and they sat and drank Cognac and smoked Seddall's Gauloises and listened to the music. When it ended Harry turned the tape over and they listened to the Jupiter.

'We're having a private wake,' Harry said.

'Yes,' Deborah said. 'That's what we're having.'

'One more drink, and then we'll have to rally round and start thinking.'

As he put the bottle down the phone rang.

'It's the Secretary of State's office,' Deborah said. 'He wants to see you.'

'Now?'

'So it seems.'

He emptied his glass and got up to go.

'Don't you want your jacket?'

'Well,' he said. 'Look at it.' It was on the floor covered with a soup of plaster and black coffee.

'You keep a clean shirt here,' she said. 'Why don't you at least put that on. You're covered with filth, and some blood, too. You're an awful mess, actually. While you change your shirt I'll go and borrow a jacket for you.'

'Never mind,' he said, 'it's not far,' as if that meant anything. But he sought and found the shirt and she went off to scout out a respectable jacket.

'Too big,' she said, as she helped him into it, 'but better that than too small.'

'Absolutely right,' he said.

'We're behaving strangely.'

'Mixture of booze and shock,' he said. 'I think I'll go straight home after I've seen the Great Man. Will you be all right?'

'I'll be fine,' she said. 'What about you, though? Do you want company or do you want to be alone?'

'Don't take it ill, my sweet,' Harry said, 'but tonight, the latter. Anyway, I've got Sacha.'

'Take care,' she said. 'You haven't washed the, ah, mess off your face and hands.'

'*Ciao*,' he said, and went off with the borrowed garment floating around his thighs as if he was setting a new trend.

Outside, he was a different man in a different day from the man who had taxied from the Tate. The sunshine meant nothing to him. The women in miniskirts and shorts and leggings, patterned or plain, meant nothing. He drifted along in his blood and dirt, or Kenyon's blood, to be accurate. For he could see it now in his mind's eye, blood on the floor where he had put his hand when he leaned over the dying man.

He looked at the hand, and saw that not all of it had been wiped off on the old shirt, so he scrubbed it a bit on the new.

'Dreadful thing,' the Secretary said, his eyes askance on Seddall, the traces of blood and the disorder of his dress.

'Kenyon?' Harry said. 'Yes. Dreadful.'

The Secretary was tall, slim, and handsome, if you liked that sort of thing. His name was Charles Little.

'They tell me it was definitely a bomb,' the Secretary said. 'What have you put in train?'

'Put in train?'

'Yes, what have you done about it so far?'

Little was still standing, but Harry looked about him and found himself a seat, and sat on it.

'So far,' he said, 'I've drunk a little brandy and

smoked a few cigarettes and listened to Mozart.'

Little had been heckled before and this went by him like a swallow on the wing.

'Are you in shock, or something?' he asked.

'Likely. My room's under the seat of the explosion. But let me say to you that all that needs doing at this minute is certainly being handled by our own Investigation Branch, by the Metropolitan Police Anti-Terrorist boys and our bomb experts and theirs. And MI5, of course. For myself, I'm on my way home.'

'But surely, Seddall,' the Secretary said, 'you must see how bad this makes us look. An office of the Ministry in the middle of Whitehall being blown up, a general killed. Surely you react to that? What was General Kenyon working on that would lead to this outrage?'

'That I know of, nothing,' Harry said.

The youngish man who had admitted Harry to the presence came into the room and handed his master a slip of paper. 'I think you'll want to see this,' he said.

Little read it, and gave it back to the youngish man, who went away.

'Not an IRA bomb, they think,' he said.

'No,' Harry said.

Little sat down, and became grave. 'That is, if anything, worse. From the point of view of appearances, I mean. We have been made to look a laughing stock and we'll have to say we don't know who was responsible for the damned bomb.'

Harry thought he was too angry to speak, but he heard himself say: 'General Kenyon is dead.'

'What else are we talking about?' Little said, and became conciliatory. 'Still, I think I should not have called you here so soon. I was not aware you were so close to the explosion. What happens in your department? Will you fill in for Kenyon, or what?'

'For the time being.' Harry refrained from any explanation to the effect that Kenyon's job would not at all suit him: even more of those committees.

Little stood up. 'I must let you go. What will you do?'

'Go home, take a bath.'

'Get some of that dirt off you,' Little said, smiling pleasantly.

'Not the dirt you're talking about,' Harry said, and a puzzle came into the smile.

The Secretary gave him a close look. 'Seddall,' he said. 'I know you've just had a hell of a shock, and I assume from the way you're behaving that Kenyon was a friend of yours. But don't take it out on me. You're a soldier, I'm a politician. We see an event like this from different standpoints. I begin to appreciate yours, and I believe that you can appreciate mine. We'll talk again, later. Meanwhile, let me get you a car to take you home.'

Seddall gave him a long look. Not, he thought, one of the overgrown schoolboys. 'Yes,' he said. 'I'd like that. Thanks.'

At Sumner Place the black cat Sacha knew at once that Harry was in a state. She greeted him from a distance and went well in advance of him to the kitchen, none of that winding dance of a progress just in front of his toes with which she made herself seductive, and had the unexplained merit that she risked being stood on, and he risked tripping over her.

He put the kettle on for himself, poured fresh milk for her, and put down some catfood. When they were in the country Sacha preferred to eat her own kill, but Sumner Gardens was not the hunting ground that Somerset was, and here in London she grew lazy and hunted only for fun, when she felt like it. She left the milk and began on her supper.

Harry made a pot of coffee and took it through the hall and up the few steps to his study. He had nothing to study, but Olivia held the view that each of them must have a work room of their own, though what she did in hers except plan the next bloody expedition God alone knew, he thought grumpily. He looked out of the window over the trees and thought about John Kenyon. He was glad the dog Bayard was down at the farmhouse with Mrs Lyon, who was getting it ready for the weekend.

Bayard would have caught his mood and put a mournful spaniel head on his knee and gazed at him soulfully. Mrs Lyon, with the best intentions, would have been bracing.

He drank coffee and lit a cigarette. Sacha came in and sat on the carpet, washing herself and stopping to fix her eyes on him, and washing herself again.

'Hi, Sacha,' he said. 'Why John Kenyon? He was practically retired, poor bugger.'

There was no sentiment about Sacha. She jumped onto the arm of his chair and stared at him, lashing her tail, the hair on her back bristling.

He interpreted this behaviour. 'Kill,' she was saying. 'Kill.'

'Well, sure.' Harry put out his cigarette. 'Don't doubt it. But kill who, Sacha? Who did it?'

The black cat stopped lashing her tail and crouched down to sit with him in comfort, and began to purr. Her eyes closed. Her ears began to twitch, a ripple would run over her beautiful body, her eyes blink open to predatory slits and close again.

Only then did Harry remember the early part of the day. 'Premonition,' he said. 'Dear God. And what good was it?'

The cat slept, but Harry sat wakeful while the night grew round him.

Chapter Four

He dialled the number and was passed through the switchboard.

'Hello, Raleigh,' he said. 'About that piano.'

Raleigh was quick enough. 'Piano,' he said. 'Ah, the Steinway man.'

'Yes,' Hynd said. 'I'm ready to listen to the story. After that I'll see. How do we arrange this? You'll want to tell Halkett, I suppose. I'm in a phone-box. Do you want me to call back when he's had time to set it up?'

'No,' Raleigh said. 'I'd like you to come to London.'

Hynd was quick enough too, listening to voice, words, emphasis. 'You have more independence in this than I thought.'

'Yes, I do. It's my operation.'

'You were playing a game with me, the two of you.' Hynd was irritated. 'I must be slipping.'

'No,' Raleigh said. 'Halkett's an old hand, and I'm a good dissimulator, which belies my honest countenance. We weren't playing a game. I'm a careful man. You knew Halkett, but not me. If you didn't want to come in, then there was no purpose to be served by your knowing I was anything more than a sideman, a heavy, if you like.'

'You're young for it,' Hynd said. 'On a level with Halkett?'

'Cresting early, perhaps. Time will tell. What do you think?'

'I could work with it,' Hynd said. 'London when?'

'The day after tomorrow. Can you do that?'

'Yes, I can do that,' Hynd said. 'I'll take the sleeper tomorrow night.'

'Then get yourself breakfast and come at eleven, say. I'll give you an address.'

Hynd put in a good six hours' sleep on the train, and once arrived in London took a room at the Great Northern Hotel so that he could bathe in comfort before his breakfast.

When he checked out he left his bag at the hotel, walked through the dining-room where he had eaten breakfast and through the service door into the kitchens until he found a way out. He walked briskly into the warren of streets west of the station and began to get lost. Sometimes he ran, sometimes walked, went through a building worksite with large, clear danger signs, ignoring questions and complaints from the hard-hats, jumped on a passing bus and then off again as he was still explaining himself to the conductor, burst through a travel agent's into a backstreet, until he was sure he was clean, and then he picked up a taxi and set off for Chelsea; the address Raleigh had given him was in the Boltons.

The driver was vexed by the traffic, the Common Agricultural Policy of the European Community, and what he regarded as the excessive number of organizations in international boxing.

As they went through the park, Hynd said, 'I don't seem to think a great deal about the kind of things you think about.'

'I can take an 'int,' the driver said, 'and what do you think about?'

'The Higher Silences,' Hynd said.

The driver thought about this. 'Fuck you too,' he said. 'No offence intended.'

Hynd smiled to himself. 'None taken.'

He paid off the taxi at the corner. 'I thought I'd scuppered the tip,' the driver said.

'Don't see why,' Hynd said.

Raleigh opened the door, Raleigh in a pale grey suit, blue-striped shirt, yellow tie, red silk in the breast pocket, the pink and white face brimming with life. Things were going well for Raleigh.

They were not going wonderfully for Hynd, but with him they were more inward, deeper: the simpler felicities which clearly, at this moment, endowed his host, he had left behind him in the history of an earlier Hynd. What Raleigh saw, therefore, was very much the man of their first meeting, the weathered face serious and enclosed, a man again in dark cords, shirt and sweater, tieless, and carrying an old weatherproof jacket.

Hynd followed the grey suit upstairs to a room whose walls, where they were not shelved with books, were painted one of the more cheerful versions of terracotta.

'Coffee, tea, beer?' Raleigh asked.

'Beer would go well.'

He went to the books: not much modern fiction, but an interest in Japan embraced novels, Mishima, Endo, Togawa; Africa and India, the Far East and South America; European history and art, but on America and Russia hardly anything.

'You learning me?' Raleigh handed him a glass mug filled with darkness under the froth. 'Wasting your time.

Not my books, not my flat, borrowed it from a man I know. He's abroad, I got the key from his girlfriend. Sanitized meeting: neutral ground, no one followed me here – I expect it's the same with you.'

'The same,' Hynd said. 'Nice beer. This crap about you pretending to work for Halkett when the two of you came up to contact me, what's the real story?'

'Oh, these people are so old-fashioned, so obsessed by their own tradition, still back there in the days of the Cold War – even earlier, some of them. They thought threats and blackmail were the only way to get you.'

'It's not only that they're obsessed by tradition. People in this business are obsessed by power. Whether it's useful to their purpose or is, in fact, counter-productive, they need to feel they hold control.'

'Quite so,' Raleigh said. 'I said I wouldn't do it their way. Nominate someone to go with me who would, and if that failed I'd try my own approach to you. Nothing to lose, I said, and a man on the committee actually came up with this: "Nothing to lose except face," he said, and meant it as a serious objection.'

'I don't remember you from SIS when I was there. Where did you spring from?'

'Gower Street,' Raleigh said. 'I didn't quite fit there; too mercurial, or something, for MI5.'

'Are you going to fit in Six?' Hynd asked him.

'Oh, I'm being used,' Raleigh said, 'I do see that, to startle all the people who might have expected to get the job they've given me. There's a wish for voluntary redundancies as well, which is rather the issue that confronts us today.'

In this way, with well-oiled social efficiency, he made

it plain that the small talk was over, and it was time for business.

Hynd chose an armchair and Raleigh sat on the couch. 'It goes like this,' Raleigh said. 'I brief you, and Peter Blaney, he's a Minister of State at the Foreign Office now, comes along for a few minutes to give an air of verisimilitude to the proceedings, in other words to show that the Government takes this with deep seriousness, to authenticate the importance of what we ask you to do.'

'I've met him,' Hynd said. 'He was at the Home Office when I last read a newspaper.'

'Moved up after the election. You knew we'd had one of those?'

'I did, I did,' Hynd said. 'Shoot.'

'Well, hold on there. You may know something I don't know, because what we know is precious little. I take it you and Caroline Swift had an éclaircissement? She must have told you something.'

'I'll tell you, or not, when I've heard what you have to tell me,' Hynd said.

'Very well. Here it is. The Cold War's over: cuts in defence spending, therefore reduction of intelligence services, not just with us, the Russians, the Americans too, and elsewhere. Russia's in the throes of disassembly and reassembly, central and eastern Europe further along that road, which means whole sections of intelligence services disbanded, reorganized. Great quantities of intelligence staff have either been axed or got fed up and quit. So what follows?'

This question might or might not have been rhetorical. Hynd left it alone.

'Not all of them,' Raleigh said, 'will go in for raising

chickens or growing mushrooms. Some of them will want to go on doing what they're trained for, what they chose in the first place because it suited their temperament. How do they do that?'

'All right,' Hynd said, joining in the game this time. 'They'll join security firms. The better ones will set up on their own account, open consultancy operations. Some will be taken on by other agencies of other governments to spill what they know. You people will have done it yourself already, and it will have been done to you.'

Raleigh crossed the room to look down from a window. 'You don't say "us", you say "you people". There's a good bit of attitude about that, isn't there? In you, I mean.'

'It's not just attitude,' Hynd said. 'It's an imprint.'

'What does that mean?'

'Raleigh,' Hynd said. 'Just tell the story. Don't flex your technical college personnel diploma abridged-for-the-simple-minded version of Games People Play at me.'

Raleigh was not abashed. 'You're the original cat that walks by itself, aren't you, Hynd? After all, that's why you're here.' He looked down into the lane again.

Hynd swallowed the last of his beer, and waited.

'What we've done,' Raleigh said, 'about our own people who've left us, is keep an eye and an ear open to see what they're doing. You'd know that.'

Hynd nodded.

'Plainly, we can't maintain surveillance. It would cost a fortune, and in any case it would be bad for morale, having our people spy on their own, just because they've gone. But we check on this and that. There's all sorts of bureaucratic paperwork and computerwork attached to any citizen of these islands, and we can make sure whether someone's doing what you'd expect if they've taken up a normal civilian life. Tax, car, TV, parking fines, house purchase, marriage, babies, divorce, travel, insurance, countless little bits of people's lives easily accessible.'

'Big Brother,' Hynd said, 'watching you.'

'As it were.'

'And some of those countless little bits of some people's lives,' Hynd said, 'have suddenly stopped being there to be accessed.'

'There you are.' Raleigh's pink and white face flushed a little. 'You have been told things by Ms Swift.'

'Uh-uh.' Hynd shook his head. 'It's what I'd make happen if I wanted to disappear. So you've lost trace of some. Any good ones?'

'It depends what you mean by good,' Raleigh said. 'One at least was very senior, and yes, very good at his job, but there was something about him that made us uneasy. The others are all good, some strikingly so.'

'How many?'

'Twenty-seven in all.'

'Oh,' Hynd said slowly. 'That's quite a thing. And what was it about the top man that made you uneasy?'

'There was something,' Raleigh looked for the word, 'inveterate about him. Owen Garrett.'

'Yes,' Hynd said. 'I know the name, but not the man. He was Southern Europe, wasn't he, Nato's right flank, in the bad old days of that Cold War of yours? What does inveterate mean, when applied to Brother Garrett?'

'That he always wanted to take a matter further up to the edge than anyone else thought reasonable. It was as if he wanted to test a situation to destruction, to see what would happen if one went too far.'

'A Faustian,' Hynd said.

'Well, possibly,' Raleigh said.

'If he was that good, I take it he cut himself loose, he wasn't pushed.'

'Yes,' Raleigh said.

'So he's disappeared himself, this Owen Garrett. How long since you knew where he was?'

'He left us eighteen months ago. Within a month we'd lost sight of him.'

'He was ready,' Hynd said. 'He had the vanishing set up before he left you, new name, new place, and escape route, as you might call it.'

'That's it.'

'And the others?'

'They weren't so quick off the mark. We have record of them for between three and six months, and then they slip out of sight.'

'I can see this would make you nervous,' Hynd said, 'but on its own it's not enough to make you paranoid. There's another strand to it, I take it.'

'We found the other strand after we got nervous,' Raleigh said. 'We'd not established a running check; we were making a spot check every four months. No, what got us going was a signal from US Military Intelligence: their computer had come up with a chain of events which it decided were all flagged with an identical signature of style, efficiency, means – you know the form. Not each of them identical in every characteristic with every other, but each sharing enough characteristics to warrant being flagged.'

The doorbell rang.

'Blaney, damn it. He's early,' Raleigh said.

'I wonder why he'd be early.' Hynd earned an unguarded glance from Raleigh. 'Tell me some of these events. Fast shorthand will do.'

Raleigh, almost out of the door, stopped and rattled off: 'Arms store in Sweden entered, tunnel through concrete, sealed long-term store, perimeter guarded but no staff inside, and four hundred automatic rifles taken. Thirteen million dollars in gold taken from a hijacked Japanese freighter in the North Pacific . . .'

The doorbell rang again.

' . . . A number of senior intelligence officers murdered, various countries, and now, just the other day our General Kenyon, bomb in his office – in his office, right in Whitehall – can you beat it?'

The voice and its owner disappeared downstairs.

There was the sound of quick greetings, and then of feet running up the stairs, and Peter Blaney came into the room on the trot, turning and coming to a standstill in a movement so fast it was almost a contortion.

Hynd understood from this rapid escalation and arrival that Blaney was to be perceived as fit and energetic, from which he took it that the man had not changed for the better.

Blaney was a trim five-ten, wavy yellow hair, arrayed in a blue suit well made but with the jacket overlong, and waisted, giving the wearer a dashing look. He did not quite carry it off, because he had the face of a perpetual schoolboy, but for all that he had the charisma of a confident and vigorous nature. There was a healthy sunburn on the skin and a vital gleam in the blue eyes.

'Hello, Blaney,' Hynd said.

'You're a damn fool, Hynd.' Blaney's smile showed

great friendliness, which was false. 'You should have stayed on. You'd have been riding high in the new regime at MI6.'

'You know me, Blaney,' Hynd said. 'I'd rather walk in the woods than ride in the circus.'

Blaney held his countenance with no trouble at all, as if the cameras were there and rolling. He and Raleigh might have gone to the same school, or wherever it was these fellows learned to believe their own bullshit.

'Where are you sitting?' Blaney said, and he sat in a chair beside Hynd's, so that they would face Raleigh together.

'That bomb that killed Kenyon,' he said. 'I was due to attend a meeting in the conference room overhead, that very afternoon. Three hours later.'

Raleigh had appeared bearing a tray and he heard this as he was about to lay it on the table in front of the couch. He faltered, almost tripped, and crockery rattled and fell over and coffee splashed out of the pot over the biscuits.

'But,' he said, setting down the tray with belated care, 'there was nothing about that bomb to suggest it was intended for anything but what it did, which was to kill General Kenyon.'

'My dear Raleigh,' Blaney said, 'you have to remember that I was at the Northern Ireland Office and that Kenyon was all his life in tanks, never served in Ulster.'

Hynd had been used to think of Blaney as a play-actor, and now realized that he had grown in this profession and wanted top billing.

Blaney in the Northern Ireland Office had been an Under-Secretary of State dealing with economic development, and had had no direct concern with combating the terrorism of the IRA or the Protestant Loyalists. He had, however, picked up the flavour of security and intelligence life while he was there, and had acquired a taste for it.

It was after that, when Blaney was at the Home Office, that Hynd had known him, and known him as one of those irritating politicians who are fascinated by the intelligence world: for its secretive power, and for its cloak and dagger aura – these two aspects being, to Hynd, very different, since the first was political, and the second a phrase which sanitized the idea of coming on a man from behind and cutting his throat.

Hynd detested politicians who fancied themselves part of the intelligence world. He held it both to impeach their judgement and to endanger practitioners like himself. A man should stick to his own trade, and respect the exclusiveness of other trades. Thinking so, Hynd was aware that he was seeing the spy's trade with the jealous protectiveness of a medieval guildsman: and self-protection was a large part of his attitude to Blaney. That the play-actor had grown more egocentric since he had last known him made him that much more likely to be a dangerous nuisance.

Raleigh had used the occasion of restoring order to the tray to collect himself. He passed Blaney a cup of coffee and said to him, 'That bomb killed General Kenyon, blew his office to smithereens, and did only marginal damage to the floor above. Though it brought down the ceiling on his deputy, Harry Seddall, whose office is directly underneath the general's. Also, there has been no IRA phone call, and the make-up of the bomb did not match IRA bomb-making methods. It is precisely because the IRA was not involved that we have been able to present it as an accidental explosion of a piece of experimental ordnance.'

'You may say so,' Blaney said, 'but I have a feeling in my bones. A man must trust such feelings, don't you agree, Hynd?'

'Depends on the bones,' Hynd said. 'Mine tell me you were listening to me and Raleigh before ever you came into this house, sitting in your car nearby; that this room is wired. You came in very prompt when Raleigh reached the point of telling me what this mission was about. I understood from him that you were to come in after I'd been briefed, and that your function was simply to demonstrate to me, by your presence as a Government Minister, that the Government is deeply exercised about whatever it is I'm to be asked to deal with.'

Blaney listened to this speech with an expression of alert interest and when it was finished said, 'You object to my listening to you and Raleigh?'

'I object to the dissimulation of it,' Hynd said. 'It doesn't worry me a lot. You're a man who likes power, and to you secrecy is power, because it's manipulative. Carried to excess manipulation is a weakness. You should watch it.'

Blaney let a grimace as of self-criticism cross his face. 'You're no respecter of persons, are you? That's why you left SIS, if I remember.'

'I don't respect persons. I respect people.'

'I wonder,' the Minister said, 'how I can disarm this hostility of yours.'

'Treat me straight, talk turkey, and don't piss around,' Hynd said.

'Asking a lot,' Blaney said, 'but I'll do my best.'

'Sit still and listen to me,' Hynd said, for Blaney was irrepressible, and the only thing to do with him was to go to war. 'Let professionals form a judgement on what that bomb was about. I can see it gives you a hit to think that bomb was directed at you, and that you feel it gives you a particular locus in this business that Raleigh is spelling out to me, but it's not good practice. It cuts out all unimagined alternatives. And a bomb that made its way into General Kenyon's office and killed him, and has not been claimed by the IRA – and they'd have claimed that one all right – or by any other group, and appears so far to be motiveless, well, that seems to me to relate with far more likelihood to what Raleigh's been laying out for me than any personal speculations that you plan to put into your I hope not yet begun autobiography.'

'I see,' Blaney said.

'So try to be good,' Hynd said. 'Remember that compared with Raleigh and me you don't know shit about this business, forget you're a politician on the way up, that you might be Foreign Secretary or Chancellor of the Exchequer one of these fine days, don't be crafty and don't be self-important, and we'll get on tolerably well.'

'You don't see me as Prime Minister?' Blaney looked amused, also natural and relaxed for the first time that morning.

'No, I don't.'

'Time will tell,' Blaney said. 'I am seized of what you say, however, and I'll digest it. Meanwhile, I'll be a good boy. Raleigh, the floor is yours.'

'What do you pick up, Hynd, from what I've said to you?' Raleigh said.

'That you think someone's recruiting former intelligence officers,' Hynd said. 'And perhaps you make a link between that and these events in which you see a common signature – the arms raid in Sweden, piracy in the Pacific, this bomb in Whitehall.'

'And you're assuming something else by this time, aren't you?' Raleigh said.

'Oh, sure. You think they've approached me or that they're going to approach me. That's why you were lurking in the heather, to spy on the approaches to Castle Hynd and see if there were signs of conspiracy afoot.'

'And have they tried to recruit you?' Blaney said. 'What about that woman?'

The look Hynd gave Blaney hardly lingered, moving on to the window where it stared unfocused at the sky, but there had been that in the touch of it which shocked the politician. Blaney held a short discussion with the watch on his wrist.

'I think you fellows could spare me now,' he said. 'Hynd will feel that what you, Raleigh, ask him to do is a direct order – I should say request, a direct and earnest request – from the Government. You do feel that, Hynd?'

'Yes,' Hynd said.

'Good.' Blaney stood up, still regarding Hynd. 'Learned a lot this morning,' he said.

'Such a learning curve, this life,' Hynd said.

This brought a cold, and this time genuine, smile, on which Blaney departed.

'You want me to join up,' Hynd said, when Raleigh came back from seeing Blaney out, 'to let these people recruit me.'

'Yes, that's what we want. Bloody risky for you, if they're doing the sort of thing we think they are.'

'Tell me why it's worth it to you, to go to all this bother to get me in there.'

Raleigh shed his jacket, and before he laid it over the back of the couch he reached into a pocket, took out a cassette, and tossed it to Hynd. 'That's from Blaney's car,' he said. 'There's no bug in here. It was a directional device from the car. Very new, very sophisticated. I asked him where he'd got it, and he just put a finger beside his nose. He should have been on the stage, that man.'

'He is,' Hynd said. 'Politicians are. He wouldn't have made a real actor, though. He acts too much without knowing he's doing it.'

'Well,' Raleigh said, wanting to get down to business, 'that kind of thing . . .'

He made a gesture which waved away that kind of thing, and settled himself along the couch – this recurring notion of the undergraduate about Raleigh – and said, 'Another event, by way of example: a former American intelligence agent sprung from a prison in Peru when it was raided by a Sendero Luminoso force ostensibly to free a number of their own who were being held there.

'This is where the pattern comes in. Two years ago Mossad sprang one of their men from a prison in Niger by supporting a Touareg raid which freed nearly twenty Touareg rebels, freedom-fighters, call them what you will. You see? Same as Peru.

'Now take the hijacking of the Japanese ship. She had berths for twelve passengers. Nine of them were occupied when she sailed from Vancouver for Tokyo, and the nine passengers took over the ship at gunpoint when she was three days out. The computer registered this as a copy of the Abu Nidal seizure of the *Achille Lauro* in the Mediterranean – you'll remember that one.'

Hynd had begun to find this interesting. 'And General Kenyon. What does the computer say about that?'

'The bomb that killed General Kenyon,' Raleigh said, 'reminded it of an exactly similar killing by the KGB in West Germany, before reunification, of a General Planfze in counter-intelligence. His office was blown up and he went with it, just like Kenyon. What do you think? There are more, but that'll do to be going on with.'

Hynd stretched out in his chair and looked at his well-worn shoes. 'All done by the same outfit, who have taken for some reason or other to imitating previous terrorist acts which were carried out by a number of different groups.'

'Yes, right,' Raleigh said. 'So why are they doing this? Why are they replicating previous terrorist acts so definitively? The National Security Agency in Washington have come up with this: advertisement.'

'Advertisement,' Hynd said, without inflection.

'It had some back-up for this,' Raleigh said. 'For example, the men who took over the freighter spoke in at least five languages – English, Russian, French, Italian, German, as well as English with an American accent. I mean they spoke a lot, they were voluble, they were making a point of it, whereas the normal thing would be to keep their traps shut except when they had to speak. So, they were doing all this multi-lingual talking for a reason. They wanted it known that they were an international outfit.'

'Did the computer say,' asked Hynd, 'who they're advertising themselves to?'

'No, it didn't, at least nothing that our own little brains can't tell us. They're advertising at large institutions which draw the line at nothing, nothing at all. That could mean they will offer their services to major criminal organizations, to business, to the governments of states, or to those who wish to subvert the government of states, even perhaps to terrorist groups.

'As to the gold,' Raleigh went on, 'in our terms, by which I mean the rate at which intelligence services spend, what they have now is up-front money, to borrow a metaphor. So they're ready to make the movie. They want backers. They're ready to go into business. They want clients.'

'Maybe.'

'Maybe?'

'Perhaps they just enjoy their work,' Hynd said. 'If so, you can expect more of the same.'

'Caroline Swift told you that?' Raleigh said.

Hynd waited before he spoke, altered by the mention of the name.

'No,' he said at last, 'that's not what we spoke about.'

'If you're going to be working for me,' Raleigh said, 'there's no point in being coy about her. I need to know what she told you. There's no need to be coy. We know her background, Hynd. You're not the first man to have been led up the garden path by a woman like that. We know she was a whore for the CIA . . . Jesus Christ!'

This last was a shriek.

In the space of a second Hynd had come out of his chair, taken hold of Raleigh's left hand, and bent back the middle finger until he knew it was on the point of breaking. And then he let the man go.

Hynd withdrew to lean against the bookshelves, where he lit a cigarette and gave himself up to thought. He paid no particular attention to the afflicted Raleigh, beyond glancing at him once or twice, but gazed out of the window opposite him with a frown on his face.

Raleigh, who had been sprawled along the couch when he was attacked, lay there for about five minutes, staring with comically widened eyes variously at Hynd and at his injured finger. At last he stirred himself, and struggled up to a sitting position, cradling the pain with his good hand.

'What the hell,' Raleigh said. 'What the hell.' Then: 'Get me some whisky, curse you.'

Hynd found the whisky and put the glass on the table in front of Raleigh, who rested the sore hand on his thigh and took two swallows, looked at what was left, and gulped that down as well.

He looked up at Hynd, flushed with Dutch courage. 'That woman's really got to you, right under your skin.'

'Be quiet,' Hynd said.

'Damn that,' Raleigh said. 'I'll say what I bloody like. Anyway, you wouldn't attack an injured man.'

'I would and I will,' Hynd said, 'if you don't lay off her. And if you think a damaged finger amounts to an injury, you must have led a deeply sheltered life. You've got off lightly, so far. Now, let's complete our business.'

'Business? You think I'm going to work with a ruddy madman like you? After this?' And he held up the hand, which was beginning to swell redly, supporting it with the other.

'Working with each other's not what's going to happen,' Hynd said. 'You're too clever for your own good, and too ambitious for mine. I've watched and listened to you long enough, Raleigh, to know I don't want to work with you.'

'Hah!' Raleigh said. 'If you think you'll be working on this one *now*, you've got another think coming.'

'Listen,' Hynd said. 'This is a serious thing we've been talking about. Your bosses take it seriously. Your bosses seriously want me. I'm going to do it, for my own reasons.'

Raleigh opened his mouth to speak but Hynd stepped towards him and lifted a hand, and Raleigh subsided.

'There are lives at stake here,' Hynd said, 'and you're not up to that. It has no meaning for you. You're not safe, Raleigh. So I won't work to you.'

'So who do you think you're going to work to? Halkett, for God's sake?'

'I'll work to General Kenyon's deputy, Harry Seddall. He's—'

That was as far as Hynd got, or indeed expected to get without interruption.

'That won't wash,' Raleigh said. 'Not for a moment.'

Hynd came close and stood over Raleigh, who recoiled into the back of the couch.

'Just keep listening,' Hynd said. 'Think of yourself as a messenger, Raleigh, just a messenger, and listen. Harry Seddall's got a stake in this. He worked for Kenyon. I don't know Seddall, but I've heard enough about him to think we might get on all right. But I'll want to meet him, to make sure.'

'Seddall's not MI6, he's military intelligence, and a damned peculiar section of it at that. It's unthinkable. This is an MI6 operation.'

'No,' Hynd said. 'It's just another operation, and I won't do it unless it's Seddall. I don't trust you people. I'm going now. Make the phone calls, see whoever you have to see. Get the OK, or not, and if you get the OK tell Seddall I want to meet him. I'll call you this evening at five o'clock. If you don't get the OK, I'll go back to Scotland tonight.'

Hynd collected his stormproof jacket and went to the door.

Raleigh stood up, as if he had forgotten the pain in his hand.

'Halkett was right about you,' he said.

'In what respect?' Hynd said.

'He said you were an utter shit, and so you bloody are.'

'That's fair,' and Hynd went out, and down the stairs, and away.

Chapter Five

Seddall found Hynd already established in the pub and chalking his cue at the pool table, while a local youth, playing under the stress of taunts from his fellows, failed with a two-cushion shot and sank his own ball into the bargain.

Hynd raised a hand to Seddall, bent over the table, and saw the game off with implacable sureness of hand and eye.

'Thanks,' Hynd said to his opponent, and laid down his cue.

'Double or quits,' said the defeated one, six foot two of brawn and muscle.

'Thanks, but no,' Hynd said. 'Best of three, that was the match. Told you I'd have to stop.' He moved his head to indicate Seddall.

'Later, then,' the young man said. 'I blew it, but you earned it.' He went into his pocket and counted out fivers. 'I'll get my revenge.'

'Another day.' Hynd took his winnings.

'Live hereabouts, then?' the youth asked.

'I move around.'

Seddall watched the youth, who had a bit of edge on but was not yet either friendly or unfriendly, measure something in Hynd, and then come up with a sudden warm smile.

'If I see you here again,' he said, and punched Hynd on the arm, 'we'll play, right?'

'Right,' Hynd said.

He and Seddall took some straightforward blended Scotch to a table in a corner.

'What kind of dead and alive hole is this?' Seddall said.

'This?' Hynd said. 'Great pub.'

'The pub's all right,' Harry said. 'In fact the pub's a find, or would be if it was on the road to anywhere that people actually go, but Acton?'

The pub was Victorian, scarred and polished panelling on the walls, wooden floor, the glass frosted or stained, the works. Somehow it had stayed free of the brewers' chains, and avoided being restored out of its mind.

'You got here clean?' Hynd said. 'No one tailed you?'

'By the time I got here,' Harry said, 'I could have shaken off the entire reconnaissance capability of the Sioux Nations.'

'That,' Hynd said, 'is why we're in Acton.'

'It's a bit extreme, though,' Seddall said, 'but then you are a bit extreme, or so they used to say.'

He had studied Hynd, tall, and not a slight man but not heavy either, when he was talking to his opponent. The hint of animosity in the loser had been ephemeral – no more than the tension of the match working out of him – but Hynd had been there, aware, ready for him, and the big man had felt it.

'A bit extreme,' Hynd said, 'doesn't mean anything to me, except that saying it defines the people who say it. You don't think it. Stop testing me.'

'I don't know you,' Seddall said. 'I only know of you. And you don't know me. Why pick on me to run this thing? You think I don't have enough trouble as it is, without you hijacking this great scheme that MI6 dreamt up, and then throwing it in my lap?'

Hynd said, 'I have a reason for doing this, and it's not for the welfare of MI6 or for Queen and country or to avenge your General Kenyon. I'm going in there myself and I'm going to run a cool, calculated, solo operation and I don't want it compromised by having Raleigh or even Halkett having their heads on it. I may get so far, though, and then need some kind of back-up – like a spare man or two or an aircraft-carrier, that kind of thing – so I want to have a bloke behind me who knows a bit about the real world, for me to call on at need. You won't be running me. No one will. You can forget it until you hear from me, and that'll be weeks or maybe months.'

'Why me?' Seddall said. 'I hear what you say, but why me?'

'Because you're not hidebound, as would become your years and station, and you're not career-motivated. I've seen a file on you, back when I was in the business. You go your own road, and mostly you get away with it because you're fortunate, in the sense that Napoleon liked his generals to be fortunate. And you seem to have some pull in odd places, as if people owe you favours or you know where the bodies are buried; I don't know what it is. Maybe it's just your old-world charm.'

'It is that, actually,' Seddall said, with the lurid and hardly charming grin of a Staffordshire bull terrier.

'Well,' Hynd said. 'You're as close as I'll get to the job description for what I need. If you'll do it.'

'I might do it,' Seddall said.

Hynd's eyes struck at him. 'Might?' He stood up and took their empty glasses over to the bar.

Watching him go, Seddall was conscious of a compelling paradox in Hynd. It was there in the posture of the body, in the set of the face, and in the life of the black eyes: these showed the man's state to be alert, almost intensely aware and active. But behind that, as in the depths of a profound pool, he gave the sense of a remote and unshakeable calm.

There was a primitive simplicity to this combination that said a lot about Hynd: it was the simplicity of a man who lived in a world without law.

With Hynd he could believe it to be not only a part of the man's nature but also of a recognition that Seddall shared, the recognition that the world was chaos and that the structures of civilization were no more real a defence against it than the walls of ancient Rome had been against the onset of the barbarians.

Whereas to Seddall, though it was a useful recognition to have made, he had the idea that to Hynd it was a creed to live by: a belief that the world was a hostile wilderness, and a man must be as ready to fight for his own hand as primitive man had been; the weapons and the accoutrements of life were more sophisticated than the stone axe and animal skin and drawings on the cave wall that was home, but in the world where Hynd moved, no man or woman could be held tamed.

Hynd knew always who was behind him in a room, what was moving in the blood of those he confronted, the always-changing configuration of a city street, and who else was abroad in the desert.

What the contradictory sense of an unplumbed peace within the man betokened, Seddall could not conjecture. He had known something of him before this, and last night had read Hynd's history from the intelligence archive as closely as Hynd had once read his. He knew that it was because he was as he was that Hynd was still alive, and other men were dead.

'You might do it?' Hynd said returning. He put the glasses on the table and sat down. 'What makes you hold back?'

'Your own motive for going into this business,' Seddall said. 'What you propose to do would scare the hell out of me, and you make it clear you're not doing it for the honour of the regiment or anything like that. You tell me you're doing it for a private reason. I've done things like this, less hair-raising than this, certainly, for private reasons myself. But I'd like to know your reason.'

'If I tell you,' Hynd said, 'you must tell no one else.'

A yellowish gleam darkened in Seddall's eyes. 'Don't threaten me.' The words came oddly from that lounging body, which displayed no superabundant appearance of being likely to win any kind of contest with the man they were addressed to, but Hynd heard in them what he had not heard from the half-aggressive talk of the local pool-player.

'All right,' he said. 'I don't threaten you. I ask for your confidence.'

Seddall reflected on this and nodded.

'I'm doing it to protect Caroline Swift. You know who she is?'

'Raleigh told me of her,' Seddall said. 'He was cross enough about your quitting on him and ringing me in, in his place, me and my dodgy little bit of Army Intelligence instead of the mighty MI6, but he was unreasonably vexed about your refusing to pass on to him what he supposes Caroline Swift to have told you. He seemed crosser about that than about your dislocating his finger.'

Hynd gave a faint smile, which had at first the air of being an ironic comment on Raleigh, but then lingered that bit longer and in a way that spoke of some direct and personal feeling.

Knowing quite well that he had shown this feeling, Hynd deliberately spoke of its cause as if his acquaintance with her were that of one professional for another. 'Swift was with the CIA to start with and latterly with the National Security Agency. Early in her work with the CIA she was called on to be a honey-trap; that was nearly thirty years ago, you understand. She was well qualified. She still is, come to that. She's quite lovely, and she's seductive, ardent, intelligent.'

He was watching Seddall like a hawk, but Seddall busied himself with lighting a Gauloise and getting smoke in his eye so that nothing about him made a comment on this recital.

'Her father, to whom she was deeply attached, was a two-star general in the US Army serving a term in NATO strategic planning. He went to Stockholm on a week's leave and hired a small yacht and went sailing single-handed in the Baltic. The yacht was found sunk in the Gulf of Bothnia, and he was in the cabin. He had been tortured to death. Swift was in Nepal at the time, taking the rays, smoking pot, wearing flowers in her hair, the sixties, all that. She went to Columbia, took her degree, and joined the CIA. It was a mission with her. When they asked her to be a honey-trap in the CIA war against the KGB, she agreed, without hesitation, she told me.'

'The KGB tortured him?' Seddall said.

'To death. Yes, I think there's no doubt of it.'

It was Seddall who went to the bar now. He came back with two glasses for each of them. 'Since we're in Acton,' he said, 'where we are as invisible as if we were in Surabaya, we might as well get slightly pissed.'

'We'll see,' Hynd said. 'She changed, she grew, and asked to be put on other work and when that was refused her she found a berth with the NSA, made a quiet career with them in Washington, and quit three years ago and moved to a cottage on the Maryland shore. She likes to live alone. She started to write. She's read me short passages, when they illustrate what we happen to be talking about; imaginative, introspective, perceptive. She won't commit herself to saying she's writing anything in particular. She was writing there, in Maryland, when they came at her last year.'

'They,' Seddall said.

'Exactly,' Hynd said. 'They do exist, this group of ex-intelligence people. They came at her. Be a honey-trap one more time, they said, one of them said.'

'She agreed?'

'She said no, so they leaned on her. There were two of them.' There was a glow in Hynd's eye now, a phosphorescence under the surface, as of a shark surging up to strike.

'Leaned on her? What with?'

'The top man said to her, apparently, "If you don't do it, my friend here will cut your throat." He spoke with an English voice.'

'Ah.'

'Yes,' Hynd said. 'The man Garrett. I got Raleigh to show me his record, and his picture fits her description.'

Seddall withdrew, and ruminated, and came back again. 'So your object in this is to take them off her back?'

'That's it.'

'Are you going to kill Garrett?'

'Certainly I'm going to kill Garrett.'

'Quite a lot of others too,' Seddall said, 'if you want to make her safe from them.'

'Well,' Hynd said, 'I don't know who they are, but they have it coming.'

Seddall sat upright to face him. 'I'm not in love with the way you approach this mission,' he said. 'With one breath you say it will be a cool, calculated operation, and with the next you talk as if you're going to wage a personal vendetta. I'll tell you where I stand. The thinking is that they're about to go into business, first big contract. We want you in there when that goes down, and the objects of this mission are, first, to find out who and how many they are and where they're based; second, to make the contract blow up in their faces so that no one will want to hire them again; third, to eliminate them as an organization so that they won't be there to be hired again. All this without it coming to light that the organization ever existed, far less that it included one-time senior MI6 men like Garrett. Therefore, it's going to call for a sudden, surgically precise, series of moves when the time is ripe.'

Seddall inhaled the remains of his cigarette. 'So, I'm not going to have you dancing in there with mythic dreams of personal vengeance coursing in your bloodstream. I want a job done, that's what I want.'

'I see,' Hynd said. 'You mean you can kill a few

people some of the time, but you can't kill all of the people all the time.'

'Was that a joke? I didn't know you made jokes.'

'It was sarcasm,' Hynd said. 'Do you think I can't reconcile my motive with your need? With the official mission statement? Do you think that I, looking for vengeance, as you put it, would be any less cool and calculating than I'm used to being when I'm out in the field? The leopard doesn't change its spots, Seddall. I'll operate on this exactly as on any other mission.'

The sun shone through the varicoloured glass of the windows, throwing prismatic flakes of rainbowed light on walls, faces, beer in mugs lifted to faces.

In Seddall unease had begun to grow from the feeling that this talk between him and Hynd was an insult to the life around them, that this space they occupied was fast becoming a neurotic corner in a group of robust and healthy humanity.

'But,' he said, 'you're in this to make Caroline Swift safe?'

'Yes,' Hynd said. 'That's why I'm in this.' He revolved the whisky in his glass and looked into the miniature whirlpool. 'We need to talk about it, I suppose?'

'Yes,' Seddall said, 'we do. If you want me to stand behind you, and I'm by no means certain that I will, then this is what we need to talk about.'

Hynd thought. 'Right.' He looked round the bar. 'We've been here long enough. Let's move. Somewhere private, if that's possible.'

Seddall came to his feet, stuffing an assortment of debris – wallet, cigarettes and lighter, a ballpoint pen, a diary – into the pockets of his jacket.

'I have an idea where we might be private, and get a decent lunch,' he said. 'Let's go and find a cab. I'm sure they have cabs in Acton.'

Hynd, unshaven, his short black hair all anyhow, and wearing jeans and a black leather jacket, looked at Seddall in his linen suit and panama hat, good clothes in their day but suffering from their wearer's indifference to his appearance, and gave a slow smile.

'I'm sure they have cabs in Acton,' he said, mimicking Seddall's voice. 'You not only look like a remittance man, you talk like one.'

Seddall was pleased, not only with the comment, but with the fact that Hynd had the understanding and the wit to ease the tension that had inevitably risen between them. It meant that at least their journey together across half London would be relaxed.

'Crystal Palace?' the driver said. 'I don't go as far as that for me 'olidays.'

'I've heard that one before,' Seddall said, 'but I'll give you five quid over and above if we get there before my lunch is spoiled.'

'Trouble with the wife, then?' the driver said as they set off down the road and stopped at a traffic light.

'Late for lunch, you mean?' Seddall said. 'Hardly that. The wife's in Outer Mongolia.'

The place was called Vincenzo, and it was Vincenzo himself who took them through a room where two dozen people were feeding off red-checked tablecloths. The atmosphere was rich with the smells of garlic, wine, herbs, fish, meat, and full of exhilarated noise.

They went into a passage and up a flight of stairs to

a room under whose floor the merriment below made a muted and euphonious din. This room was much smaller than that below. There was one table, laid for them at an open window.

Vincenzo rapped on a door. 'There is a bathroom in there,' he said. 'Through the bedroom.'

Hynd went as a matter of course to inspect the adjacent spaces, and came back with an expression of serious pleasure on his face.

'What an excellent thing,' he said to Vincenzo. 'That bedroom is absolutely charming. Flowers and all, complete.'

Vincenzo, a lanky, fair-haired North Italian, responded to this encomium by taking a card from his hip pocket and presenting it to Hynd.

'Fresh flowers every day,' he said. 'Now, gentlemen, your salad is on the table. The fish will be ready exactly when you have finished, so you must begin.'

He settled them at the table and poured them some white wine from Piedmont. 'Too dry for you?'

'Dry?' Seddall said. 'It's arid.'

Vincenzo looked at Hynd.

'My kind of wine,' Hynd said.

'Then it will do,' Vincenzo said. 'I'll serve you myself. Your meeting will be disturbed by no one else.'

Seddall stared at the closing door. 'The things I've done for that man,' he said. 'Well, one thing, to be precise. Now, all of a sudden, you're his blue-eyed boy. Why's that?'

'Beats me. Maybe it's because I like the way he's got this floor set up as a place of assignation.'

'Assignation?'

'For lovers,' Hynd said.

'I've got to see this.' Seddall got up, and did so. When he came back to the table, he said, 'Yes, it is charming. New since I was last here. It was just a bare room, then. You don't think it's vulgar?'

'What's that got to do with anything?' Hynd said. 'And, no, I don't think it is, not in the least.'

'I must be getting stuffy in my old age,' Seddall said. 'Still, the fact that you and Vincenzo experience a rapport over the question is no reason why I should get stuck with a wine that turns my tongue inside out, just because it suits you. Let that be a lesson: favours don't last for ever.'

To Seddall's surprise – for sitting by this open window looking out over the sunny street, with a breeze refreshing his brow, he was not yet ready for business – Hynd took his idle moralizing about favours as a cue, and went straight in again to the question of Caroline Swift.

'I've been out of the game for a while,' was how he came at it, 'been living solitary, well, more or less solitary.' It was inevitable, no doubt, that with these words he would favour the door of the delightful bedroom with a fleeting glance. 'More or less solitary,' he repeated, 'but all the same, I have an irrational feeling that you can be confided in.'

'I'm not a gossip, certainly,' Seddall said. 'These olives have been stored in oil.'

'Gossip would be the least of it. I'm talking about trusting you with personal stuff.'

'Well, damn it, I'm trusting you as well,' Seddall said. 'If anyone knew that I knew why you were taking on this mission, and that I let you go ahead with it – if that's what I do – I'd be dropped to corporal overnight.'

'You can't stop me.'

'Maybe not,' Seddall said. 'But I don't have to sponsor you, do I? Which, as I say, it remains to be seen if I do. Fantastic bread. They bake it here, you know, and he won't sell it. He's a hard man, that Vincenzo.'

This distracted Hynd briefly. 'Yes, he is a hard man. I'm assuming you count him reliable.'

'No question. He wouldn't be so offhand with me otherwise.' Seddall picked up an olive and sniffed and felt it as if he were shopping in the market at Cuneo. 'You're being evasive about Caroline Swift.'

'Evasive? Am I?'

'Evasive,' Seddall said. 'I haven't heard you tell me she's the love of your life, for example.'

'Does that matter?'

'That,' Seddall said, 'is what I mean by evasive. Of course it matters. You are about to embark on a mission which the Great and the Good and, it must be said, the Godawful, have asked you to accomplish for high-flown reasons concerning the security of the State. You want me to be what amounts to your case officer for this mission, and the only reason you're going into it, risking your life and God knows what else about yourself, is the existence of this woman. That is a fragile basis, Hynd, upon which to establish a foundation of belief that you are the right man for this. No one but me would still be contemplating the thing.'

Hynd wiped his mouth with his napkin and swallowed some wine, and stared down into the street. 'I know. That's why I chose you.'

'Terrific,' Seddall said crossly. 'So what is it about her? Are you in love with her?'

Hynd moved impatiently. 'Love,' he said, and it was

81

as if Seddall had confronted him with an algebraic equation that had baffled him even when he was at school.

'Love,' Seddall said firmly, but thought dubiously about Olivia, footloose in wildest Mongolia.

Hynd said, 'It may not be the love of my life, it's certainly not hers, but it is the meeting of my life.'

'Whatever that means. Is it mutual? Is it the meeting of her life?'

'I don't know,' Hynd said. 'I don't think so. But those are my words for it, I don't know what words she would use. And anyway, I have difficulty even with my words, since the meeting of my life is with me. Perhaps it is simply that I meet more of myself when I am with her, and I meet more of her than I've ever met of any other human being. I don't mean narcissism, you understand. It is that she is very self-aware and clear-sighted about herself, in a pretty tough way, a hard way. And she gives me that for myself.'

'She sounds like a female guru.'

'Watch your damn mouth,' Hynd said.

Seddall had known as soon as the words were spoken that they might have been acceptable if he'd said them right, and that he hadn't, that he'd got the tone wrong.

'Let me try to get hold of this,' he said. He went to the bell by the door and gave the signal to Vincenzo, then he went into the charming bedroom and lay on the bed with his hands behind his head.

The meeting of his life, Hynd had said. What a moderate word to use, as against love or passion. A recall came to him, that at some time long ago he had been to a play in which one of the characters had said, 'I have missed the meeting that my life was for.'

He heard the door to the passage open, saw Vincenzo

pass by and heard him exchange words with Hynd. A smell of fish decorated with subsidiary odours came to his nose.

He got off the bed and said, to himself but out loud, 'The man knows what he's doing, that's what counts.'

He waited till Vincenzo had left again and then rejoined Hynd at the table. Fish lay there in a light sauce, and new potatoes and spinach.

'Bream,' Hynd said. He seemed to have resolved something in himself, for there was an appearance of peace in the way he sat, and in the way he looked up, unsmiling but amiable.

'Simple fare,' Seddall said, 'always the best.'

'Oh, yes,' Hynd said, 'simplicity that has been reached and understood, worth attaining and rarely achieved.'

'I know you're right about that kind of thing,' Seddall said, 'but I can't handle it this minute. I understand about Caroline Swift, though.'

'Tell me,' Hynd said.

'The risk of getting killed is the least of it,' Seddall said. 'You'd risk your – I don't know how to put it – your whole nature for her, your whole sense of yourself.'

'You're afraid that because I've declared vendetta against these bastards I might run amok, go blood-mad, and end up with a lot of dead men on my conscience. That I might go over the top.'

'Yes,' Seddall said, 'and do something appallingly cold-blooded which would make you feel seriously weird about yourself afterwards. A lot of dead men and women, all for the sake of Caroline Swift. Does she know this?'

Hynd ignored the question. 'It's not just for her sake,

it's for the sake of Caroline Swift and me. So long as this organization of theirs stays in being she will feel unsafe and be unsafe. I want her to feel safe from them, and be safe from them, and I want her to be alive in the world.'

'That's not how we'll do it,' Seddall said. 'We'll use our little brains.'

Hynd laid down his knife and fork and, with his chin a little tilted, regarded Seddall. 'So you're in.'

'Yes,' Seddall said.

'Why?' Hynd said.

'Because you'd go to the wall for Caroline Swift. I find the whole concept of you calling up the primitive in you and undertaking formal feud unspeakably embarrassing, and I won't go on about that. But it's not that you've *decided* to do it, it's that it's simply happened in you that you're *going* to do it. It's fallen on you like one of those tasks in a fairy-tale, a kind of fate. You've become an implacable force. I think it makes you right for the job. I think with you at the sharp end and my cunning and sagacity behind you, it is not unreasonable to suppose that something might be achieved.'

'Good,' Hynd said.

His black eyes were on Seddall but there was a blankness on them as if they were seeing an image not in this room.

Hynd lifted his glass and tilted it so that the wine in it poured out of the window. A faint cry came from below.

'Libation,' Hynd said, and tossed the glass, rather than threw it, so that it passed through the air in a scintillating arc and shattered in the empty fireplace.

This was not Seddall's kind of lark at all, but he took it that he was being asked to seal an alliance, and must not fail the mysterious spirit across the table.

'*Hoch*,' he said, raising his own glass, and drained it and threw it over his shoulder.

'I think I might ring for the profiteroles,' he said.

Chapter Six

Hynd scudded through the night lying in the back of a Citroën ambulance with the blinds drawn about him. On the opposite bunk his guide, or guard, sat with knees up and a book propped on them reading.

He was a dashing young man, well over six feet, with dark hair cut *en brosse* and an obsolete pencil moustache, who had introduced himself at Orléans as Pierre Aschaffenberg, which Hynd took to be an assumed name.

They had dined at Tours and the young man had revealed himself to have a reckless and cheerful nature, to be much given to insolent wit, to have a laughing mouth and a cold eye, and to have the inquisitive nature of a man on the make, for he alternately mocked the Hynd who sat across the table from him and met with a kind of equal respect the Hynd he had heard of by reputation: so that altogether he reminded Hynd of the cynical and cheerful rascal in *The Prisoner of Zenda* – Rupert of the Rhine? No, dammit, Prince Rupert was a historical figure. Rupert of Hentzau, that was it.

'We dine here,' the cheerful rascal had said, 'because roads come into Tours from all points of the compass, so you will have no way to guess where we are going.'

'What about the stars?' Hynd said. 'Or am I to be blindfold?'

'No,' Aschaffenberg said. 'We'll be eight hours on this drive. It would be intolerable to blindfold you for so long; besides that it would be the height of ill-manners to blindfold you at all. No: the blinds of the car will be drawn.'

'I could manage a look out behind the blinds now and then,' Hynd said.

Aschaffenberg became grave, but not disconcerted. 'Best not,' he said. 'Truly, I don't advise it. Especially since I have told you what I have about our organization. No, I do not advise it.'

'Or what?' Hynd said.

'Or,' Aschaffenberg said, smiling, 'you and I will not part friends.'

Hynd, since he was not much of a one for badinage, had been astonished to find himself laughing.

'You're a cool son of a bitch,' he said. 'I've never had anyone offer to kill me so euphemistically in my life.'

Aschaffenberg had let most of the smile depart from his long thin lips. 'So long as you understand me. I would do it without hostility, since it seems to me we get on rather well together, but also I would do it without a moment's hesitation.'

Hynd looked through his Grand Marnier at the sconcelight on the wall behind Aschaffenberg.

'Were you to decide it was necesssary to kill me,' he said, 'then extraordinary rapidity of execution would certainly be your best course.'

The young man bit his lip and threw down his napkin and signalled for the bill, and then his ebullience came back. 'We are two of a kind,' he said. 'Let us embark.'

So now Hynd lay in comfort in the back of the Citroën, which ran along the roads of its mysterious journey as if it rode on silk. And while his companion read a novel with the title *Une femme qui ne disait rien,* Hynd turned on his side and got comfortable, and fell asleep.

They must indeed have travelled for something like eight hours, for when Hynd awoke at their journey's end the sun had been up for an hour; and they had dined early, the night before, and had set off nearly two hours before midnight.

When Hynd emerged from the Citroën and looked at the house before him he was hard put to it not to smile, for the secrecy with which he had been brought here had been a waste of time. This was one of those fortified farmhouses. This was Burgundy.

He looked at the forest of oak and beech and chestnut, and at the Charollais cattle in the meadow, and at the lowering sky, and he sniffed at the air heavy with the smell of summer rain that had fallen overnight, and knew he was in Burgundy.

Having bathed, breakfasted with a slightly weary Aschaffenberg, and being in a tolerably good humour, Hynd went now to be interviewed.

There were three of them ranged, wide-spaced, behind a long table: the inevitable defensive, power-taking barrier. In the middle, an American; on the American's right, a man who was a Russian if Hynd had ever seen one, and in any case he knew he had seen a photograph of this man in the files in some briefing or other; and the other man, since he inclined his head towards Hynd and said in a pure French accent that he was enchanted to make his acquaintance, he knew for a Frenchman and not a Belgian or a Swiss.

They looked at Hynd, and Hynd looked at them. The Russian was a large and heavy man with thick white hair and a pasty face, as if he kept his secrets even from the sun, but it was a strong and ruthless face; the American had a wealthy tan on a bland countenance, and Hynd read a lot in the cant of the head, the look of the eye, and the small actively pensive mouth, cunning and insecurity for a start; the Frenchman was tall, slim, fit, and handsome in a sharp-edged way, with black hair coiffed and blow-dried like a politician's, and the ungiving expression of a professional diplomatist.

When he had finished this survey Hynd found that they were still looking at him as if they had gone into a trance, so he got up and went to look out of a window at the day, which showed hopeful signs of lightening, and then turned and leaned against the wall of the embrasure.

'I used to get this kind of crap when I was in the Service,' he said. 'It's a symptom of the reason why I quit. Why don't I go out into the garden, and you can send me a postcard when you're ready to start?'

The American frowned and shifted impatiently, the Russian stared at him like a man who had been told what a joke was but had never understood one, and the Frenchman coloured as if Hynd had spat on Napoloen's tomb. Off to the right, where Aschaffenberg sat on the sidelines, Hynd saw out of the corner of his eye a flash of white teeth.

'Let's get to it,' the American said. 'Aschaffenberg has told you about us?'

'That you are ex-intelligence people,' Hynd said, and walked back to his chair, 'who have gone into business for yourselves, in order to use your professional expertise, the knowledge acquired in the course of your service, the useful fact that you are of any number of nations, and the advantages of being men of unscrupulous greed and a wilful lust for power, to win a rich harvest in the Indian summer of your lives.'

'Poetic,' the Russian said.

'A wilful lust for power,' the American said, and looked at Aschaffenberg. 'That is how you described us to Hynd?'

'No,' Aschaffenberg said. 'That is his own perception, but hardly a false one. We should recognize it. Not to know yourself is a weakness.'

'When I want lessons from you,' the American said, 'I'll be sure and let you know.'

He faced Hynd again and tapped the papers in front of him. 'I have here,' he said impressively, 'your personnel file from your time with the Secret Intelligence Service.'

'Of course you have.'

'What do you mean by "of course"?' the man said. 'It's classified secret material.'

'I mean I would have done the same,' Hynd said. 'I'd either have got hold of it, or pretended to have got hold of it.'

'Are you telling me,' the American said, 'that you could have got my file out of Langley?'

'Certainly,' Hynd said. 'I may have done so already. If you gave me your real name I might be able to remember.'

'He is talking rubbish,' the Frenchman said, and lit a cigarette.

Hynd looked round the room, and saw no other ashtray than the two on the table. He lit a cigarette himself, stood up, lugged his chair over to the table opposite the space between the American and the Russian, and hooked towards him with a finger the ashtray that sat there.

The American's face scrunched up and he said, 'Why do you want to join this organization, Hynd?'

'Two reasons,' Hynd said. 'First, because you have threatened a woman called Caroline Swift, and I think you'll harm her or kill her if I don't join up. Second, because until I met you guys, I thought it might be quite a lot of fun anyway.'

The Russian said a sensible thing. 'If the woman means as much to you as that, you'll carry a grudge against us for threatening her, will you not?'

'My dear comrade,' Hynd said. 'Just think how many operatives you have run successfully simply by threatening their nearest and dearest. You want me on your strength because I'm one of the best, and if my being one of the best makes you nervous for your own health, then all you have to do is send me away.'

'My dear Comrade Hynd,' the Russian said, 'if being so close to such a dangerous man' – and he smiled like a wild boar being challenged by a hedgehog – 'makes me nervous, then all I have to do is have you buried in the forest.'

'First of all,' Hynd said, 'you would have to make me dead.'

'That would not be difficult,' the Russian said. 'Each of us here is armed, and you are not, and there are thirty others in this house.'

'Well, you've got me there, certainly,' Hynd said, 'but why are we sitting here playing verbal poker. You wanted me, and here I am.'

'I don't trust him,' the Frenchman said.

'Speak to that, Hynd,' the American said.

'I don't trust you either,' Hynd said. 'I distrust you severally and together. Do you trust each other? I doubt it. Who trusts anybody in this business? And this set-up of yours, where you're doing it only for the money, has displaced any common loyalty. As to your Monsieur X' – here he indicated the Frenchman – 'the fact is that he and I have taken against each other, but that kind of personal antipathy doesn't matter, unless we have to work together.'

The American sat back and looked out of the windows where the sun shone now and sparkled in the raindrops on the unshorn grass that ran away to the trees. His lips were clenched as if he was trying to hold them still, and then from somewhere in him the humour came up and the shape of his mouth became, if not merry, certainly a smile.

'You wouldn't, by any chance,' he said, 'be pitching for the post of personnel officer? You've done nothing but put us right about the way we're handling this since you came into the room.'

'Personnel officers,' Hynd said, 'are people who know nothing about people in businesses whose business they don't know.'

The Frenchman said, 'He is too glib, this man. It is true I don't like him, but also, I do not trust him.'

Hynd ignored this, and said to the American, 'No one's mentioned money. I don't know what you'll want me to do, but I rate high. How long will you want me to work for you? A month? A year? Longer?'

The Russian came in. 'Mr Hynd is right. There is no trust in this business. But Jean-Paul is right too. Mr Hynd does not feel to me like one of us, he is too much his own man, too full of himself. In Moscow I would never have employed him. But,' and he made a deprecating movement of the face, 'he did us much damage, so to this organization he may be useful. So, I have a proposal: a one-month trial. And after all, reflect that it is to Casson we send him, and Casson is also an Englishman, and was also with their Intelligence Service, and will know better than us what to make of him.'

The American's brown eyes, which were as dirty as the Mississippi in flood, rested on Hynd for so long that he had a fastidious impulse to go and wash his face clean.

'Yeah,' the American said at last. 'I would have no problem with that. We've gone to a lot of trouble to attach Mr Hynd to us because of his reputation in this business. It would be a pity just to write that off, and not to have him now, when we are engaged in our first venture in the market with our first, shall I say, client, and such a difficult and dangerous client, which is why we went after Hynd in the first place. What do you say, Guesclin?'

The Frenchman had found a way out of being the dissenter that also saved his face. 'Well,' he said, 'loyalty can always be bought, and it sounds as if this man's loyalty can be bought. We know he is not rich, so money will mean a lot to him.'

Hynd did nothing to correct this misapprehension.

'You're talking my language,' he said. 'This probationary month. What do you offer me for that?'

They fell silent. It was the Russian who broke the silence. 'Ten thousand dollars,' he said.

Hynd waited, but neither of the others spoke, so he did.

'Bullshit,' he said.

'Pounds,' the Frenchman said.

'We don't seem to play at the same tables,' Hynd said. 'You do not offer me a long engagement. We are talking of a fee for one month. If there's anyone better than I am in this business, for what you want of me, name him. If I work for you I take all the risks – death, prison, whatever.'

'You forget,' the American said, 'that we have leverage.'

'What would that be?'

'The woman.'

'Ah,' Hynd said. He got up and went over to Aschaffenberg and said a ridiculous thing. 'Give me your pistol,' he said.

Aschaffenberg put his hand in his jacket and drew a small Colt automatic and looked up at Hynd very gravely, nothing of the laughing scapegrace about him now, with the weapon pointing at Hynd. Then he flipped his hand to catch the Colt by the barrel, and presented it, with still the same seriousness in him.

Hynd turned before any of the other three could react and went back to the table and stood across from the American with the pistol raised and held rocklike in the aiming position and pointing at the left eye.

'Listen to me,' he said. 'I am here because you threatened Caroline Swift. You said to her that if she did not persuade me to join you you would cut her throat. I have come here to join you. She has done all that you demanded of her. You will not threaten her again or harm her.'

Something happened to the American's breathing and his fists clenched against his chest.

'He has a bad heart,' the Frenchman said.

'You're telling me,' Hynd said. 'But that's not what ails him. He's just angry.'

Whatever it was that ailed him, the American came out of it with no visible symptoms except that his colour was high and his hands shook a little as he laid them on the table and looked down at them until they stilled.

'You're such a shitheel,' he said to Hynd. 'You're not worth the trouble. And you,' he said to Aschaffenberg, 'why did you do that? Why did you give him the gun?'

'I don't know,' Aschaffenberg said. 'I think I was liking him better than I was liking you.'

'Jesus,' the American said. 'Why'm I not sitting in the sun in Florida instead of dealing with assholes like you?'

'Money,' Hynd said. 'I want twenty thousand pounds, ten down and ten at the end of the month, and if we're going further after that then we'll talk again.'

'Deal,' the American said. 'Now go away. I want him on the way to Italy tonight. I want him out of here. Let Casson have the fun of working with him. I'm going upstairs. Jesus God.'

He stood up, and, standing, appeared suddenly to be a meagre and wasted man, as if he had developed a slow puncture and was etiolating as they watched. He went to the door, and out, leaving it open behind him.

The Frenchman said, 'I didn't know Englishmen had such passion in them.' For the first time his voice was not quite unfriendly. 'Are you finished with that?' He nodded at the pistol.

'Yes,' Hynd said. He went over to Aschaffenberg and gave the weapon back to him.

'Our American friend has a vindictive streak,' the

Russian said to Aschaffenberg. 'If I were you I'd stay out of his way for a while.'

The young man shrugged.

'If I'm on my way tonight,' Hynd said, 'I want the money moved by bank transfer today.' He took the cheque book from his wallet and tore a cheque out of it. 'That's my bank and account number. Now I think I'll go for a walk.'

'I'll come with you, if I may,' Aschaffenberg said.

'By all means,' said Hynd, who had not seriously expected to be allowed to walk around this place unescorted.

They crossed the meadow, and the cattle, impelled by the meaningless and eternally unfulfilled curiosity of the bovine herd, gathered and followed them as they went.

They walked in silence, they walked under a clear sky, and left the cattle behind at the fence and went into the forest. A few birds sang, not so many as there would have been in an English wood because of the French passion for *la chasse*, but enough to sweeten the air, and magpies chattered and a pheasant broke from under their feet. They walked beyond the dappled shade into the depth of the trees and came to a space where the sun shone again.

There was a fallen beech and Aschaffenberg sat on it. 'You must be careful,' he said. 'These men have taken on more than they are good for. You realize that? It makes them nervous, and the American, though I am no psychologist to say this, is as good as paranoid.'

'Thanks,' Hynd said. 'I'm a careful man. But you yourself – how careful can you be, living in that house

96

among that garrison? They will not pass over you giving me that pistol.'

'I'm a careful man too,' Aschaffenberg said. 'I have had enough of this bunch. They are not my kind of men. Desk warriors, what can you do with them?' He smiled a brilliant smile. 'There is a car that I can borrow not far from here. I shall go on through the wood. You will go back to the house by yourself. By the time you are in Italy, I shall be in some other country.'

So Hynd walked back alone through the wood.

As he passed among the trees he had out of nowhere a vision of Caroline. Her eyes and her beautiful face were laughing into his. His breathing stopped and pain went through him like a shaft of darkness. The pain did not go, but something in him smiled, and it was as if he had remembered who he was. He lay on his back on the grass, heedless that here in the wood it was still wet, and lit a cigarette, and looked up through the beech leaves to the sky distant above the treetops.

After a while he stood up and brushed himself down, and went on towards the meadow, towards the house: towards Italy.

Chapter Seven

Out of a turmoil of dreams Caroline Swift found herself, abruptly, wide awake. She lay on her side, startled and bewildered, staring at the wall, and then became aware that a pale radiance filled the air around her, and knew what it was that had woken her.

It was the night of the full moon.

She got out of bed and put her arms on the window-sill and leaned out.

It was one of those electric nights of utter stillness that come only in the country, and which itself would have woken her, but she knew that tonight it was the moon that had done it.

This hung low to the sea, so large and white and bright that she was astonished. She pulled on jeans and a shirt and sweater and ran downstairs and outside.

As she went across the rough grass to the sea her walk slowed, for where she had at first been astonished now she was awed: the moon was more than large, it was immense, a vast and luminous orb, and in the light which came from it there was so much force that she felt it strike, not just her eyes, but her body and her spirit.

The potency of the moonlight quickened the land about her as if it had been transformed to an original state, transformed into a night-world unknown to all of humankind but her, so that even the sheep that roamed from here to the shore – and there was nothing, it seemed to her, more ordinary and palpable than a flock of sheep – appeared to sleep, to stand, to move in thrall to the aura of the moon fallen now upon the earth.

She accepted this thrall to herself, accepted the pull of the moon and the call of the sea, and walked on towards them both, coming at last to the shore to find the tide at the full and the sea as still as the night itself, still and calm and waiting.

Waiting: that was the rub, because she knew the sea off these rocks was cold, but she knew too that this was why she had come here, this was what had drawn her.

She stripped her clothes off and stood there bare to the night, feeling its cold on her skin until she began to shiver; and lifted her arms and dived well down into the dark and sudden chill of the sea, and came cleanly from the dive to the surface and swam in a strong breaststroke along the silver path that ran before her towards the moon.

This was fear, and she defied it. For the vastness and brilliance of the moon both drew her on and appalled her spirit. She swam on for another quarter of a mile, aware but reckless of the risk of cramp, and then turning on her back she began to kick her way back to the shore: so that still she faced the moon, acknowledging the presence of its life in her, but taking her own life back into her own hands and turning over again to break back for the land in a fast crawl, with her heart in her mouth when she saw how far out she had come.

But she steadied her stroke and lifted her head now and then to be sure she was swimming for the mark, which was the light in the cottage window; and the shore was there, suddenly within reach, as it always was when she came in from a long swim; and she put up her speed and found that she was no longer cold, her muscles fuelled by the energy she was using. Until at last she climbed onto the rocks and found her clothes, and, shivering again in the night air, bundled them under her arm; putting out the last of her strength she alternately ran and walked, ran and walked, up to the cottage.

She went straight into the kitchen and found embers still glowing in the remains of the fire and built on them carefully until she had a blaze going, then towelled herself vigorously in front of it, threw on a dressing-gown and collapsed into her armchair.

She felt wild. She felt vigorous and exhilarated and, on top of that, ecstatic, full of life, of herself, of the joy of being herself.

She found the cigarettes and as soon as she was smoking she felt ravenous. 'What I want,' she said aloud, 'is bacon and eggs and fried potatoes.'

She locked the door, fried the food, and ate heartily at the kitchen table, and then she refreshed the fire and sat in the armchair with her feet on a stool and a rug wrapped round her.

She knew this was a night when she would not want to go upstairs to bed. So she sat there and thought her thoughts, and among her thoughts was that she liked being alone with herself.

'Is it over in me, with John?' she asked herself. And answered that she did not know, but perhaps not yet over, perhaps not yet.

*

In the morning she came out of her sleep slowly, pulling the rug round her and feeling too snug to move, looking at the bundle of clothes on the floor and the remains of her night-time fry-up on the table, able to be warmed by the slovenliness of it since the rest of this tolerably spartan abode was scrupulously clean.

At last, having established that there was no more sleep in her, she came out of the armchair, let the rug fall, gathered the dressing-gown round her and made coffee.

'Wow,' she said, as she sat down to drink it, for she was stiff in places she'd never been stiff in before. 'That must have been quite a swim. A hot bath, and then to the shop.'

Outside, the sun was already high. The bath and the two-mile walk down to the village put paid to the stiffness. She stocked up at the shop, as much as her knapsack could carry, and walked across the main street and went into the pub for a pint of beer.

It was barely noon; such holidaymakers as wandered off the beaten tourist track were not likely to get here for another hour. She exchanged a few words with Fergus MacPhail behind the bar. Apart from him, the place was empty except for two local men she knew well enough by sight to say hello to.

She sat in a pleasant state of peace and ebullience derived from the experience of the night, with a notebook and pen on the table in front of her as a psychological wall to discourage casual intimacy from such strangers as might stop here for lunch.

She sat thinking of nothing very much, idly caressing the pub dog, a black and white collie which pushed at her with its head when she neglected her duty.

This tranquillity was broken by the slamming of car doors and the entrance of a young-middle-aged couple, all tan and energy, work-out people, a wiry red-haired woman in chinos and a plaid shirt, and a chunky tough-looking bald man in long shorts and a tee-shirt.

They said 'Hi' to the room in general and sat at the bar to order drinks and discuss the bar-lunch menu.

To Fergus's friends the woman said, 'I guess you're fishermen.'

One of them said no, they were with the Forestry.

The man began talking about the lumber business in Washington State, about hunting trips, bears – 'Don't get uphill from a brown bear, he feels threatened and he'll come after you' – riding along precipitous ledges in the Rockies.

'I guess you don't get a lot of Americans round here,' the woman said.

Fergus turned to pick up another glass to polish and slanted a questioning eye at Caroline, and she made the most minimal negative movement of the head, and he said, 'No. Not a lot.'

The relentless patter went on, until to Caroline – still held in her experience of the night, of the full moon and the sea, as if it were a dream that continued within her – it became a hectic and alien noise, and she got up to go.

The dog came with her, to walk with her on her way home as far as it felt like and then come back to the pub on its own.

As she went by the American couple, the woman said, 'I like your dog.'

She lunged for the animal as if to pat its head but the dog skittered away nervously. At the same moment

Caroline caught the woman's eyes, not on the dog but on her. The expression in them was so avidly searching, so acquiring, that Caroline felt she had been photographed against her will.

She said nothing and moved on. The man, who was still displaying himself as the garrulous extrovert, lifted his glass and said to her, with a good-fellowship so gratuitous that it fell oddly between them, almost a parody of the familiar banality, 'Have a nice day.'

Caroline went on out, having said nothing to either of them. The dog was peeing on the rear wheel of a red Ford hire car that stood in the street. She settled the knapsack and swung into a long stride, heading for home and sanity, with the dog running on before.

Later, she was sitting outside in the last of the day, when she saw a red car pass slowly along the road at the bottom of the field. It went to the road-end by the sea, and the man and woman got out and looked about them. They looked long at the hill at whose foot the cottage stood, and briefly at the sun setting over the sea. But then there had been nothing sensitive about them at the pub; perhaps they had seen all the sunsets they needed.

They got into the car again after a while, and drove back past and out of sight, no doubt on their way to their hotel.

No doubt; yet that night she got out the pistol John Hynd had left with her and, although she examined it with distaste, when at last she went to bed she took it with her. She put it on the chair beside the bed but threw a sweater over it, to pretend it wasn't there.

For a long time she sat up hugging the quilt round her knees, trying to exclude from herself a world in which the Americans were anything other than tourists; to cling to the reality of her world, the world in which she swam out to sea when the full moon called to her.

As she sat there the moon began to move across the window. It was not the colossal and intimidating moon of last night; it was a moon returned from its wild state to normality, a moon of ordinary size and reduced wattage, remote and self-effacing among the clouds.

Caroline knew better. She had met it high with entropy and refulgent with chaos. She had seen its different faces and knew they would not be reconciled.

She tossed the sweater from the chair to the floor, so that the pistol was ready to her hand, and went to sleep.

Chapter Eight

The man in the white raincoat strode into the lobby of the hotel in Savona. He was a man all vigour and purpose, but for a fraction of time it was as if these deserted him and he stopped and stood where he was.

This was because he had seen the sea.

The lobby ran right through the hotel from the street door to the wide doors that opened on to the beach. When you entered at the front you saw nothing of the beach, so acutely did it slope from the back of the hotel to the Gulf of Genoa. What filled your view was the sea, and so freakish was the foreshortening of perspective caused by the lines of the lobby, the invisibility of the beach, and the height of the horizon, that when the wind was blowing hard onshore the short steep waves of the gulf came pouring down at you, imminent to overwhelm you, the hotel, and the whole littoral. It was as if the deluge had come again.

So the man in the white raincoat, of whom it might have been remarked that he had seen everything, was taken aback, and stood for that moment poised, wary, alert to the unknown.

His body balanced on the balls of his feet and became buoyant with energy: he was at once roused, and filled with stillness, like a lone swordsman who confronts a gang of assassins with his back to the wall.

The life force running in him passed through the air to a woman leaving the hotel, and as she looked at him her eyelids came down while her eyes went over him, and she smiled into herself.

'Excuse me,' she said unnecessarily, simply to make him speak.

'By all means,' he said, and the moment of inspired tensility of being left him. 'By all means,' he repeated, but the voice was abstracted, the black eyes had not registered her.

She had registered him, a man contained, private, compelled, indifferent to the passing world; a man, in fact, walking in armour, she thought, and let the thought turn her off.

'Who needs it, sweetheart?' she said to herself, and went on her way to Bologna.

The man crossed the lobby to the reception desk.

'Check-in,' he said. 'I have a room. You speak English?' He put down a passport and a credit card.

The man at the desk was piqued by this curtness of style. 'I speak English,' he said. 'Your room is 314, Mr Hynd, overlooking the sea. The elevator is there.' He pointed. 'Do you wish assistance with your luggage?'

The visitor met the clerk's hostility – if indeed he had detected it at all – with a blank and impervious eye. 'No,' he said, and went to the elevator.

In 314 he threw his bag on the bed and went to the window. It was June, but not a sunny day. A thick haze lay heavy on the littoral of the gulf, as if the weather was going to break up in thunderstorms. Under it the waves of the Mediterranean threw themselves onto the beach, the dull green sea piling up into breakers in which a few swimmers defied the auguries of the sky.

The phone rang and the man called Hynd turned from the window and picked it up. 'Hynd,' he said, and a little later, 'Tell me where and when.' At what the telephone said then he smiled. 'Yes,' he said, 'I'll find it.'

He loosened his tie and took his shoes off, and laid himself on the bed, and looked at the watch on his wrist, stared briefly at the ceiling, and slept.

Hynd put the Lancia up the track as if it were a rough-terrain vehicle. He liked driving. He liked to see what he could do with a car and what it would do for him. This one hurled itself round the bends with loose stones whacking at the chassis and bouncing off the paintwork. Below him the hillside fell steep to the valley, and above him as the small car climbed the windscreen was alive with change: now his vision was filled with the pale clay and rocks and sparse trees of the mountain and glimpses of blue and white and yellow flowers; now, as the gearbox howled with effort, nothing but the brilliance of the sky; and now, as the car wired into a turn, the flash of sunlight blinding him.

The car flew up the last stretch to the plateau where the house stood and when it shot onto the white gravel he kept his foot down until the last moment, and threw the car round in a cloud of pebbles and white dust just short of the edge of the gorge on the far side.

Hynd sat there as the dust subsided about him. Full of pleasure, he looked deeply serious. He switched off. 'Yes,' he said. 'Yeah.'

He got out of the car and stretched himself full out, his arms reaching upward as if to touch the empyrean. He was perfectly aware that the noise of his tempestuous arrival had brought men running out of the house with guns in their hands, but he ignored them.

He walked across the gravelled terrace to look down at the road he had driven, a white ribbon of spectacular bends that vanished into the coastal fog far below.

Up here in the mountains the wind that had brought the waves pounding onto the beach at Savona was no more than a breeze, a refreshing complement to the heat.

He gave the winding road a last look. Nothing moved on it.

'Hey, you,' a voice said, at the very instant that he turned towards the house.

He considered the source of the voice, one of that race of short men with massive shoulders and limbs that proliferates on the Mediterranean. This one had that simple kind of authority that comes from obedience to another: sure, Hynd thought, one of those, irritating guys sometimes.

'You,' the man said. 'You should not drive in like that.'

Hynd walked right up to him and into his space, so that the man's pistol arm had to move aside.

'Send a man down the track,' Hynd said. He pointed. 'To that bend there. And put another man here. The first man to signal to the second if a car comes, or a motorcycle, or a troop of horse, anything.'

The man smiled at him. 'No, no,' he said. 'You don't give orders here.'

'In case I was followed, you understand,' Hynd said.

That was all he said, and when he had said it he left the little incident behind him and walked to the house.

It was not a house of great character, but the architect (at the time of the Risorgimento) had not been ambitious and it was unmarred by excessive decoration;

and since it was built of white limestone from a local quarry it was pleasant enough. In this climate, on this hot day, it was a house that would have suited Hynd.

It was built on two floors with a tower above the door ascending another two, and a bare flagpole on top of it – raised, perhaps, to fly the flag of united Italy, thought Hynd, playing again with the nineteenth century. He hummed a bit of patriotic-sounding Verdi and went into the house's cool shade.

There were three men waiting for him. One abstracted, in repose and a pale blue tussore suit and with black glasses hiding his eyes, sitting at the piano playing softly 'The Continental' as if he were George Shearing, but with vivacities and rallentandos all his own. Hynd could have listened to this till the sun went down; and would have, despite the news he brought, if the two others had not converged on him as soon as he was in the room.

'Well?' one of them said.

He was planted right in front of Hynd, a tall and big-faced, confidence-exuding man in a conservative business suit. The other hung off in his right rear, a man wearing the same kind of suit, but a heavily built man, of too much bulk for his clothes to sit on him successfully.

Hynd gave his attention to the man in front of him.

'I flew into Genoa this morning,' he said. 'I drove to Savona. Now I've driven up here. I have come fast and far.'

'What are you talking about?' the big man said.

Down the room the man at the concert grand filtered through two changes of key, moving the music along on its way home but with the sense that he would give

109

it a plentiful waste of time of day (as the other song said) if he felt like doing that. Beyond him long white curtains stirred prettily at an open window, and beyond the window a garden showed, statuary and flowers sheltered by trees, pine and cypress, lofty, older than the house, and away past them a lawn that spread to the edges of a mountain meadow.

The pianist's way with the piano, and the picture he and his piano were in, composed of the tall cool room with the garden beyond, were so agreeable to Hynd's senses that he gave the involuntary smile and turn of the head that is not made but happens.

To the big man in front of him, he said, 'What I'm talking about is that I'm tired.'

'I don't follow,' the big man said, but he followed all right. His big red face grew redder.

'I want to sit down,' Hynd said. 'I want a drink. I want to be courteously received. I don't want to stand here in the doorway with you barking at me.'

The big man passed a hand over his grey hair. His grey eyes were hard, and he was not fazed.

'You're a bit sensitive, don't you think?' he said, moving aside.

'More than a bit, I hope,' Hynd said.

He went to a chair by the piano and sat sideways in it, with one leg over an arm of the chair, and flirted a hand at the musician. The black glasses looked at him and the head bowed, and the hidden eyes stayed on Hynd while the music ran out to its end.

'That was nice,' Hynd said. 'Goes back a long way.'

'*Si*,' the pianist said. 'So do I.'

He did not look it. His hair was jet black, but perhaps it was dyed. His skin was the brown of a hot climate man. His face was wide and primitively made, as if it had been run up in a hurry. Instead of taming it, the black reflector glasses added to its threat. The hands were huge.

'You play the piano?' he said. He had a deep but husky voice, as if before he took to the piano he had sung his vocal cords away.

'Not since childhood,' Hynd said. 'But I'm in the process of acquiring one.' He doubted if that process was still in train, after the way he had treated Raleigh.

'If you were any good at it,' the pianist said, 'you should take it up again. It is good for the soul.'

And to Hynd's surprise he fell to playing the 'Chapel of William Tell' from Liszt's *Years of Pilgrimage*. Hynd wished he could see the man's eyes: his playing of it was infinitely sad, the enormous hands as apt and delicate on the piano keyboard as if it were a loved creature dying.

The big man came close, into the pianist's line of vision, and raised a deprecating hand. The music stopped.

'Señor Arrando,' he said. 'It distresses me to interrupt you, but we have only so much time.'

The pianist shrugged, and said, 'Business is business.'

'Regrettably,' the big man said.

The bulky man intervened.

'Casson,' he said. 'You have no manners, no respect.' He addressed himself to Hynd. 'My name is Guercio,' he said. Hynd knew at once that Guercio was Mafia, just as he would have known the Devil by the smell of sulphur in his aftershave. 'And this,' Guercio indicated the pianist, 'is Señor Arrando, from Peru.'

'My name is Hynd,' Hynd said. He nodded at the

pianist, who inclined his head. Hynd turned back to Guercio. He did not stand up.

Guercio stared at him from eyes that were chasms filled with ancient and untroubling sins.

'Apart from that,' Guercio said, 'who are you?'

'I am a man of Casson's,' Hynd said, and let the leg that hung over the arm of the chair begin to swing gently.

Guercio went on staring at him, but his words were for the big man. 'Casson,' he said, 'what does this one do for you?'

Casson put himself in another chair facing out of the open doors down the long garden. 'He is a newcomer to my organization,' he said. 'He will, however, do anything that needs done. Hynd is a man of great abilities. As you have seen, he is self-willed and temperamental.' He looked for a moment at Hynd. 'But he will learn how to work with me.'

'Temperament,' said Arrando, who had not seemed to belong in this conversation, 'is sometimes a mark of talent.'

Casson's gaze went past Hynd to the pianist. 'There speaks the artist,' he said, with so much indifference that what might have been meant as sarcasm had no sense of insult in it at all. He returned his eyes to the vista down the garden.

'Temperament,' said Guercio, 'is for the men at the top. You are not a top man,' he asked Hynd, 'of Casson's organization?'

'Not yet,' Hynd said. 'I'm only the best at what I do.'

The mafioso fixed those fathomless but unhiding eyes on Hynd's, for so long and with such intensity that

Hynd began to feel that looking back at Guercio was like looking into the dark places of his own soul.

'I know one of the things you're best at,' Guercio said.

'Yes,' Hynd said. 'I think you do. It takes one to know one.'

'I wonder who he wants you to kill,' Guercio said.

'I don't,' Hynd said. 'He may not know himself yet. When he wants it done he'll tell me.'

'Whoever it is?' Guercio said. 'If he tells you to shoot Guercio, or shoot Arrando, then you will do it?'

'No,' Hynd said. 'Nobody tells me how to kill. If he says to me "Kill Guercio," I might shoot you, I might prefer to break your neck, or cut your throat. And I would not kill Señor Arrando. He plays the piano too well.'

'For God's sake,' Casson said. 'Can we leave out the social chit-chat. Guercio, I take it you will tell your people we are going ahead?'

Guercio shrugged. 'I will tell them what you have said, and they will decide.'

Casson stood up. The force in his anger was startling. It not only showed in his face and sounded in his voice, it emanated from him and struck at those in the room like a force-field, as if it were the discharge from a nuclear pile gone wild. And yet the words he used were, in themselves, ordinary, almost mild.

'I don't like this,' he said. 'It is not what I understood. We had a deal. Have we not demonstrated to you that we can do anything we say we will do? Señor Arrando, for example, and his distribution in Eastern Europe. He seems satisfied.'

'Completely satisfied,' said Arrando, who was still seated at the piano.

'You have done what you promised,' Guercio said. 'I don't deny that. You have penetrated Whitechapel—'

'Whitehall,' Casson said.

'Whitehall,' Guercio said. 'You have penetrated security there and successfully exploded a bomb. You have—'

Casson interrupted: 'We asked you to think of a seemingly impossible mission. You came up with the idea of a bomb in a British Military Intelligence office. We accomplished it.'

He had moved close to Guercio and squatted in front of him, balanced springily on his toes with his hands on his knees, as if he was getting in a bit of yoga; but despite this posture the effect of his anger so magnified his presence that he was as a giant about to fall upon a dwarf. Guercio waved an impatient hand at him and walked away, and drew a long thin cigar from an inside pocket of his jacket and lit it.

'Very well,' Guercio said. 'And also you have arranged the, ah,' and he glanced at Hynd, as if unsure that Hynd should know about this one, 'the Baltic acquisition. You have done all. That is not in question. I report to many interests, Casson. It will be up to them to decide.'

Casson regarded him across the space Guercio had left between them like a duellist wishing the seconds would give them their pistols so that he could shoot his balls off. Then, as if his attention had been caught by the dance of the white curtains in the breeze, he went to the french windows, and stood there with the white muslin drifting about him, and went off down the garden.

Guercio went slowly to the window and stood there, smoking his cigar, and watching Casson walk away.

'Hynd,' Guercio called out. 'Come here.'

As he reached Guercio the sound came to Hynd and then went away again on the wind. 'No,' he said, as Guercio began to move onto the terrace. 'Stay inside.'

He held a fold of the curtains clear of the window and he and Guercio looked out at the bright sky.

The Peruvian came up behind them. 'What is it?' he said.

Hynd gave him a quick glance. 'Mixmaster,' he said, 'all-same Jesus Christ.'

'What?' the Peruvian said.

'Helicopter,' Hynd said, 'and there she blows.'

The machine had come up over a ridge about half a mile off and hung there, as if it was looking at the house.

'See one here before?' Hynd asked Guercio.

'No,' Guercio said. 'I, we, have never used a helicopter here. I don't know who it can be.'

'If we don't know, we go,' Hynd said. 'Have you got a place to hide up here?'

'No,' Guercio said. 'What about Mr Casson?'

Hynd watched the helicopter lift and choose its course and come towards the house.

'Mr Casson is out of sight. I'm not going hunting in gardens this size for Mr Casson. Let's go. Ride with me.'

'Because we see a helicopter?' Guercio said.

'Oh, yes,' the Peruvian said unexpectedly. 'First we get safe, then we find out. Come.'

Arrando went fast through the house with the others at his heels. As they went the clatter of the helicopter grew.

'What's up?' the man on the door said.

'Carlo,' Guercio said. 'I don't know what's up. There is a helicopter, they think it smells bad. Take the Merc from the garage and get out, or hide in the bushes. Tell Benedetto.'

'I think it smells bad too,' Carlo said. He scooted across the gravel towards a cleft in the rocky hillside.

'That?' Arrando said, when he saw the small Lancia.

'Mister,' Hynd said, with the key in his hand, 'it's small, but it makes up time on the corners.'

He flung open his door and got in. Guercio threw himself into the back seat and Arrando sat beside Hynd.

The car started first kick and Hynd turned it round and ran it back gently over the gravel.

'Faster,' Arrando said.

'Be cool,' Hynd said.

He drove along the front of the house and stopped the car short of the corner.

He opened his door and left the engine running. 'What we want to do,' he said, 'is see if the 'copter lands. If she's hostile, then when she's on the ground is the time to leave. So sit tight.' He got out of the car.

The noise of the helicopter was loud now. He began to move along the side of the house towards the sound.

'Hey, what is this?' a voice said behind him. It was the voice of the leader of Guercio's security squad, who had accosted him when he arrived. The man, presumably, known as Benedetto.

Hynd kept moving.

'What's going on?' The man came round in front of

Hynd. The words had been shouted into Hynd's face against the racket from the sky.

Beyond him Hynd saw the helicopter hovering over the farthest stretch of the villa's gardens, not more than a hundred feet up and on the point of ... no, yes, descending.

'Watch!' he yelled to Benedetto.

They watched. Hynd thought for a second about Casson, but only for a second.

As the helicopter touched and jounced and touched again, men came leaping out of it with weapons in their hands.

Hynd turned and ran for the car, the other man after him, shouting his questions. At the corner of the house they ran into the bewildered group of Benedetto's men, three of them, talking to Guercio who was out of the Lancia.

'We're leaving now!' Hynd shouted the words at Guercio as he passed. 'Get in.'

'I can't leave my men,' Guercio said.

The bull-bodied Benedetto came into his own. 'You must forgive me,' he said, and lifted Guercio from the ground and laid him in the back of the car. 'Go,' he said to Hynd, who was already behind the wheel, and slammed the rear door and thumped his fist on the roof for a farewell.

Hynd ran the car across the gravel and down onto the rough track. From above and behind there came an outburst of gunfire.

'My Benedetto,' Guercio said. 'They will pay for this. Whoever they are, they will pay.'

A bullet came through the rear window and through the passenger seat and hurled the Peruvian forward. His head bounced on the windscreen and he slumped back into his seat.

'Well, sure,' Hynd said as he lifted the speed and set himself in the seat for some real driving. 'Sure you'll make them pay. The question is, though, who's paying them now?'

'You'll find out,' Guercio said.

'I'm driving you out of here,' Hynd said. 'That doesn't mean I work for you for ever.'

Guercio leaned forward and elbowed the Peruvian's head out of the way so that he could fold his arms on the back of the dead man's seat.

'For ever can be a short day,' he said.

Chapter Nine

There was no pursuit, and Hynd had not thought there would be. After a while he said, 'Where are we going? It's only ten kilometres to the main road. We'll have to do something about Señor Arrando.'

'Where did you hire this car?' Guercio said.

'Genoa.'

'That's good. First we go to Genoa, then to Putignano.'

'Putignano? Where's that?'

'When we get to Bari,' Guercio said, 'ask me again. Ah! Stop here. Get one of those rubbish bags.'

They were approaching civilization. Nature, or road-building so far back in time as to be part of nature, had made a lay-by, and man had made it a collection point for garbage.

Guercio got out of the car and looked about him. First, warily, at the sky, and after that, with care and suspicion, all round him. Up the track, down the track, at the hills, folds in the hills, ditches, trees and bushes single and in clumps. Then he climbed the bank above the lay-by and did it again.

He jumped down from the bank and took the keys from the ignition and opened the boot, and Hynd caught on. He emptied one of the rubbish bags of tins and wine bottles and chicken carcases and God knew what all onto the ground. By the time he got to the car Guercio had the passenger door open and took the bag

119

from him. He pulled it over Señor Arrando's destroyed head and down as far as he could round the shoulders.

Then he hauled the Peruvian's body out of the seat by the armpits, Hynd took the legs, and they had the corpse in the boot and out of sight with the lid shut on it in less than a minute.

Guercio climbed up the bank and made another faster survey of all the country round and came down again and said, 'Let's go.'

As they whacked along the autostrada Hynd said, 'Bari's at the other end of Italy. How are we going there?'

'We'll go by road,' Guercio said. 'I want a new car. That Mercedes at the villa, do you think it will still be in one piece?'

'No, I don't,' Hynd said. 'That was a punitive raid. They didn't seem to need to kill you, but they'll have shot up everything they saw worth shooting up.'

'They didn't try not to kill me.'

'They would not have minded if they'd killed you. I don't think it mattered to them one way or the other. The raid itself was the warning.'

'That's what I think,' Guercio said. 'A warning to me and to my friends, if I survived, and to my friends if I was killed.'

The Friends of the Friends, Hynd thought. Quite so.

Guercio was in the seat where the Peruvian had died, relaxed and comfortable, with the back lowered to an obtuse angle. 'They're very violent,' he said.

Hynd quelled the impulse to laugh. 'Yes,' he said. 'I think they want you to know they are as violent as you are.'

'More violent,' Guercio said. 'They want me to know

that they will be more violent than I would be.'

'More violent than your people would be?' Hynd said. 'Who in Italy is more violent than your people?'

Guercio brought his seat upright and put his back against the door, and for a long time stared at Hynd. Hynd glanced at him once and went on driving, and let him get on with his staring.

At last Guercio relaxed again. 'The purpose of violence,' he said, 'is to make it so absolute that it carries a message, that it says: "Nothing is beyond us. We are a force of life, as inevitable as the seasons, as uncontrollable as the weather." And now this message is being sent to me. Now they are sending this message to us.

'Ha!' he said, almost a laugh, and shook his head. 'The world is turning upside down.'

'You know who sent the message, don't you?' Hynd said.

'I do now. At first I couldn't believe it, but I do now. It was Casson's people, your people.'

'Yes,' Hynd said. 'I believe it too.'

Guercio laughed outright, and hit Hynd on the shoulder. 'You too. They didn't care one way or the other whether you died or whether you survived.'

'We can't be sure if that's true, you know,' Hynd said, 'about either of us. Only one shot came into the car. It might have been a mistake, they may just have meant to hurry us on our way.'

'Oho,' Guercio said ironically. 'You think you're important to them, even if I'm not?'

'Yes, I rather think I am.'

'Good.'

'Good?' Hynd said.

But Guercio did not speak again until they were well into Genoa, when he began to navigate, his directions taking them to a part of that ancient seaport not far from the docks.

It was that ideal part of the heart of a city that is dedicated both to commerce and to habitation. Cafés, shops, and restaurants were busy, there were new cars and old rustbuckets parked along the streets, businessmen and waged workers sat in the cafés and at pavement tables in the evening sun and children played in the dust.

Death, in the person of Guercio with Hynd at the wheel, passed among them, perfectly at home.

Guercio said, 'Round this corner. Here, this is it. Drive straight in.'

Hynd drove straight in, into a garage whose cement floor had been collecting oil for fifty years but passing at the entrance new high-speed petrol pumps, into a brick barn of a building with a high roof of corrugated asbestos on steel frames, with tatty posters on its walls going back to the 1939 Lancia Flavia, but with the service bays and equipment of today's Fiat dealer along one wall.

'Right to the back,' Guercio said.

The working day was over, but at the back of the garage there were still two mechanics working on the engine of an old Peugeot 604 drophead coupé.

'Park there,' Guercio said, 'beside the office.'

He got out and went to speak to the mechanics, and came back to Hynd's window. 'The Peugeot is theirs,' he said, 'their treasure. They work on it in their spare time. They'll be gone soon, but stay close to the car.'

He went into the glassed-in office, and Hynd saw him exchange greetings with a giant-like man, who ushered Guercio into an inner sanctum and then closed the door behind them.

Hynd had no intention of leaving the car, not with that corpse resting there in the boot. He was pretty interested in Guercio. He thought that for a man in his sixties the Mafia boss was full of go: he had taken the action at the villa in his stride and ever since he had been making all the necessary moves as if he was on automatic pilot.

The two mechanics put down the bonnet of the Peugeot and vanished offstage right. They emerged a few minutes later, overalls gone, wearing their street clothes. '*Ciao*,' one of them said as they passed, and Hynd nodded. He watched them in the mirror walking away down the long garage. As they left, they switched off lights and then pulled the big doors across.

Hynd had the place to himself. He and the Lancia and the venerated Peugeot were the only occupants of the lit stage that was his end of the garage, with the rest of it faded to an artificial twilight. He got out of the Lancia and found a battery of light switches on the wall behind the Peugeot, and doused the rest of the lights, so that the only illumination now came through the glass of the office.

When Guercio and the giant came out of their conclave, Hynd came out of the shadows.

'Why are you in the dark?' Guercio said.

Hynd said, 'They put the lights out at the other end – dark down there and me spotlit up here, and I don't know these people.'

123

The man laughed. 'One of the careful ones. A wise one.' He was a man of great girth with arms like tree trunks, a fat face with many chins and large dark eyes. 'Let us not know each other at all,' he said.

He opened the passenger door of the Lancia and inspected the interior. 'No problem there,' he said. 'That will clean up, Hertz won't know a thing. That's Item One: clean the car and return it to Hertz at the airport?'

He looked at Hynd, who nodded.

'Let's look at Item Two,' the man said, and went to the back of the car, where Hynd unlocked the boot for him and lifted the lid.

'He'll begin to smell soon, in this heat,' the man said. 'I'll take him sailing tonight, and sink him deep.'

He brought the lid down and closed it with a respectful minimum of force.

'Item Three,' Guercio said.

'*Momento*,' the man said.

He went down the garage into the dim light and started up a car and reversed with the verve and accuracy peculiar to garage hands. The car was an Alfa Romeo V6, three-litre engine, dark blue.

'A demonstrator,' he said, emerging from the driver's seat. 'Beautiful car. Tank's full.'

Guercio said, 'You are a good man to deal with. I wish you could eat with me, but tonight it would not be discreet, and besides, you will be busy.' They shook hands, and Guercio got into the Alfa.

The giant shook hands with Hynd. 'Continue to be one of the careful ones,' he said, and pointed with his chin at Guercio through the roof of the car. 'I'll open the doors for you. You'll like the Alfa.'

'I like it already,' Hynd said.

Out on the road he liked it a lot. If he had to drive the length of Italy, this was the car for it.

Guercio had changed his mind about dinner. 'We'll eat in Lerici,' he said. 'It would be careless to eat here and let people see us, in case anything goes wrong. Nothing will go wrong; Ettore knows what he's doing, but why be careless, eh?'

'Why indeed?' Hynd said.

'One of the careful ones,' Guercio said. 'That's what he called you. You know how to act fast, and you're one of the careful ones as well. You're going to be useful to me.'

'You're useful to you already,' Hynd said. 'Four hours ago we were attacked from the air and our South American friend bought it. You've arranged for the body to be dumped, the Lancia's going back to Hertz cleaned and purified, and you've got yourself a new car, all without thinking about it. What do you need me for? I thought you Mafia bosses were gloomy old men who deliberated long and hard about policy and left action to lesser mortals; but not you, you're the original Action Man. You don't need me.'

Guercio laughed, but it was such a laugh as might have come from a scorched throat. 'I came up here with my best, these boys are devoted to me – were devoted to me – how can I tell? They're dead or running still, maybe they'll come home. What do you mean, I don't need you? You got me off that hill. I cleaned up the loose ends, that's all. We make a team. I'm going to buy you a good dinner in Lerici, and then we're going down to my country.'

'What makes you think I'm going to do this?' Hynd said.

'Because you're interested,' Guercio said. 'Because I'll pay you as much as Casson's corporation is paying you – so you'll get paid twice. And every now and then I'll give you a bonus. But most of all, Hynd, because it's better to be a friend of the Friends than to turn them down. We get bigger, while the world gets smaller.'

'What about the corporation? I'm hired to them, not to you.'

'You will be the liaison between us,' Guercio said. 'Listen, when they have a better use for you, we can talk about it. Till then, you're with me.'

Hynd took the car down the motorway and turned off after La Spezia, driving into Lerici while the sun went down, a Made Man, going to have dinner with his Don.

Chapter Ten

Lerici was a holiday town, and it was jumping. The top road was alive with boys and girls in cars, hooting and flashing their headlamps, as if the thing to do in Lerici was to herald the night by going nowhere and back again. It was so spontaneous a celebration of life that, passing through its carefree ebullience, Hynd felt himself and Guercio to be alien and incongruous passengers, and the crawling motorized *passagiamento* to be a damned nuisance.

Guercio, however, was enlivened by it. He had a cigar going and his window down and shouted to a girl in an open Fiat which won him a flash of smile and eye and a toss of blonde hair from her and a dirty look from the boy at the wheel. 'Beautiful children,' he said.

'Sure,' Hynd said, as the traffic seized up and came to a stop. 'How do we get out of this?'

Guercio looked at him with the face of a witty middle-aged satyr. 'You are too serious,' he said. 'You are out of your element here.'

'That is possible,' Hynd said. Surrounded by cars and pavements alive with this adolescent tribe of brown bodies and bright clothes, white teeth and laughter, a generation of vibrant youth issuing its mating call in a unanimous cacophony of klaxons, shouts, jeers, and enough jollity, as it seemed to him, to serve for a lifetime; he did feel, running as he was out of the frying-pan (so to speak) of the encounter with Casson and the helicopters into the fire (as it were) of life with Guercio and the Mafia, out of his element.

And what was Guercio doing, this Man of Respect who had survived death only this morning by the skin of his teeth, making coarse jokes – he was doing it again now to the black-haired child alongside in a Mercedes two-seater – to children young enough to be his daughters or even, at a pinch, grand-daughters? You'd think the girl would despise him for it, but no, she was enjoying it: she was even interested in Guercio.

He caught her eye, and then Guercio's, and felt his aloofness wittily recognized by both of them. The traffic began to move again.

'You take women too seriously,' Guercio said. 'They won't thank you for it. Look, put the car over there, and we'll walk.'

Hynd, who knew he was taking a woman too seriously, who was resolved to go on doing it – in the name of what gods or goddesses only heaven itself could have told him – and who was here because of it, said nothing.

He turned off the engine and got out and stood looking over the roof of the car, over Guercio's head, into the passionate depths of the darkening blue of the sky, and accepted the image of Caroline. He watched the grave and lovely face, and the brown eyes, ravishing in their seriousness, turned his heart over; he saw the smile full of delight and the wanton flash of the eye that Aphrodite first taught. He stood on the very brink of the mill-race of that incandescent abandon with which they met, and then he brought himself back, with his hands working and his breath-rate doubled, and found himself nodding, private and alone, and looked at the ground and gave himself a smile, and brought the force of his will to command himself, and returned to the present.

Guercio had come round the car and was in front of him. 'What's the matter with you?' he said to Hynd.

Hynd met this with a look in his eyes that Guercio had never had from man or beast.

Guercio, who had wished a thousand deaths, and had by his own hand or the hands of others seen to a hundred of them, turned his head a little away and stared at Hynd's shadowed face.

'That's not how people look at me,' he said. 'I don't like it.'

Hynd put his arms out to the side and shrugged the ease back into his shoulders. 'Then don't step onto my ground,' he said, 'and perhaps nobody will look at you like that again.'

They walked down a steep alley into a different world. They went round one corner and the noise above and behind them subsided. Ancient walls flanked them, at doorways men and women stood or sat on kitchen chairs doing nothing with an immemorial grace.

The midsummer heat came off the walls but a light breeze came up the alley off the sea, a perfect evening.

Guercio was wearing his suit over a white shirt, the collar open, striding down the hill with an energetic spring to his step. A sturdy man with a brown and cheerful countenance, his dark hair speckled with grey, thick and tousled, his full mouth with a humorous lift to it, still infected, no doubt, by the mood for by-play which he had indulged with the girl in the Merc.

An unexceptional man, a good bloke on vacation, you'd have accounted him. But as he passed the people loitering away the last hour before night, Hynd saw the change in them. It was not that they knew Guercio, whose home was five hundred miles to the south and on the other side of the country, on another sea; but they knew, with the certainty of a herd of deer watching a wolf go by, that the man was a predator.

Hynd too was a predator, but he knew that if he had walked down that alley on his own these people would never have known it of him. Something atavistic ran from Guercio to and from the citizens of Lerici; something in race memory came awake as he went by them.

He gave a greeting sometimes as he made his way down the hill. '*Buona sera*,' he said, and received unfailingly the civil reply, but it came through an invisible curtain of reserve.

When Guercio passed by, it was as if the shadow of the hawk had touched them.

'Ah,' this sublime being said, 'here we are. What a memory I have!' And Hynd followed him down three steps into a place of eight tables and a bar, and an atmosphere of grilled fish, garlic, oil, alcohol, and tobacco.

Guercio stood there, content, confident and unassuming, for five seconds before the man behind the bar – a fat man with a completely bald head but a flourishing grey moustache – came to him. Hynd knew the man was about to greet Guercio by name, but a signal clearly passed, and the welcome, though earnest enough to catch the attention of diners at tables nearby, remained anonymous.

There were two empty tables, and Guercio pointed to the one at the back of the room. 'Sit there,' he said. 'I will go with Carlo and choose the fish.'

'I have red mullet, for you,' Carlo said. 'And Anna will want to know it is you she is cooking for.'

'Ah, you see!' Guercio said, and the two of them went into the kitchen, where Hynd could see them through the open door with a slim young woman who must be fat greying Carlo's Anna, talking all three of them at once, voluble and boisterous with gesture.

Hynd gave himself a cigarette and looked round the room. There was no sense here, as there had been on the walk down the alley, that with Guercio's entrance an Ominous Presence had come among them. This was a gathering of the prosperous, a more worldly and less intuitive species of humanity, and less submissive to fate, unless one day fate should actually knock on the door and announce itself, saying (for example), 'My name is Guercio, and this thing in my hand is a gun.'

Here the mafioso was unidentified, anonymous. It occurred to Hynd to wonder if Guercio, as he came down that narrow walk between the people of the tenements, had out of mischief and some evil merriment of spirit deliberately released from himself, like an animal discharging musk, the scent of who he was.

Guercio was not what Hynd had expected of a Mafia don. The habit of death had not brought morosity or taken from him the lust for life. At this moment the man would be boiling with anger at the violent onslaught on his house, had sworn vengeance even as Hynd whisked him away down the mountain road, must be devilling away in his head at the questions: who had done it; could it really be Casson; what was this deal he was in with Casson's people worth now; who could he trust (well, nobody, ever – forget that one); how would he get back at them? And yet here he was, revelling in this meeting with Carlo and Anna over the red mullet, and there he had been, not half an hour ago, flirting with salacious gusto with these girls up on the road.

What sort of man was this, who with fury raging within him could plan his vengeance with part of himself – and Hynd had no doubt he was both planning vengeance and, more immediately, working out how to defend himself against whatever other hazards he might now face – and at the same time give such complete exhilaration to the business of living?

Were it not that Guercio's business was killing, extortion, drug-dealing, corruption, Hynd would have believed that at last he had met that miracle, the whole man. Yet this exuberance with which Guercio lived, was this what was meant by the wages of sin? Hardly. He sought for and found a line from Samuel Johnson: 'He who makes a beast of himself gets rid of the pain of being a man.'

It would surely be too easy an option to write Guercio off simply as a man who had made a beast of himself. Surely? After all, to argue the other side of the case, man was an animal, and if he refused to be that he became – what? No more than a suit, a cultivated-seeming, seemingly respectable sort of fellow? Or at the far end of the spectrum, say, a saint? Who would want to be either of those creatures? Not Hynd.

On the other hand, he would not choose to be Guercio.

Well, he said to himself, there were animals and animals. Hynd raised a hand to the waiter and ordered beer.

By the time Guercio came in again Hynd had relaxed from his contemplation of human nature, and had gone back to work. After all, right now, he was a bodyguard, and he and Guercio were on the run – with or without cause, they had no way of knowing yet, so to be on the run was the wise course until they knew better. He was sitting back with a foot up on the chair next to him, his left hand was absently revolving the beer glass on the table, his right had checked that the pistol lay easy in the holster and now held a cigarette, and he was imperceptibly taking stock of the other diners.

Guercio sat and put a bottle of wine and a half-full wineglass on the table. 'Have you ever seen red mullet die?' he said.

'Never,' Hynd said.

'Carlo had it in the salt water tank,' Guercio said. 'While they're dying the colours change, an excellent thing to see, a living rainbow, a dying rainbow.'

'Death of a Rainbow,' Hynd said. 'Good title for a sad book.'

Guercio regarded him and produced a slow and remarkably amiable smile. 'You going to write it?'

'Who knows?'

Guercio's smile became wider. 'If you wrote it, I'd want to read it. Would I get credit for the title?'

'How could I refuse you?'

'That's right,' Guercio said. 'How could you refuse me? We understand each other.'

'We understand each other,' Hynd said.

'Good,' Guercio said. 'Listen. Tonight we'll drive to Cassino. It's a long way, we have breakfast at Cassino. Two good men will meet me there with another car. I don't know if that Alfa I bought will have been tagged to me yet. If I was after Guercio, if you know what I mean, I'd have tagged it and I'd have it spotted somewhere on the road south. So we'll keep our eyes open tonight. Tomorrow I have some business in Naples. You know who I mean in Naples?'

'Yes,' Hynd said. 'I know who you mean in Naples. You mean the Camorra,' and he said this in a quiet voice.

'I want to be sure I have enough friends,' Guercio said. 'I have many friends. By that I mean that yesterday I had many friends and I want to be sure that after that foulness today I have the same friends. Who knows who is playing in what game? That is always the thing to know. The only way for me to be sure is to meet certain people face to face. So I will go to Naples.'

'With these two good men, and in another car,' Hynd said. 'Where do I go?'

'You take the Alfa. You take the autostrada across to Bari, and from Bari you take the Taranto road and go to Putignano, and from there to Bissino, to my house. My family is expecting you.'

Hynd thought about this. 'Then they're more confident than I am. You want to set me up, driving your nice new Alfa, to see if anybody's laying for you on the road home.'

Guercio's face now was completely still, a carved mask, and his eyes stark and inhuman.

'Do this for me,' he said.

'It's a useful thing for you,' Hynd said. 'I can see that. If the Alfa's been tagged, as you say, they have only to watch the road to Putignano, or the last stretch, that road to Bissino. If they go for the car then we'll have smoked them out and there's a chance we'll learn something. If not, we can suppose the attack on the villa was only a demonstration.'

'Yes,' the graven image said.

'And you want me to do it,' Hynd said. 'You want me to do it because I insulted you up there,' and he nodded up the hill. 'I told you to shut your mouth.'

'It was not a deep insult,' the mask said, 'and you had a reason of your own which I know nothing about, but it was an insult. Do this for me, and the insult will be wiped out, and we can be friends. Men like us can be useful to each other. There are men who would kill their grandmothers to be Guercio's friend.'

'My grandmothers are all dead,' Hynd said.

Guercio knew now that Hynd would do it, and the face came out from behind the mask. It bore a grieved expression. 'A man should not speak so lightly of his family,' he said.

'As to that,' Hynd said, 'you are only saying that I have different hypocrisies from you.'

'Hypocrisies.' Guercio shook his head and poured himself some wine, and with the arrival of the Parma ham and a bowl of pears became again the jovial man revelling in the senses.

He took a huge bite out of a pear and slurped it into his gullet. 'Carlo,' he said. 'These pears! You will be able to give me a few for my journey?'

'For your journey?' the fat man said. 'Bah! You shall have a box to take home with you.'

Tribute wore a smiling face, but to Hynd the smile wore some only-just-noticeable elements of strain.

'I will do this thing for you,' Hynd said, 'of driving the Alfa to Bissino, but I shall exact a price.'

'A price?' Guercio said, and his expression was that of one deeply shocked by a display of bad form. 'Money?'

'Certainly not,' Hynd said. 'The price is that the pears go with me in the Alfa.'

Guercio's big face broke into laughter and the hair fell into his eyes. He swept it back with both hands.

'But, my friend,' he said, 'this is a risk for me. What if you and the car are blown up or shot to pieces? Then I lose the pears.'

'Quite so,' Hynd said. 'It seems appropriate to me that you should share the risk.'

Guercio had put too much food in his mouth, and Hynd thought the merriment would choke the son of a bitch to death.

When his oesophagus was clear again, Guercio said, 'I knew you and I would do well together.'

'That may be,' Hynd said. 'I can see what I gain from having the standing of a friend of Guercio's – for one thing it means you will not now have me shot and thrown in a ditch for being rude to you – but since I am not the sort of man to kill my grandmothers, even if they were still alive, I am curious to know what profit you anticipate from friendship with a man like me.'

Guercio became serious. 'I am a great man where I come from,' he said. 'I am respected.' He meant that he was feared. 'Why am I playing with words like this? We are a closed society at Bissino. I am *capo*, supreme. Do you know what I have found? I have found that too much respect makes a man suspicious. I trust my people, you understand, but always I know that somewhere among them will be one I cannot trust, and I do not know which one it is, or will be. None of them would dare to insult me to my face. A man who will do that is a man I can trust.'

'There's a flaw in that logic,' Hynd said.

'Logic?' Guercio said. 'I do not think about such a thing with logic. I think about it here.' He smote his breast, but despite the fact that his fist fell upon his heart the look in his eye was so far from being sentimental as to be actually menacing.

Hynd had finished his prosciutto. He lit a cigarette and gave the look back. 'I know what you mean,' he said. 'You were as close as dammit to being shot to shit and sent on your way to Hell today, and you don't know how much good work the other side – maybe it was Casson, but maybe not – have done on you. They may have done a deal with someone else, close to home: a man like you, there's always some other mogul around who wants your territory for himself.

'And closer to home than that, even inside your own home, you're afraid the palace guard back at Bissino, or some of them, have been got at. That's one thing. The other is that you're going back to Bissino in one piece, but with your tail between your legs because someone is after you and you left your men up there to die or get away as best they could. That makes you feel bad. It makes you ask yourself if the moment has come when power begins to turn away from a man.'

Guercio was sitting frozen and still, as if he had been encased in ice, but the anger in his face was seething.

Hynd said, 'You're a great man at Bissino, you said so and I knew it anyway, it's a thing that shows itself. A bit more than that, for all I know: from Bari down to Brindisi and across to Taranto, I would think.'

Some of the anger went away. Guercio felt himself accurately perceived.

'But when you get home,' Hynd said, 'your people there will be watching you because of what happened at the villa. If Benedetto and the boys don't come back your people at Bissino will expect you to do something about it. They'll expect you to have the blood of the people who did it, and that's not going to be easy until you know who did do it. And whether they know it or not they'll be watching you in another way too: they'll be watching to see if you've been weakened by this little disaster. If there's doubt in you they'll know it, and if there's fear they'll smell it.'

'Fear?' Guercio said, and his teeth bared as he spoke the word and the sound he made was like the growl of a dog.

'For all these reasons,' Hynd said, 'I am a good thing for you. I'm strange, I don't belong, I'm the guy who escaped with you. When I turn up it looks as if you've started to respond to the attack already. You will show me special trust and the people there will know that if there is anyone, inside or out, who is trying to get you they will have to go past me first.

'And what they'll think, up there at Bissino, is that you're telling them you trust nobody so you've brought in this stranger. Not just a hired gun, a friend they've never heard of. They'll resent it but they'll respect you for it. That's why you want me along. And don't make faces at me; you were thinking all this while we were driving down that hill with Arrando dead beside us. I hand it to you, I've never seen anyone adjust so fast to anything. Just don't think I believe everything you say to me.'

'I'm a liar?' Guercio said, but the fire of his anger had died down.

'Of course you're a liar,' Hynd said. 'You people are all liars. Hell's teeth, Guercio, I'm a liar.'

'Don't call me Guercio at Bissino,' Guercio said.

'What?' Hynd said.

'It's not respectful,' Guercio said.

'What do you expect me to call you, for God's sake? Padrone?'

He knew his man, but all the same he was startled when Guercio actually considered this. 'No, no,' Guercio said. 'It is as you said, it is important for us to be seen as allies. Call me Andrea, and I will call you . . .' He snapped his fingers impatiently. 'I think of you as Hynd. What is your Christian name?'

'John.'

'John,' Guercio said. 'Good.' He held his hand out across the table. 'Andrea,' he said. 'Call me Andrea.'

Hynd shook his hand, and something in him shuddered. He knew that Guercio was now determined that Hynd's bones should be buried in Italy, but it was not this which had awoken the qualm within him, it was the gift of treachery. 'Andrea,' he said.

The red mullet came. Guercio smiled upon the fish whose death throes had given him such pleasure. 'How beautiful it was when it was dying,' he said. 'I feel I have lost a friend.'

He cut a huge piece out of its side and put it on Hynd's plate, and then another for himself.

'And now you're going to eat him,' Hynd said.

Chapter Eleven

They were seven soldiers round a table in New York, twenty floors up in the Secretariat Building of the United Nations. They were conscientious men in their different ways, but they were bored, and Harry Seddall was as bored as any of them.

They were a sub-committee drawn from a committee representing over forty countries whose task was to work towards setting up the UN's very own Intelligence Service, a project which none of them, since they were practical men, expected to see carried to fruition.

They were also conscientious men, and within the framework of futility which encompassed their brief they had made the best of it by engaging with each other as if they were embarked on a serious exercise.

The windows of their conference room looked over the East River, and the sun had long gone past their windows. It was the cocktail hour.

'Our lucubrations seem to have reached a natural lacuna,' said the chairman, a Frenchman called Hérisson.

'What did he say?' This was Charles Woolpit, the American.

Ben Bussay from Niger translated for him. 'He said it's quitting time. Back again at ten o'clock tomorrow.'

'Thanks,' Woolpit said. 'I can understand American, but English sometimes has me floored.'

Ben Bussay turned to his left. 'Are you going back

to your hotel?' he said to Seddall. 'Shall we walk together? I am going that way myself.'

'Good,' Harry said, 'and let's stop for a drink on the way.'

'My idea exactly.'

When they got out of the elevator Bussay said, 'Up Third Avenue, I think.'

'Why not?' Harry said. 'Why don't you just tell me who we're going to meet, Ben?'

Bussay laughed. 'Am I so transparent? An acquaintance of yours, Charles Doffene.'

'Ah.'

'But first we have to make sure we are not being followed.'

'*D'accord*,' Seddall said.

'Doffene has arranged it,' Bussay said. 'We get into a car and drive around for an hour, and then the car drops us at the meeting place.'

It was a hot June evening and they did not walk, they strolled. They had reached 57th Street when a police car pulled up beside them. The man beside the driver got out and spoke to them across the roof.

'In the back,' he said.

'Why?' Seddall said.

The man came round the car now with his hand on his gun.

'Do it,' he said. 'Don't even think about it.'

'Harry,' Bussay said. 'This is our transport.'

Seddall climbed into the back and Bussay followed, and the patrolman slammed the door and got in the front. The car pulled away and immediately began making a noise like a banshee and doing hair-raising things with the five o'clock traffic.

Seddall's nerve went, and he got out a bent pack of Gauloises and extracted one and lit it.

'What the fuck's that?' the police spokesman said. 'Shark shit?'

'Gauloises,' Harry said. 'Try one, or don't you smoke on duty?'

'I'm always on duty,' the man said. 'I thought I was the only living human being still smoking in New York.' He held a hand over the seat and Seddall put a cigarette in it.

He lit it and puffed. 'Jeez,' he said, and after a moment, 'I like your suit.'

'Thanks,' Harry said, brushing ash off his knee. Perfectly ordinary suit, he thought, dark but lightweight.

'Not yours,' the policeman said. 'Yours I wouldn't be seen dead in. Well, maybe I would. How can you tell what they're going to dress you in? The other guy's suit.'

Ben Bussay was wearing a scarlet safari suit and had a yellow silk scarf at the throat. He also had a red Borsalino hat.

'Thank you,' he said.

'You look like a black pimp,' the policeman said.

'Good,' Bussay said. 'I come from Africa. I took advice. I wanted to fit in.'

'You're doing fine,' the policeman said. 'All you need is the Cadillac.'

'I have that back home,' Bussay said.

The policeman said, 'I bet you're a cool cat back home.'

'I'm chill, man, chill,' Bussay said.

'Way'ull,' the policeman said, deeply pleased.

The car had been cutting its way in fits and starts

through the traffic but now the driver made a false move. The police car slammed to a stop with two wheels on the sidewalk, and a man in torn jeans and a grubby sweatshirt who hadn't shaved for three days jumped for his life.

'I'm an innocent pedestrian minding my own business,' he yelled at the driver, 'and what do I get for it? Murdered by the New York Police Department.'

'Get a job, buy a car,' the driver snarled at him as he got the car going again and streaked off.

'My partner's Polish,' the spokesman said. 'No manners.'

'You know,' Harry said to Ben Bussay, 'this is the best thing that's happened since I got here.'

'It has been a tiresome week,' Bussay agreed.

A message came over the car radio and the two policemen looked at each other. 'This one's ours,' the driver said. 'You guys can get a cab from here. If anyone's been tailing you, they're long gone. I'm good at this. Give them the bit of paper, O'Hara.'

Seddall looked at the address on the scrap of paper. 'Where's this?' he asked.

'Upper West Side,' the driver said. 'You could walk it in ten minutes if you know the way.'

'Which I don't,' Seddall said.

'You'll make out,' the driver said.

Seddall and Bussay watched the black and white tear off with its roof light flashing and the siren yelping.

'After that it will be all downhill,' Bussay said. 'Here's a cab.'

The name on the piece of paper was a fish restaurant on Broadway. When they arrived it was the time of the early evening clientele, most of whom were in there to drink, but in the middle of the chattering crowd at the bar a black man on his own sat on a stool eating oysters.

He was a tall man with a fierce and aristocratic countenance: a large swooping nose, a ruthless set to the mouth and jaw, and black eyes, sombre and cold. He wore a conservative blue suit to which he imparted the gift of elegance, as you saw when he slipped off the stool and walked towards them.

'Harry,' he said. 'Good to see you. Ben, thanks for bringing him here. What can I get you?'

'I'm off, Doffene,' Ben said. 'I have people to meet.'

'Next time,' the tall man said, and the colourful Bussay departed.

'Scotch and soda,' Harry said. 'Let's find a quiet corner.'

'I'm holding one,' Doffene said, and they went to a table at the back of the room, which the tide flowing from the city's offices had not yet reached.

'I used Bussay to bring you here,' Doffene said, 'because at any one time half of you intelligence people from overseas are being followed or bugged by one or other or all of the gallant intelligence and security agencies of these United States.' He made his intelligent face wide-eyed and naïve. 'And, would you believe,' he said, 'those of half the rest of this mistrustful globe. There's no sense in it, but what's that got to do with anything? And I used the police because, though as a rule they don't like us government people, I have friends there.'

'Well, it worked,' Harry said, 'and I take it, from this elaborate routine, that our message system's working too.'

'Yup,' Doffene said. 'I had a fast phone call from your friend Hynd. He was in a café on the autostrada between Naples and Bari. The owner's private phone; he said it was safe.'

'Secure at his end,' Harry said, 'but how about yours?'

'Do me a favour, Harry,' Doffene said. 'I'm an assistant director at NSA now. And I worked my way up. There are electronics guys who still condescend to play poker with me even if I have succumbed to being upwardly mobile. My phone is safer than the Director's.'

'So tell me,' Harry said, 'what's going on with Hynd?'

Doffene told him.

'Working with the Mafia,' Harry said. 'Jesus Christ, the boy's not nervous, is he?'

'He didn't sound nervous to me,' Doffene said. 'He didn't sound any more nervous than a pike in a trout farm. Where did you find him?'

'He found me,' Seddall said, and explained this.

'So he's a maverick.'

'You've gone pompous. And a maverick's a steer. Hynd's a lone wolf.'

'Yes, yes,' Doffene said, and rapped his knuckles on the table, indignant with himself. 'You're right. Too many committees, too much shared wisdom. But I'm not over the hill yet. You know it was me who caught onto the pattern about these terrorist acts, the Japanese freighter hijack, Peru, Sweden, and your General Kenyon, the latest one? I'm sorry about the general.'

Seddall's face had gone dull for a moment. He honoured Doffene's expression of regret with a movement of a hand. 'I knew it was the National Security Agency computer,' he said. 'I didn't know it was you in person.'

'Yes, sir, me in person. I like computers and they like

me,' Doffene said. 'Hynd described this person Casson to me. After he phoned I got out our files of your MI6 early-retirement disappeareds.'

'You have such files?'

'You think we haven't penetrated MI6?' Doffene said. 'What do you think the special transatlantic relationship is about? It was only this afternoon I looked at the files, you understand, after I heard from Hynd, but I have a tentative match for Hynd's Mr Casson. A man called Owen Garrett. MI6 seem rather concerned about the vanishing of Owen Garrett. He was a crack hand in the field but inclined to over-commit to an assignment.'

Something relaxed in Seddall. He sat back in his chair and finished his whisky. 'So,' he said, 'we're on the right track. Hynd's on the right track. Garrett. Let me think.'

He went to the bar and came back with plenished glasses.

'I've met Garrett,' he said, 'an over-ambitious man. Plenty of empressement and capable too, but he thought every job was going to kick him three steps up the ladder with the result that he messed up once or twice. He was running Southern Europe but they had to pull him out, and sent him to South Africa for a spell to cool him down.

'Yes,' he went on, 'I remember. Do you know what the worst fault in an ambassador is? Identifying with the country he's stationed in instead of putting his own country's interest first. Garrett had acquired a version of that. He got to thinking that the French and the Germans – and the Israelis, he was a great admirer of the way Mossad goes to work – knew what realpolitik was about and the British didn't any more, so whatever station he was on he'd work closer with their people than he should have.'

'File tells us,' said Doffene, 'that he'd reached his level and wasn't going no place, ran out of promotions, and that's why he quit.'

'The attack on the villa,' Seddall said. 'He could have set that up, all right. I wonder if he did. Our trouble is we don't know what deal these people he's with have made with the Mafia or where the Peruvians come in.'

'I'm looking at drugs,' Doffene said.

'That's too limiting, don't you think?' Seddall said. 'All this knocking off of Swedish arms factories and Japanese ships and poor Aubrey Kenyon. They wouldn't pull all that out of the hat just to cut themselves in on the drug trade.'

'The Mafia,' Doffene said. 'The Peruvians.'

'I know, I know. Drugs may be part of it,' Seddall said, 'but these boys have been demonstrating that they can and will do anything, absolutely anything. They're saying to anyone who thinks power comes out of the barrel of a gun, anyone who's into direct action, that they're the people to sign up. They really go to war, these people. They're advertising themselves as the fighting edge. I think they must be into some utterly unimaginable project.'

'Then I'll tell you why they attacked the villa,' Doffene said, 'if it was them. And I think it was them, now that I can make sense of it.'

'Why?'

'Price,' Doffene said, 'or a mixture of price and extortion. I think our guys, they want money and power both. I think any deal they go into, they'll want big money and they'll want a piece of the action. Maybe that's where drugs come in. Drugs are big with the Sicilian Mafia.

'Like they've negotiated a deal but the Mafia's holding off from going through with it, trying to hold them down on price while they think about this deal some more. So our guys – we'll need to find a name for them, we can't keep calling them our guys and these guys—'

Seddall interrupted him. 'I call them the Masterless Men.' He shrugged. 'They honour no flag. Filed under THEMM.'

'Kind of poetic,' Doffene said, 'but you're right. It fits. So these Masterless Men mount an airborne attack on this Guercio's villa to tell the Mafia anything they can do THEMM can do better, to say to the Mafia a deal's a deal and if the Mafia don't come through it's going to be a bad war.'

'They do this to the Mafia?' Seddall said. 'Wreck one of their houses, kill their men? They think that's going to work?'

'I think it would work,' Doffene said. 'The Mafia's impressed with them already, or they wouldn't be dealing with them. They know their track record, hijacking thirteen million in gold off a ship at sea, breaking Shining Path people out of jail in Peru, killing top intelligence people in Europe. That's heavy metal and it's versatile, Harry, and it's big scale.'

'You want me to believe,' Harry said, 'that shooting up the house and the bodyguards of a capo di Mafia, or whatever these big white chiefs of theirs are called, would make the Mafia toe the line? They'd lose face, they'd be too angry to see reason, they'd go to war and to hell with it.'

'You don't know as much about the Mafia as you should for this one,' Doffene said.

'Instruct me.'

'In the first place, it doesn't sound to me as if Guercio's Mafia. Guercio's home country is Puglia, up there in the hills behind Bari and Brindisi. Now, what you have in Puglia is quite new, it's a bunch of bandit gangs that's grown up there in the last three or four years. They have a pretty name for themselves, the United Holy Crown, but that doesn't mean they're part of one joint enterprise.'

'How do you know these things?' Harry said.

'These committees I sit on, with the Secret Service and the FBI and the CIA and the Drug Enforcement Agency and a dozen other agencies and departments, do you have any idea how much paper I have to read to keep up with them? This I have from the DEA.'

'I can see it's good to be well informed,' Harry said, 'but what's this got to do with the National Security Agency?'

'God, you Brits are insular,' Doffene said. 'Since you lost your empire you've got no perspective on the world view, have you? The Mafia are into finance and industry right through Italy, even into the government. Italian politics, the whole life of the state, are destabilized by the growth of the Mafia. Are you going to tell me a modern state can't fall to pieces? Look across the Adriatic at Yugoslavia. Look at Italy's position. Below it Africa – well, look at Africa, at least you don't need lessons from me about Africa. Across the Adriatic Yugoslavia and Albania – do you want to bet Albania won't be drawn into that war? Then Greece and Turkey and you're into the Middle East.

'I'm not saying Italy's ready to go to pieces yet, but that's a country that's had a hundred governments since the war, and it's only been a country for a hundred years. Do you feel that the south of Italy and Sicily are the same country as the north of Italy when you're there yourself? No, you don't. Nobody's calling for it to be partitioned, of course not, but states in Europe are changing. Germany's united. Czechoslovakia's broken up. There's no natural law that says the world will hold together as we know it. So, Italy, we have to keep aware of what's going on there, and the Mafia is part of it. Where was I?'

'You were telling me about the man Guercio,' Harry said, but he found he had to clear his throat before he spoke – he was fascinated by Doffene's exposition. Italy going to hell in a handcart? Surely not. He went there for his holidays. But dammit, he'd been to Montenegro on holiday.

'Right, Guercio,' Doffene said. 'Guercio's is one of these Holy Crown mobs in Puglia. He's got links with the Camorra in Naples and with 'Ndrangheta, which is the Calabria outfit, next door to Puglia. Now, 'Ndrangheta has an alignment with the Sicilian Mafia, just across the water, and do you know what, it often acts as broker between the big Mafia clans. Suppose, Harry, suppose that Guercio has been acting as the negotiator for the Mafia between them and Casson's guys.'

'All right,' Seddall said. 'I'm supposing it.'

'Well, Casson's guys want to make the Mafia see reason and persuade them to come through on this deal Hynd tells us about, and to show they're getting impatient and mean business they mount a helicopter attack on Mr Guercio's villa. The Sicilian Mafia, the Neapolitan Camorra, even the 'Ndrangheta in Calabria don't give a shit about Guercio's villa. Guercio is a big man where he comes from maybe, but he's a small man in Puglia to them. The message is as clear as it could be, but it has been delivered with discretion, and this is the kind of language the Mafia understands. Guercio is nothing to them, except their negotiator. No *infamita* has been committed, the Mafia's pride and honour have not been impugned.'

Doffene rounded off his exposition with an air of triumph, but this faded as he came to realize that the look he was exchanging with Seddall was one-sided: that behind the Englishman's bland exterior his attention was in fact withdrawn, as if he was listening to a wavelength Doffene could not receive.

Doffene made an effort to sustain the charge of energy he was bringing to the meeting, but this inwardness of Seddall's made him ill at ease, for he was contemplating being less than candid, and he knew that Seddall had an instinct that could find its way like a cat in the dark.

There was a part of Hynd's message that Seddall would want to hear, and Doffene was not going to give it to him.

'This is the last thing,' Hynd had said to Doffene, 'but to me it's the most important. Tell Seddall this: I want Caroline Swift protected. I want her taken out of that house and away from there and I want her protected. Say it back to me.'

Doffene said, 'You want Carolyn Swift . . .'

'Caroline.'

'Caro-*line* Swift. You want her taken out of that

house and you want her put into protection. And the house,' he said casually, 'is where?'

There was a pause. 'Seddall knows,' Hynd said.

'Right.' And though he was beginning to have an inkling, Doffene asked, 'Why do you want this done?'

Hynd said nothing, and went on saying nothing. Using the weapon of silence all the way from Italy, Doffene thought, and fuck you too.

Into the phone he said, making his voice quiet and a little bored; 'Mr Hynd, you can trust me as you trust Seddall.'

'I don't trust that easily,' Hynd said. 'I don't know you, Doffene, except as a message centre.'

'Well, I ain't sensitive,' Doffene said, and tried another tack. 'I knew already about the connection between you and Ms Swift.'

'Seddall told you?' And at the tone in that voice Doffene was glad of the distance between them.

'No,' he said. 'He did not. This is the NSA, Mr Hynd. Ms Swift worked for us once. To me that makes her one of ours. If you're worried about her safety, then so am I.'

More silence, then: 'I am worried about her safety.'

'I'm not clear why you should be,' Doffene said, though it had been growing more clear to him by the moment.

'Doffene,' Hynd said. 'Just do it. Give that message to Seddall. I want your promise.'

The voice of conscience is the voice of God, Doffene said to himself, and he could not believe there was the least discernible flavour of falsity in his reply. 'You have my promise.'

'*Ciao,*' Hynd said.

'Good luck.'

Doffene had worked it out like this. Hynd had gone south down Italy with Guercio, a fact which either was now, or would soon become, apparent to this Casson guy. Casson would not know whether he could rely on the belief that Hynd had, on the spur of the moment, put himself alongside Guercio on Casson's behalf on the chance that it might prove to be a useful initiative so far as Casson was concerned; or whether he had seen some advantage for himself and switched allegiance to Guercio.

So he knew what Hynd's fear was – that Casson's people, who had already threatened the Swift woman, would take her and hold her hostage to make sure Hynd stayed true to his salt.

This had given Doffene an idea. So far as he was concerned, the salt he wanted Hynd to be true to was that represented by the red, white and blue flags of America and Britain. Hynd did not sound to him like a man who saluted flags. To Doffene he sounded like one of the other kind, the dangerously individualistic kind.

For the purposes of the mission, therefore, it might be quite the best thing if Caroline Swift was taken under the care and protection of associates of Doffene's, who, in the event that Hynd needed to be whipped into line at any point, would use her to apply pressure on him without a qualm. Whereas if she were in Seddall's care, it was not that Seddall would have qualms about using her in such a way, it was simply that Seddall would never dream of being such a shitheel as Doffene, by now, had decided to be.

Hynd had made himself a Trojan Horse among these terrorists without cause or country who were blowing holes in the fabric of the civilization that Doffene was sworn to defend – for as Doffene saw it, if America did not defend it, then who else would or could? – presumably those terrorists who went in for assassination, piracy at sea, and raiding military armouries, in any country they chose, and who did not shrink, apparently, from kicking the Mafia in the balls as a way of cementing an alliance with them.

What an alliance between two such forces could lead to he did not want to contemplate. All he knew was that Hynd was in there, a solitary champion in the camp of the barbarians; and that Hynd must stay there.

Doffene wanted a lock on Hynd, and Hynd himself had shown him the way to get it. Even in trusting Doffene as a messenger, Hynd had trusted Doffene too far.

Within the half-hour of hearing from Hynd Doffene had a conference call in being with Defense Intelligence, CIA and FBI participating. Within the hour they had agreed that the CIA would take Ms Swift under their protection, or, to put it another way, kidnap her for her own good; for her own good, at least, in the first instance.

Ten minutes after that Doffene was on his way to meet Harry Seddall.

Chapter Twelve

After he had made the phone call Hynd went outside and sat at a table in the sun with a double espresso and a bottle of mineral water. The hotel was a mile from the autostrada but the traffic sound washed the ear, a poor and unmelodious imitation of the sound of a flowing river.

It was noon and the sun was as hot as he'd known it in Italy. He had bought some clothes and a razor when he drove into the village; he would shower and change in the hotel before he set off again. He smiled to himself. Always a good thing to freshen up before driving into an ambush.

He thought of the road ahead, first to Bari, and then the road to Putignano and Bissini, the stretch where Guercio thought he might be waylaid. He did not expect to be ambushed, but he thought there might well be a meeting somewhere along that road.

At Bari he would send a cable to Caroline. It was the best he could do, since she had no telephone. That man at the other end of the line in Washington, Doffene, he did not trust him an inch. If ever he'd heard a shit-eating voice on the phone, it was Doffene saying Hynd could trust him as he would trust Seddall. Even without the warning that such a promise would raise in any man of sense, Hynd would not have been going to put an atom of trust in Doffene.

There was little chance of Hynd relying on the word

of anyone in government service (never mind government itself) in London – he had made an exception for Seddall, since on that day when he spent a good many hours in the man's company his instinct confirmed what he already knew of him – so how much more meagre was the likelihood that he would put any faith in their counterparts in Washington.

If there was a threat to Caroline a cable would get to her faster than he could. Meanwhile, he looked north into the blue sky and the heat haze over the distant mountains and sent her messages through the ether, and when that was done he crossed the gravel to the car, collected his bag with the morning's shopping in it, and went into the hotel to change.

He had sent the cable at Bari and now in the early evening he drove out of Putignano on the Bissino road. The cable had said simply: 'Time to go.' She would know what that meant. She would know he meant it, that it was a warning, that it was serious. He had a grim feeling in him as to what else she would make of it. Now and then, she had said to him he knew her better than she knew herself. The grim feeling was telling him that Caroline's spirit, finding her on the move again, would urge her to seek fresh fields and pastures new; call to her to move onto the next place in her life; away from what she had known there in Scotland and what she had known with him, to find new things to know. It was a roaming spirit, he knew that, an outlaw spirit.

If that was what she did he would bear her no grudge, or, to be more honest, he would fade the grudge as soon as he could. He had embarked on this enterprise for her sake, and for her he would take it as far as he could go. It was a strange and passionate commitment he had made to her, and a bit crazy, he knew it. He was behaving like a knight-errant, wandering round Europe like Don Quixote wearing Caroline's favour on his helmet, true to a pact he had made with himself alone.

He blinked into the sun on the windscreen and brought his mind into the present. He would fight the campaign, and then he would see what the future held.

He had come to a hill village and he brought the car to a stop at the side of the road and got out to stretch himself and clear his head.

He had hardly walked twenty yards along the street before he smelled two things: poverty and hostility. He passed two men leaning against the wall of a house, and gave them good evening. He was favoured with no reply, but each of them met his eye with the same look of pure ill will. It was extreme ill will, as if there was nothing they would rather do than stick a knife in him, and there was no reservation or embarrassment in it, as you might expect of men who thought to kill you without cause. For there was cause, and he recognized it: he was a stranger, an intruder, an alien who did not belong here. That was cause enough.

When he had passed them he stepped into the middle of the street and looked all round him. His thoughts had been elsewhere when he drove into the village, but he could have sworn the scene had been what you would call normal, men and women and children out and about. Now there were no women, only men standing in groups of two or three, and all of them looking either at him or the car. He had an odious awareness that the price of the Alfa was more than the whole village earned in a year.

He was the enemy, he felt it. He had the curious belief that he was all their enemies in one, and that any stranger would be in this formerly much-invaded and now utterly neglected land. He was the Greeks, the Saracens, the Normans, the French, the Germans, the British and Americans, any of the invaders who had come and gone.

He thought that if he stood there long enough, in the end something would break and he would be a corpse, lying there in the middle of the street. A cat appeared from nowhere, a sorrowful and skinny animal, and began winding itself round his legs. He squatted down to stroke it, determined to have it purring before he would depart; one assurance of contact between another living creature and himself.

The cat began to purr, at last, and, as if it had understood the pact between them, sat down in the dust and began to wash itself. He walked down the centre of the street, and got into the Alfa, and drove on out.

After the village the road ran narrow and almost straight along a rocky plateau, a barren landscape with hardly a house to be seen, nothing growing but parched grass, here and there acacia or ilex or wild olive, with nothing living but a flock of tenacious goats, once a surprising field with a few cattle in it; an unexplained donkey standing beside the road, waiting, as if it had been waiting there for years.

When he had passed over this terra incognita he found himself descending a steep pass that coiled back on itself, so that sometimes he saw below and behind him the path that the road took. As soon as he saw the nature of the terrain he made a quick calculation. Bissino would be ten kilometres or so ahead. If anyone was watching for him this would be the place to do it.

He assured himself of the pistol in the holster on his belt, and drove on. The hillside above him now was a flourishing olive grove; down the road ahead of him he could see the leafy crowns of forest trees. There would be a river in this gorge. He went round a corner and there was the ambush, a hundred yards ahead: a three-ton truck with a canvas hood over the truck bed, set slantwise across the way and no room to get by.

Between him and the roadblock the picture was of the brief straight stretch of downhill road, with the olive trees rising on his right, and on his left the ground falling away in a grassy, rock-strewn slope with a few trees on it.

He did not slacken his pace until he had halved the distance and then he braked, threw the gear into neutral, flung open the door beside him and executed not a bad fall from the moving car onto the roadside, a hard blow on the shoulder when he landed but rolling over without cracking his head on any evilly placed chunk of stone and coming up into a crouch and breaking at once for the shelter of the little stand of trees that had decided his disembarkation point.

He drew the pistol and made a quick scan all round the compass and then focused on the extraordinary and unanticipated sight before him, for the Alfa had gathered speed again on the slope and instead of careering off up the hill into the olive trees on the one hand or down into the gorge on the other, it was clinging to the road and heading with a reckless determination of its own, or as if steered by some sublime agency, for the truck.

Hynd did not often produce a wide smile, but he did that now, although he knew the Alfa was bound to swerve off the road at the last minute. The gods could not be so amusing or so amiable . . .

But the gods were, and he had a sight of at least two disconcerted human figures hopping around near the truck before the self-willed car reached it.

The noise of the crash was not a resounding one. There was no shriek of tearing metal or thunder of exploding petrol, but the Alfa was a big car and had gained enough velocity to hit the truck with a solid thump that shocked the senses: unless they were men of exceptional fixity of purpose, that moment of impact must have shaken the wits of the ambushers.

In that moment, therefore, Hynd was out of the trees and ten feet downslope from the road and sprinting as fast as he could go for the scene of the ambush.

He had marked his spot, a white boulder beside a patch of dried reeds, where there must be an outflow of water draining off the hill in the rain or after winter snow.

He went to ground there. Looking upward he could see the roof of the van not twenty feet from him. He waited and listened, but no one spoke.

Very well: outflank them and come in from the rear. He made a loop downhill and up again, covering another hundred yards or so. The slope he was moving on curved round to the right and he went on further, so that when he came up to the road and looked back down it the bend in it concealed the van, the Alfa, and the aspiring citizens who had lain in wait for him.

The shortest way there from where he was now would be over the shoulder of hill through the olive trees. He crossed the road and climbed until he was looking down on the disaster scene.

He had everything he could want, a clear view of the enemy's chosen ground, the advantage of height, the disposition of his own forces (himself) unknown to the enemy.

The Alfa had hit the truck near its back end and swung it round, tearing off a rear wheel, and so changing the geometry of the truck bed that the hoops on which the cover was stretched had sprung, and the canvas lay all anyhow like bedclothes on an unmade bed.

The front of the Alfa was stove in and jammed under the tailgate of the truck. The windscreen was smashed. Coolant from the radiator made a glaucous pool on the tarmac.

For the rest, one man was making a wary approach to the clump of trees where Hynd had made his jump from the moving car; another was directly below Hynd, forty feet from him, snugly ensconced as behind a parapet, in a fold of ground that sheltered him from the road. Hynd could have put a bullet in the back of his neck with no trouble at all. Twenty feet beyond this innocent were the wrecked vehicles, and across the road, in the very patch of dried reeds that Hynd had passed not five minutes before, a third man crouched with a rifle or shotgun resting on top of the white boulder.

Having established the locations of these three men in front of and below him, Hynd took in the lie of the land to his rear and on either side, and reckoned that he was secure. Such were the rewards of quickness of thought and execution.

It was a ravishing evening. The ground was warm under his hand, the air warm on his face. The blue of the sky was fading but the sun was still hot on his back. On the hillside before him was the dusky grey-green of the olive trees, on the far side of the road the rocky meadow fell towards the tree-strewn gorge, and when he looked straight out to the horizon made by the jagged crests of the hills he saw that birds of prey – eagles or large hawks, he could not tell which – were floating in slow circles on the sky.

The men below him, wretched exponents of the ancient art of the ambuscade, seemed to him unworthy figures in this landscape. The man who had been sent to sniff around the clump of three trees had circled them craftily and came forward through them now waving his hands as if to indicate that he had drawn a blank. He had a pistol in one hand. He began to run back to his colleague beside the white rock.

The man in the reeds stood up slowly and looked about him. The man immediately below, having more sense than his comrades, went down behind his cover, and lurked, and no doubt put his mind to work. The movement showed Hynd that he was armed with a sub-machine gun. That was the man to deal with first. He had the firepower, such brains as there were among the three, and he was, from these indicators, the boss man.

Hynd made the calculations appropriate to firing a pistol downhill at a range of forty feet, came up in a well-founded kneeling position, made his aim, fired four times at the man's back, and went down the hill like a gazelle without waiting to see what effect the shots had had or what effect the noise of the firing had had on the outlying troops.

The man was still twitching when he got there but he was dead, heart and lungs gone by the look of the holes in his back. Good shooting, sitting duck or no.

Hynd lifted the sub-machine gun off an open palm. An Uzi, of course, the international currency in this type of weapon. He found a spare magazine in the dead man's pocket. He put his head over the parapet and saw that the enemy had lost it. The running man's comrade had plainly advanced to meet him, but had gone only a few paces when he was stopped by the sound of Hynd's fusillade. The two men stood now about five yards apart staring up at him, the one with the rifle or shotgun lifting it slowly to his shoulder.

Time to take prisoners and interrogate. Hynd fired two short bursts from the Uzi at their feet, holding the gun down, against its tendency to climb, for all he was worth. Then he stood up and fired another burst into the sky in a visibly debonair way, and held the Uzi ostentatiously not pointing at the foe; but ready, and they knew it.

They were hopelessly exposed, he had the drop on them, and unless that was a rifle they were outgunned. The man with the pistol had thrown himself to the ground, which wasn't going to do him any good, and at that range Hynd had no fear of his pistol. The other man was a chump. He fired what turned out to be a repeating shotgun three times. By the time the shot reached Hynd the spread was hopelessly wide, and Hynd took only a couple of pellets in his left arm.

He was deeply irritated, but what was he to do? Consult the Queensberry Rules? He fired the Uzi till the man with the shotgun fell. Then he changed magazines and went down the hill.

When he got there he found the pistoleer, his weapon lying discarded on the grass, tending his companion.

'You look English to me,' Hynd said.

'I am English.' The man was probably in his middle twenties. He had taken his shirt off and was tearing a bandage out of it with the help of a knife.

'How is he?'

'You've blown a hole in his thigh. I'm worried about the artery. I want to make a tourniquet.'

'You're being over-dramatic,' Hynd said. 'I haven't blown a hole in him, I've made a hole. This is a sub-machine gun, not a French seventy-five. And that's not arterial blood. There's a first-aid kit in the Alfa. He's not English.'

'No, he's Italian. He's the local knowledge.'

Hynd picked up the shotgun and the pistol from the grass. 'Come with me and get the first-aid kit. I'll see if that lorry's going to work for us, while you dress that wound.'

They walked towards the truck.

'Perhaps you'd better do it,' the man said. 'I've never dressed a wound before. And what about Pat Spender? Is he hurt?'

'He's dead.'

The young man looked at him.

'You were a desk man, I take it,' Hynd said.

The man's face flushed. 'A desk man? No. What's that got to do with—' He broke off.

'You're one of us,' Hynd said. 'Casson set this up. You weren't sent to get Guercio.'

'We were to contact you, and make it look like an

attempt on Guercio. You are John Hynd?'

'Yes, I am John Hynd. Who are you?'

'Sanderson,' the man said. 'Ben Sanderson.' Then he became embarrassed. 'For this,' he waved a hand in an encompassing gesture, 'I have a cover name. False passport and everything. Bill Naude.'

They had reached the vehicles. Hynd threw the pistol and the shotgun down the steep pitch beside the road. He opened the boot of the Alfa and gave the young man the first-aid kit.

'I rather expected it,' he said. 'I thought Casson might want to make contact, and do it something like this. He could hardly phone me at Guercio's house and things have moved fast; we had no line of communication set up.'

The man looked up the hill. 'But you killed him, for God's sake.'

'Well, what difference does that make?' Hynd said.

'God in Heaven.'

'Go and look after your wounded,' Hynd said.

He climbed into the cab of the truck. The engine turned over. He put it into gear and to the accompaniment of some tragic metallic noises from behind drove it out of its entanglement with the Alfa.

He got down and looked at the rear end. The wheel that had been sheared off in the crash was one of the twin wheels on the left side of the truck. If the inner wheel and the axle held up, the truck might take them as far as they had to go.

He shifted such possessions as he had from the Alfa into the cab of the truck and then went to help Sanderson bring up the wounded man. They settled him as comfortably as might be in the back, hacking off the collapsed canvas to make a bedplace for him, and left him staring bitterly at the sky.

'Now,' Hynd said to Sanderson when they were in the cab. 'Where do I take you?'

'To the car, I suppose,' Sanderson said. 'But we must take him to a doctor or a hospital.'

'I'll take you to your car,' Hynd said. 'Then you take him to a doctor or a hospital.'

'You don't care what happens to him, do you?'

Hynd stashed the Uzi between his seat and the door. 'Hardly at all. The bugger wanted to kill me, and that's only a flesh wound he's got. On the other hand, laddie, if I'd left it up to you the poor sod would probably have died of starvation before you got your act together. Where's your car?'

'Halfway between here and Bissino. About six kilometres. You have a filthy manner, you know that?'

'I do have a filthy manner,' Hynd said. 'That's true. But let me tell you something. When I'm held up by men with guns I don't think I'm in the audience at La Scala watching *Forza del destino*, I think I'm up there on the stage and I want to come out of it in one piece, which is by no means a thing a chap can be sure of in a Verdi opera, and a thing he can be a lot less sure of in real life. And as to the wounded left around after it's over, well, good luck to them.'

'What does that mean?'

'It means that if someone's out to get me, I put a knife or a bullet in him and leave him lie. If I think he'll come after me again when he's got his health back, I'll like as not make sure of him.'

'Kill him, you mean?' Sanderson said. 'In cold blood?'

'You would say so,' Hynd said. 'In fact I wouldn't hang around waiting for my blood to cool. Mortal combat is a tremendously *now* kind of business, believe it or not.'

Hynd let the man beside him chew on this; he hoped he was playing him right. He drove along slowly. The truck rattled and groaned probably no more than usual, for it was an ancient of its kind. In Italy, at least, Fiats go on for ever.

After a bit he said, 'You've never been in action, have you?'

'No.'

'Why are you here, anyway? This business doesn't seem to me to be your cup of tea.'

Sanderson spoke with sudden and open candour. 'It doesn't seem like it to me either. I only came along for the ride. I can't actually do anything until we get the boat, and Spender thought it would be a useful exercise for us to work together. I fit in because I was in fast patrol boats in the Navy. They sold half of them off and I took early retirement.'

The boat? What was this about a boat? About a fast patrol boat, presumably? Hynd became cunning, and showed no interest in the boat. 'Now that Spender's dead,' he said, 'I guess you'll be the Pony Express from me to Casson. Tell him I'm sticking with Guercio. Tell him there seem to be some uncertainties between Guercio and the other Italian colleagues, and I'd better be around to pick up what I can. And tell him I regret Spender, but that ambush set-up was a disaster waiting to happen.'

The truck was showing no signs of collapsing. The road had emerged from a continuous succession of Zbends, following the windings of the river that ran down the gorge, and now ran beside the river into a hill valley. Hynd kept the truck at about thirty miles an hour. He had a wounded man in the back, and he had a rear wheel that might fall off at any moment: but the chief reason he drove slowly was that he wanted time to talk with this youth. He was learning things here.

'You regret Spender? I suppose that's as far as you would go. Well, to be honest,' Sanderson said after a moment of thought, 'the ambush idea was a fuck-up.'

'The ambush was fucked up,' Hynd said. 'But I'm not sure that the idea was a fuck-up. It's perfectly possible that Casson did want me dead, and had told Spender to kill me.'

'Why would he do that?' Sanderson asked.

'In case. To be on the safe side, that's all. In case I had thrown in with Guercio and his friends in preference to Casson.'

'You say Casson would kill you just in case?'

Hynd thought that yes, Casson very well might. Look at it from Casson's point of view. He had gone to great lengths to enrol Hynd – probably, very probably, because he was dealing with the Mafia and wanted the best man he could get to stand at his shoulder. And now, damn and blast it (from Casson's standpoint), simply because Hynd was so damn smart he had got out of there as soon as he saw the helicopter and taken Guercio with him.

Guercio would love Hynd for this, and if the two of them put their heads together and worked out that Casson had set up the raid on the villa to pressure Guercio to make the Mafia stick to its deal with Casson – and so far Hynd was going along with this explanation

– then Casson now had not only an angry Guercio to reckon with but an angry Guercio with Hynd in his camp.

So, yes, Hynd thought Casson very well might want him killed, just in case. Better safe than sorry.

Hynd, however, was not going to complicate the mind of the young innocent beside him with all this stuff, not when he was so wonderfully innocent that it hadn't even occurred to him there might be things Casson didn't want Hynd to know and was showing such willingness to talk about them.

So he simply said, 'Never mind about that. It didn't happen, so maybe we'll never know.' And he tossed in his negligent question. 'The boat's due pretty soon, isn't it?'

'I should have it a week today. N-Day is twelve days from now. I call it N-Day after the island.'

'You're in over your head rather, aren't you?' Hynd said. 'One minute in the Navy and the next a mercenary for hire. It's a bit extreme, surely.'

Sanderson gave a short laugh, a bitter sound.

'I was in love with this girl,' he said. 'And she went off with someone else. It was an impulse. A cousin of mine knew Spender and Spender was looking for a skipper for the boat. Mercenary is how I thought of it. It didn't sound too bad, and I felt like doing something heavy.'

Hynd had taken to this kid, which was a shame, because now he was going to have to kill him. Sanderson, restored to the Casson milieu, would certainly tell the tale. He would be asked if Hynd had questioned him and what he had divulged, and, with the same innocence he was showing now, he would tell them.

Then Casson would come up with a different scheme, and what Hynd had just learned would be wasted. If Casson thought Hynd had killed the three of them straight out in the ambush, he'd replace Sanderson somehow and stick to his original plan – whatever that might be. A fast patrol boat; an Italian (presumably) island beginning with the letter N: Seddall ought to be able to make something of that.

'Do you have a good crew?' Hynd said. 'Who's your second-in-command, or does that not figure with a boat that small?'

'She's not that small. She's four hundred tons. SAM missiles and a three-inch gun, though I don't know if we're getting the missiles or not. Yes, I've got a good second. Canadian fellow. The crew's mostly coming with the boat, but the guy bringing her in isn't a naval man, no experience of naval operations. You need a professional, that's why they wanted me.'

So that was it, Hynd thought bleakly. Casson would have no trouble replacing Sanderson.

The lorry gave a lurch and wobbled perilously close to the river. 'Hang on,' Hynd said. 'I'll check that wheel.'

He jumped down with his pistol in his hand and shot Sanderson through the head, stone dead. He went to the back of the truck and leapt up and shot the wounded Italian as the man sat up to see what was going on.

Then he climbed back into the cab and turned the truck away from the river and bumped onto the rough ground on the other side of the road, completed his circle, and headed back the way he had come, this time as fast as he could make the thing go.

He met one car coming down the gorge. Whoever

was in it would have seen the wrecked Alfa and got out to have a look, but they would have seen nothing to denote a gun battle. If there were people at the scene he would simply have to drive on through; but this was barren country, it was not twenty minutes since he had set off in the truck; he was in with a chance.

Sure enough, there was no one there. He drove up to the clump of trees and stopped. Sanderson's head was a mess of blood and bone and brains, and he did not want that on him. There was no point in compunction now that the boy was dead, so he took him by the feet and dragged him out of the truck and in among the trees. He did the same with the Italian.

He left them there and got back in the truck. Even from the height of the cab, the two murdered men were out of sight of the road. He put the truck in gear and set off again for Bissino. He wondered if the Italian, the man with the local knowledge, was one of Guercio's men, if he was Mafia, if there were sons or brothers or a father, if he would find himself in among vendetta. That would do it, all right.

For a long succession of long moments Hynd wished he'd never met Caroline Swift. If he hadn't met Caroline Swift he wouldn't be here. Sanderson and the Italian would be alive. No, face it, he didn't give a shit about the Italian, the man would have killed him without a qualm. The boy would have been alive. He would not have murdered the boy.

But hell, Sanderson had been planning to use his three-inch gun, and SAM missiles if 'the boat' had them, on whom? Since he would have been serving in Casson's navy, commanding a crew recruited by Casson, in cahoots with the Mafia, the people under Sanderson's firepower on N-Day would presumably have been a lot less deserving of sudden death than Sanderson.

Hynd was out of the gorge now, starting along the valley at the end of which lay Bissino. The sun was down and the sky that had faded earlier was now deepening to the dark blue of night.

Hynd stopped the truck and got out and walked a little away from it onto the arid field beside the road. He must stop this nonsense. If there were worse things to do yet, he would do them. He had chosen to immolate everything within him, if that was what it came to, for Caroline Swift. He was surely mad, but he knew that his purpose, within that madness, was inflexible.

If, afterwards, there was anything left to shrive, then he would seek to be shriven. For this season of his life, however, he had chosen to be the other Hynd, and hypocrisy was not an indulgence he could allow himself.

He went back to the truck. He remembered that his pistol was empty, so he loaded that. He found a rag in the truck and soaked it in the river and wiped Sanderson's blood and brains off the door and wall of the cab; it took several soakings, several trips to and from the river.

Then he threw the rag into the river and washed his hands in the grey-green water, and drove on down the valley before him as it filled with the long shadows of the ending day.

Chapter Thirteen

In the silence that returned to the room after the racket made by pouring the fuel into the stove there came a break in the storm, as if the wind had paused for breath, and in this space she heard the trace of a sound followed, like an echo, by another sound. She stood there, with the empty hod still in her hand, trying to recall what the sounds had been.

The gale struck again at the gable end of the house and she was held transfixed, baffled by the urgent need in her to put a name to these sounds, so faint and distant that their character seemed to have faded and gone before ever they reached her consciousness.

What she felt was a wrongness, that there had been an alien note to them, but one that struck a harmonic somewhere within her, that stirred uneasily in her memory. There had been an animal sound, not the bark of a dog, the cough of a sheep, the lowing of a bullock, the call of a bird. She had set the hod down beside the stove and was at the front door drawing the bolt across before she realized what her mind was saying to her – that what her memory had heard was the crack of a firearm and a cry of pain.

She could not credit this. It was long ago that she had heard these things; her mind and memory, and whatever part of her that had taken her to the door to bolt it, must have got it wrong.

She bit her lip: credit it or not, the sense that it was

true, might be true, had taken hold of her. She went swiftly down the passage and locked the back door. Then she went to the kitchen and grabbed her Barbour jacket from its hook. She looked at the typescript of her book and nodded once and lifted it from the table, and then ran upstairs into the darkness. She had left the lights on in the kitchen, for it was best to make no change in how the cottage looked to anyone outside.

She put the typescript in the daybag, and her wallet. She took her cash from the drawer and put it into the hip pocket of her jeans, then the pistol that Johnny had left with her. This went into a side pocket of the jacket, and the two spare clips of ammunition went one in the other side pocket and one in the deep poacher's pocket inside the jacket.

She went to the window, not too close, and stared out until her eyes were used to the dark. Nothing moved except the clouds flying over the moon, and the rowan tree at the gate thrashing in the storm.

'Come on,' she said to herself. 'Do it. You'll feel a damn fool tomorrow if there's nothing out there, but I feel it in my water so that's that. Let's move.'

She ran down the stairs to the back door, took the pistol from her pocket and put it off safety, eased the key round in the lock and opened the door a crack to look and listen. She did not plan, in the first instance, to go far. There was a rock she liked to sit on halfway up the hill behind the house where the heather was deep and thick. She would throw herself into the heather behind the rock, and from that vantage point await events. Assuming, that was, that events had not come so close as to prevent her getting there.

She went out, pulled the door to, and waited for a

moment. Nothing, no sound, no figure looming out of the dark. Only the beating of the sea to her left and the surge of the wind all about her. The clouds had covered the moon. She put the safety back on, pocketed the pistol, and went low to the ground up the slope. After a hundred yards she was in the heather and climbing more steeply. She slowed, knowing she was invisible at thirty feet so long as she kept low, and came at last to her chosen rock. She lay down and worked her way in among the heather.

This was her rock. She would sit on it in the evenings and watch the land change as the sun went down, and sometimes when she could not sleep she would come up here and sit under the stars. That piece of land below her, bounded by the sea, had become her home.

She looked down on it, where it lay, under the now unclouded sky, bared to the light of the moon. The moon was not bright, and touched the earth with no more than a loose mist of light that was not enough to penetrate the dark. The effect was to give to this perfectly ordinary bit of country which was the tip of the peninsula – this patch of bog and grassland and bracken so scoured by the Atlantic gales that trees would hardly grow on it, and in the day had no character at all – an aspect hidden and mysterious.

In the normal way of things to be out on a night like this would have appealed to her. Hers was a nature variously restless and calm, and she had come to accept such restlessness of her spirit as a kind of questioning going on within her: she would seldom know what the question was that she was asking herself, and would not always look to find words for it, but here at night, especially a night of storm, with the sea sounding on the rocks and the wind flying across the sky, she would let the unknown question search for its answer, and then go back down to that light which was the welcoming kitchen of her home, sometimes with new knowledge of herself, sometimes eased of she knew not what.

Tonight, however, she found that Land of Cockayne down there, which had so often spoken to her spirit as if it were the landscape of a familiar dream, alive with danger and menace.

Tonight she was not the woman who waited for unphrased answers to wordless questions. Now that she had reached her chosen position, her mind was working. She lay in the lee of the boulder with her hands flat on the hummock before her and her chin on her hands, asking herself what she planned to do if the going got dirty, if there were strangers roaming about down there who meant her harm.

'Make yourself a mission statement, Caroline Swift,' she said to herself. 'Making for the high ground was a good instinctual response to the feel of danger, but if there are serious badmen down there you must at least know what you are prepared to do about it.'

She discarded the idea of planning what course of action to follow should the imagined enemy do this or that. What she had to establish was: Am I willing to shoot people with this pistol? To which the answer was, Not if I can help it. Am I carrying enough courage to engage in an actual gunfight? To this the answer was, Perhaps, but I don't feel charged with that kind of aggression. Do I plan simply to lie low? And to this the answer was, You bet. And if that doesn't serve? Then I shall see.

The glow in the back window of the kitchen gleamed

at her, a beacon recalling her to the reality she had become used to. Beyond the house, weapon-flash imprinted on her vision a human figure, an image mean, crouching and hostile that was gone as soon as it reached her, and then came the pistol's distant crack shredded by the wind.

There was a display of flashes from three or four places, and a trivial rattle of sound from the explosions that had made them. In front of her cottage, then, a small war was going on. And since it was in front of her cottage it must have something to do with her. Meanwhile, however, these people were busy with each other.

A hundred feet behind her the hill crested, over that and she would be into dead ground and after that, the whole world to hide in. She went up it, slow and circumspect, still low to the ground, for busy though the warriors below her were, there might be a nightsight down there that would glimpse sudden movement. At the crest she rolled over and down the blind side, and waited there to let her nerves quiet and her heart slow.

She lay on her back and stared with large eyes at the moon. She said to herself, This is no way for a girl to spend her evenings.

She came to her feet and set off towards the southeast, aiming for the the neck of the peninsula, bound for the Border, for England, for Europe. She had nothing but what she stood up in, the old trainers, the washed-out jeans and sweater, and the Barbour jacket. She had the typescript in her bag and the pistol, for what that was worth, in her pocket. She was running for her life. She laughed to herself and tossed her head at the sky as if she was flirting with the stars – she had her toothbrush, even that. And she had about a hundred and fifty pounds sterling in cash and she had her credit cards, when she might feel it safe enough to use them.

She was fit, she was a walker, her long legs would carry her through the night. She was a woman in advanced middle-age and she knew what she was going to do, she was going to go down into Europe like a hippy of the sixties. She was going to Spain, to bask in the heat. She'd find a place there in the hills between Saragossa and Madrid. Somewhere inside her she had known all this even as she decided to quit the cottage.

This bit of her life was over. God, she had loved Johnny Hynd, still loved Johnny Hynd. But he loved her too much. He put a value on her that she didn't understand, or want, and in doing it he took something away from her. He had gone to war because he loved her and might die of it, but if a man had to do what a man had to do, that was his choice, not hers.

She had no idea who the opposing forces fighting it out before the cottage might be, and she had not the least interest in knowing, or speculating about it. That was their world, not hers. It might be that they represented large and efficient organizations, in which case she might have difficulty in slipping out of Britain, but Johnny had given her a man's name and a number to phone in a crisis, and as fallback the number of a woman who worked for the man: a man and a woman she could trust, Johnny had said.

A man she could trust in the world she used to play in? In the world Johnny was playing in now? That would be a freak of nature, that would.

Leaving the killing-field which these unknown enemies were making of the land that had belonged to this latest bit of her life further behind at every step, she walked on.

At noon on the next day, the postman parked his van and walked up the field with a cable in his hand to the house she had left. Here and there he found smears of blood in the grass, in one hollow a dried pool of it. He trod on a patch littered with cartridge cases.

He walked up to the cottage and knocked on the door, but no one came, and the door pushed open under his touch. He went inside and called out, and had no answer, so he explored it, every room, and found it empty.

He went slowly about the field after that and found more cartridges, more blood. He thought that in such a battle there would have been men killed as well as wounded. He picked up a couple of cartridges – 'Nine mil,' he said, for he had been in the Army – and put them in his pocket.

He reached his van and leaned on the roof and looked out over the sea, then up at the sky. He turned for a last look up the field to the cottage.

'Dear God,' he said to it. 'What went on here?' Then he got back in his van and drove off to find the law.

Chapter Fourteen

From Tallinn on the Baltic the road ran south across the Estonian plain to Tartu. It ran between forests of birch and fir, over drained marsh and flat farmland, under a low sky that shed its rain to the wind. Out there only the black grouse were having a good day, because despite the weather it was the height of summer and the cranberry season was in.

Along this road a Mercedes 200 proceeded at a decorous pace, driven by Valentin Murashov, who had crossed by ferry from Helsinki on a passport that said he was an American named Ray Trotter.

He jerked a thumb to his right. 'Collective farm, that was,' he said.

'Really,' said the man who called himself Casson, very bored. 'Nowadays I suppose it makes money.'

Murashov laughed. 'You were never in the economic section, were you? It's possible it makes money, if the Estonians have shaken off the habits of third-rate Soviet management and the infection of Russian habits of laziness. Everyone in Russia has forgotten how to work, and you know a third of the inhabitants of Estonia now are imported Russians.'

'You don't think a lot of your fellow-countrymen,' Casson said.

'Emotionally I am a Russian,' Murashov said. 'Pragmatically I am a citizen of the world, or of nowhere, as are you. It is why we now work together.'

'Humph,' was the sound Casson made. He stared beyond the windscreen wiper into the rain. 'I do not consider myself a citizen of the world, or a citizen even of nowhere.'

'It is true,' Murashov said. 'You are an anti-citizen. You are anti-everything. You are an anarchist.'

'Almost an anarchist,' Casson said with a smug air, 'not a thorough-going anarchist. I shall not want to play this game for ever. Two or three years, perhaps, and then I'll have had the fun of it. I'll be wealthy and will retire and enjoy myself. I like the fleshpots, Valentin.'

'You won't retire,' Murashov said. 'You are too much the professional to spend your days in idleness.'

A gust of wind hit the car and this extraordinary outburst of summer rain intensified, so that Murashov was obliged to slow down and put the wiper to full speed.

Casson, though it was as warm as toast in the car, reflexively huddled down into his coat collar and scowled at the weather. 'You're right,' he said. 'A professional is what I am, certainly; a professional who wants to bring his career through to its completion. And when I have done that, assure yourself, I shall be ready to relax.'

A sceptical look passed over Murashov's face. Murashov was Casson's junior by a good ten years, a man in his thirties with yellow hair, an unremarkably good-looking face with a pleasant expression, and for a Russian he smiled a good deal. He looked like an American businessman in a suit, and there was a quality in both the pleasant expression and the open-seeming smile which suggested that they were no more to be counted

181

on than those of any other businessman in a suit. His eyes were blue and pale and habitually bland, as if he was hiding himself behind them.

He said now, 'This completion you talk of for your career, what will it bring you apart from professional satisfaction and, conceivably, wealth?'

'What else should it bring?' Casson said.

Murashov sensed the emotion rising in the man, and flashed one of his large smiles out of the side window onto the bleak countryside. 'Well, there,' he said, 'I do not know, but it will be a fulfilment that eluded you when you were working for your government.'

Casson was silent and the feeling of tension from him increased. Then he opened his hands and looked at them as if he were a fortune-teller reading both palms at once, and laughed. 'Yes,' he said. 'My government did not know what they had.'

'You mean to let them know,' Murashov said. 'That will be your fulfilment?'

Casson turned his florid countenance upon the Russian, and then back to the rain-swept road in front of them. 'Murashov,' he said. 'There are disadvantages to learning too much about a man like me. Reflect on this.'

Murashov reflected, and Casson withdrew into his own thoughts, and the car ran on into the Baltic summer rain.

The two Frenchmen in the Café Pussirohu-kelder in Tartu were playing chess. It was a cavernous chamber, it was lunchtime, and there were a lot of students in the place, for Tartu was a university town.

From time to time some of these would drift up and

study the chessboard, but when they saw the low level of play they lost interest. Before one disenchanted couple moved off, the girl, who had heard the two men exchange a few words, asked them in French: 'What do you do?'

'We drive a truck,' said Goubert, and gave her a pleasant smile, but she saw that he meant nothing by it and shrugged and took her boyfriend away.

'One of us should be better at this game,' Rénouvin said, and moved a bishop.

'I am better at this game,' Goubert said, 'but it is wiser to offer an uninteresting spectacle.'

'It is too slow a game for me.' Indeed, Rénouvin looked as if it was. He was a tall thin man with a cadaverous face, and with restless eyes and a body full of restless movement, running a hand through his hair, shifting in his seat, leaning his chin first on one hand then the other.

They were the classic pair, for Goubert by contrast was Rénouvin's opposite: he was short and heavily built, and he sat foursquare to the table with his hands planted solidly on his thighs, and his hair, also black, was cut to within an inch of his head.

He took, phlegmatically, Rénouvin's surviving rook which had been guarded by the bishop. 'Now I can mate you in five moves.'

'You mean you can win whatever I do?' Rénouvin said. 'But you have lost many more pieces than I have.'

'It is not a question of force. It is all in here.' Goubert tapped the side of his head.

'You are welcome to what is in there,' Rénouvin said. 'You have the brain of a mechanic.'

'You are a sore loser,' Goubert said.

Rénouvin came up with a rueful smile which transformed his face. The girl who had been brushed off by Goubert saw it from three tables away and wanted to go to bed with him. 'Yes, I am,' Rénouvin said. 'Whatever I play, I am a sore loser.'

'Be easy. You are not going to lose this morning. They have arrived.'

Goubert stood up and raised an arm. Casson and Murashov came to their table and sat down. Murashov looked at the board. 'Mate in five moves,' he said in English.

'Of course,' Goubert said.

'I want a drink,' Casson said, 'and lunch.'

'You should have the veal,' Rénouvin said. 'We had it last night. Unless, of course, you are sensitive about how they rear the calves.'

Casson lay back in his chair and stretched hugely, easing out his body from his toes to his fingertips. With his eyes on the far height of the vaulted ceiling he yawned and said, 'If it made better meat I wouldn't care if they put their eyes out and cut their legs off and flogged them every day of their short lives. I shall have the veal.'

The two Frenchmen looked at each other sideways and said nothing.

They gave their order to the waiter. When his whisky had come, Casson said, 'Herschel and Konig are with the van?'

'Of course,' Rénouvin said.

'You're very edgy today,' Casson said. 'That's not how you were sold to me.'

Rénouvin's hand came off the table and went to the top of his boot where he kept a knife. His head tilted

lazily to one side and his eyes went soft. He looked like
the Marseillais killer which Goubert knew him to be,
but the words he used were not congruent with that
image, for Rénouvin had lived many roles in his time.

'You lack sufficient evidence for that comment,' he
said. 'It is no more than an attempt to take control.'

'Don't talk to me like that,' Casson said. 'You work
for me, Rénouvin. Don't forget that. Bad things could
happen to you.'

'Blow it out of your shorts, Casson.' Rénouvin smiled
like an angel.

At this sign Goubert knew the moment was dangerous, and intervened. 'Rénouvin is all right. It is only
that he doesn't suffer fools gladly.'

Casson's large face, already red by nature, grew
redder and seemed to swell. 'You're telling me I'm a
fool?' he said, in a voice expecting the answer no.

Murashov was watching them with an air of
detached and speculative amusement. From the pla-
cidity with which he sat there, you would have said that
if the other three fell to shooting and stabbing each
other, Murashov would simply wait until it was all over
and sit on, expecting his veal to be brought.

Goubert's phlegmatic countenance continued to
manifest no expression. 'It is foolish to ask if we have
left the van unattended. We know our business.'

Casson leaned his hard grey eyes on the Frenchman.
'I don't like your attitude,' he said.

Goubert shrugged. 'Life is not always what one
would wish,' he said. 'If you take first-rate men into
your organization, they will not accept to be treated as
second-class.'

The grey eyes opened very wide, and suddenly

Casson threw away his temper as if it had never been. 'Let's get on. We have you two, the two with the van, and the six crew waiting at Parnu. You are content, André, that you can sail the ship with ten men?'

Goubert inclined his head. 'She has a complement of thirty as a warship, but a crew of ten is ample to sail her.'

'Sanderson said he could fight her with a crew of twenty, which is what she will have for the operation,' Casson said. 'Could you?'

'Could I what?' Goubert said.

'Fight the ship with a crew of twenty.'

'You mean command her?'

'Precisely that.'

'Why do you ask,' Goubert said, 'since we have Sanderson?'

'We don't have Sanderson any more. He's dead.'

'What did he die of?'

'He was shot in the head,' Casson said, 'and that's all you need to know.'

'Here's the food,' Goubert said as the waiter arrived. 'Let me have a little think about this.'

Murashov pulled in an extra chair and put the chess board on it to make room for the waiter. They ate in silence while Goubert had his little think, and Murashov studied the chess board by his side.

After a while Murashov said to Rénouvin, 'You know, I think you could turn this game round.'

'Not me,' said Rénouvin. 'I am no chess player, I am too impetuous and anyway, look at all those pieces of mine he's captured.'

'Ah,' Murashov said. 'Then perhaps when we are at sea I shall have a match or two with Comrade Goubert.'

Goubert finished eating and wiped his mouth with the back of his hand. 'It is like this,' he said to Casson. 'I have the ability to command that little ship, but I was only a sub-lieutenant in the Canadian Navy's intelligence branch, and I was not long in a sea-going berth before I transferred. After that I was ashore. I could command her, if the crew know their jobs.'

'They know their jobs,' Casson said. 'Those that Eugène recruited,' and he nodded at Rénouvin, 'he will vouch for them.'

'Yes,' Rénouvin said. 'They're good men, André.'

'That's what ...' Goubert said, 'eight men out of twenty?'

Casson said, 'Nine. Rénouvin's nine Frenchmen, two Irish, a Scotsman, three English, five Americans. So there's no language problem, since you have English and French. You can take it from me, this crew has been well chosen, radarman, wireless operator, gunners, the whole boiling, all experienced for what we need.'

'OK,' Goubert said. 'I'll do it.'

'Good,' Murashov said. 'I'd rather serve with you than with Sanderson. He was too simple, that one. And you did well with the Japanese ship. I enjoyed that.'

'Very well.' Casson was not into the fellowship of comrades-in-arms or mutual respect or any rubbish like that. 'Meeting's over.'

He put both his arms in the air until a waiter saw them, and when the man came he asked for the bill.

As they drove towards the docks in Parñu, with the truck coming along behind, Casson extracted a piece of paper from his wallet.

'What's that?' Murashov asked him. 'A laissez-passer?'

'No. It's our destination. We go to the north side of the harbour, as I said. These are the words we look for when we get there. Estonian for timber wharf. Apparently there are signs.'

'A wooden pier?' Murashov said. 'I thought this was a real seaport.'

'You know nothing about your empire, Murashov,' Casson said. 'You Russians deserved to lose it. Parnu was a seaport before Russia ever had a navy. And timber wharf does not mean wooden pier. It refers to the fact that Pärnu once did a thriving trade in timber, among other things.'

'Well,' Murashov said. 'You can be damned glad that Russia has a navy now, or you would not be buying this ship.'

'I concede it.' He was insufferably smug this morning. Why should he not be? He had slept for much of the journey while Murashov drove through the dark and rain. Now, for their arrival at Parnu, the persistent rain had stopped and the waters of the Gulf of Riga sparkled in the sun. And Casson was carrying a million US dollars with which he was going to complete the purchase of a fighting ship: his would be the only private organization west of Suez with a warship of its own.

Yet the glory was Murashov's, or so it seemed to him. It was Murashov who had been in the KGB and had been able to make the vital contacts in the first place. It was Murashov who found out that the KGB – which was also the Border Guard and in that function, therefore, had its own fleet – had possessed exactly the type of vessel called for by the Italian operation: a warship that could masquerade as a civilian vessel until the moment of action, and could thus sail freely across the oceans.

The *Baikal* was an attack craft of the *Svetlyak* class, 450 tons, with twin diesels giving her a speed of 30 knots, a 76 millimetre gun firing 120 rounds a minute to a range of fifteen kilometres, and a six-barrel 30 millimetre gun firing three thousand rounds a minute. She would not have the SAM missile launcher or the torpedoes, but they would not need those, and in any case they would have had to be dispensed with, because the great thing about the *Baikal* was that with her elegant lines, with the squat but raking funnel on her upperworks and that long afterdeck free of any armament at all, she looked like a yacht: at that size a millionaire's yacht, a tycoon's yacht, but once in the Mediterranean, where tycoons' yachts made their natural home, she would, with the guns convincingly housed or shrouded, be as good as invisible.

It was Murashov who had known where to go, whom to see, who had to be paid off. It was Murashov who had learned of the *Baikal*, commissioned for the Border Guard fleet, left in limbo even as she was completing her fitting out at Tallinn, when the KGB was stood down.

Murashov, therefore, who had spent too long in the company of a self-congratulatory Casson, sounded a discordant note.

'Uh-huh,' he said. 'I'll believe we have secured her when we are at sea, or rather when we are out of the Baltic altogether.'

'Shopping on the black market is always a dicey business,' Casson said. 'That's why you and I have come in person, after all. To see that nothing goes wrong.'

There was the lightest susurration of irony in his delivery which suggested that if anything went wrong it was not unthinkable that he would hold Murashov to account and save his second-last bullet, so to speak, for him.

Murashov was used to Casson, and ignored this. 'It's not the KGB I don't trust . . .'

'There is no KGB now.'

'A rose by any other name,' Murashov said. 'They may be playing chamber music in the Lubianka these days, but would you bank on what music they'll be playing there two summers from now?'

'No,' said Casson. 'I would not. Whatever kind of music it is, I won't be playing it or listening to it, so I don't very much care. You were saying it's not your old chums from the KGB you don't trust. They've been paid their first tranche and today they get the rest. They put you on to this vessel. Built for their Border Guard fleet but not commissioned. Perfect. So who don't you trust?'

'The Navy,' Murashov said. 'The Baltic Fleet. They might be active. A flotilla out of St Petersburg might come over the horizon and say what's this, a warship, one of ours, and take her over.'

'What a perfectly absurd idea. In any case they've been paid too. I paid that fucking admiral fifty thousand pounds.'

Casson's wellbeing was unshakeable.

'By God,' Murashov said, 'there's no guard on the dock gates. Do we just drive through?'

'It's what I would do,' Casson said, 'unless you want to push the bloody thing. You've been in the West long enough. What did you expect? It's not a naval base.'

Murashov gave him a heavy smile. 'Colonial habits die hard.' He drove into the docks and turned right, and the lorry followed. The tyres swished on the wet stone of the pier.

Casson, having made sure of the lorry, turned back again and produced an electric shaver and began to smooth his skin.

'Timber wharf,' Casson said. 'Down this quay. Well, look at her, the beautiful creature, she looks like a yacht right now.'

The *Baikal* did indeed look like a yacht. More than a hundred and sixty feet in length, she gleamed in her new coat of white paint, and the funnel was painted primrose yellow. The ship shone in all this pristine glory as if she was bursting to get away from these northern climes and show herself off in the Mediterranean.

'Mine,' said Casson.

Chapter Fifteen

For once Harry got in some sleep on the flight back from New York. On the run-in to Heathrow even that bit of England looked welcoming in the long light of the sunrise.

He would go down to the farmhouse for the weekend and let the country nourish him. Get some of Mrs Lyon's cooking inside him, go for a good long walk or two with the dog. Take it easy at the office today.

He took a taxi into Sumner Place, turned on the hot water for his shower, and while it warmed up sat in the kitchen with a cup of coffee for an intelligent conversation with the black cat Sacha. When he was away for no more than a few days Sacha fended for herself. She would have found any other arrangement insulting to her independence and these days, possibly sexist as well.

The sour twist in this last thought was provoked by finding a letter from Olivia, riding her ruddy camels in Mongolia, as he riffled through his mail. He took it from its envelope, and sat with it unopened in his hand and looked at Sacha, who sat a yard away from him on the table. She was washing herself, having accepted with an air of marked indifference a meal of tuna out of a tin.

She stopped and sat with a paw in the air, waiting for him to speak. 'Do you know, Sacha,' he said. 'I don't think this is a lot of fun any more. It's one thing for a woman to want her own space, but it's quite another to spend half the year in the back of beyond.'

Sacha put the paw on the table top and gave him a look of contempt. 'I walk by myself,' the look said, or so Harry interpreted it. 'It is my nature. You are merely a human, one of a weak and effete species. I can't help you with this.'

He read the letter. They were now, by God, riding not camels but ponies, descendants of the animals on which Genghis Khan had ridden to empire. The letter was a travelogue of desert life, hoped he was well, and ended with love.

'Love,' he said to Sacha. 'What does she mean by love? I tell you, Sacha. I think this will hardly do.'

At this Sacha gazed at him deeply as if she had at last heard him issue a proclamation that made sense to her, and then went back to washing herself.

Seddall showered, dressed, went out and found a newspaper and breakfasted on coffee and croissants, and took a taxi down to Whitehall.

At the office, his prospects of an idle day began to go downhill.

'You have a meeting,' said the fair Deborah.

'What's all this stuff?' Harry said. There was a pile of mail, two inches thick, sitting on his desk.

'And these are phone calls to be answered.' Deborah put two sheets of A4 paper stapled together on his desk.

'I can't live like this,' Harry said. 'Is this what the general did all the time? Read mountains of paper and answer phone calls from strangers?'

Deborah put a cup of coffee beside the pile of letters.

'You must just be brave,' she said.

'Don't patronize me, you insolent filly.'

A man called Fawcett wandered in and said, 'Wonderful smell of coffee.'

'Give him some,' Seddall said.

Fawcett, who was enormously tall, lay down rather than sat in an ancient leather chair that was low everywhere, low to the ground and low in the back, so that he was able to extend himself fore and aft in a long, slow, relaxed sigh of physical pleasure.

'Grand coffee, Dodo,' he said.

'Dodo?' Seddall said.

'It's what she was called at school,' Fawcett said.

'Don't sit there talking about me as if I was a dumb animal,' said Deborah, now becoming Dodo in Seddall's mind.

'Quite right,' Fawcett said. 'I apologize. Shan't do it again.'

'Why are you here, Mick?' Seddall said. 'Do we have a thing to discuss?'

'Lord, no. Just dropped in for coffee and a chat. I must say,' he swung the hand holding the coffee cup in the direction of the paperwork on the desk, 'you seem to have a lot on your plate. Are you running the section, or what?'

'That's how it seems to be,' Harry said. 'I'll do it for a little, but I'm not going to get stuck with it.'

'Too adult for you?' Fawcett said. 'All that responsibility?'

'Responsibility? Is that what you'd call it?' Harry knocked the neat pile of paper into a sprawl. 'Not my kind of responsibility, anyway. What I need is an adjutant.'

'If it's only for a week or so, why don't you rope me in? I'm good with paperwork. All it needs is fast

194

response. Doesn't matter to me what it's about. And there's nothing happening upstairs just now. Drury won't mind.'

'Detached to me as temporary acting personal assistant?' Harry reached for the phone. 'Won't do much for your standing.'

'My standing? What's that mean? Good room this, I'd like to work here. We should have some flowers in, though.'

Harry gave the phone to Deborah. 'Get Drury for me, will you?'

She did this. 'Joe,' Harry said into the phone. 'I propose to relieve you of a burden. How would it be if Fawcett came to work for me for a week or so, till they make their minds up about this section? Good news, thanks.'

He put the phone down. 'You're on. He said he owes me a dinner for taking you out of his hair.'

'I'll get a desk in here today,' Fawcett said. 'We can plonk the sofa against the wall. Suit you?'

Seddall rubbed his hands. 'No, it doesn't, as you perfectly well know. You'll bunk out there with your girlfriend, which is what you want to do anyway.'

'Girlfriend.' Fawcett endeavoured to look discountenanced. 'Bunk?' he said. 'Surely an ill-chosen word.'

'I know when I'm being engineered,' Harry said. 'God bless you both, but don't pretend I'm a blithering idiot. Flowers, though, you're right about that, why don't we have flowers around? See to it,' and he waved a hand as if he were a magnate of great wealth and power, and those before him were his social secretaries.

'Dodo,' he said the new name experimentally. 'Dodo,

what is this meeting you announced to me when I came in?'

'Peter Blaney, Foreign Office Minister, and Raleigh of SIS, and I don't know who else. And as for you,' she said to Fawcett, 'why did you have to tell him I'm called Dodo? He'll take the piss out of me from now till Christmas.'

'Well, that's only six months,' said Fawcett, clearly a man with a light sense of obligation to others.

'All very exhilarating, to be sure,' Harry said, 'but I'm not going to be able to work like this. You two can play your games in your own time. Deborah, withdraw and be useful. Major Fawcett, you too may leave the presence, and kindly find out about this meeting with the Messrs Blaney and Raleigh, et, presumably, al.'

Fawcett rose and bowed languidly, and let Deborah hold the door for him as became his rank.

The meeting took place in a small conference room in the Foreign and Commonwealth Office. The room was in the process of being spiffed up. The walls had just been stripped by the painters and on his way in Seddall had passed by tarpaulins and ladders stowed in the corridor.

'We apologize for the state of the room,' said young Mr Wilson. 'There's a frightful lot going on here just now.'

John Wilson was a short and sturdy lad, but smooth and well turned out, in the regulation blue suit, silk handkerchief, and unknown school tie, the dapper career-maker to the life.

The Home Office was represented by a senior official,

a Deputy Secretary called Jane Kneller; Commander
Kenna of Special Branch was there for the police. The
others were Raleigh of MI6, as well as an assistant
director of Six, a Diana Cole.

Peter Blaney came in at speed wearing a black pin-
stripe and dark glasses, steered straight for the chairman's seat, put his black document case on the table,
and sat down, all in one movement.

The whole appearance and style of this arrival put
Seddall in mind of one of those small black GTi cars
with tinted windows scudding into sight and nipping
into a parking place, except that the Minister of State
did not behave as if he had come to rest but sat there
with his engine running at high revs.

'Good morning,' Blaney said. 'Beautiful day. This
working group has been called into being to deal with
the developing situation that has arisen from a mission
initiated by MI6 but operated in the unusual circum-
stance that a former MI6 officer on temporary re-
engagement is being run by an officer of Army Intelligence, namely Mr Seddall.'

Here he looked at Seddall with the bright cold eye
of a sparrow. Seddall took kindly to being addressed as
Mr instead of by military rank, and would have held it
to be rather courtly and eighteenth century of Blaney
but for the fact that nothing else about Blaney recalled
the courtly or echoed the eighteenth century; he had a
feeling too that Blaney was ready to do some hard
driving, and accordingly prepared himself by slouching
lower in his chair and gazing out of the windows at the
sky.

The sky was a brilliant blue, and the fact of being
stuck here in yet another Whitehall meeting made the

idea of being out there under it infinitely alluring. Distance lends enchantment to the view, he sang silently; but disenchantment expanded within him as the meeting proceeded.

Blaney named names round the table, since not everybody knew everybody, and got down to business.

'Ms Cole will give us a run-down from the MI6 P of V,' he said.

'P of V?' This was Jane Kneller of the Home Office.

'Point of view,' Blaney said.

'Good heavens,' she said, and won Seddall's heart.

'If we can proceed,' Blaney said. 'Ms Cole?'

'I appreciate the political correctness, but please call me Miss Cole, or Diana. I have no objection to either.'

Blaney said at once, 'Very well. Surnames only, please, ladies and gentlemen.' Looking at her, he said, 'I'll call you Cole and you'll call me Blaney. Does that suit?'

'Forget it,' Diana Cole said.

For Seddall, the exchange had been about nothing at all, but he was struck by Blaney's reflexive need to retain the high ground; and he was struck even more by Miss Cole's ability to shoo Blaney's verbal rubbish out of the way as if he were a child playing King of the Castle.

'We all know why we're here,' Diana Cole said, 'so I'll only sketch. We had cause to suppose, and of the accuracy of this supposition we are now certain, that former intelligence officers of various nationalities had combined to form an organization to sell their expertise, and that they were responsible for several acts of violence and terrorism: the assassination of General Kenyon here and of his equivalent in Germany, piracy in the north Pacific, armed robbery, raid on a military arsenal in Scandinavia, prison-breaking in South America.

'We had cause to believe that these people would seek to recruit a former officer of MI6, John Hynd, and persuade him to accept such recruitment on our behalf. Profile of Hynd is that he's resourceful, callous, and intrepid, but that his usefulness as an intelligence officer in the field or on the desk is offset by immaturities of character such as undisciplined wilfulness, an excessive solitariness of habit, and a neurotic and brooding temperament, and lately he appears to have developed an obsessive passion for a woman; a bundle of immaturities, in short.'

'Hold on,' Jane Kneller said. 'Can we be sure of the merit of these interpretations? It could equally be that he's self-motivated, self-enquiring, and not scared of his emotions.'

'The nature of the work he is asked to do directs the interpretation,' Cole said. 'The question is not whether he is the kind of man you like to know, Mrs Kneller, but whether he is at this moment well fitted for the task in hand.'

'Most men are a bundle of immaturities,' Blaney said. 'The differences come in how they deal with them and how they play them out into the world.'

Diana Cole looked up at him with strong, and slightly surprised, grey eyes. 'Be that as it may. We were not, therefore, distressed when Hynd left us. On the other hand, in many respects he was the right man for the assignment and so far he has demonstrated that. However, in a characteristic display of independence he insisted that he would not work directly to MI6 but that he would report to Harry Seddall. It seems he felt they had something in common.'

This was a smart crack and Seddall met the grey eyes coldly. Diana Cole had a broad forehead, a straight nose, a round chin, and sleek black hair cut middling short that curved in under the beginnings of her jawline. He could not determine whether the eyes showed her as formidable or merely hard, but he discerned enough to know he would not like her as an opponent.

'We have now learned, but we have not learned it from Mr Seddall, that having engaged with these people Hynd found that they had in fact made an alliance with the Mafia in Italy to execute a definite project whose nature we do not yet know, but which, in view of the scale of their previous operations, and in view of the fact that we regard these previous operations as no more than displays of their capacity to be competent and ruthless, and to commit what amount to acts of war to achieve their ends, we cannot but believe may be a project of some magnitude and probably destructiveness.

'The state of Italy being what it is, this gives rise to apprehension. We have also learned that Hynd,' and here she smoothed with her fingers the immaculate sleeve of her black blazer, an act which in so controlled a woman amounted to a gesture of vexation, 'that Hynd has identified a leading member of this organization of ex-intelligence officers as Owen Garrett, a former senior member of MI6, who is using now the name of Casson.

'Finally, when last heard from Hynd was in the south of Italy crossing from Naples to Bari, and is possibly making his way into the confidence of a minor member of the Mafia, a minor don, I should perhaps say. So clearly he is taking appalling risks, and we may want to consider our options in the event that he fails to survive.'

There were ashtrays on the table and Seddall took this to mean smoking was in order and lit a cigarette. Through the smoke, he said, 'John Hynd's chances of failing to survive seem to me to be improving with every word I hear.'

'Thank you, Miss Cole,' Blaney said. It was not clear to Seddall whether Blaney had understood what he said or not. Whatever the case, Blaney simply went on with the programme.

'Italy,' he said. 'Two thousand people in jail awaiting trial on corruption charges, from Milan to Palermo: ministers and ex-ministers, politicians in general, distinguished academics, directors of world-famous companies, and members of the Mafia. A country that's had a hundred governments since the war. And so forth.'

Blaney's eye crossed Wilson's, no more than that, and Wilson began to speak.

'We don't know,' he said, 'what holds a state together. We don't anticipate, we don't measure the possibilities of a state disintegrating. We can account for it when it has happened, but only to a degree. That is to say we can explain to our own satisfaction the separate causes. But what we cannot do is pinpoint the element which leads to the relaxation of parts from the centre, a thing which happens, in historical terms, in a breath.'

Wilson, without any embarrassment at all, was delivering this exposition with the confidence of a tutor to a group of students at a polytechnic.

He went on: 'The civil wars in the former Soviet

Union and Yugoslavia; we can see where they have come from but we did not see them coming. Even the split in Czechoslovakia, we did not expect that. We can, however, see that instability is, worldwide, running a good race against stability. Countries in South America, Africa, the Middle East, the Sub-Continent, South-East Asia, all demonstrate that.

'Italy is unstable. The Northern League wants to hive off from the south. The Mafia in Italy has survived every attempt to oppose it and has expanded until it is a force in the public and political and business life of all Italy. Now, with the drive against corruption in Italy, it confronts yet another threat. What will it do about that?

'I think we have to consider that Owen Garrett aka Casson and his merry men have come up with a well-timed proposition that makes sense to the Mafia in this context.

'We have to consider that between them they may destabilize Italy further than it has destabilized itself already, and we have to consider whether, after the experience of Yugoslavia, we would not be foolish to let that happen. We're getting close to home, are we not? How stable, after all, is the newly unified Germany? A strong currency, you know, takes no account of the invisible psychology of the people. It is the psychology of peoples that we are looking at, and it is from there that comes the relaxation of a nation's nervous system which happens, as I said, in a breath, and which can be diagnosed afterwards but is not susceptible to prognosis.'

He glanced up at the clock on the wall. 'We can't deal with the psychology of peoples,' he said, 'but we can perhaps pre-empt this liaison between the Mafia and Casson and his friends.'

It was pretty much what Doffene had said in New York, except that it had been enunciated at pompous length. That, however, was no more than irritating, and Seddall was in a state of growing fury.

'Mr Wilson,' he said. 'What's your security rating?'

Wilson was mildly surprised, that was all. He looked at his boss.

'Wilson has my full confidence,' Blaney said.

'The animals in Regent's Park Zoo have my full confidence,' Seddall said, 'but what's that to say to anything?'

'I find that offensive, Seddall,' Blaney said.

'Well, then, by God,' Harry said, 'I'm glad to think I'm getting through to you, and I hope it's not just to you. I am running an agent in the field, undercover, I repeat undercover, and I find myself in a meeting where I hear the whole goddamned ship's log of his progress down to his last known location recited to this haphazard collection of human beings,' he waved a hand to indicate the assembled functionaries, 'in utter violation of the most basic rules of secret intelligence work.'

'This is unconscionable language, Seddall,' Blaney said.

'What's this meeting for?' Harry said.

'It is the introductory meeting of the working group, as I made perfectly clear at the start.'

'It's more than that,' Harry said. 'You had a reason for calling it now, today, this noon. What was it?' He looked at the woman from MI6. 'What was it, Miss Cole?'

Yes, hard was what they were, those grey eyes of

hers. 'At MI6 we think Hynd has got about as far as he's going to get,' Miss Cole said. 'He's taking extreme risk and exposing himself recklessly. He can't last. They'll catch on to him at any moment and he'll be killed. Perhaps he'll be tortured, but we can't help that—'

Seddall interrupted: 'When you say "We can't help that," what do you mean?'

'Simply, that if he talks it makes it a lot more difficult for us to work the next phase.'

'I thought that was what you meant.'

'Therefore,' she said, 'we must be prepared to act. We need to have an alternative strategy in place now. The object of this meeting is to assess the position and draft a mission statement.'

Seddall was reaching out his arm to extinguish his cigarette. At the phrase 'mission statement' he paused and his arm hung for a moment in the air. Then a private smile turned his mouth and he stubbed out the burning tobacco.

He knew what was going on. The political implications of the operation had become apparent, and this had made it clear to the politicians and their civil servants that they must Think. The great minds at the Highest Levels of Government had begun to deliberate already; they would seek to establish an Objective. They would then perceive that there might be unforeseeable consequences from that Objective, and they would endeavour to foresee all possible unforeseeable consequences. It was with paradoxes such as these that the Foreign Office nurtured its impotence.

They would settle, with every satisfying feeling of resolute determination, upon a Limited Objective with

Minimal Risk of Complications, and congratulate themselves upon their mature and sophisticated wisdom.

They would then want to mount a meticulously prepared, thoroughly paperworked operation and to feel secure that they were totally in control of it. Hynd could be written off, now that he had made contact with and identified the enemy. Seddall was only in it because Hynd had made that a condition. With Hynd out of the equation, Seddall would be sidelined in short order.

His temper had dissipated. He felt calm, clever, and wicked. He was glad Mrs Lyon had put out this facetious summery suit for him to wear. He was pleased to be an alien among these seriously suited people.

He smiled like a basilisk at Diana Cole. 'I admire the rapidity of your thinking,' he said.

She waited.

'You perceive Hynd to be a loose cannon.'

'Yes,' she said, watching him.

'He was chosen as being uniquely qualified to do what he has done,' Seddall said. 'He's done as much death or glory stuff as you think you need of him, and now it is time for more adult and balanced minds to take over.'

'That's right.'

'I understand you now,' he said. 'Wisest thing, quite possibly.'

He was not sure if he was up to the dissimulation required to present this appearance of being reconciled to the merits of Consensus Planning by the Best Minds. He felt Gerald Kenna's eye on him and exerted himself not to meet it. Commander Kenna and he had known each other these ten years, and this picture of a conciliating and accommodating Seddall was not one Kenna had seen before.

He was having enough trouble meeting Diana Cole's cold gaze. That was a hard woman if ever he'd met one. He wondered how good she was, how capable, how perceptive. He knew he could not shed the pugnacity from his face and he did not try, offered no false, palliating smile, just looked across at her as if he was trying to assess her, which indeed he was.

'Perhaps, now,' Blaney said, 'we can move along.'

'However,' said Jane Kneller, earning her keep as a mandarin of the Home Office, 'a question was raised about Mr Wilson. Does he have security clearance?'

'We really must try to abandon these outworn shibboleths,' Blaney said. 'The Cold War is over. We are emerging from the era of State secrecy and bringing the work of the security and intelligence services into the light of day, making them openly responsible to Parliament. We can hardly confer usefully among ourselves unless there is openness and confidence among those taking part. Mr Wilson, as I have said, has my full confidence.'

'No, Mr Blaney,' Kneller said. 'That won't do. I readily believe that Mr Wilson is as discreet as any member of the Foreign and Commonwealth Office, but security considerations go far beyond discretion.'

Wilson stood up. Clearance or not, Harry thought, the man was worth something. His face had gone tight, but that was his only visible reaction, and he was being infernally embarrassed by his Minister.

'I must withdraw,' Wilson said.

'Very well,' Blaney said. 'If you must, you must.'

Wilson left the room swiftly, and with no sign of

discomposure in the carriage of his body.

'Commander Kenna,' Blaney said. 'What can you tell us about the events at the house of this woman,' he refreshed his memory from the documents in front of him, 'Swift, Caroline Swift.'

Events at the house of Caroline Swift? Seddall, metaphorically and physically, sat up.

'What's this about Caroline Swift?'

Diana Cole came in: 'This is exactly the kind of thing I object to in the man Hynd. We should not have to distract our attention or waste our time talking about this Swift woman simply because Hynd has this obsessive passion for her.'

Seddall felt himself give her a look of contempt that Sacha would not have disclaimed. He sat back in his chair again.

'Gerald,' he said in a controlled, drawling voice to Kenna, 'what's this creature, what's her name, Cole, talking about?'

'The thing is, Harry,' Kenna said. 'Caroline Swift seems to have disappeared.'

Chapter Sixteen

Seddall heard this with his eyes still on Diana Cole. She did not go white to the lips, or scarlet with indignation, but he saw from the look of hard fury on her that he had made an impressive enemy.

He turned to Kenna. 'Tell it, Gerald,' he said.

Kenna was a large man who looked as if he might still have much of the strength he once had, but no longer the physical energy to use it. He sat with his shoulders hunched up and his head stooped forward, the posture of a man who worked stressfully at a desk. He was one of those Celts with a big angular head, and the black springy hair was now almost all white. But from the set of his face he was still the tough Gerald Kenna that Seddall had always known him to be.

'What it comes down to,' Kenna said, 'is that two small groups of people encountered each other a couple of hundred yards in front of and below Miss Swift's cottage, which is in a lonely place, and engaged each other with small arms. There were serious injuries because we found blood in several places, as well as indications of bodies, living or dead is unknown, having been dragged across the turf.

'Forced entry was made to the house. A sheep on the hill was killed by a long shot and died. We found seven-millimetre and nine-millimetre cartridges. We don't know who was engaged on either side or what they were on about in the first place. Miss Swift has disappeared. Either she was kidnapped, or went of her own will with one group or the other, or she was killed, or she decided that her solitary retreat was no longer the peaceful place she had taken it to be, and responded to this by leaving, somehow eluding the two parties of gunmen.'

He rubbed a big hand down his craggy, choleric-complexioned face. 'Miss Caroline Swift's name was flagged on our computer, so the Scottish police notified us and we notified the Home Office. I was in Glasgow two hours after we were notified and on site, courtesy of a Strathclyde Police helicopter, an hour after that. They worked fast and smart, the police up there. The sheep was privily removed before the shepherd learned of its demise. One way and another, the thing has not become known to the public or the press, which we take it is what you'd want. The postman who reported the signs of the gunfight to the local police is an ex-army man and willingly agreed to keep his own counsel, and from his record, he can be relied upon.'

They waited, but no more came from Commander Kenna.

'Well, man,' Seddall said impatiently, 'who was involved in this gunfight?'

Kenna gave him a dark look. 'As to that, Harry,' he said, 'you must look to Miss Cole or Mr Raleigh, but I'll tell you this. The postman had gone to the house to deliver a cable. The cable was unsigned and said only: "Time to go." It was sent from the south of Italy.'

'Hynd was warning her,' Harry said. 'He feared she was in danger. Therefore in danger from Casson, formerly your man Garrett.' He directed this last at Cole.

'I wonder why—' He broke off and ran through the timing in his mind.

Yes, the timing served. So why did Hynd not tell *me* if he thought Caroline Swift needed protection? His thought slowed and ran off on a loop-line. Well, Doffene was the message-taker. It would have been Doffene he told.

He went into recall, back to New York. He remembered Doffene across from him in that bar on the Upper West Side. He had sensed a wrongness in Doffene, a disingenuousness, lurking unease; but he had failed to identify its cause, and, failing, had neglected to use his imagination to discover where Doffene's deceit lay.

He was sure of it now. Hynd had asked Doffene to pass on a message that he was worried about Caroline Swift's safety, and Doffene had kept it from him. The more he went back to how Doffene had been, sitting there across from him, the more certain he was that the American had received such a message from Hynd and concealed it for some purpose of his own; that Doffene had decided to take a hand in the game.

Which meant that the Americans as a whole had decided to take a hand in the game. Which here in Britain probably meant the CIA. And if there was one thing Harry did not want, it was to have the CIA getting under his feet.

Suddenly, Harry wanted to get out of there. He wanted to get away from this world of meetings, whether in New York or London, meetings at which everyone had an axe to grind, openly or secretly. He wanted to run this operation not from a desk but out there in the field.

Jane Kneller said, 'You began to speak, Mr Seddall,

and then you interrupted yourself. It was as if you had remembered something germane to the disappearance of Ms Swift.'

Seddall began to tell her. 'I was in New York at this UN committee,' he said. 'I'd promised Hynd . . .'

Then he found his voice was nothing but husk, and he had to cough his throat clear and start again. In that moment's pause he made up his mind to say as little as possible. If there was one person in that room he might have been willing to rely on it was Jane Kneller, but he was not alone with her, and in any case, his faculty for trust was diminished since his recent conjecture, and then certitude, about Doffene.

Thinking on his feet he moved forward nimbly. 'Strike that,' he said. 'I think I get the smell of this. What happened, Raleigh? CIA London station took a hand in the game?'

'They wouldn't dare,' Commander Kenna said, and his head was at a curious angle, like a bull trying to make up its mind if it was going to charge.

'Yes, they would,' Harry said. 'It was them, I know it. I'm only surprised they failed to take a vacuum cleaner over the ground afterwards. They must have been in a bit of a panic. What about it, Raleigh? CIA the other players in this shooting match?'

'Yes,' Raleigh said. 'I'm afraid they were. They should have called on us if they thought Swift was in any danger. So that we could deal with it appropriately. Fortunately, they came out on top, the other fellows were beaten off.'

'You are telling us,' Kenna said, 'that the CIA, perceiving what is in fact the case, that they had no colour of legality behind them, simply let the other side take up their casualties and depart without let or hindrance. Both parties being in fact criminals under British law and liable to prosecution. That is what you are telling us?'

'Ah,' Raleigh said. 'Yes.'

'Well then, dammit,' Kenna said, 'can you kindly tell me, what is their story about Miss Swift? She was, after all, the only innocent party involved, and I am, after all, a policeman, and I am concerned to know whether I have to act on her behalf. Since I take it,' and he looked, not so much daggers as blunderbusses, at Blaney, 'that we shall not be encouraged to prosecute our American allies.'

'It would not do, Commander,' Blaney said. 'The strongest representations are being made this very day. We have had the most profuse apologies from Grosvenor Square, the ambassador himself in person. The gravity of it is fully realized.'

'Miss Swift,' Kenna said to Raleigh.

'No sign of her after the gunfight,' Raleigh said. 'Cottage empty.'

'Took to the bushes,' Kenna said. 'Wise woman.'

'It would be deplorable, if it were indeed the fact, that the CIA should set themselves up as armed bodyguards to anyone in this country,' Jane Kneller said. 'American citizen or no. But it makes no sense. They must have had an urgent warning about Miss Swift's safety, if they sent a party of armed men up there. They wouldn't have that kind of facility standing by in Scotland, they'd have to send. So why not call on us? We could have had her safe out of there in an hour, and a trap laid for whoever was after her. There's no sense in it.'

'That is to assume,' Harry said, 'that the CIA's intention in this was benevolent to Miss Swift.'

'Mr Seddall echoes my thought,' said Jane Kneller.

They looked at each other.

She saw a man in a crumpled summerweight suit, oldish probably, but whose cut deserved better of its wearer, a round face that created the same impression on her as the suit, an indulgent mouth set off by a mulish jaw, brown hair starting to go thin on the ground, and light brown eyes in which a yellowish feral gleam had sprung as his anger grew, but where an ironic and scornful humour now began to show, as if he had withdrawn from them all, and made some decision of his own.

He saw a woman with sandy hair and a long face of elegant good looks, with blue-green eyes the colour of the sea, whose matured intelligence was public for all to see but where he, in this moment, saw some privacy of her own thought swim up to study him from just below the surface. She wore a white suit with a blue stripe on it and a white scarf at her throat.

An exchange passed between them, and was ended by Blaney.

'I don't follow you,' the Minister said. 'What other intention could the CIA have here that was not benevolent?' And Harry saw that the poor man could not, in truth, make such a leap in his mind. Kenna, on the other hand, unclenched his hands, which had been locked together one over the other as an expression of the tension in him, and threw himself back in his chair with a huge sigh, which could have meant anything from despair to relief.

Harry, who had already begun to have an inkling of what he himself might do after he had got out of this meeting, continued to keep his mind hidden.

'An idle speculation, Minister,' he said, all deceit and self-deprecation, with his face as open as the day. 'I had just the taste of an idea on the tip of my tongue, but it's gone.'

He surveyed the table then: Gerald Kenna, lounging back, a picture of disillusionment; Edward Raleigh, pink with confusion of the mind over what had just passed; Diana Cole, hard and strong physically and by nature, her grey eyes hostile with scepticism; and Jane Kneller, too confident in herself to evince any of these characteristics, regarding him still with interest and intelligence.

'Why,' said Harry, to throw a distracting cat among the pigeons, 'is there no one from MI5 here? I'd have thought that gun battles fought by aliens on British soil was a matter for the Security Service.'

Cole nearly looked at Blaney but caught herself. She saw that Harry had picked up the aborted movement and stared him down.

'Perhaps we should have them next time,' Blaney said. 'This was held to be a delicate matter concerning foreign relations. I was not aware of the extent to which it had affected these shores.'

'Is it not appropriate now,' Diana Cole said, 'for us to have a report on the Seddall–Hynd operation at first hand? We have to plan for the future, now that things have got into such a mess. For my part I should particularly like to know, since he has clearly won the confidence of John Hynd, if Seddall has any idea where Caroline Swift might have gone.'

'Yes, Seddall,' Blaney said. 'Would you be so kind?'

'It's the damnedest thing,' Harry said, with all the tact and grace he had left in him, which was not a great deal, 'and I'm most awfully sorry, but I'm feeling rather unwell. I do have to ask you to excuse me.'

He pushed back his chair, stood up, looked into the calm face of Jane Kneller, nodded at Kenna, walked slowly from the room as if he was already unconscious of those present, was already elsewhere; made his way down through the building and onto the pavement.

Once outside and standing in the sunlight, he shook himself like a dog, lifted his head and sniffed the air like a warhorse, and strode, with the vigour of a trapped man suddenly set free, towards the rest of the day.

Chapter Seventeen

Fawcett, with a vase of white lilies, of all things, on his desk, was dictating to a typist. Deborah followed Harry into his office, which was enriched by nothing more exotic than a mixture of red and white carnations, though these were in vast quantity.

'Messages,' she said. 'Sorrel Blake says she plans to eat at eight but she'll be ready to receive you from seven on. Call her to confirm.'

'I'm dining with Sorrel?' he said in a bewildered way, still coming down from the fury engendered in him by the meeting, and a bit slow, therefore, on the uptake. Then he understood that this was Sorrel's way of letting him know she had news to give him. 'Ah,' he said. 'Of course. Yes. Sorrel's, between seven and eight.'

'Your meeting,' Deborah said. 'How did it go?'

'The customary, expectable bullshit,' Harry said. 'But things to discuss. I shall call a council of war with you and Master Mick Fawcett first thing tomorrow.'

She went out, and he sat down to think, but he was in a muddle and wandered out again to the outer office and sat on Deborah's desk. 'I begin to feel I should have lilies,' he said.

'You can't have these,' Deborah said. 'Mick gave them to me.'

'Then why are they on his desk?'

'Because if they're on mine I sniff them, and it makes pollen smudges on my nose.'

'A peculiarity of lilies,' Harry said.

'How will you be getting to Sorrel Blake's tonight?' she said. 'You didn't bring the car in today.'

'Hadn't thought. Except that I want to be sure to get there unfollowed; unfollowed by MI6 or the Americans, in fact. It's become time to play the cards close to the chest. I expect I'll dive in and out of buses and taxis, that sort of thing. Why?'

'I'll take you.' There was a note in her voice: this was not merely an offer, she wanted to do it. What was that about? Well, time would tell.

'That's decent of you,' Harry said. 'You know the sort of driving this calls for?'

'I'll probably be better at it than Mick would.'

'Better than me too, I dare say,' Harry said. 'We'll go straight from here. I ought to sit in my office and try to think, though I must say I'm finding it hellish difficult. Is there a decent bottle of sherry on the premises?'

'I know where I can steal one,' Fawcett said.

'Do it,' Harry said, and retired.

At seven Deborah came into his room. She took his jacket off the stand and waited for him to take it. She handed him his hat.

He had been right. He knew from her manner that she had things to say. 'You have an agenda, or I miss my guess,' he said.

'Yes,' she said. 'I want to ask you something.'

'Sit you down then, and ask me.' He dropped his jacket on the desk and sat down himself, with his hat on the back of his head, and lit a Gauloise.

'Sorrel Blake,' she said. 'She works with you in the field. She's not stuck behind a desk like I am.'

'Yes, what about it?'

'I wish you'd let me do that kind of thing, the kind of thing she does.'

He had no idea what he felt about this, and played for time. 'Sorrel may look like a sweetheart,' he said, 'but she's a tough cookie.'

'So am I, I'm as fit as anything. I left Mick standing on a twenty-mile hike last Saturday.'

'That's not the kind of toughness I mean. Sorrel plays hard and rough, when the chips are down.'

She blushed furiously. 'I'm in the Army,' she said, 'I'm not a goddam Girl Guide.'

'I know that. I'm taking this seriously. Let me think for a minute.'

She appeared to him as a slight, slim, hundred and twenty pounds of bright-eyed schoolgirl with black hair cut to a trendy one inch from the scalp. He knew from his experience of her that she was intelligent and capable. He knew from her file that she was tough, fit, and gutsy, that she was a member of an Army rock-climbing team, that she'd been snow-holing in Norway, that one of her sports was judo, that she swam like an otter. But what did she know of life and death the way a woman like Sorrel Blake knew about it?

'The thing is,' he said, extinguishing the cigarette, 'I think you might be very good, and I do need a team, but for this one I need you and Mick to hold down the office. It's what I want to talk about to both of you tomorrow. There's John Hynd, up to his neck in it out there in Italy, and MI6 and the Government are getting ready to back off from him and move in on the operation with ten planning committees to the acre, which will leave them with the usual preferred options, either to let it wither on the vine on purpose, or to foul it up by mistake but with the very best of intentions.'

He found he was smoking another cigarette and looked at it with surprise. He could not remember lighting it; must be feeling the heat. 'And Hynd,' he said, 'has got his toe in the door already. That's all it called for, it's all that would have done. A simple operation to get one man in and a small unit to call on when he needs it. The smell I get is that they find Hynd expendable, a risky man to employ, don't you know, and not one of us.

'They want the comfort of doing something powerful *en masse*, liaising at high levels all over the shop. And whether they choose in the end to be effective or to be nugatory will make no difference to Hynd. Power can lead hotshots like these to make frightfully brave decisions with other people's lives.'

He doused that cigarette and sighed. 'I'm getting pompous in my old age. The long and the short of it is that so far as I'm concerned the game's afoot and we're going in there to play with Hynd. By the time the policy-makers know what they're about the thing will be over, one way or another. This time, though, I'm afraid you and Mick will be the HQ Company. But consider, Dodo, that your application has been favourably received, and if I don't get sacked after this one, then, yes, we'll let you loose upon an unsuspecting world.'

'Well,' she said, 'at least you didn't say something patronizing like, "Good God, girl, I know your father. How could I explain it to him if anything happened to you?"'

'Your father? I don't even like your father.'

'Oh,' she said.

219

'Exactly so,' he said. 'Anyway, you're going to be taking quite a risk even holding down the office, if you're willing to do what I want you to do. Same applies to Mick. First thing tonight or tomorrow when you see Mick, tell him that from now on neither of you will be giving out the slightest bit of information about this Hynd operation, or telling anything we know about these Masterless Men, to anyone at all, from the Cabinet down, or up, depending on how you view the Cabinet.'

He gave her a long cold stare. 'You may come under a lot of pressure, and this may end your short career, young Deborah. We're going out on a limb. I've done it before and got away with it but times have changed rather, and we may end up in the doghouse. Think about that before you volunteer.'

'I've thought.'

'No,' he said, 'you have not thought. Tell me tomorrow. Now let's get going.'

Once they were in the car and running through the traffic, in a Peugeot 205 which she handled with revelatory skill and speed, he said, 'Well, you can certainly drive a car.'

'I'm putting on a show. I thought you'd feel I was too young to go into the field, all protective about the fresh-faced innocent.'

'I never met an innocent woman in my life, of any age. And life corrupts sooner or later. It won't matter a damn to me if you get corrupted sooner rather than later.'

'That's telling it,' she said. 'Are you trying to put me off now?'

'No,' he said, 'I'm not. I'm just letting you know

what an unfeeling bastard I am to work for.'

'I know *that*.'

'Oh,' he said, in his turn.

They completed the journey in silence, and when she pulled up at Sorrel's house, he said, 'Thanks for the ride. Are you sulking?'

'No, of course not. Are you?'

'Me? I never sulk. Nine o'clock tomorrow.'

She gave him a hug and kissed him on both cheeks.

'You're an insubordinate officer,' he said.

'I should hope so,' she said. 'Goodnight, boss.'

She drove off and he rang Sorrel's doorbell.

Sorrel greeted him barefoot, wearing a yellow skirt which echoed the colour of her short curly hair, and a white sweater.

'You're a sight for sore eyes,' he said. 'You look younger than ever. How do you do it?'

'I'm in love.'

'Not again.'

'Mind your manners,' Sorrel said. 'I don't fall in love all that often. Anyway, this is who I'm in love with this time.'

She bent down and picked up a small bundle of fluff that had bounced into the doorway. Harry perceived it to be a Cairn terrier puppy, of the grey, not the ginger, persuasion, less than three months old.

'Isn't he a darling?' Sorrel presented her darling towards Harry, so that the creature licked his weary face entire in two seconds flat and was beginning all over again when Harry ducked out of the line of fire.

'Actually, yes he is,' he said. 'Give him here. What's his name?'

'Colin.' She handed over the small grey dog. During the transfer Harry's jacket fell from his arm and the hat, dislodged by the eager inquisitive nose, off his head.

'Go on in and sit down,' Sorrel said. 'You look a wreck. I'll get us a drink.'

Harry sat on the couch and planted the infant terrier on the cushion beside him and pushed it onto its side. The bright eyes looked at him and then closed, and young Colin fell asleep on the instant, refreshing himself for the next bout of ecstatic energy.

Seddall liked Sorrel's flat. It was in a commonplace terrace in the basement, but it was well windowed and full of light, long, low rooms furnished, pictured, and flowered with easy grace. He went over to the glass sliding door that led to the large expanse of common garden at the backs of the houses and went up the steps and sat on the grass, and, with his spirit enbowered by the smell of cut grass, by the presence of the tall trees that grew round about, and the high blue sky overhead, he began to unwind.

He saw Sorrel come into the sitting-room and went to join her. She put his drink on the table in front of the couch and sat in an armchair with her feet pulled up under her.

She said, 'Caroline Swift called me.'

'Thought that was it,' Harry said. 'What's the scoop?'

'Well, hardly any,' Sorrel said. 'She was on and off the phone in twenty seconds. She just said, "Caroline Swift. I'm near London and I need help. Can I see you or Harry Seddall? I'll call you again about ten tonight." And hung up.'

'Sensible woman.'

'Well, brief and to the point, certainly.'

'No,' Harry said, 'more than that. She's on the run and she doesn't trust your phone. She was trying to avoid a trace. I don't trust your phone either, or mine, for that matter. MI6 are going to start messing this affair up, and the CIA have moved in on it, so we're back on the old lay, Sorrel, we're going to do our own thing.'

'Goody,' Sorrel said. 'Life's been awfully dull lately. Why's Caroline Swift on the run?'

Harry finished his whisky at a gulp and got up to help himself to more, lit a cigarette, and walked about the room as he told her the story of the gunfight at the cottage in Scotland.

'It sounds as if she just walked out and left them to get on with it,' Sorrel said. 'I like the sound of that. She'll want a place to hole up until she knows what she's going to do next.'

'Yes, I should think she will. The trouble is that with any of the people you or I know who have spare houses they could lend us, security would be blown before we start. They and their abodes, few or many, could be traced through us.'

'You could just put her in the farmhouse, and throw in a garrison. Ready to eat? I'll go and play in the kitchen. Shan't be long.'

They ate in the kitchen, and while they ate he told her everything he knew about the Hynd mission, about Hynd and Swift, about Hynd's history and Swift's history, and about the meeting at the Foreign Office.

He told her about young Deborah's wish to be out there in among the action.

'She sounds like the right stuff. Got to start some time. Nobody worth their salt wants to sit around in offices all day moving paper and answering telephones.'

They went back to the sitting-room for coffee and Seddall mixed Cointreau and brandy for them, and they talked about idle nothings as the clock moved towards ten o'clock and the expected phone call.

The clock moved on; ten o'clock went by, and eleven. The puppy, worn out by the exertions of the day, lay flat out in his basket. Harry began to yawn. 'Lord, I'm sorry,' he said.

'Don't be a chump. You were in New York this time last night. No wonder you're tired. What'll we do? Give her till midnight? You can bed down here if you like.' Then, as if she had been biffed by some osmotic imp she said, 'You've not said a word about Olivia.'

And this confused them both, because they had been lovers once.

'She's off riding her bloody camels in Mongolia, Sorrel,' he said. 'You know that.'

The door to the garden was open to let out the smoke of Harry's Gauloises and the night chill had come in. Sorrel broke the awkward moment by going through to her bedroom to get a sweater.

Harry looked at the small dog in his basket, and smiled, and went to the kitchen to put the kettle on for more coffee.

As he entered the sitting-room again Sorrel was coming in from the bedroom, pulling on a dark blue sweater. When her head emerged from it she stopped, frozen in the act, and stared.

'Good God,' she said.

There was a woman at the other end of the room,

engaged at the moment when they saw her in pulling the curtains over the garden door and the glass panels that flanked it.

When the curtains were drawn she turned and faced them. 'Hi,' she said. 'Sorrel Blake and Harry Seddall, right?'

She looked at the pistol in Seddall's hand. 'You won't need that,' she said. 'I'm . . .'

'Caroline Swift,' he said, and put the gun away.

'Yes.'

'How did you know this was the right house?' Sorrel said.

'I sussed it out. I counted the houses along the street and then did the same at the back. I had your name and phone number from Johnny, but that was just in case of a crisis, which I didn't really expect to happen. I got your address from the phone book. Are you angry? I know it's not the way to behave but it seemed a safe way to get to you.'

'No, no, I'm not angry,' Sorrel said. 'It's only the surprise if it.' She went over to the other woman. 'Come and sit down. You've done bloody well, ducking out of that gunfight and finding your way here. What would you like? Coffee and a drink? Something to eat? And you'll spend the night here, of course.'

Caroline sank into the sofa. 'Coffee would be great,' she said, and as Sorrel went to make the coffee, 'and to stay here would be wonderful. I've just about run out my string.' She looked up at Seddall. 'So you're Harry Seddall?'

'Yes.'

He was astonished by her beauty, the face paled by the fatigues of fear and the long run – indeed, the long

225

escape – from that northern cottage to London, and flushed by the excitement of her arrival here, the grey-streaked ash-blonde hair all anyhow round her head and shoulders, the long body in worn blue denim. The strength of spirit in the deep brown eyes.

Harry felt as if he was in two states of being, and that one of them swayed slightly on its feet.

'I really made it,' she said.

'You did that,' he said. 'Put your feet up. You're safe here. You can let yourself go now.'

'If I put my feet up I'll fall asleep,' she said, but she was already pulling off her trainers.

'You're allowed to fall asleep,' he said.

She stretched out on the couch. 'God, that feels good.'

There was something particularly likeable about the way she gave herself up to her exhaustion as if she had known him all her life.

'How did you get here?' he asked her.

'You know about the gunfight, don't you?' she said. 'Sorrel mentioned it. I don't know who they were but I decided that at least one lot must be after me, so I got out. I just took what I could carry' – she gestured at the bundle by the windows, a small knapsack and a sweater thrown on it – 'and walked out over the hills, and in the morning I got a local bus and after that I hitch-hiked.'

'This won't keep you awake very long.' Sorrel was back, bearing coffee. 'You look absolutely flat out.'

'I am. Can you guys hide me?'

'Yes,' Harry said.

'And can you get me out of the country? So that no one knows?'

'That too,' he said. 'Don't worry about things any more. Take it easy.'

Whether it was that, or that the Cairn terrier puppy came to life and jumped up and began licking her face: whatever the cause, Caroline Swift burst into tears.

She wept heartily, and then wiped her face and smiled radiantly. 'Lord,' she said. 'Sorry about that. Release from strain, I suppose. What do you know about Johnny?'

'Johnny's doing brilliantly,' Seddall said, 'and as soon as we hear from him again we're going to go and help him finish these people off.'

'Who's we?'

'Sorrel and me, and a few others,' he said.

'It's what your Johnny would want,' Sorrel said. 'A small group, but the best. You can join us, can't she, Harry? You have the intelligence experience and you know some faces.'

The lovely face closed as hard as stone. 'No,' she said. 'Count me out. I'll go to bed now, Sorrel, if I may. And can I have the little dog for company, please, if he'll stay with me?'

Just like that.

She got up, gathered her belongings from the corner, and stood expectant.

Seddall watched Sorrel's reaction with amusement: the disapproval in the wide blue eyes, which was almost at once over-ridden by the dictates of her upbringing.

'Of course,' Sorrel said. 'We shouldn't be nattering to you like this, you must be ready to drop. Come on, Colin, you can help us make up the bed.'

And she gathered up the puppy and led the way.

'Breeding will tell,' Harry said to himself, and lay

full length on the couch vacated by Caroline Swift.

When Sorrel came back she closed the door and sat down with her back very straight.

'I must say,' she said, 'I find that pretty disappointing.'

'What?'

'Well, the way she just said "Count me out." When you think what that man's doing for her. And what we're doing, come to that.'

To his own amazement, Harry was up in arms in an instant. 'For Christ's sake,' he said, 'why should she if she doesn't want to? It's not her job, and I'd have thought she's shown enough guts already not to have to prove anything to you or me.'

Sorrel's eyes went to the door through which she had conducted Caroline Swift to bed, and then returned to Seddall.

'I think you were right,' Seddall heard himself saying. 'The best thing will be to take her down to the farmhouse and put it in a state of defence. I was going down tomorrow anyway.'

Sorrel stared at him.

He met, resolutely, her eye. 'So if you don't mind,' he said, 'I'll use your phone to call Mick Fawcett, get him to recruit a garrison. And don't look at me like that, woman. Damn it, it was your idea in the first place.'

Chapter Eighteen

The hotel was late sixteenth-century Apulian Baroque. In its first incarnation it had been an abbey standing in the country off the road to Taranto. Now, reborn into the nature of a hotel, it hung on the western edge of the city of Lecce, built of the pale yellow stone that gave Lecce's baroque architecture its particular glory.

As the car drove up the long curve of the drive the building shimmered through the trees. Enlustred by the last beams of the declining sun, it showed itself to Hynd as an invitation to a dream, evoking images of one of those ideal passages of place and time stolen out of life which, when they come, echo in the present as if they were memories from an enchanted past.

Such reincarnations as this from abbey into hotel were not achieved without the caress of the Mafia. In this case Guercio's local equivalent, one Bagnone, had extorted from the developer a fee for allowing the sun to continue to shine, the breezes to blow, and the rain to fall, as these had done in their seasons, always and forever, from the sky under which the building stood.

Bagnone had formed a consortium of his fellow-chieftains of the Apulian limb of the Mafia, the Sacra Corona Unita, and when the hotel was on the point of completion had, in the space of half an hour, inspired the proprietors with an earnest belief in the merits of accepting the consortium as majority shareholders.

This was the hotel's inaugural weekend, but it was

not the kind of opening that any normal hotel manager would have wished, since it had been proposed by the Holy Crown, and accepted by the Mafia itself, and by the Camorra of Naples and the 'Ndrangheta of Calabria, as the place where they would meet for this weekend to deal with matters of common interest and mutual dispute.

No publicity, therefore, could attend the opening of the hotel. The enterprise was being brought to birth away from the light of day.

Guercio was a member of this consortium of Bagnone's, a part-owner of the hotel, so you would have thought it was with a pleasing sense of participating in the business initiatives of the community that he came to see the hotel for the first time, and to stay in it on the very weekend of its opening.

Business worries, however, lay on him too heavily for the simpler pleasures to touch him. They were business worries of such gravity that in the car with him, as well as Hynd, were Troilo Perroni and Paoli Valori, men with long histories of ferocity whose faces wore, like scars, the darkness of their being.

In addition to this immediate bodyguard Guercio had placed in a farmhouse a few kilometres away (which belonged to a cousin of his wife) a squad of nine men with three cars: a flying column in waiting, ready to spring into action at the first sound of a cellular phone.

These dispositions made, Guercio clearly felt he had done the best he could. Valori stopped the car at the hotel entrance. Guercio got out, shrugged the jacket of his silk suit foursquare onto his shoulders, and with Hynd at his back went inside.

They walked across the flagstones of the lobby,

passed the reception office with a nod to the man and woman behind it, and went up the flight of stairs. The lobby and stairs were as they had been for three centuries. There were no rugs on the floor, nothing on the walls, only the coolness of the pale yellow stone, and space so generously used, and shaped with such art, that even the soul of a Guercio might, here, have found peace, if the mafioso had ever understood it might entertain such a wish.

'They think,' Parentucelli said, 'that they are bringing the world down about our ears.'

He addressed a gathering of seventeen men, from the centre of the long, heavy, black oak table which, it seemed to Hynd, must have been built in the room as part of the original furnishing of the abbey. Eight men faced him across the table, four sat on his left and five on his right. It was only these men he spoke to. The twenty or so who were standing, like Hynd, with their backs to the walls, were understood to have no ears.

Parentucelli's appearance astonished Hynd. He seemed as mild as milk. He was tall but lightly built. He seemed a man of neither physical force nor demonic character, yet he dominated those around him, some of them men of twice his bulk, some of them men of such chaotic spirit that you knew that to cross them was to risk instant death. All of them wore suits, from the elegance of Armani to the down-to-earth plain black cut by the local tailor, as if to say that what was good enough for their fathers was good enough for them.

After fifteen minutes in the room, before the meeting started, Hynd thought he knew where each of them carried his pistol, either from the hang of their jackets, or from the way they stood, or from absent movements of the right hand, and in two cases the left.

Parentucelli carried no pistol, Hynd was sure of it. Nor was he wearing a suit. He wore a silk tweed jacket of a pale ginger colour over a natural linen shirt open at the neck and pale grey flannel trousers. He wore these clothes as if he had been born with the gift of elegance, and was unaware of it.

There was nothing elegant, though, about that head and face. The head was large, almost too large for the body, and covered with a careless mass of black hair. The brow was broad and low, the eyes were set too far apart, the ears were large and stuck out from his head, the nose thrust down and to one side as if it had been broken, the mouth was fleshy with the upper lip too long for the lower, the jaw large and square. The whole effect was discordant, as if the pieces had been jumbled together in a hurry.

And yet the ugliness of this ill-designed mass of uncouth features was quite overset by the force and energy of its expression, which displayed themselves not as evidence of the power of his personality but in a kind of radiance of wellbeing and good humour. If he had not known Parentucelli for who he was, Hynd would have said this was a man who had the secret of happiness.

It was the eyes that showed his power. They were black, alive, and lambent not just with intelligence but knowledge; they said he knew everything about every man in the room, more than the men there knew about themselves. They said that to him life was a simple business, that he understood it and always had. They said that nothing he set his hand to failed.

They said, above all, that there was no point in going up against him, either with guile or openly, because in the first place he would see you coming, and in the second, he would brush aside your efforts with no more difficulty than if you were a puppy not yet weaned.

When those eyes had first met his own, Hynd had experienced an alarm he could not recall knowing before. They had not searched into him, they had simply rested on him for longer than he would have expected, and knew more of him, by the time they moved on, than he would have wished. How much more, this day or the next, presumably, would show.

'They have arrested our people in their hundreds,' Parentucelli said. 'From the high to the low. They think they have cut off our head and our limbs. Well, we grow new heads and new limbs. We always have, and we always will.'

He smiled, apparently with humour. 'Any of us may be arrested tomorrow, arrested today, arrested here in this agreeable hotel.' He gave a pleasant look to Bagnone, as head of the consortium that had moved in on the hotel. He touched his breast over his heart. 'I may be arrested even before we have had our lunch, and it may be said that today I represent the head.' He shrugged. 'If so, then tomorrow we shall have a new head. This is excellent coffee.'

The man leaning against the wall behind him went quickly to the buffet at the end of the room, poured coffee, took it to Parentucelli and removed his empty cup.

Parentucelli circled those at the table with that humorous look of his again. 'If they come to arrest any of us,' he said, 'I for one shall do my best to escape them. Let our motto be *sauve qui peut*. I expect each of us has made his own arrangements, and, beyond that, what precautions can be taken have been taken. We have spies watching all the prefectures and all the police stations round about, likewise all the special police intelligence units, so that if they send out a party large enough to deal with those of us gathered here, or several small parties from several such stations intending to surround us when they arrive, we shall have warning of it. We are even watching the autostrada in case they might run a convoy from as far away as Naples.'

'Well,' said one of the Armani suits, 'who has done all this? Where have all these spies come from? I am the chief man in Taranto, I believe, and no one has called on me for men to watch the prefecture or the police.'

'I have done it,' Parentucelli said. 'You think that because I am a Sicilian I have no friends here in Italy?'

'I think,' said Bagnone, 'that what Vitelli means is that he would have liked to be called on to produce men for this. Each of us has our territory, he is saying.'

'And you are saying it too?' Parentucelli said.

'You fancy you are pushing me to the wall?' Bagnone said, who was a strongly built man with a heavy, phlegmatic face. 'Why ask me a question like that when you know the answer? Yes, I am saying it too. It would have been usual, it would have been proper. There are courtesies to be observed in such things.'

'I acknowledge it,' Parentucelli said. 'Do not suppose that I have any wish to intrude upon either your territory, Ferranti, or on yours, Bagnone, or on yours, Guercio. What I have done is brought men down from as far north as Milan. Since they were to act as spies upon the police, I wanted men whose faces would not be known to the police here in Puglia.'

'You could, perhaps, have told us sooner,' said Ferranti, he of the Armani suit, 'but perhaps you do not trust us.'

'Trust is not a commodity to be wasted,' Parentucelli said simply. 'Why spend it when there is no need to do so?'

'Ah,' said Ferranti, and offered the conciliatory tribute that had now become appropriate. 'It is for such things that you are the chief among us.'

'Maybe,' said Parentucelli, with a dismissive gesture. Behind the face of that habitual state of wellbeing which came off the man like an effulgence, far behind it, Hynd detected the presence of contempt. 'Let us get on. We are here to endorse finally the plan of the man Casson to strike back at our enemies. Casson and his associates will be here this afternoon. First, though, there is something for us to reach agreement on so that we can put it behind us, one way or the other.'

He turned his countenance on Guercio, and so did everybody else. 'We have to thank you, Guercio, for acting as our ambassador to Casson.'

'Please,' said Guercio, and moved a deprecating hand. There was nothing to suggest that Guercio had any misgivings about what was now to come. He gave the impression he always gave, of being tough, capable, and up to any man's weight. It was clear, in the look exchanged between him and Parentucelli, that as far as Guercio was concerned Parentucelli might be the top man, but that nevertheless he was only the first among equals.

'We have to deplore,' Parentucelli went on, 'that your villa in Savoy was attacked and ruined. That men of yours were killed. That you yourself might have been killed. It was an outrage, against you and against us. I am certain, as you know, that it was done by this man Casson's people, at a time when we were debating the merits of going through with our agreement with them. They wanted to show us that they are not to be trifled with, to lean on us, and they wanted us to know something else as well.'

He stopped talking and bent forward over the table, communing with himself. Then he sat up and went on. 'They wanted us to know that they have no country, that they are outside society, that they will behave, and have the resources to behave, like an army. I think if they had a nuclear bomb and thought it would be useful to them to explode it, then they would explode it. That is their strength, that they are content only to destroy. We do not have that strength. We are part of society, and that is our strength. We cannot destroy indiscriminately.'

At the bottom of the table, one of the men in black suits raised a hand, a gaunt man in his age, perhaps seventy, with his long bony face burnt dark by the sun. 'These people will not last,' he said. 'When we have used them, we can make them pay in blood for what they have done to Guercio.' He raised his eyes for a moment as if to some god of his own. 'We will do it, but it would not matter if we did not. They will not establish anything, these people. They will do what they do for a while, and then pass away. They will be gone, and we will still be here.'

This view was well received. 'They shall pay,' a beautiful young man from Naples said. 'Our honour demands it. It is true that we are talking serious business, and for that we need them. But when it is over, then I say this: it is not business that ensures and justifies, yes, justifies,' he said, nodding in agreement with himself, 'our survival. It is because we keep faith with our honour, that is why we survive. I speak for the Camorra. Perhaps I do not speak for all.'

'I agree,' said the old man. 'You speak for all. They must pay. They have spat in our face, and they are without honour, they are not serious people, they are ordinary people.'

Over Parentucelli's face came a particularly merry look. 'Not all of them are ordinary.' He looked at Hynd, and Hynd looked back at him. 'That one is not ordinary,' he said, and they all followed his look.

'He is my man now,' Guercio said.

'You,' the old Sicilian said to Hynd. 'Who are you?'

'My name is John Hynd.'

'You are Italian?' the old man said. 'You speak Italian like a Lombard.'

'I am English,' Hynd said.

A chair scraped on the beechwood floor as first one, and then another, of the wild primitives among these masters of the modern business world reacted to this news. Half of them came to their feet, or began to rise and then sat down again. Men standing against the walls stepped forward, hands going to the waist, or inside the jacket, or to the back of the neck.

'English?' the first man to stand said. 'What are you

doing here? What is he doing here? What is this madness?'

The room was full of noise and menace. Hynd stayed where he was, almost sideways to the room, his shoulder leaning on the wall and his body off balance, in a hopelessly undefendable stance. He was full of the adrenalin rush, his mind running everywhere like quicksilver, calculating angles, looking for the way out. But there was no way out, he knew that. So he stayed there, relaxed and negligent against the wall, doing his best to look as if he had withdrawn into himself at being so ill-used.

The tumult reached its crescendo and then, having failed by the merest margin of physics to convert itself into action, it began to subside.

'Come, come,' Parentucelli called out, still as merry as the Devil, which Hynd could see now was what he was. 'Hynd saved Guercio's life at that villa in Savoy. He is Guercio's man. What do you say, Guercio?'

'I trust him with my life,' Guercio said. 'When we came away from the raid on the villa, I had no way of knowing who had done it.' He looked up and down the table, and his head turning on those massy shoulders was like a bear poised on the edge of losing its temper. 'So I went on into Naples to talk with my friend,' he nodded at the man who had spoken for the Camorra, 'and hear what I might hear.

'I had bought a new car up north, but we thought it might be known by this time. I said to John Hynd, you take the car to my home. That way, if the car has been spotted by the people who attacked my villa in Savoy, and they want to try for me again, you may flush them out. He might have been bombed, or run off the road and killed, or ambushed.

'He said, sure, he would do that for me. And he was ambushed. There were three men in the ambush, and he killed them all. He is a good man.'

It was a brilliant piece of special pleading. Guercio had changed Hynd from being an outsider into being one of themselves. A man who would accept without question the risk that belonged to his boss, and who had known, when he ran into the ambush, how to deal with it.

'How did he kill them?' the old Sicilian asked. 'How did he overcome an ambush with three men in it?'

Guercio turned towards Hynd and ducked his head sideways, as if to apologize for talking about him to his face, then went back to his audience.

'He came round a corner,' Guercio said, 'and saw a lorry blocking the road at the foot of the hill in front of him. He went down the hill and rolled out of the car and let it crash into the lorry. Then he hunted. He stalked two of the men and killed them. The third he took prisoner and questioned, then he killed him.'

Hynd closed his eyes against the memory of shooting the young man, but in the context of such a narrative they took this for modesty or boredom.

The whole room had relaxed. Indeterminate sounds of approval came both from those sitting – all had resumed their seats – and the lesser men standing round the walls. The old Sicilian looked as if he was reliving his youth.

'If he gets tired of Guercio,' he said, 'he can come to Sicily with me. An Englishman, ha!'

Hynd thought he knew what it was with the old

bastard. First of all, it was that Hynd had stalked these men out in the country – none of this modern crap of remote-control bombs planted on the motorway. But for the Sicilian, the best of it was that he had questioned his prisoner and then shot him: for him, only the man who would murder callously in cold blood was a man.

'What did he tell you, before you killed him?' the Sicilian asked Hynd. 'Who ordered the ambush?'

Hynd came off the wall and bummed a cigarette off the man next to him, who was in the act of lighting one for himself. The man lit the cigarette he gave to Hynd, watching him gravely over the flame.

Hynd nodded his thanks and spoke to the Sicilian. 'He answered the questions I asked him,' he said. 'They were my questions, and now they are my answers.'

Ottavio listened to the words a second time, to be sure what he had heard, and scowled. They did not seem to him to show respect. 'But you told these answers to your don?' he said.

'If that is what I should have done,' Hynd said. 'Then that will be what I did.'

'Enough of this,' Parentucelli said. 'If we decide, when we have concluded our deliberations today, that we do not trust Hynd, then we can perhaps arrest him until this operation with our new allies is over.'

'If we want to hold him,' the old Sicilian said, 'he can come to Sicily with me. While he is my prisoner, I can get to know him.' He tapped his head significantly. 'If, in the end, it is necessary, I can have him fed to the fishes.'

'Yes, yes, Ottavio,' Parentucelli said. 'I was talking about these allies of ours. All I'm saying to you is that

Hynd was one of them, and you have seen him, and heard him speak. They are not ordinary people. They will be worthy allies, and therefore they would be worthy opponents. We will not, therefore, trust them like brothers.'

He drew a cigar case from his pocket, and took a cigar for himself and slid one across the table to Guercio. It seemed to Hynd that this was promising, that Guercio's misgivings were not going to be realized. To his surprise, however, Guercio let the cigar lie on the table for a long moment before he put his hand out and took it.

Parentucelli nodded, as if pleased to be spreading sweetness and light. 'Well,' he said, 'we have decided to fulfil our agreement with Casson and his people, but not because of that foolish attack on Guercio in his own house – not his home, it is true, but a house that is his own. They will think they've pressured us into this, but what they think means nothing to us. It is only that they are a tool that offers itself to our hand, and we will use them because the campaign against us has escalated and provokes us to retaliate.'

He raised the hand with the cigar in it and pointed it at Guercio. 'Now, Andrea,' he said, 'we have a little business to get out of the way. You negotiated with Casson for us, and you have our gratitude, and you suffered loss on our account, and we give you our sympathy. But what you offered Casson was more than we authorized you to offer. We authorized money. We have more money than we know what to do with. Money is nothing to us. But you offered also a deal concerning yourself and Casson, and cocaine from Peru.'

Guercio drew on the cigar, and held the breath, and when he exhaled he fanned the smoke with his hand. 'That was on my own account,' he said. 'It is my business.'

'No,' Parentucelli said. 'It is my business, since I am in this chair. It is my business because it is the business of all of us. I say it was wrong of you to make a private deal on the side while you were acting as our representative.'

He waited. He drew on his cigar. Guercio considered his own cigar and drew on it again. He contemplated the growing ash on the tip, and revolved the cigar gently, as if to say to Parentucelli: I am listening, continue.

'I say also,' Parentucelli went on, 'that we do not deal with the Peruvians. We deal with the Colombians. If we decide to deal with the Peruvians, it is a decision we make together, among ourselves.'

A few chairs shifted, and here and there inarticulate sounds recorded agreement with this sentiment.

Guercio went on smoking, and kept his eye on Parentucelli.

'However,' Parentucelli said, 'we are on the point of going to the next stage with this agreement that you have made for us with Casson. We are going to strike a blow that will resound throughout Italy. We are going to defend ourselves. It is a time for us to hold together.'

He cast one of his merry glances over the company, his black eyes glowing as if he was giving them a blessing from the fountain of wellbeing that sprang within him.

'What I propose is this,' he said. 'Had it not been for this private deal you made with Señor Arrando and Casson, we your brothers would have compensated you for the damage to your villa and for the loss of your men, we would have cared for their widows and children. As it is, we leave those at your own charge. And as for the drug market you are ready to open in Eastern Europe, we, all of us, will undertake to supply it, and we shall do so with the help of the Colombians. And for the rest, since you have done us great service, we shall let bygones be bygones. That is what I propose. What do you say?'

'It is a good cigar,' Guercio said.

'You will give a box to my friend Andrea before we leave,' Parentucelli said over his shoulder, but kept his eyes on Guercio.

Guercio nodded, as if to say they understood the same things about life. 'I like what you propose.'

'Does anyone disagree?' Parentucelli said.

There was a long silence, then a small man who had not spoken before cleared his throat and began to speak.

'Excellent,' Parentucelli said before the man had got a word out. 'We need no speeches to convey a unanimous agreement. You know,' he went on, his ugly face irradiated with benevolence for himself and all around, conceivably for all the world, 'it was perhaps no bad thing, that raid on Guercio's villa, perhaps not too high a price to pay, because it is just possible that our anger at the insult has determined us to have a closer look at these people, who would do such a thing to us, and that behind their minds – without their knowing it, as it were – those of us who were uncertain whether to go ahead abandoned their vacillation, and so are now united with the rest of us in the determination to strike this blow for our own hand.'

This was merely a complex way of saying that he,

Parentucelli, had been in favour of the Great Counter-
blow (whatever that might turn out to be) all along,
and that some of the more diffident spirits had in fact
been so alarmed by the military-style raid on the house
of one of their own that they had caved in and agreed
to go through with the deal they had made with these
madmen.

At a time when informers were informing, and not
only Mafia men at all levels but also their political
protectors were being rounded up day by day, who
needed to live with the prospect of war to the knife
with a bunch of maniacs who would do such a thing
to a man of respect like Guercio?

Watching Parentucelli, glowing with cheerful mischief, Hynd was suddenly seized by the conviction that
the great man had taken part with Casson in planning
the raid on Guercio's villa. For the shortest space he
could not believe it, and then he was unshakeably sure
of it. It made simple quite a lot that had been undefined.
That Parentucelli should be co-operating secretly with
Casson, to bring about what each of them desired, could
explain how he knew about the Peruvian, how he knew
the details of the proposed expansion of the cocaine
market. It might explain, too, though Hynd very much
hoped not, the interest he had taken in learning about
Hynd from Guercio, and in seeing how Hynd would
conduct himself at that first moment of exposure.

He had lingered too long, while these illuminations
came to him, on Parentucelli's face, and he saw now
that it was laughing at him with that silent laugh, and
cutting into him with those excessively penetrating
black eyes.

He turned away and offered a cigarette to the man

who had given him one before. Hynd had never thought of the Devil as merry before today, but he could see that he might be. He would think about it later, if there was a later. In Sicily, say, before the ancient Ottavio had him fed to the fishes.

Parentucelli addressed himself to Guercio. 'Perhaps, Andrea my friend,' he said, 'you will consider Ottavio's kind invitation to take this English stranger into his household. And now, my stomach tells me it is time to eat.'

Chapter Nineteen

Hynd knew it would be Sicily, or worse: the knife or the bullet or the garrotte. The appalling instinct of Parentucelli had begun to find him out.

It didn't take instinct to notice that there was something unusual about an Englishman taking up with a capo of the Sacra Corona Unita like Guercio, or to notice that in doing so he had changed masters. He was changeable, a man who changed when the weather changed, a man to whom loyalty was a negotiable bargain; and to those imbued with the hierarchical tradition of the Mafia, the psychological forces of that tradition made mincemeat of any logic in Hynd's change from one master to another.

In the afternoon, while the great men were in conclave with the Casson group, Hynd had found himself moving among his peers – the men who had stood with him around the walls – and sponsored as it were by Guercio's men Perroni and Valori. He learned that he was perfectly acceptable both to those who had made their judgement of him during the morning's meeting and to those who, like Perroni and Valori, had remained outside to man, as it were, the ramparts; but he understood that he was accepted, not as one of themselves, but as a mercenary.

There was nothing disconcerting about this, it was right and reasonable. What disconcerted Hynd was his certainty that Parentucelli had not written him down as a mercenary and left it at that. What was a mercenary, in the eyes of these men? One who played for excitement and money in the life where they fulfilled their destinies, their souls, and their role in the society of their tribe. In that balance, a mercenary was to them a lightweight. Whatever his attributes and qualities, and even if those equalled or excelled their own, he was still a lightweight.

The wayward factor in this equation was Parentucelli, who was not regarding Hynd as a lightweight at all. During luncheon – the debut of the hotel's kitchen and dining-room staff – he sometimes saw and sometimes felt, far oftener than he liked, Parentucelli's sinister and laughing eye on him over many tables and from more than half the room away. To Parentucelli Hynd was not a mere whimsical and feckless mercenary, and the man was sniffing him out.

In the afternoon had come Casson – whom Hynd had not seen since the assault on Guercio's villa – with a driver and five others, in a Toyota eight-seater: no suggestive limo with smoked-glass windows, and indeed there wasn't a vehicle in the hotel car park to suggest that the mob was here.

Guercio and old Ottavio and Hynd were on the hotel terrace when they arrived, one group among many taking their coffee and smoking classy cigars and noisome cigarettes. As Casson and company came towards the terrace Hynd felt a hand on his shoulder, and when he turned his head to look it was Parentucelli.

Since it was to Parentucelli that Casson inevitably came, he came also to Hynd. As the hand left his shoulder so that its owner could advance to greet the leader of the newcomers, Hynd felt the pressure of the fingers that meant: stay.

To Hynd it was a remarkable meeting. Casson came on, all importance and presence, florid-faced, stony-eyed, a ponderous caricature of closed, inflexible man, and down the steps to meet him ran Parentucelli, fluid and wicked with grace, dark and open and mercurial as the Great God Pan.

The distinguished host shook hands with the distinguished guest and brought him up to the terrace.

Hynd was interested to see how Guercio would speak to the man who had been willing to kill him simply to make a point. Guercio did not shake hands with Casson. He first embraced him, and then gripped him vigorously by the upper arms as if the pair of them were blood-brothers who had discovered that both of them had survived a furious battle.

'My dear Casson,' he said. 'It is a pleasure to welcome you to Puglia, to my own country.'

The words and the iron grip conveyed, with more force than Hynd could have imagined, the fearful and ambiguous embrace of the Mafia.

However much it might go against the grain of his nature, Casson rose to the occasion.

'It is an honour for me,' he said.

Guercio, with nothing in his face at all, went on holding him and looking at him, until it began to seem that Casson was confronting an old-fashioned camera requiring long exposure.

Then he let him go, and said, 'You remember John Hynd.'

'Of course he does,' Hynd said, taking what little initiative there was to take.

'From way back,' Casson said, which was quite a message if you took a good hold of all its possible implications, and grinned heartily at Hynd, which could have meant anything.

'From way back?' Parentucelli said.

It was clear neither to Hynd nor to Casson whether this scenario of Hynd's being down here in Guercio country should be interpreted between them to mean that Hynd had deserted, or had joined up with Guercio to put himself in a useful place in the service of Casson. To Parentucelli's question, therefore, Casson returned in effect no answer at all.

'Yes, certainly,' he said. 'Shall we get down to it? I want to be in Paris tonight.'

Parentucelli was so put off by this offhand reply that for once in his life he became obtuse. 'Paris? That is where your headquarters are?'

'Paris' – Casson had exhausted what little gift he had for the diplomatic dissimulations – 'is where the French are. Let's go and have this discussion.'

Parentucelli reassumed the mantle. 'Present your colleagues to me.'

All along the terrace the men of the Mafia, the Camorra, the Sacra Corona Unita, and the 'Ndrangheta sat, drinking and smoking and either contributing to the effervescent noise or drowsing in the sun, according to temperament.

And on the gravel below the terrace, Casson's five colleagues, men of considerable power by Mafia standards, namely the violence they had committed and the money they had gathered from it, stood and waited while this colloquy proceeded.

'I will present them to you inside,' Casson said. 'In the room where we meet. Your top men only, right?'

'You exclude Hynd?' Parentucelli said, still fishing away.

Casson peered at him as if astonished.

'Hynd? Of course I exclude Hynd,' he said. 'Hynd is a hired man. I do not admit him to my inner counsels. All my professional life I've worked on the need-to-know principle. In the terms of my profession this mission we're going to discuss is Top Secret. Hynd does not need to know.'

That made two probing questions from Parentucelli about Hynd. Whether the doubt about Hynd that was apparent in the mafioso's questions had reassured Casson that Hynd was still in fact on the team – or at least that Hynd had not gone over to the Mafia and might therefore be useful to Casson, planted as he was down here among the demented dons – or whether, from whatever motive, Casson had done his best to diminish Hynd's importance, which as far as Hynd was concerned was the best thing he could have done to ease Parentucelli of some of his suspicion.

'I am puzzled,' Parentucelli said. 'Is Hynd your man or Andrea Guercio's man?'

Guercio was standing opposite Hynd, facing out across the gardens, a sturdy figure like a rock, giving no ear to these exchanges. Now, however, he turned towards the group, as if what was about to be said would be worth hearing.

Casson laughed, a fierce mixture of humour and anger. 'Hynd works for me. If he is being helpful to Guercio, that's a satisfaction to me, though I could have borne to have him back with me before this. That's how it is, isn't it, Hynd?'

Hynd looked at the three of them, and hated their

several sets of guts. It didn't matter too much to him what he said. He knew that whatever happened this afternoon he would be going to Sicily with Ottavio. He was already working on the idea of getting a message out to Harry Seddall, who would be back in London now, by his reckoning. He could put no call through the hotel switchboard, that was sure. It would be monitored and possibly even taped.

'Hynd?' Casson said again.

Hynd met the hard eyes in the big choleric face. 'When the villa was shot up,' he said, 'Guercio and I ran for it with the Peruvian. We got out by the skin of our teeth, except for Señor Arrando. He bought the farm. We kept running. We ran all the way down to Puglia. We didn't know who'd done it, except that it was someone who either wanted us killed or didn't care if we were. It might have been you, it might have been friends of Guercio – the kind of friends he has around here, anything could happen to him—'

He was interrupted. 'You are insulting us, you are insulting us all,' said Parentucelli. Hynd saw that a curious change had taken place in Parentucelli. He was still wearing that strange face of one who exhilarated in life, but the exhilaration was getting tired. The Devil was in danger of losing his temper. Hynd wondered what that would be like.

'Insulting you? I doubt it. You know what you are; Casson knows what he is.' Hynd was liking this speech. It might not be the way to make friends and influence people, but it was sure God not the speech of a man who was trying to keep in with these scum for some hidden purpose of his own. 'So here I am, Casson, doing what Guercio wants me to do. I'm a hard case, but all that friendly fire at the villa made me nervous. When we'd finished running I thought I'd stay here where I felt a damn sight safer than I did when those helicopters came at us. When I'd calmed down I thought maybe you'd find it useful, both bunches of you, to have a liaison man here.

'If you think that's a bad idea I'll move out. Maybe I should go to Marseilles and join the Foreign Legion. Life is very uncertain down here too. I ran into an ambush on the way to Guercio's house and had to kill three guys. I still don't know who they were, whether they were after me or him. And they had no ID and I had no time to hang around to find out more.'

Despite himself, Casson's face had tensed at the reference to the ambush, and then relaxed again when Hynd disclaimed any knowledge of the men he had killed.

Hynd was interested to see what Guercio might do about this barefaced lie of his. Guercio was the only one who knew that Hynd had identified the men he'd shot at the ambush. Guercio, he thought, would keep quiet. Guercio was out to get his revenge on Casson, when the time was right: he would give him nothing.

Not that it mattered a lot to Hynd. Down here was where the scent was hot, down among the mafiosi. He did not expect Casson to think he loved him like a brother; he had lied about the ambush only because it seemed a good idea not to lay it at Casson's door. Guercio or no Guercio, Hynd had a score of his own to settle with Casson, as atavistic as Guercio's but less coded in these Mediterranean mystiques of honour; and anything Hynd could do to give Casson a false sense of security about him was worth trying.

Guercio did not refer to the ambush. He had other

fish to fry. 'Casson,' Guercio said, still with a face like a stone, and with no inflection in his voice. 'It was your people who made that air raid on my house?'

Parentucelli was back in the upbeat mode again; perhaps his hilarity had been refreshed by the tension that was running around the other three like an electric current.

'Andrea,' he said, pouring oil on the flames, 'let us not embarrass our friend Casson. That is all in the past. We are partners now in the same enterprise.'

Casson was not in the least embarrassed. 'I don't say they were my people,' he said. 'But I'll tell you, when I make a deal with someone I expect them to stick to it. When they don't, I play rough. You fellows were about to walk out of our agreement. Now, as you say, Parentucelli, we're back in business.'

A private joke passed between Casson and Parentucelli, and Hynd knew he had been right, Parentucelli had been in on the raid on the villa.

Parentucelli became witty. 'But, my dear Casson, we are back in business, not because someone attacked Andrea Guercio in his villa and nearly killed him, but because we see that the situation demands it.'

'Fair enough,' Casson said, and to Guercio: 'Where do you stand?'

'I am back in the business too,' Guercio spoke as a rock would speak if it was covered with ice. 'And I keep all my bargains.'

'Good,' Casson said. 'So do I.' It was clear that he had read the darker significance of Guercio's message. 'So let's get down to business. My colleagues are being kept waiting, and we have things to talk about. We have to set the day and the hour. The *Baikal* has sailed.'

Parentucelli put a finger to his lips and shook his head at Casson, and then pointed the finger at Hynd. 'Not here. Come, let us go inside.'

Casson gathered his flock, who were, after all this time, being entertained by Ottavio and one or two of the older men, who had a sense of what was seemly. Parentucelli shot Hynd a glance that was positively coquettish with evil. Guercio, for some reason, gave Hynd a pat on the arm. And all the men of importance went into the hotel.

And Hynd said to himself, Thanks a lot, Casson. 'The *Baikal* has sailed,' just like that, out in the open. A useful thing to know, if he could get word out. But that look of Parentucelli's meant that Casson had put Hynd's life on a knife-edge.

So now, up in his room at the end of the day, Hynd knew it would be Sicily, Sicily and perhaps death. Well, death had been avoided before, and they would be unlikely to kill him tonight with the hotel opening tomorrow to clients from the real world.

Sicily was not such a bad idea. He might learn something from this Ottavio, unless he was going to be cast into a dungeon and left to rot. He didn't expect that. Ottavio's place, wherever that was, would be guarded like a fortress. Ottavio neither trusted nor distrusted him. Ottavio would simply have him around to see what developed, have his boys keep an eye on the Englishman. And Hynd would get to know these boys; he might find that one of them was susceptible to a bribe, that he could make a run for it.

He was carrying plenty of money; on the job he made sure always to be cash-rich. He got out his wallet and counted: over two thousand pounds in lire, not counting the value of the stamps. He had thought he might get a letter off to Caroline, but that was not how it had worked out. He got up and went over to the window and looked down. He saw her in the dark, under those trees down there, he saw her being in the night, being one with the night, he saw . . . he saw the letter-box at the reception desk downstairs.

What kind of nonsense was this? Well, was it nonsense? The fact that it was simple didn't make it nonsense. He had to get word out, the telephone was barred to him, and there was that letter-box at the reception desk. Tomorrow the Mafia would be gone and the hotel would start operating as an ordinary hotel, which would mean the letter-box would be cleared every day and the contents put in the mail. It would be a gamble, but not a bad one.

Look at the gamble: as far as he knew, even Parentucelli had not firmed up his view of Hynd enough to suppose that he was working for a third and unknown party. The sense he had from him was that he thought Hynd was, if anything, playing a game of his own, playing off the Mafia against Casson and company, for some conjectured gain, or some other private reason. In which case, Parentucelli would not think of him wanting to get a message out. Parentucelli was still playing a waiting game, playing cat and mouse, and enjoying it with a kind of malevolent ribaldry.

As to the rest of them, Hynd did not see the Mafia mind being meticulous enough to think of security as being an imaginative matter of covering hypothetical angles. Yes, the letter-box was not such a bad bet. It was extra risk, but placed as he was, everything was risk.

He was in deep, sure enough, and it was time to think about getting out. It might well be that he would know enough soon, and it would be time for action, time to link up with Seddall and whatever forces Seddall could bring to bear. The letter would pass on the gen about the *Baikal*, and at the same time say he wanted help to extract himself from Ottavio's clutches.

His room was provided with paper and envelopes. He wrote the letter, addressed it to Seddall's private address in London which was lodged in his memory bank, stamped it, and put it in the inside pocket of his jacket which was hung over the back of a chair. Then he lay on the bed with his hands behind his head and settled to wait until most of the hotel had gone to sleep. Not everyone would go to sleep. There would be a night porter for one thing but there would also be a serious night watch. None of these men would sleep easy in their beds unless they had men patrolling in the hotel and out in the grounds as well.

Time passed. He emptied his mind. He did not want to focus on Caroline; it would spoil his efficiency. The moon came to the window, waxing, three or four days from the full. Along his corridor robust voices made each other ebullient goodnights. He waited. The hotel became quiet. He would give it another three hours. The later the better, the less time the letter was in the box, the safer for him. When he went down he would encounter the night men but he would deal with that easily enough, say he was looking for a drink, or had run out of cigarettes, and he would be unlucky if he couldn't find a moment to slip the letter into the letter-box.

Time passed, and still he waited. The moon had

moved. He heard an owl working its patch, the squeal as a predator pounced on the victim. The moon went on across the sky, leaving his room illumined palely in its passing.

There was a distant sound, and the sound became voices, the voices became shouts with panic in them. He got off the bed and put on his jacket. He settled the feel of the gun at his belt and went to the door but it flew open even as he reached for it.

'Downstairs!' said an urgent and unknown voice. 'Take all your things, leave no trace. The police will be on us any moment.'

The man vanished. Hynd had no more than an airline bag with him, and he slung it over his shoulder and went out into a maelstrom in the corridor. Men throwing themselves out of doorways, bodies colliding, cursing fate and each other. Parentucelli had said, *sauve qui peut*, and there was certainly no sense of organization to deal with this crisis.

Hynd went downstairs in amongst the mob. When he got to the lobby he made his way to the reception desk and put his back to it, like a cool head taking stock. With the letter in his hand he felt behind him for the slit and got his hand in and let the letter go.

Men were moving to the door, forming as they went molecular groups of those they had come with but not hanging about for anyone who was lagging behind. The room was full of shouts and the smell of fear and anger. Guercio came at him out of the scrum, with Valori behind him.

'Hynd!' he said. 'It was my people, they were driving the road between here and the farm and they ran into the police. They phoned from the car and then shots,

Valori heard the shots, and then Simone called from his car, a different road, and then he was cut off. So they are closing in. I am losing men as if I were Napoleon. Come, Perroni is getting the car.'

All this as they went towards the door, till out of the ruck Ottavio appeared with three men at his back.

'Hey, Guercio!' he said. 'The Englishman goes with me.'

'Who says so?' Guercio demanded.

'I do,' said Ottavio, and at the words his three men had guns in their hands. 'And it is Parentucelli's will.'

'In that case,' Guercio said, 'fortune go with you.' And he and Valori went out of the door.

'You will come easily?' Ottavio said.

'Of course,' Hynd said.

'Then we go,' the old Sicilian said, 'but we go a different way. Leopetto, show us.'

Leopetto led them into the empty restaurant and on into the deserted kitchens, down past a row of stainless steel-topped tables, a quick impression of pans, fish kettles, dishwashers, refrigerators, utensils on steel hooks, aprons on hooks, out through the nether regions, out of a back door, out through the trees, through a kitchen garden, out onto a hillside under the last of the moon.

'Leopetto, run on ahead and scout,' Ottavio said. 'For the rest of us I'll set the pace. I am the oldest, I know what I can do. Silvestro, come last and keep an eye over your shoulder.'

They went up the low hill and over its crest. Down into a small valley and up another hill through a scattering of cork oaks. They went on, and on, up hills and down, over the undulating landscape.

When the sky began to lighten they entered a wood which was edged with white poplar, and here, under a canopy of chestnut trees and beech, they came to a stop.

Leopetto came running back through the wood. 'The van is there,' he said.

Ottavio glanced a punch off the side of his jaw. 'Well done, Leopetto. It was Leopetto,' he said to Hynd, 'who planned the escape route.'

'It was you who had the foresight,' said Leopetto.

The two of them stood and grinned at each other.

'I wonder what trouble they ran into back there,' Ottavio said, 'running everywhere in their cars with the police on all the roads.'

Silvestro came up from the rear. 'Nothing behind,' he said, 'and I can see a good way. Back at the beginning I heard a few shots. We did the right thing.'

'We are country boys,' Ottavio said. 'We understand these things. Let us have breakfast.'

'And then?' Hynd said.

'We will wait here till the afternoon,' Ottavio said, 'and then, if all seems well, we shall drive to the coast, and there we shall find a boat to take us to Sicily.'

Chapter Twenty

Somerset was in its glory. Seddall put the car into the arcade of trees that ran the last mile to Old Spring Farm and they ran through dappled shade and glades of bright sunshine. A pheasant scooted along the verge of the road before swerving into the wood.

Caroline Swift freed herself from the seat-belt and sat forward with a face of delight. Harry looked at her and met in the mature woman's eyes a sixteen-year-old rejoicing in the sheer pleasure of life. He had glimpsed it in her before, when they stopped for a pub lunch on the way down.

The pub was called the Royal Oak and must have been built almost as soon as Charles had got safely off across the Channel. The meal was simple, steak and salad and summer pudding, but the beef was grass-fed and full of taste. And he had seen it in her then, as she ate the food and drank her pint of bitter: the immediate sensuous enjoyment of the moment.

He had been amazed at her resilience, to see her move so swiftly from three days and nights with little sleep and in a state, presumably, of some fear, to being that cheerful and vivid creature who sat opposite him, enlivened, now, even to a spirit of mischief: for if those brown eyes across the table from him were not flirting, whether with him or simply with the moment, then Harry Seddall had never eaten beef before this day . . . nor no man ever loved.

As he turned through the gateway that led to the farmhouse, she said, 'Harry, what a beautiful place to live.'

It was. The old stone house with its thatched roof sat in the bright sunshine, its two acres of ground – which included the old farmyard on the west side that was now a lawn; the rambling garden in front of it part grass, part orchard, part vegetable patch, part flower beds; and Harry's treat to himself, the swimming pool that lay now where the old cattle-barn had been, beyond the new-established lawn – were bordered by oak and beech and ash, and over all this the blue sky threw its unclouded span.

Harry had never seen it look better, and it always lifted his spirits to come here; but today his spirits were not merely raised, they were exalted.

'A swimming pool,' Caroline said as the car ran round to the back of the house and stopped. 'I haven't got a suit.'

'You can get one in Bridgwater tomorrow,' he said.

'I can't wait till tomorrow,' she said. 'A day like this? I'll swim nude.'

Mrs Lyon appeared at the back door.

'Will your housekeeper mind?'

'Why should she? In any case, I'd like it a lot.'

She gave him one of those flashing looks and coloured, but just a little. So, he thought, did he. 'You say what you mean, don't you?' she said.

'Mostly. So do you.'

She got out of the car and stretched herself in the heat.

'It feels as if there's no one about for miles. It's a heavenly place to have brought me.'

As Mrs Lyon approached from the east and the dog Bayard came galloping out of the bushes to the north, he said to her, 'I seem to be liking you an awful lot.'

He had not meant to say anything like this to her, for he was not certain of how she stood towards John Hynd and of how he himself stood to the eternally travelling Olivia, but he had spoken on impulse and was glad of it.

She looked at him across the roof of the car, lifting a hand to shield her eyes from the sun. 'I know,' was all she said.

The black cat Sacha leapt from the back of the car onto the driver's seat and thence to the ground, walked into the path of the oncoming spaniel, and found something to amuse her in the form of a fruit-gorged and intoxicated wasp.

Bayard gave Sacha a wary greeting as he reached her but he was not wary enough, and she bopped him on the nose, arched her back with satisfaction, and went to meet Mrs Lyon.

In the event all five of them met among Harry's baggage as he unloaded the car – one bag, and half a dozen cases of wine which were first to settle, then end their days here. Caroline had all she presently possessed slung over her shoulder.

With Bayard's paws on his stomach, Harry presented the incomer to the incumbent, and saw as he did so that Mrs Lyon knew at once that his heart was somewhere on the other side of the windmill.

'What a wonderful place,' Caroline said.

'Aye, it is,' Mrs Lyon said. 'Ye'll enjoy yerself here.'

'I've no swimsuit,' Caroline said. 'Do you mind if I swim naked? I see it will be under your windows.'

'Sae lang as ye dinnae expect me tae join ye,' Mrs Lyon said. 'I'm bye wi' sichlike capers. Ye'll be a sicht for sair een, I mak nae doot.'

Reassured that mutual acceptance had taken place, Seddall stooped to the first of the wine cases and left women and animals to make their meeting.

Mrs Lyon gave them tea in the garden, and then from his bedroom window, having changed into swimming trunks and wrapping a bathrobe round himself, he saw Caroline walk naked as Diana, with a towel in her hand, across the lawn to the pool.

He felt a lurch inside him that was almost like faintness, and went downstairs and so, more sedately clad, crossed the lawn and dropped the robe and dived into the pool where she was already swimming back from the far end towards him.

'Looking good,' she gave him the jogger's greeting as they passed each other, and they swam back and forth until after about twenty lengths he saw her sitting on the edge of the pool waiting for him.

He hung on the rail and looked up at her. The body was as lovely as the face.

'Will you have dinner with me, Caroline Swift?'

'I don't have anything smart to wear.'

'Oh, we don't stand on ceremony here,' Harry said. 'Just come as you are.'

She put her face up to the sun and laughed, and put a foot on his head and pushed him under.

'Yes, Harry Seddall, I'd love to have dinner with you.'

They dined on Mrs Lyon's coq au vin with a bottle of claret, and sat in front of the drawing-room fire and talked, and after a while, as he sat in his armchair and she across from him on the hearthrug looking into the flames, a silence fell.

It was the silence that says this part of the evening is over, it is time to go to bed. And as it went on, and she sat there gazing at the fire, and he sat there gazing at her, the tension grew.

At last he leaned far forward in his chair and put out a hand and brushed the hair off her face.

'Let's go to bed,' he said.

She pushed the hair off her forehead herself, as if to claim it back, and looked at him; her eyes were deep and bared, and he felt he saw everything that was in her, hurt and joy and fear and hope and courage, and something far within, that he could not fathom.

'I don't want to sleep with you, Harry.'

'I didn't say that,' he came back at once, and heard the defensiveness in it.

'Cop-out,' Caroline said.

'All right,' he said. 'It's what I meant. But I wasn't coarse about it, was I? I left it open.' He watched her face change. 'You look as if you're angry.'

'Of course I'm angry.' She quoted him. ' "I left it open," indeed. You mean you thought there was a good chance I would want you to sleep with me and left it to me to say so. Harry, we've had a lovely day and a lovely evening and I like you a lot, but that's all. I love Johnny Hynd.'

He wished he was upstairs alone in his room, or outside in the dark, this very minute, because he knew this crisis he had created would not talk itself successfully away.

'Well, I wasn't sure about that,' he said, 'about you and Hynd.'

'Why ever not? You've met Johnny. You know what we've been to each other.'

'Yes,' he said, 'but I know you don't like what he's doing, and I got the impression that you might leave him because of it. That you probably would.'

'I don't want to talk to you, or anybody else, about me and Johnny.' She was scarlet with vexation. 'I hate him doing this, and I don't know what will happen with us, but I don't fall into bed with a man just because I like him and fancy him, and I do fancy you, if the truth be known. But, damn it, Harry, I was feeling just great about you. I've been being happy for the first time since Johnny went away.'

She was almost crying now and her speech became muddled. 'I've never felt more about anyone than I have about you that I could trust them as much as I've been feeling I could trust you; except Johnny, perhaps not even Johnny, no, not even Johnny.'

'Well, good God,' he said, 'I don't know what you mean by trust, but what do you expect to happen when a man falls half in love with you all in a day, and the first thing you do when you get here is start swanning about with no clothes on?'

To his astonishment she burst out laughing, a ringing laugh which was, irritatingly, absolutely captivating both to hear and to see.

'Don't be such a prude, Harry,' she said, and put a hand on his knee. 'It doesn't suit you.'

'A prude?'

'Harry, a girl can swim in the nude without it meaning she's ready to make love to a man.'

'Yes, I know, I do know that really.' He felt himself blushing and smiling as well now, though against his will. 'It's just that I got carried away. I haven't been so happy myself as I was today since God knows when.'

He couldn't go on sitting here. He had to move. He got up and took a cigarette from the box on the mantelpiece and lit it and went for a small walk and ended up leaning on the back of the chair he had been sitting on.

'It's been such a day, the whole day,' he said. 'It's been such a simple day, all clarity and light and laughter, like a day out of life. Perhaps it wasn't real.'

'I don't like that very much,' she said. 'It was a great day and it was real, and I'm real, Harry, I'm not . . . Just because I was once a honey-pot for the CIA twenty and more years ago doesn't mean I'm anybody's for a hot dinner and a bottle of wine.'

He was angry himself now. 'If that's what you think I think of you, it certainly tells me what you think of me.'

She looked at him and then stood up and leaned an elbow on the mantelpiece and looked at him again.

'Yes,' she said. 'That's not you, is it? No, I don't think that of you, and you don't think that of me, do you?'

'No,' he said. 'Not for a minute have I thought of you like that.'

'Then let's stop this,' she said, 'and make friends.'

'Yes, let's have one more cigarette and then go to bed.'

He went round the chair and sat in it, and she took a cigarette from the box and chucked him one.

'Harry, that half-in-love you say you fell with me today. It was only the lovely day we had, and it was only one day. And I know me, whether I stay with Johnny or not, I won't fall in love again for ages. But do you want me to go away? I mean, will it be difficult for you to have me here?'

'I do absolutely not want you to leave. The object of this exercise is to keep you out of harm's way. Nothing else matters. And as to the rest of it' – he waved a hand about – 'I mean all this, we're both grown up, we can look after ourselves.'

'Thanks, Harry.'

She looked down at the fire and after a moment said, 'Did I tease you today? Did I make you think I wanted you?'

He shook his head as if to clear it. 'I dunno, all I can say for sure is that you were a hell of a lot of fun to be with, and it got to me.'

'Well, so were you,' she said, 'and it got to me, I told you so. Where does that leave us?'

'It leaves us,' he said, 'baffled by ourselves but knowing where we stand with each other, and perhaps ready to be friends, once we've slept on it.'

'I'd love it if we could be friends. Friendship's more important than anything, and you're important to me.'

'We'll see what we can do. Why don't you toddle off upstairs and let me sort of clear up and turn the lights off. No, no. Don't hug me or kiss me on the cheek tonight. I have several decompression chambers to pass through.'

'Tomorrow,' she said, with a kind of difficult lightness.

'Tomorrow I shall embrace you as if you were my favourite borzoi.'

'Borzoi?' she said.

'It just came into my head,' he said. 'It conveys the

idea. There's nothing offensive about it unless you want to make it so.' He was getting testy.

'I've got nothing against borzois,' she said. 'I don't even know what they look like. Sleep tight, and, Harry, thanks for a really great day.'

When she had gone he emptied the ashtrays into the fire and put the lights out and went up to bed. He fell asleep at last as the birds began to sing.

When the sun was high Harry got up and went to the window to meet the new day, then he looked at the clock. Dear God, the garrison were due in fifteen minutes. He went to the phone and called Fawcett.

They came in a Range Rover, three of them, the fruit of a score of nocturnal phone calls by Fawcett. Two of them were desk-bound officers eager for a weekend that might provide some real action, and the other had recently quit the army and was at a loose end.

Seddall knew one of them, a stocky Highlander, name of Kit Fraser, with a tough head, a man of quick movement and eye who was taking in the house and the lie of the land even as he came up to say his hello.

'Hi, Harry,' he said. 'Nicely isolated here. Good place for a private brawl.'

'Good to see you, Kit,' Harry said. 'Present the troops.'

'I didn't know these guys till this morning,' Kit said. 'This is Tony Carver. I don't know how good he is. He was a fusilier but they let him go without complaining.'

'So long as I can keep my head below the parapet,' Carver said, 'I'm sure it'll be all right. I can load the muskets while the rest of you do the real fighting. How d'you do.'

He was a tall man with black hair on a narrow head, a long sunburned face, and a clipped unfashionable moustache no wider than his nose.

The third one was a young Adonis with a rosy complexion and fair hair and a shy sweet smile, who had recently completed a tour with the SAS.

'Mark Sedgwick,' he said, introducing himself. 'Awfully good of you,' he said to Harry, as if he had been asked down for a couple of days' fishing. 'I'm not much of a hand at loading muskets, but I can cook a little.'

Caroline came out of the house wearing shorts and a shirt, and at the sight of this long tall beauty the garrison evinced, by some mysterious and silent principle, the sense that they were pleased to be enrolled in so good a cause.

'This is she whom you are to protect,' Harry said, and when the courtesies had been exchanged asked if the three had breakfasted.

'We stayed not for brake, and we stopped not for stone,' Kit Fraser quoted with patriotic fervour. 'Seemed best just to get here.'

By the end of breakfast the atmosphere was euphoric. The table had been cleared, which gratified Mrs Lyon. The soldiery had eaten like horses and were looking forward to whatever scenario the weekend produced. Caroline felt utterly confident in her garrison, and therefore safe. Seddall was satisfied that these three were worth a hundred ordinary men. And Carver, who in other people's houses was a pet-spoiler, had given half a kipper to the cat and a grilled kidney and a rasher of bacon to the dog. The euphoria, therefore, was universal.

'Well, this is very jolly,' Seddall said. 'Let's get down to business. Who's to be the boss among you three?'

'Kit,' said Sedgwick and Carver together.

'Right,' Harry said. 'Weapons. I've three shotguns, one rifle – a .243 Ruger – and two pistols, a Browning and a .38 Smith. I'll use the Smith, the rest are up for grabs.'

'I'm good with a rifle, and I like the Ruger,' Carver said. 'Unless there are any other offers I'll take that.'

The Ruger went on the nod.

'I'm a close-action man,' Sedgwick said. 'I'll take a shotgun, and I've got a pistol. Picked up a Beretta 93 on my travels.'

'Neat weapon,' Kit Fraser said. 'Three-round facility. Where did that come from?'

'Italy, of course,' Sedgwick said. 'Other than that I don't know. The man I took it off was dead.'

'Silly question,' Fraser said. 'Subject to your approval, *mon colonel*, the operation will go live at 1300 hours, which is to say in sixteen minutes.'

Seddall nodded. 'I'll just say a word,' he said. 'Three or even four different lots of people may come after Caroline. First of all MI6 and the CIA.'

Carver raised his eyebrows and smiled a little. Sedgwick said, 'I love it.'

'Do you, Mark?' Seddall said crossly. 'Well, I don't. It's great of you people to rally round and I deeply appreciate it, but don't take these intelligence orgs lightly. They can be as dangerous as all Hell, and I don't know what they want with Caroline, except that at the least it's probably to kidnap her and use her as a hostage

– why, I shan't explain now. I shall later if I think it's warranted.

'Anyway, these two are perhaps the lesser of a number of evils. The others are a job lot of maverick ex-intelligence characters who go in for skulduggery in a big way. Among other things, and this is for your ears only, it was their bomb that killed Aubrey Kenyon.'

His auditors were still, and their expressions became dark. General Kenyon had been one of their own. They were now actively hostile to the, so far, merely imagined enemy.

'The fourth lot,' Seddall said, 'and I don't really expect this, are the Mafia, who are in cahoots with the Masterless Men.'

At the mention of the Mafia, Carver turned a sardonic face to the sun coming in at the window as if to say that if the day brought him any more gifts he wouldn't be able to bear it, and the young Adonis looked down and sideways at the floor with a deadly, sluttish glaze on his face.

Fraser merely raised an eyebrow, but said, 'The Masterless Men? Sounds very romantic. Who are they?'

'I needed a filename. It's what I call the mavericks,' Harry said. 'The ex-intelligence hooligans. Who are multi-national, by the way. A consortium of many tongues. That's all I want to say, Kit. Take it away.'

'Right,' Kit Fraser said. 'Tony, I want you to learn the country up to a one-mile perimeter. Take the Ruger and the Browning too, if you want it. Expect the enemy at all times from now, in God knows what shape or form. They may look like gangsters or they may be herding a flock of sheep. Can you tell the difference between a real rustic and a fake?'

'Yes,' Carver said. 'I'm a rustic born.'

'At four hours from 1300 hours I'll start doing the same thing myself,' Fraser said. 'Meanwhile I'll stand by the house and immediate policies. You come in at 1700 hours and get some sleep. We'll be working nights, of course.'

'Got it,' Carver said.

'Mark,' Fraser said. 'You can prove the country tomorrow. What I want you to do now is take the car and go into Bridgwater. Nearest town of size, right?' This to Seddall, who nodded again. 'Walk around, do some shopping, eat a cream tea, go to a pub or two. Look for anything strange. You've done stuff like that before, I think.'

'Yes.'

'Get yourself some supper in one of the pubs,' Fraser said, 'and be back in time for dinner, say between 1900 and 2100 hours, depending on how it goes. I want you outside there on the prowl while we dine. Want any shopping done, Harry?'

'I'll ask Mrs Lyon to make a list,' Harry said. 'Always useful to stock up.'

'I'd like a swimsuit,' Caroline said. 'Should I go into town with Mark?'

'No,' Fraser said explicitly. 'Not the thing at all. Not the safest thing for you, and it would blow Mark if the enemy saw him with you.'

'Give me your size,' Mark said, 'and I'll do it. Do you want a bikini or a Speedo sort of thing?'

'Both, really. It seems rather facetious of me while you lot are going to such trouble to look after me.'

'Look, lady,' Fraser said. 'In the first place this is what we like doing best. In the second, in weather like this we need you swimming. Everything must seem to be normal.'

'I like shopping for women,' the young Adonis said to Caroline. 'I'll assume I have carte blanche. I'll get you something wicked.'

'I doubt if you'll find anything too astonishing in an English country town,' Caroline said, with her chin up and that mischief in her eyes and the slight flush and the delighted smile. She was fifty years old, Harry thought, but give her the hint of sexual challenge and she flirts and colours like a girl. It was a lovely thing to see, and it reminded him of the idea he had had in the night that she was a bird of passage, which was one of his ways of steering himself free of where he had been yesterday.

Fraser said, 'Collect yourself, young Sedgwick. Harry, you agree these dispositions?'

'Yes. Sounds good to me.'

'Good,' Fraser said. He looked at his watch. 'Then let's see this armoury of yours.'

'You must tell me, Kit,' Seddall said, 'when you need an extra man.'

'Will do, but meanwhile the thing is for you and Caroline and Mrs Lyon to proceed exactly as you were doing before we turned up. For the rest of us we'll keep out of sight as far as we can. We can't be invisible, but every little helps. I suggest we stow the Range Rover in that shed at the back, Harry, when she's not out on the road.'

The day passed. Caroline sunbathed in a quiet corner of the garden between the gooseberries and the orchard, with Bayard on watch beside her. Kit roamed the house, particularly the top floor, watching the curtilage. Harry took a gun and a gamebag and postured in the woods and fields immediately about the house, potting a couple of rabbits and a woodpigeon, every inch the country-man, but in reality a self-appointed sentinel. Tony Carver went off on his expedition, and young Master Sedgwick went on his shopping trip.

Mrs Lyon was in her element, with so many to look after, and roasted a sirloin as the mainstay of the night's dinner.

The black cat Sacha, curiously, sat on a wall and watched the road as if she was expecting someone.

Carver came in from his reconnaissance and went to bed. Fraser went out in his stead. Harry came in from the meadow and took Fraser's place as house patrol, and Caroline helped Mrs Lyon with dinner.

Caroline, making horseradish sauce, experienced a baffling exchange with Mrs Lyon, who was egging the pastry on her apple pie.

'Ye'll no hae a special interest in riding camels?' Mrs Lyon said casually, with her eye on the pie-top.

'Camels? No, I'm not especially interested in camels,' Caroline said. 'Why do you ask?'

'Fine, that,' Mrs Lyon said enigmatically.

Caroline was much mystified, but understood from Mrs Lyon's conduct towards her that so far, at any rate, she continued tolerably high in the housekeeper's esteem.

Adonis, the wandering boy, came home and garaged the Range Rover in the shed and shut the door on it. Sacha abandoned her vigil and followed behind him at a respectable interval.

He put a box of various canned and jarred and pack-aged goods on the kitchen table, and beside it a glossy pink bag patently designed to hold clothes for women. He made himself a cup of instant coffee and sat on the table, swinging a leg and looking expectant and extremely pleased with himself.

Caroline washed her hands at the sink, knowing what was expected of her. 'Let's see what you've come up with,' she said.

He had come up with a pale blue racing swimsuit and a white thong bikini.

Harry came into the kitchen as she unwrapped it. She burst out laughing. 'Look what he found,' she said, and examined what there was of it. 'Well, it's my size,' she said. 'Thanks, Mark, I'll wear it tomorrow, and then I won't feel I have to skulk behind the gooseberry bushes.'

'Glad to have been of service,' Mark said, and they sat around the kitchen being a nuisance to Mrs Lyon until Kit Fraser came home.

'You fed and rested?' he said to Sedgwick. 'Then into the trees, if you please, and play the Last of the Mohicans.'

Mark went through the house and came back with his chosen shotgun, the Beretta on his belt at the back, and a knife in his boot.

'Come on, Sacha,' he said, which Seddall thought was ridiculous, but to his astonishment the cat let Sedgwick get out of the door and then followed after.

'Aye, the laddie's got on the richt side o' yon wee black deil,' Mrs Lyon said. 'Now if ye'll gie a body some room I'll have yer dinner on the table in no time.'

They put the shutters up and drew curtains throughout the house, and dined, and talked, and went to bed.

Sunday was much the same, except that the Range

Rover stayed in the shed. Caroline variously swam in the pool and sunbathed on the lawn between it and the house in her white thong, which Kit said was good for the morale of the troops, when they were around the house on, or in the spaces between, their appointed missions.

No strangers came to the house, or were seen within a mile of it. Seddall made a circuit of the roads about in the Saab but saw nothing strange.

They dined on cold tongue and ham, and salad and new potatoes, and Roquefort and Stilton and Cheddar, and champagne and port and all of them but Sedgwick went to bed.

Outside in the trees the young Adonis prowled and lurked under the sickle moon, as silent and easy in the night as the black cat Sacha who moved with him: two predators in their own element, each lusting for the kill.

At a time when both sat on a mossy stump listening to the sounds of the darkness, the man passed the black blade of his knife across his forearm while the black cat gazed at him in the light of the stars.

'Be patient,' he said to her quietly. 'We will kill soon, I know it.'

Chapter Twenty-One

On Monday afternoon Mrs Lyon departed in the Renault 5 to spend the night with friends in Devon.

'Ye'll hae tae fend for yersels,' she said, 'for breakfast as well as dinner. It's ower far tae come back the nicht, and besides, I'll no can drink my dram and drive efter.'

It was to be duck for dinner. Seddall, this time, had driven into Bridgwater and wandered about the town, seen nothing untoward, and returned with a couple of brace of mallard.

Caroline and young Sedgwick, who had proclaimed himself a cook, studied the recipe for duck bigarade: it had a lot to tell them.

'Rub the duck over with the spirit (this was orange liqueur). Tie string round the thighs, leaving enough over to suspend the duck from a broom handle laid across two chairs, or from a convenient drawer knob. Put a large dish underneath to catch drips. Train the cold blast of a blow heater onto the duck for an hour. Alternatively, rig up a hair dryer. If the weather is blowing a dry gale from Siberia, hang the duck outside in the wind, out of the reach of cats.'

'Shouldn't they be farmyard ducks for this?' he said. 'Seems a pity to gussy up mallard like that.'

'You're just nervous because it's so complicated,' Caroline said. 'If you can't stand the heat, get out of the kitchen.'

'No way,' he said. 'It seems a lot of malarky just to

cook some duck, but I can see it's kind of irresistible.'

They found two blow heaters, and hung the curaçao-smeared duck between them from two broom handles.

Kit Fraser came in. 'Dear God,' he said, looking at the four carcases swinging in the wind. 'What an undignified way to go.'

'This,' Mark said severely, 'is *haute cuisine*.'

'I'm going up the north end,' Kit said. 'Carver's not due in for half an hour, but it does no harm to break the routine. Harry's playing gardeners out front, so stick with Caroline until further notice.'

He sprinted from the back door, and was lost to sight in the trees inside ten seconds.

'I was going to have a swim,' said Caroline, who was wearing shorts over the blue swimsuit.

'Have to wait,' Sedgwick said.

'You mean that?' She was surprised and put out.

'I am inflexible. We've two men out. I'm supposed to stay in the house. I can't have you out there on your own. Nothing's happened yet, but that doesn't mean it's not going to.'

Their gazes locked, her deep brown against his pale blue. 'I don't like being told what to do.'

'That's only because I'm young and I look like a softie,' he said. 'You've no idea how many men are sorry they thought that.'

'Women too?'

'Not women. I'm a sucker for women, you know that. Women always do know that. But this is business, Caroline. It's why I'm here.'

'I do believe you'd keep me here by force.'

'Certainly, if I had to.'

'I might enjoy that,' she said.

His eyes went so odd that she had to turn her head away for a moment.

'Don't fuck with me,' he said. 'Flirting is one thing, it's fun. But I don't mess with another man's woman.'

She flared up. 'I'm no man's woman.'

'Slice it how you like. I'll debate the individuated being with you some other day, but a man called John Hynd is laying his life on the line for you and that makes him my kind of man. There's a line I don't cross, and that's where it's drawn.'

'Why are you talking like this?' she said. 'All over one perfectly innocent remark? You're making me feel like a shit.'

'Well then,' he said. 'Think about that for a little while.'

'Christ almighty. Who do you think you are?'

He nodded. 'Yes, that's a question, I can tell you.'

He walked past her towards the open door, giving her a quiet, withdrawn glance as he went, and the flicker of a smile. Then he stood leaning against the doorpost, brooding. Still in his hand was the kitchen knife with which he had cut the string to hang the ducks from the broomsticks, and he looked out into the sunlight, tapping it lightly against the back of his knee.

Sacha ran suddenly through the doorway into the kitchen and in the same moment Caroline went rigid.

A shape appeared between the young Adonis and the sun, and a man stood there with a pistol in his hand.

The man looked at Mark Sedgwick, who gave him the shy, sweet smile and said, 'Hello, how are you?'

The man opened his mouth and the knife went in under the rib into the heart and twisted, and the man began to die.

Sedgwick took the gun before it fell, and pushed the corpse from him to let it bleed outside.

He jumped out into the sunlight and looked all round him. Then he ran back inside and locked the kitchen door and threw the two bolts across, grabbed Caroline and pulled her to a corner of the room where he thrust her down, so that she was squatting with her back to the wall where she was part hidden by an oak dresser, took the Beretta automatic from its holster at his back and gave it to her and said, 'Safety's off. Finger on the trigger, please. Watch the windows. Don't move from here. Back in a jiffy.'

She had never seen anyone move so fast in her life.

Sedgwick checked the dead man's pistol and lifted the shotgun off the kitchen table, and she heard him run up the passage to the front of the house and shout out, 'Seddall. Get in here.'

She heard their voices in a quick exchange, feet flying and doors slamming on both floors of the house, and then Harry's voice saying, 'Caroline, it's me, Harry,' and he came into the kitchen.

'You all right?' he said.

She put the Beretta on safety and laid it carefully on the floor. 'Yes,' she said, emerging from her crouch. 'But, Jesus! If ever a borzoi needed a hug, I need one now.'

Outside a shotgun went off twice, then twice more.

'It's OK,' Harry said, as her body stiffened. 'That's Sedgwick signalling to the others.'

She came out of his arms.

'I think this is a hot sweet tea situation,' she said. 'I'll fill the kettle.'

'Good,' he said. 'We're going to fort up in the house

until Fraser and Carver get in. Sedgwick's watching the front. What happened here exactly, or would you rather let him tell me?'

'Give me a cigarette,' she said, and sat on the table hugging one knee while she told him.

'That boy doesn't hang about, does he?'

'No,' she said. 'He doesn't.'

She remembered that during their quarrel she had asked Mark who the hell he thought he was, and how he had gone broody and said something like: 'That's a question, I can tell you.'

Well, now she knew. Knew a part of him, anyway.

The kettle boiled and Harry made the tea and while it brewed he moved from one window to another to see what, if anything, was going on outside.

Sacha appeared from nowhere and jumped up on the table beside her, and sat looking at the ducks and drooling at the mouth.

'Can I ask you,' Harry said. 'What's with the ducks?'

'*Yes*,' she said. 'Let's talk about real things.' Which was not quite what she meant, since nothing could be more real than a man stabbed to death in front of your eyes, and this extraordinary way of cooking duck had something fantastic about it.

'Here's the recipe,' she said. 'Read what happens next. Read it to me aloud.'

She put her chin on her knee and watched him while he read to her.

He was an interesting man, he went his own way (though in Caroline's view he had let Olivia take him for a ride), he got into muddles with himself, but in the world he was capable and self-reliant; he was self-indulgent but self-mocking as well; he was intelligent, reckless, and witty; and a lot more.

'Put the honey and leek or onion,' he read, 'into a self-basting roaster. Add enough water to give a four-to-five-centimetre depth. Bring to the boil. Using the string, put the duck into the liquid and leave for thirty seconds. Put back to blow-dry again, for a further hour. The skin will look very smooth, with a faint sheen.'

He looked up at her, the tough, weathered, life-tired face merry. If it hadn't been for Johnny, she'd have wanted to take this man to the Caribbean for a month and remind him that life should be a holiday some of the time. Face it, she said to herself, you do want to take this man to the Caribbean for a month, but that's not how it is, you simply don't know where you are with yourself. There's too much sex running in this bloody house, so be a good old borzoi and settle down.

'All this,' Harry said, 'and nothing's gone into the oven yet.'

'I know. It's the most fun I've had from cooking since I learnt to make popcorn as a kid.'

'Well, I dunno,' he said. 'Will we eat tonight?'

'Of course we will. It'll be ready in lots of time. Goodness, I'm starving right now.'

He caught himself quick enough not to throw a look at the door outside which the body lay in its blood. For he knew why she was hungry and saw no call to pass it onto her.

'So am I. How does crumpets swimming in butter sound to you?'

'It sounds perfect.'

So that, when Fraser and Carver came back, first checking with Sedgwick at the front door, they found the two of them guzzling toasted crumpets and smeared with butter like children who were being licentiously reared.

Carver took three dripping crumpets in his hand and went out to the front to free Sedgwick for de-briefing.

Caroline watched Mark Sedgwick as he came in. He looked to be in a state of marvellous wellbeing, like a man who has just been to a stunning performance of *La Bohème* and has a date with Mimí after the show.

Mark told Fraser pretty much what Caroline had told Seddall.

'You didn't ask him any questions?' Fraser said.

'I asked him how he was,' Mark said, 'but that was just to win me the vital second. I wasn't that keen to get to know him.'

'Well,' Harry said, 'we'll see what we can find out about him in a minute. Let's consider first, though. There's nobody around the house, front or rear hemisphere. But that fellow didn't come alone. A car waiting for him a mile or so down the road, I would think, and he took a shortcut across the fields. Will they still be there? Do we want to send a patrol out to see? Yes, we do. The Range Rover can go along the top parallel to the road and crew can debouch and with luck take the car unawares, if it's still there. I'll do it, if you'll lend me the vehicle.'

'No,' Fraser said. 'Divisional commanders don't go out on patrol. I'll send Carver. Mark, here's the key. Tell him what Harry's just said, and you hang around up front for a while.'

Adonis went off to sit in the front garden and commune with the roses, and, as it turned out, with Bayard and Sacha, who were of a like mind.

Seddall was pleased to see that Caroline, although a trifle pale, was single-mindedly chopping leeks into honey. Come what may, they were going to eat well tonight.

He put a hand on her shoulder and said, 'You take care.'

'You do the same. And I mean, you guys be *careful* out there. I want you all here for dinner.'

'I'm not going anywhere,' he said, 'and we'll all be here for dinner, give or take a bit of guard duty.'

Fraser unlocked the back door and drew the bolts.

Harry looked down at the corpse. City suit, grey; brown shoes; fair hair. 'What do you think?' he said to Fraser.

'How deeply interesting,' Fraser said, with much nonchalance in his voice. 'I don't have to think. I know. This man comes from Grosvenor Square.'

'The US Embassy?' Harry said. 'My Lord, what a morning.'

'Yes, indeed,' Kit Fraser said. 'Military attaché's office. Met him at a conference. I forget who he was, but he wasn't just nobody. We are in deep shit, or we have hit the jackpot, depending on how you look at it.'

'I'll tell you exactly how I look at it. Thou wretched rash intruding fool, farewell, that's how I look at it. The man had no business coming to my house with a gun in his fist, and he deserved everything he got. Perhaps he was CIA, perhaps US Army, but it would make no difference to me if he was chaplain to the White House. He came to the open door of my kitchen with a pistol ready to fire and Caroline twelve feet from the muzzle. We'll bury him tonight a long way from home. I expect we'll get a phone call from Six or CIA themselves but I'm having no amnesty to collect corpses. I'll know nothing about him. We have never seen him. He'll go down unshriven and unsung, and that's how it will be.'

He said all this very quietly, looking around him at his home, at the hedges and the trees and the fields, lifting his head to find a lark that was singing in the sky.

'God, you're angry,' Kit said.

'Yes,' Harry said, 'I am. Are you with me on this, or do you want to pussyfoot with the diplomatists and the bureaucrats?'

'I'm with you. We'll stash this lad and forget he ever happened. Where shall we dump him just now?'

'I've got a tarp in an outhouse that locks,' Harry said. 'We'll roll him in that and lock him in till we're ready to move him out.'

'So,' Kit said. 'Let's do it.'

They did it. Adonis was released to help Caroline with dinner.

'You may not want me here,' he said.

'You probably saved my life. It was awful, but you couldn't have done anything else.'

'You saw me do it,' he said.

'Of course,' she said. 'I was there. I was riveted. And it's far too much to be able to thank you for, but I am deeply and intensely grateful.'

He turned a hand, acknowledging that. 'Then you saw that I'm good at it, that I like it.'

She sat down. 'Goodness. I've come over all tired, right out of the blue. Delayed shock, I suppose. Listen to me, Mark Sedgwick, my boy: I think you're bloody weird, but I like you, and I'm running out of steam, and if you'll do things while I tell you what needs to be done I'll be grateful for that too. I'll tell you this, I feel safe with you around.'

Then she laughed on a slightly higher note than usual, and he saw a gleam of the old spirit, but with a touch of hysteria in it.

'I think you ought to wash your hand, though,' she said, 'before you get into doing dinner. There seems to be blood on it.'

Carver came back. He had found nothing but the place where the car had stood, and the usual cigarette butts.

The phone rang, and when Seddall picked it up, Deborah said only, 'The fawcett's come unstuck. You can expect an overflow.'

Keyed up by having the war brought to his doorstep, so to speak, Harry was brilliantly quick on the uptake: 'Hot water or cold?' he said.

'Ah,' Deborah was clearly taken aback by this rapidity of mind, 'hot water, definitely the hot water.'

'When did it come unstuck?'

'This minute, really.'

Fawcett, therefore, had just left, was on his way down, and had something of serious import to say.

Seddall looked at his watch. Sedgwick had just announced dinner. Fawcett would not be here till midnight or later, and he would no doubt stop to eat on the way, which would mean later.

The mallard bigarade was worth every act that had gone into its preparation. The mood at the dinner table was cheerful but there was a quality of seriousness in the air as well, since with the advent, however short-lived, of the man from Grosvenor Square, the preliminaries had ended and the game was afoot.

Besides, later tonight some of them would be tossing a man with a knife in his heart into a furtive grave in some forgotten wood under a waxing moon.

Not long after dinner Caroline went up to bed, and as soon as she was gone Fraser said, 'Let's get it done.'

So the saturnine Carver, and the beautiful and murderous Mark Sedgwick, took the man away to lay him in his long home.

Bayard and Seddall and Fraser kept watch, and Sacha lay out on the top of the wall, and waited for her fellow-spirit to come home.

It was long after midnight when Fawcett arrived, and by that time Harry had turned in. Fawcett told Kit Fraser his news, and Fraser decided the morning would be time enough to tell Seddall. 'You look as if you've had a long day,' he said to Fawcett. 'Go and get some shut-eye.'

So upstairs Morpheus ruled, downstairs Mars waited, and out there in the night, Charon was given a soul to ferry across the dark river.

Chapter Twenty-Two

Fawcett walked with Seddall in the garden before breakfast.

'This,' he handed over an envelope, 'is why I'm here.'

'It's been opened,' Seddall said. 'Sweet heaven, it's from Hynd.'

'I opened it,' Fawcett said. 'Extraordinary thing happened yesterday afternoon. A woman came to the office and said you might want to know there was a two-car stake-out on your house.'

'Came to the office?' Seddall said. 'Who was she?'

'That's the extraordinary thing,' Fawcett said. 'It was Jane Kneller, that rather top person at the Home Office who was at the grisly conference you went to.'

'She came to the office just to say that?'

'Yes. Laid it out, made sure I'd tell you soonest, and went off again.'

'I wonder why she did that?' Seddall said.

'Don't know,' Fawcett said, 'except that I had a sense that she thinks you're on the side of the angels.'

'That makes her a rare species these days. I must say, I liked her style. What did she say?'

'That she'd had an MI5 report that the Americans were watching your house. Two cars.'

'The Americans? What infernal bloody cheek. So then what?'

'Well, I was taking Dodo out to dinner at La Bouchée in Old Brompton Road,' Fawcett said, 'so the two of

us thought we'd look in at Sumner Place on the way
and see what was going on. Dodo took your spare keys
from your desk; making a bit free but we thought you'd
want us to do it.'

'No, no, absolutely,' Harry said. 'Go on.'

'Kneller wasn't kidding. We spotted two cars at
opposite ends of the street and two men and a woman
who may have been watchers. What do you suppose
they're watching for?'

'Caroline Swift,' Harry said. 'I'm getting quite cross
with these people, but they'll do no harm at Sumner
Place. Did you play dumb or did you leave them bleeding in the gutter?'

'Played dumb. Went into the house, which is when
we found the letter. We opened it because it was from
Italy, and though it was a long shot that Hynd would
actually write to you, it is, after all, a sound and simple
way to communicate. That was rank impertinence,
opening it, but I had to know, to see if it was worth
breaking my date with Dodo to fetch it down to you.
It's full of news. That Hynd must be quite a guy.'

'He is. So that's the lot?'

'That's the lot,' Fawcett said.

'You go and have breakfast. They're eating in the
kitchen this morning. I want to fill them in on all this
– they don't even know the full strength about Hynd's
mission yet – so since you've read his letter would you
mind going on watch after you've eaten so that I can
have them all together?'

When he had read Hynd's letter he sat on the bench
at the top of the herbaceous border for as long as it
took to smoke three Gauloises.

Everyone, except Caroline who was not yet down,

had breakfasted by the time he went into the kitchen, and Fawcett had taken the dog and gone out on his roving patrol.

'Things are moving,' Seddall said, and poured himself coffee. 'I'm going to ask for volunteers for service abroad, but first I'll fill you in.'

He gave them the whole story about Hynd and then offered the gist of the letter. 'Item one,' he said. 'We know that Mr Casson and his Masterless Men have acquired a vessel called the *Baikal*, and that they plan an operation on or against an island, presumably Italian, beginning with the letter N. And we know that when he wrote the letter John Hynd was in imminent expectation of being carted off to Sicily and being held there – under house arrest at the very least – by a capo de Mafia in his seventies called Don Ottavio.'

'Which means,' Kit Fraser said, 'that if we can identify the ship, the island, and the ancient mafioso along with the location of his permanent residence, we can form a plan of campaign.'

'Exactly,' Seddall said.

'I seem to recall,' Tony Carver said, lying back long and languid with his weight on the back legs of his chair, 'that there's an island a goodish bit south of Sicily that might fit the bill.'

'Tell,' Fraser said.

'Group of Italian islands on a line between Sfax in Tunisia and Malta,' Carver said. 'One of them's called Isola di Nasa.'

'I didn't realize Italy had islands that far south,' Fraser said.

'Oh, yes,' Carver said with an offensive display of self-satisfaction. 'What's more, I read somewhere that

it has an old prison on it, or a kind of fortification that's
been turned into a prison, and that they're using it to
hold two or three hundred of these Mafia blokes they've
been arresting this last year or so.'

'How on earth do you know things like that?' Seddall
said. 'I didn't know that.'

'Then you're just not earning your keep, old son,'
Carver said. 'Either that or I'm unusually abreast of
what's going on in the world, which is, in fact, very
much the case.'

'Give that man a cigar,' Fraser said.

'Actually, I'd love a cigar,' Carver said.

'In the drawing-room,' Harry said. 'Help yourself.'

Carver brought his chair down with a thump and
went foraging.

'Good for him,' Harry said. 'Until I hear further I'll
assume that he's got it in one. But I'll have to get Fawcett
and Dodo to run through all Italian islands to make
sure. In fact I'd like to brief Fawcett now; there's a great
deal I'll want him to do as a result of Hynd's report, so
now that you know the score, Mark, will you go and
take over from him outside and send him in?'

'Sure,' Mark Sedgwick said. 'This service abroad you
referred to. If you mean Sicily and the Mafia, or this
Isola di whatever, count me in.'

'Mick,' Seddall said when Fawcett came in. He told
him about Carver's contribution. 'You must scoot back
to London, rope in Dodo, and start working. I want
Dodo to run down all Italian islands beginning with N.
She can go to the Royal Geographical Society. I want
you to go and see Gerald Kenna at Scotland Yard and
ask him to identify an ancient mafioso called Don Otta-

vio in Sicily and give you his address. If there are more than one, obviously, we want them all.

'I don't want either of you to be making any phone calls about any of this. And about this vessel, the *Baikal*, let's see, who can tell us about her? There's a man called George Whittam in Naval Intelligence, Mick. Call in on him too, will you, and see what he can come up with.'

Fawcett departed, Caroline appeared, Seddall made scrambled eggs for two and Kit Fraser acquired for himself an extra ration of toast and marmalade. They were just settling down to this when a car drove up outside.

Caroline vanished upstairs again, taking her breakfast with her, and Fraser went to the front door and Harry the back.

Fraser returned. 'I've put them in the drawing-room,' he said. 'Three of them, Americans. Carver's in there with them. I'll watch this end of the house. They've left a driver outside but Sedgwick will be keeping an eye on him. Carver's rodded-up. Are you?'

'Yes,' Harry said. 'It's under the sweater.'

He entered the drawing-room in the state of mind of a wolf going into a sheepfold. He was exhilarated by John Hynd's communiqué, which portended action and possibly success, and he felt arrogant, vicious and cold towards these yahoos who kept getting under his feet and who were so damned stupid they were dangerous.

They were standing in a group near the door and Carver was at the other end of the room, leaning against the wall and in the act of lighting himself another cigar.

Seddall sat himself on the piano stool with his back to the piano, a position which gave him ready access to his pistol.

'Sit down,' he said to the visitors.

'Melman,' said one of the newcomers, a tall, grey-haired man with a refined countenance and an impressively confident bearing, who as he spoke touched on the arm the man who stood to his right, 'why don't you go and—'

'Your Mr Melman isn't going anywhere,' Seddall said. 'You misunderstand me. When I said sit down I meant it. Do what you're told.'

The leader frowned. 'That's a pretty offensive way to talk, Seddall.'

'I'm an offensive man,' Harry said, 'when I have cause. I have cause. I don't want you here. Sit down and speak your piece or go back to the Bronx, or wherever you come from.'

'Connecticut, actually,' the man said.

Harry lit a cigarette, reached himself an ashtray from the top of the piano, and said, 'You're not handling this very well, and you're not going to manage it. I'm too much of a shit and you're on my ground. So sit down and speak, or go.'

Melman was large and muscular and raring to have at it. The third man, a slight and black-haired figure, looked like the only one worth knowing. He stood at peace, regarding Seddall with quiet and serious interest.

This man sat down now in an armchair and said, 'We've lost a man.'

The leader looked at him and then sat down himself, and a wave of the hand told Melman to do the same.

'Yes,' he said. 'We're missing a man. We believe he came to this house yesterday. He hasn't been seen since.'

'Fellow in a grey suit?' Harry said. 'Yes, he was here yesterday.'

'You admit it?' the American said.

'Admit it?' Harry said. 'No. I don't admit it. I simply tell you that for a short time yesterday my household experienced the misfortune of his presence.'

'If harm has come to him,' the American said, 'I'll . . .' and left his sentence hanging in the air.

The small dark man said, 'Can you tell us what transpired?'

'He came,' Harry said, 'to the kitchen door at the back of the house. He had a pistol in his right hand with the safety off, and he pointed it into the room. The man who confronted him at the door took his pistol from him and sent him away.'

'I find this hard to believe,' the leader said.

'So do I,' Harry said. 'It's a damned odd thing to come to a fellow's house ready to shoot up the occupants.'

'That's not what I meant,' the man said.

Seddall extinguished his cigarette and waited.

'I want to know what happened to him, goddamn it,' the leader said.

'No doubt you do,' Harry said. 'For my part I wouldn't care if he was stung to death by a nest of vipers, or if he fell into a pond and was eaten by a giant pike. But it does seem to me that if he was going about the place with a pistol ready to fire he must have thought this was unsafe country for him. Perhaps he was right.'

'You won't get away with this,' the leader said.

'Carver,' Harry said. 'I think that was a threat.'

Carver came lazily off the wall. He did not look the least bit alert, but a dangerous feel came from him.

'What do you know of Caroline Swift?' the man said. 'Do you know where she is?'

'I see,' Harry said. 'So that's what all this is about. I understood you had already been forced to apologize to HM Government for acting illegally over Caroline Swift. I don't think you people know what you're doing or even, when you get down to it, why you're doing it. What am I to expect next, an assault by the 101st Airborne?'

The man looked at the ceiling for a moment and then at the air in front of him.

'Let's go,' the small dark one said.

The leader stood up. 'You won't get away with this,' he said again. 'I've checked you out. You don't have a lot of clout in Whitehall these days.'

'My dear man,' Harry said. 'You are absolutely right, so hang onto that, if it's the sort of thing that comforts you. See the fellows off now, will you, Tony? I want to have another stab at getting some breakfast.'

The scrambled eggs had been given to the dog, but Caroline had a pan of water on the stove and he regaled himself on boiled eggs and cold ham.

'Than which there are few better meals to start the day,' he was saying when Carver came in.

'Well,' Carver said, 'that was fun.'

'Of a sort,' Harry said. 'I felt rather cheap, to tell you the truth. They set themselves up, but I suppose they were willing to suffer that. All they wanted to know was if their man had bought it, and now they know.'

'And we know that their chief concern is me,' Caroline said. She stood withdrawn at one of the windows, her arms folded, her expression sombre and uncertain, looking out into the trees.

'We thought that anyway, Caroline,' Kit Fraser said. 'That's why we're here.'

'I know that,' she said, 'and it will bore us all if I keep saying thank you for it, so I won't say it again now. But it's not a lot of fun for me, it scares me stiff.'

'Well,' Fraser said. 'We'll be moving out soon, now that things are hotting up, down to Sicily. Hanging around waiting for things to happen is always more trying than carrying the war to the enemy's camp.'

Caroline turned and looked at him as if from a vast distance. 'You don't think for a moment that I'm going with you all to Sicily? I'm not a soldier. I'm not a secret agent. I don't live this kind of life. I want back into real life again.'

'Where do you want to go?' Harry said. 'The only way for us to get these blighters out of your hair is to deal with them for good, and that means we have to go to where they are. And, once we've dealt with them, the CIA and everyone else will lose interest in you too. But meantime, you won't be safe here from harassment, not on your own, or even with Mrs Lyon.'

'You're going to Sicily too?' she said, and her eyes were dark.

'It's my job,' he said. 'I can't send these fellows off to do my job for me.'

'They'd do it without you, though,' she said, and looked at Carver and Fraser. 'You would, wouldn't you?'

'Of course.'

'Sure.'

'That's not the point,' Harry said. 'I'm in charge of this operation, and I'm not going to walk out in the middle of it. And I'm not going to leave you unguarded.

We need to find a way of making sure you're safe.'

'Why does this keep happening,' Caroline said. 'I'm a free and independent woman and now all of a sudden I keep needing men to protect me.'

It was a strange, sad, passionate *cri de coeur*, but so quietly said that somewhere inside each of them the three men sensed doubt touch their certainty of belief in what life was about.

'Lady,' Carver said, 'it's up to you. What you need to do doesn't fit with what Harry needs to do, but that's not the end of the world. Why don't you decide where you'd like to be till it's all over, and we'll see you get safely there, with no one knowing you're there, and someone handy to be with you, if you want that.'

Seddall, whose view of Carver was already formed, was amazed to hear so much understanding unmarred by sympathy in the way he spoke.

Certainly it had gone down well with Caroline. She tossed the hair off her face and said to Carver, 'I want to have a serious swim, clean my mind out. Can you be the bodyguard? Can he?' This last was to Fraser.

'Yes indeed,' Fraser said. 'We're kind of blown here anyway, Tony, so you can sit out there in comfort so long as you keep your eyes peeled.'

She went to Carver and said to him, 'Tony, you're gay, aren't you?'

He looked down his long nose at her and said, 'Yes, lady, I am.'

'I'd like to go to Spain,' she said. 'If they can get me out to Spain, will you come with me instead of going to Sicily, and be my bodyguard there too?'

A kind of question came into the pale eyes – regret

for the Mafia, or a private mystery of his own, who could say? – and then was gone.

'I'm your man,' he said. 'And Spain's good. I've got friends among the Catalans, and I know a place where we can hide out until the heat's off.'

She put her arms round his waist and leaned her head on his chest and relaxed onto him. 'How absolutely wonderful,' she said. 'How perfect. Let's go and have this swim.'

She detached herself and gave a quick, half-shy smile to the others, and went out, with Carver, shotgunned and pistolled, moving like a bandit in her wake.

'Carver's a good idea for her,' Fraser said. 'That's a woman with a flying spirit and a flying heart, and it brings her a lot of pain. Tony will be a kind of refuge for her.'

'What does that mean?' Harry said.

'I'm not sure I know, but it feels right.'

'I had no idea Tony was gay,' Seddall said. 'How did she know?'

'Don't ask me,' Fraser said, 'and what does it matter?'

Mrs Lyon came back and drove them from her kitchen and set about preparing lunch.

In the late afternoon Fawcett phoned. 'Harry, how would it be if you went to Wearth crossroads and I called you there in twenty minutes.'

'Not bad,' Seddall said.

Twenty minutes later he stood at the phone kiosk and Fawcett came on. 'I took down the number as I came past this morning. I'm in a callbox too, so we're secure.'

'What have you got?'

'First,' Fawcett said. 'Only one aged Don Ottavio where we're looking. He lives in the hills near Cefalu, not far from the coast.'

'Name and place,' Seddall said, and wrote them down.

'Second,' Fawcett said, 'and you're going to like this one a lot. *Baikal* was the name of the vessel Hynd gave you, right? Well, there's an attack craft built for the KGB but overtaken by events called the *Baikal*. She was fitting out at Parnu in Estonia when the Soviets disintegrated. Get this: she sailed last week, left the Baltic, out into the North Sea and down through the Channel. Seems to have been sold, officially or black market, but who cares.

'Your friend Whittam and his buddies have been watching her, since that class carries real metal and they want to know where she goes, who's bought her. *Svetlyak* class, 450 tons, 30 knots, torpedoes, SAM missiles, and two guns, one 76 millimetre and one 30 mil.'

'That island, by George,' Seddall said. 'Do you think they're actually going to raid the island and try to free those Mafia prisoners?'

'I do think so,' Fawcett said. 'I should tell you, Whittam was really keen to know how I'd come to focus on a ship that he's watching. I mean, they usually know who's bought what. I had nothing to tell him, so I just gave him no comment, didn't explain. There was no point in flannelling. He may broadcast our interest to those we don't want to know about it.'

'That won't matter,' Seddall said. 'We can't handle warships. We'd have to pass it on anyway, and Whittam's the man to tell. But not yet, I want to get me and my mob out of the country first. What I'm concerned to do is to rally round Hynd and put paid to Casson and his Masterless Men as such.'

'Right,' Fawcett said. 'More news about the *Baikal*. One, guns visible on her when she went through the Skagerrak, but no torpedoes and no SAM missile launcher. The guns would do it for them, though, with a surprise attack. Two, she's been painted white, which is odd. Three, I've had a thought.'

'What's the thought?'

'Whittam might close up on us, since all we're doing is asking him for help and not giving anything back. But I know a man on Gibraltar who is, so to speak, appropriately placed. I thought I might ask him to tell me if she passes through the Strait.'

'Please do. Well done, Mick, all round. Any other N-initial islands?'

'Dodo says no likely starters,' Fawcett said. 'That's her judgement. Do you want to make your own?'

'No. She's got a head on her shoulders. Take her out to dinner tonight.'

'Actually, she's taking me.'

Back at the house, Harry said to Fraser, 'Do you know what I think, Kit? I think we need a boat. I wonder if we can dig up someone who keeps a boat anywhere near Sicily.'

'What's in your mind?'

'We need a convincing reason for some idle strangers to be stamping around near Cefalu. If we just appear ten or twenty miles or so from Don Ottavio's ancestral stronghold, while we're getting our bearings and sussing things out, we're going to look a bit too like what we are. Sailing chaps are different, they're expected to turn up unexpectedly, if you take my meaning.'

'Good notion,' Fraser said. 'I should think, between us and Fawcett and his Dodo, we ought to be able to come up with someone who'll oblige.'

'Since Caroline wants to go to ground in Spain,' Seddall said, 'we can slip her out of the country easily enough. But since Tony's going with her we'll be three instead of four in Sicily. Do you think we should recruit someone else?'

'No,' Fraser said. 'I like what we've got. With your cunning, my intelligence, and Sedgwick's deplorable gift for, what shall I say, total war, we'll do all right.'

In the middle of the night Carver, keeping his watch among the trees, saw Harry Seddall come out into the garden and walk up and down, up and down, smoking endless cigarettes.

'Alone and palely loitering,' Carver said to himself. 'Well, that's the way the cookie crumbles.'

Chapter Twenty-Three

It was in July that he sailed into the bay at the helm of a little wooden cutter, picked up the mooring below the Marinelli house east of the village, pulled ashore in a rubber dinghy, walked up the beach, unlocked the front door, with a key which he could only have had from the lawyer in Cefalu, and made himself at home.

On the second day he was seen to swim to the yacht, which was about five hundred metres offshore, and spent some time diving to inspect the state of the mooring: so he was a careful man.

On the third day, when unsatisfied curiosity in the village was about ready to turn into irritation, he walked into Agnello's and in a comprehensible mainland Italian said good evening to Agnello, ordered a glass of wine, and asked if he might borrow the copy of the *Giornale di Sicilia*, which was lying folded at the end of the counter.

He had a hard eye, but you would say his manner was neither offensive nor polite, or perhaps that he had no manner at all. His self-contained stillness was that of a man serious and absorbed in some deep questions of his own, so that what appeared as reserve might be grief, if he was that kind of man, or might be thought, if he was a profound thinker.

He sat himself at a table on the street and variously read the *Giornale* and looked out over the sea, and perhaps into himself, for they knew, in Ciascia, that the two go well together.

He was a man above middle height, somewhere in middle-age, with a round head and a stubbly brown beard and moustache shot with grey, not unkempt but not clipped by the barber either. He wore cotton trousers and shirt. There was nothing to tell whether he was rich or poor, who he was, where he came from, what he did, or why he was here.

He drank his wine and smoked a few Gauloises, and took the glass back into the bar for a refill. The room was very plain. The wooden top of the bar counter was polished and scarred by a century or more of use. It was dark, pickled by age and alcohol, scorched by cigarettes. The floor was stone, the plaster of the walls a neutral colour that had been white, patched with faded red and green where the original decoration still survived.

There were twenty and more men there, half of whom had taken in the newcomer as they passed him when he sat outside in that reverie of his. Most of them sat at the table, a few stood at the bar. They wore old trousers and shirts, some wore waistcoats. In a corner was a table of older men in dark suits. Poverty, as well as custom, made its own uniform.

Behind the bar was Agnello, dark and thin, even skinny, who listened and worked, and spoke little.

It was Paolo Sciandri, standing beside the stranger as he waited for his drink at the bar – or rather above him, for Sciandri was a man of unusual size – who found the question.

After the opening greeting, which was met with a look and a nod from the stranger, Sciandri was silent for a while. Then he said, 'You have been here before?'

The stranger acknowledged the delicacy of the approach. Across his mouth a smile came and went as fast as a dragonfly.

'To Ciascia? No,' he said. 'I wanted a quiet place to work. Some peace, some sun. This is a quiet place.'

Yes, it was a quiet place. 'I myself am a fisherman,' Sciandri said. 'All my family have been fishermen.'

This laid an obligation on the stranger, who answered it. 'I am writing a book,' he said. 'I have been a solider, and now I am writing a book.'

'You will write about soldiering, I suppose,' Sciandri said.

'I am writing about myself,' the man said, 'and as yet I don't seem to be writing about soldiering.'

Sciandri had a black moustache that drooped at either end. He stroked his hand down it, and again, thinking about this.

'Perhaps you have stopped being a soldier,' he said, 'and grown wise.'

'I doubt that,' the man said, 'but it's a nice idea. Do you think I'd find someone to clean the house now and then? Sometimes, perhaps, make a meal for me that I can put in the oven at night for my dinner?'

'Of course,' Sciandri said. 'You are talking to the right man. I have two daughters. Either of them could do these things for you. Shall we discuss this? My name is Paolo Sciandri.'

'Henri Leconte,' the other said.

There was an empty table at one of the windows and they sat there, connected now by the personal question of caring for a man's home, however temporarily; and by the commerce of the transaction. When this had been completed – so many hours a day at so much – Sciandri frowned.

'My Caterina is very beautiful,' he said. He gave the Frenchman a shrewd look.

Leconte was two moves ahead of him. 'Send your other girl,' he said.

'Amelita is also very beautiful,' Sciandri said.

Leconte shrugged. 'Then send them both. They can chaperone each other. One can cook while the other sweeps and dusts – they can sort it out between them. And there is the garden. Vegetables need watering, and there are too many weeds. There will be plenty of work for two. I could pay a little more for that.'

The deal, so satisfactory to both parties (whatever the Sciandri girls might think of it), having been concluded, the two men sealed it with a few hours of conviviality. Before the night was out, Henri Leconte had drunk with everyone in the bar, which was most of the men of the village of Ciascia.

He arrived back at the house under the Sicilian moon in the company of a tall dog, which adopted a melancholy air when he turned the key in the door and was astounded with joy when he said to it, 'My house is yours.'

The dog ran inside and lurked respectfully in the dark.

Leconte made his way upstairs. He had enough moral integrity left to take off his clothes before he fell into bed, and when his head had steadied after the abrupt move to the horizontal he yawned with a kind of satisfaction, and waited for sleep.

As he was nodding off something landed heavily on the bed and pillowed its head on his feet.

Leconte looked down the length of his body and saw the dog's eyes shining at him.

'Sometimes, my dear Henri,' he said, 'you are such a damn fool.'

On the day after that alcoholic night Leconte sculled out to the yacht and brought ashore a small library of books, and after that he lived an exemplary life. At night he read, and every day he worked at the desk where his portable Olivetti typewriter sat. At first, there were long spells when the machine was silent, and he would walk about the house or garden with his face so contorted by thought that he seemed to be in a rage.

When the Sciandri girls encountered him in this state they looked at him askance and became particularly busy. Amelita, who was in the habit of singing when she worked, stopped singing in the house altogether, and if he came out to the garden when she was there her song faded away to nothing.

Three times in two weeks he hired Agnello's car with Agnello's son Piero to drive him, and went to Cefalu. He would have Piero let him off in the middle of town just in time for lunch, and pick him up at that spot at five o'clock.

He would buy newspapers and then regale himself with a meal of many courses, in a different place each time. In the evening, when Piero brought him back, he would drop in at Agnello's and discuss the news in the French papers and the merits of the cooking in Cefalu. He gave little time to the town itself. The long lunch, the newspaper for company, were his chosen relaxation from the furious spells of work on his history.

He would stay not more than an hour at Agnello's, and then he would walk home to the Marinelli house to put in some work before his evening meal. On such days Amelita and Caterina were told to prepare him only a light supper, and on such days the lights in the house went out earlier than usual. He drank well on these expeditions, as you could tell from his benign condition after them.

He never got seriously drunk again, as he had that first night in Agnello's, but on most evenings he would come to the village and talk to Sciandri and Agnello and whoever was there. One night Ottavio came down to have a look at him. He watched and listened to the Frenchman discoursing on the battle of Magenta and went away again.

After two weeks of this, on the Friday, he received a telegram and the Sciandri girls were told to prepare bedrooms for two visitors who were expected to arrive during the weekend.

'Well,' Leconte said grouchily to Sciandri, 'that's what happens when you find a good place to work and enjoy some peace. Before you know it your friends find you out and tell you they are coming to break in on your solitude.'

'Frenchmen like yourself?' Sciandri said.

'A woman and a man,' Leconte said. 'She is French and he is English. It's a sad story. He is her brother-in-law. Her husband was killed in a car crash. The brother thought a quiet sailing holiday would be a good thing for her. They will have a crewman as well, but he can stay on board and look after himself.'

He went to the bar and came back with more of the dark red wine. 'I am not that selfish,' he said. 'I am just set in my ways.'

'You will be pleased once they arrive,' Sciandri said.

'A man's friends are a man's friends, as are a woman's. They need each other in the bad times as in the good.'

'Well, they will stay a few days, I expect,' Leconte said. 'I will bring them to meet you.'

On the Sunday morning a ketch half as big again as Leconte's cutter came into the bay, and dropped anchor. She was painted duck-egg blue and from the shore looked very spick and span, not like the Frenchman's little old cutter.

'The woman is naked,' said Amelita.

'No,' said Caterina, having taken her father's old telescope from its place on the window-ledge. 'She is wearing a yellow bikini, but it is very small.'

After a while Leconte went down to the beach and waved, and rowed out to the ketch in his dinghy.

When he came alongside Leconte said hello to Sedgwick, who was up forward, doing crew-like things which seemed to involve getting inextricably wrapped up in foresail and jib, and then hauled himself aft to where Fraser was leaning over the rail.

'Welcome aboard, Harry,' Fraser said. 'We mostly drink gin on this boat. Sorrel has this old-fashioned thing about dry Martinis. She knows how to fix them too.'

He was wearing a pair of faded blue cotton shorts which were reduced to the detritus that comes just before complete disintegration.

'You're supposed to be brother-in-law and sister-in-law, and in mourning,' Harry said, 'and you're both sailing round the Med half naked. These are simple folk around here. You should be in black to the ankles. What will they think?'

'They'll think we're decadent types from the corrupt

metropolises up there,' Sorrel said, with three glasses held by the stems between her fingers, and waving a jug frosted with ice in a northerly direction. 'And if you think I'm not going to take the chance to spiffy up my tan, you've got another think coming.'

'A woman's place is in the nude,' Fraser said, 'sweating gently, which Sorrel does very nicely.'

'This is the most sexist boat I was ever on,' said Sorrel.

'What news?' Fraser said.

'This is the place, all right,' Harry said. 'An evil old bugger came in the other night and sat among the ancients when I was laying forth about strategy and tactics as exemplified in battles long ago, and except for the voice of Seddall a deathly hush fell when he came in. I was half pissed, and he listened to my garbage for an hour and then went away again. I'd lay anything you like that he was Ottavio.'

'Wow,' Sorrel said. 'We're in the front line.'

'We will be, when we've found out where he lives,' Harry said. 'I've been frightfully uninterested in exploring the countryside, it wouldn't have done. Now you lot are here we can undertake a few earnest walks and go a-picnicking. God send Hynd still lives. And as to Hynd, what have you found out about the dynamic little fighting ship that sailed from the Baltic?'

'Hang on,' Fraser said, and dived into the cockpit and went below. He came back with a bit of paper. 'The *Baikal*,' he said. 'Fast attack craft, built at Vladivostock for the Border Guard fleet, finished fitting out at Parnu in Estonia, which I think is not usual, but I guess that for black market purposes they wanted her out of the

CIS – Commonwealth of Independent States – this week's name for Russia.'

'Thank you,' Harry said. 'I have been at least minimally aware that we are no longer in the days of Peter the Great. And I knew that stuff about the *Baikal* already. Apart from that all I know is that she's out at sea somewhere. Is that all we know?'

'No, it's not all we know,' Fraser said. 'Being keen to make an impression I got on an aeroplane and went to Helsinki, and picked up Doddie Gogarty to interpret for me – you know Gogarty? No. He's doing something in the academic line now and speaks Finnish, which is as you know a Finno-Ugric language, as is Estonian. Don't fret. He's as close as an oyster.

'We got the ferry to Tallinn and drove to Parnu. Learned that the *Baikal* was indeed painted white before she sailed. Beautiful, rakish-looking ship, just like a yacht in her new coat of paint. Did not, in fact, have missiles mounted. Sent Gogarty back to Finland, flew home.

'And yes, the *Baikal* is in this very sea. She came through the straits into the Med last week, and she was actually dressed as a yacht sure enough. Awnings fore and aft and looking as innocent as you like.'

Harry had been listening to this last part with bated breath, and he let it out in a long sigh and lay back and stretched his length luxuriously on the deck while pulling his T-shirt off at the same time.

'You've done wonders,' he said. 'Is there any more of that hooch?'

Sorrel vanished into the cabin and was back in no time. Seddall lay and gazed at the sky. Fraser looked round the bay, across the pellucid, unbelievably beautiful sea at the white houses of the village, at figures moving slowly in the heat of the July afternoon, the foothills that rose into mountains.

What a place, he thought. It was heaven on earth, and up there somewhere, if he still lived, was a man who was taking risks that were to Fraser unimaginable: a man he wanted to meet, to see what he was like, this kind of man – no, he would be one of a kind, a man like that, a man who was doing all this for a woman.

'Extraordinary thing,' he said.

'What is?' Harry said, still dazzling his eyes with the brightness of the empyrean.

'That so much hinges on that man,' Fraser said. 'And his only reason for doing what he's doing is that these people threatened the woman he loves. She's quite a woman.'

'Yes, indeed,' Harry said, and sat up. 'Sometimes you find women of astonishing beauty who have qualities in them that they've not found fulfilment for. They can be confusing to a man. They can be very strong, tough even, but the lack of fulfilment leaves them with a sense of loss that's like a hurt they carry with them, and it has a terrible appeal to some men. They feel they can heal it. They're being asked to heal it, not in words but across the space between the man and the woman. They can't heal it, of course, because it becomes part of the woman and it's her hurt, and she won't, in the end, let a man heal it for her. It's her own to deal with, part of herself. But it puts an irresistible hold on the man.'

Fraser stared at him with an expression of utter astonishment, and even Sorrel, who had emerged from the cabin and sat herself on the coaming of the cockpit with the refreshed jug in her hand, was looking at him with surprise.

'I didn't know you knew stuff like that, Harry,' she said.

'I don't know stuff like that. John Hynd told me. Is it true?'

'Yes. I don't know. I think perhaps it is,' Sorrel said. 'I'll have to think about it a bit more. It's rather terrible.'

'I don't know that I understand it,' Fraser said. 'But it sounds as if Hynd is saying that he knows she'll not want him that long. That she'll be up and away, looking for whatever it is.'

'Yes,' Harry said. 'He said that too.'

'And he's putting his life on the line for her all the same,' Sorrel said. 'I don't know that I like it.'

Harry said, 'Hynd said it was worth it to him. It wasn't down to her. He would do it, because nobody had ever done it for her before.'

'I should bloody think not.' Sorrel was indignant. 'It's like him putting his head into a hornet's nest so that she can get out of the garden without being stung.'

'I do like it,' Fraser said unexpectedly. 'I haven't grasped it in the way you two have, but I rather go for it. It's beyond my ken, I think. I think it's a thing older than I am.'

'What does that mean?' Sorrel said.

'I'm not sure. As soon as I'd said it I was baffled by it.' He looked up at the hills beyond the bay. 'I hope we get that man out of there.'

'Well, he must be an odd sort of man. He's up there dicing with death among the ungodly and she's off to Spain and whatever's the next excitement.'

Harry said, 'Enough of this. I've been thinking. If

Hynd's confined to barracks, I mean free to move within limits, he might be able to get himself out. In which case the thing is for us to let him know we're here so that he can come to shelter. If he's locked up, then we'll have to break him out. The first thing is to get a sight of Ottavio's house and see what we think of the set-up. Give us a drink, Sorrel.'

The pitcher went round again.

'How do we let him know we're here?' Fraser said.

'Come in sight of the place,' Sorrel said, 'and see what occurs to us.'

'That's not much of a plan,' Fraser said.

'Hell's teeth, Major,' Harry said. 'You're not in the army now. However,' he amended, inspired by alcohol, 'even if we were, first thing would be recce. Who knows what might not happen? Remember Blondel and Coeur de Lion. Sorrel might sing "Come into the garden, Hynd," to which he would reply "I am here at the gate alone." Thus we would know he was free to walk about the garden.'

'Well, sure, it could bear that interpretation,' Fraser said. 'I would need to study it. But what if he sang "For the black bat night is flown"? Besides which, we were talking about coming in sight of the place. You're talking about being in earshot.'

'You're a real wet blanket, Kit Fraser,' Sorrel said. 'I think gin makes you morose.'

Fraser wrestled her into the sea. Harry slapped him on the back and the two of them hugged each other like footballers. Sorrel, since she was in the water, went for a swim.

'He's getting drunk,' said Amelita, passing the telescope to her sister. 'The ones at the stern are getting drunk. The young man working on the sails is very beautiful.'

'Yes,' Caterina said. 'He is very beautiful. He is like a god. We may see him tomorrow, if they come ashore before they are all completely drunk, and do not drown themselves.'

They did not drown themselves.

The next day at breakfast Harry said to Amelita, 'We're thinking of going on a picnic, perhaps today. Do you know if Piero's free to drive us?'

'He is out in the boat,' Amelita said, 'with Papa.'

'Oh, what rotten luck,' Harry said. 'Still, today does feel like the day for it. We'll walk.'

An hour later the expedition set off.

Chapter Twenty-Four

Hynd was not in the mood to sing Victorian Irish ballads, whether about the need for Maud to come into the garden, or about anything else. He was getting restless and a vicious temper was growing inside him. He had been here for nearly three weeks now, living in an illiterate household with no books worth speaking of, no music worth listening to, and no conversation worth a damn.

That was not the worst, though. The worst was that Ottavio was beginning to assume towards Hynd a curious form of paternal affection; curious, because it appeared to have a hidden design in it.

Ottavio had once had three sons, but they had all been murdered in a war with an interloping neighbour. Ottavio went to talk peace with his rival, who also had three sons, in a restaurant in Cefalu. He had arrived bowed down by grief, snivelling with a cold or influenza and a handkerchief to his face in the act of blowing his nose, a scarf round his neck and an overcoat over his shoulders.

He had sat down at the table just as he was, pushed his chair back a couple of feet on the wooden floor, thrown the coat back with the arm that held the sawn-off shotgun, and blasted the father and one son with one barrel and the other two with the other. Then he had got up, shedding coat and handkerchief, pulled out a pistol, shot each of them, dead and dying, in the head, and walked out with a spring in his step.

The dead man's heir was a nephew, a shopkeeper in Cefalu, whose uncle's death, along with that of the cousins, had made him rich. Ottavio went to see him the next week. He took the shotgun with him. 'Consider,' he said, 'what you have inherited because of me. Look into this' – the gun – 'and look at me. Do you want peace, or blood feud? I think you want peace. You are not a man of your hands.'

'What about my honour?' the shopkeeper said.

'You are full of fear,' Ottavio said. 'You do not need honour.'

'Nevertheless, what about my honour?' the tradesman said, although he was indeed white and trembling.

Ottavio had been impressed by this. 'Let us reach a compromise,' he said, 'and declare a truce between us, a truce of fifteen years. I shall be dead by then. But no harm to the womenfolk. What do you say?'

'Ten years,' the man said, 'and no harm to the womenfolk, yours or mine.'

Ottavio had smiled. 'Ten years,' he said. 'I shall be old in ten years. If you come, I shall be pleased to see you. But I shall not come to you.'

That had been three years ago, Leopetto had told Hynd, when Ottavio was seventy-two.

'He has no sons,' Leopetto said. 'He has taken a liking to you.'

'That's nice,' Hynd said; then, 'Just a minute. What do you mean?'

'You know what I mean,' Leopetto said. 'He thinks to adopt you.'

'That is either mad,' Hynd said, 'or a trick.'

Leopetto frowned, since one did not insult the Don.

316

His was the face of a man in his late fifties, an alert and lively face with the lines of experience and of his character marked clear on it, harshness and vigour, contentment and wit. A long face, ruddy as much as brown, with grey hair going white, and bright blue eyes: a throwback to the time when the Normans ruled Sicily.

'Well,' Leopetto said. 'He has had enough to make him mad.'

'All of you have had enough to make you mad,' Hynd said. 'Sicily makes you mad.'

'We are alive,' Silvestro said. 'To be alive in Sicily is a kind of madness, but it is truly living.'

Silvestro was younger than Leopetto, a tall man, full of energy and temperament, a man impetuous in laughter or rage, a nature without constraint. He was as brown as a Moor, with a narrow face and a hawk nose and rich black hair and deep brown eyes.

The four of them who had escaped from Puglia with Ottavio were eating their midday meal in the shade of three beech trees at the back of the house. The fourth and youngest was Carmine, a quiet lad in his twenties, smooth-faced and well-groomed, a man of the town rather than the country, a man who thought much and said little.

'It is truly living,' Hynd said, 'until you are dead. You are always at war, against each other and the State.'

Carmine answered this. 'It is our life,' he said. 'And what of you? You have come into this life of your own choice, and you do not seem so very out of place in it.'

'What were you doing before you came here?' Silvestro asked Hynd.

'I was at peace,' Hynd said. 'I lived in my house,

read books, listened to music, caught fish in the rivers
and in the sea, walked on the hills.'

'Then why did you come away from there?' Carmine
said.

Hynd looked at him with eyes that would have taken
the heart out of any number of ravening Rottweilers.

'That is not the question,' Leopetto said. 'The question is, what did you do before you lived in that solitude
of yours?'

'I was in a kind of British Mafia,' Hynd said, and
could not help smiling a little at this description of MI6.

Leopetto nodded. 'You see,' he said. 'Your life in that
peaceful place was not enough for you. What is his
name? Casson. Casson called to you and here you are.
A man has to live the life of a man.'

'This is all very interesting,' Hynd said, 'but it does
not deal with this madness of Ottavio's. For one thing
I am a foreigner, I have no place in his family. For
another, you, Leopetto, must feel yourself that you are
the man to step into his shoes when he dies. For another,
no one here would accept it, and none of the other
families would accept it. For me, the most important
objection is that I don't want it.'

'All of that is true,' Leopetto said. 'Well, it is an old
man's whim, and these things come and go in their
season. For me, what he says is, is. And as for me, so
it is for all the others.' He swept a hand through the
air in an extended gesture that included first Carmine
and Silvestro; then the house and those within it; the
men lounging at the gate into the courtyard that was
composed of two wings of outbuildings, stables and
coach-houses in their day; and then with both arms he
conveyed the world outside, the sweep of land down

to the coast and the meadows that sloped up to the mountain.

'And meanwhile, I have nothing to complain of,' Hynd said in order to cut all this grandiloquence down to size. 'I may be a prisoner, but I continue to live.'

According to the prevailing social code, this reference to the fact that one of these fine days his throat might be cut was gross, and Leopetto without a pause threw it back in his face.

'It will not be long now,' he said. 'Another week, perhaps two, will decide it.'

The girl Bianca, Ottavio's grand-daughter and his only living descendant, came out of the kitchen with a tray and began to collect the dishes. As she went about it she brushed the back of Carmine's neck with her hand, and he closed his eyes. She was dark-eyed and black-haired, nubile and voluptuous with sex, and the young man was infatuated with her.

That conversation had been at the end of the first week.

During the second week Ottavio took Leopetto and Silvestro and they drove off in the big armoured Mercedes with the bullet-proof tyres.

Hynd and Carmine went for a stroll along the hillside as far as the limit that was permitted to Hynd; the rule was that he be always in view from the house. They sat themselves on a wall and watched a herd of goats forage on the vetch and bent-grass on a meadow strewn with white asphodel. Beyond that the sea, blue and glittering, and the little group of islands that lay on the horizon in the haze.

Hynd took out his wallet and extracted his wad of lire, and began counting.

'Why are you doing that?' Carmine said, and laughed. 'You don't need money here.'

'It helps me to think of the day when I will be a free man again.'

'It's a lot of money for a man to carry about with him.'

'You think so?'

Carmine laughed again, but there was a quality to the laugh that struck Hynd as encouraging. He put the money away and they went back to the house.

Ottavio did not return that evening. That night, when Hynd was in his bedroom, leaning out of the window and having a last smoke before going to bed, and watching the companionable glow of the cigarette in the mouth of the man who would guard that side of the house till dawn, the key on the outside of the door turned softly and the door opened.

'It is I, Carmine,' the voice said on a whisper. 'Come away from the window,' and he closed the door silently behind him, and came, a shadow in the darkness, into the room.

'What is it?' Hynd said.

'I want to talk to you.'

'All right.' Hynd let his cigarette drop out of the window. 'You take the bed, then,' and he found the wooden chair for himself.

'What you call this madness of Ottavio's,' Carmine said.

'Which I do not share.'

'Nor I.'

'Ah,' Hynd said. 'A man who lives in the real world.'

'Maybe. I don't know how real I am these days. But

no matter. The Don will want you to marry Bianca, so as to bring you into the family.'

'Jesus Christ,' Hynd said, acting like anything. 'You know this? It is a fact?'

'I know it for a fact,' Carmine said grimly, 'and I will not allow it.'

'How will you prevent it?'

'I will kill you,' Carmine said, 'if that is what it comes down to.'

'That is an imperfect idea, surely,' Hynd said. 'What would happen after you had killed me?'

'The Don would probably kill me. He is hot-tempered and crotchety, and you are a guest in his house, which is one thing. And if he is still devoted to this madness of his I will have thwarted him, and he will kill me for that. Yes, everything says he would kill me, it does not even have to be explained in these ways. It was what he would do. He would do it first and think about it later.'

'Be assured, I shall not marry Bianca.'

There was a silence.

'How can I be sure of that,' Carmine said, 'while you are still here?'

There was another silence. Carmine gave a deep breath. 'She is mine,' he said. 'We love each other.'

'How do we know the Don is not playing with me?' Hynd said. 'Perhaps it is merely a pretence to keep me quiet until he decides what to do with me.'

'I have thought of that. Even if that is true, it's not all there is to it.' Another of those deep breaths. 'Bianca says to me that she loves me, but she wants to be sure. She says she has never seen a man like you.'

'Hell and death,' Hynd said. 'She might as well say

she's never seen an elephant. She knows nothing at all about me. She would hate to know a man like me. And to me she is only a child, and men of my age do not find children interesting: they are callow and unformed, and ignorant of life. Tell her that, if you like. All the same, I wish to God I was out of here.'

'Yes,' said Carmine. 'So do I.'

'I need time to think. When does Ottavio come back?'

'Tomorrow,' Carmine said, and added incautiously, 'when everything is settled.' He stood up. 'Do your thinking. I will go now.'

He slipped from the room as quietly as he had entered it.

After he had gone Hynd sat motionless in the dark, doing his thinking, as Carmine had said. He was thinking, though, not about Ottavio's ideas in regard to him, whether real or pretended; but that Carmine had said Ottavio would be home tomorrow 'when everything is settled'.

If he could learn in the next few days what it was that had been settled – presumably the where and when of the Casson–Mafia joint operation – then he could get himself out of here. Beyond that, he could not make a plan. He could not see himself being able simply to walk onto a plane at Palermo, or any other airport on the island. He thought he knew how he might get away from the house, but after that not a road would be safe, no house or hotel would be a safe shelter. He would in every respect be in the position of a man on the run in enemy country.

He knew that he would be likely to manage that and escape the island in the end, but time was important.

Whatever he managed to learn he would want to pass onto Harry Seddall. He would not be able to use a telephone anywhere in this countryside, at any kiosk or in any café or restaurant. Even if he were rash enough to go to Palermo, it would be the same there. Parentucelli would see to that. Among them Ottavio and Parentucelli, and all the other Ottavios who acknowledged Parentucelli's sway, would have half the population of western Sicily looking out for him.

This time, he thought, a letter would hardly do. The date set for the operation must be close, and he would have at most two or three days' notice of it. He wondered if the letter he had sent from Puglia had reached Seddall, and doubted it. At first, when he had heard them talking about a man who had turned up in a nearby village, he had thought it might be someone sent by Seddall. But, since visitors were so unusual here, first Silvestro had gone to inspect him and came back saying it was a Frenchman with a taste for the bottle, and then old Ottavio had gone down to see for himself, and said yes, it was true, the Frenchman was indeed a military historian, as a man of theirs in the village had reported soon after the newcomer sailed into the bay and set up house. Ottavio listened to him babbling about the battle of Magenta and then came away.

Well, Hynd could still justify the faint hope that Seddall had got the letter and might be able to make a useful move. In any case, he was counting rather a lot of chickens at the moment: he had yet to acquire, if he could, the vital news he wanted to take with him out of the house, and even if he got hold of that, he would still have to achieve the great escape.

Pondering, therefore, these imponderables, he went to bed.

The next day at noon, with the blinding sun high in the sky, the expedition returned, and Ottavio summoned Carmine into conclave over lunch with Leopetto and Silvestro.

Hynd ate in the courtyard in solitary state, alone except for the presences of Niccolo and Ercole, who lounged on old cane chairs, one in the gloom within a stable door to Hynd's left, the other under the lintel of a coach-house to his right, each with a sub-machine gun on his knee. These were in addition to the two men at the gate, whose protection from the sun was provided only by the pair of embittered beech trees at the gate and their straw hats.

Hynd was too stunned by the heat to speculate on what might, or might not, happen when the meeting was over. Affairs were moving towards their crisis, and he would deal with that when he knew what he had to deal with. In the meantime he ate his seventeenth lunch under house arrest. He fed scraps from the antipasto and then the veal to the dog which lay panting under the trestle table, a huge beast with wolfhound in its genes and crossed with some ancient, unknown breed that had probably sprung full-grown from the Sicilian rock, and whose friendship he had diligently cultivated.

He watched the lizards move in their sudden unpredictable courses across the walls, and his mind emptied. The silence of siesta descended on the house. Hynd went to the garden and lay on the grass in the shade of the ubiquitous laurels. The dog lay close by. The two guards with the sub-machine guns came too, and made themselves comfortable at a decent distance, and all four fell asleep.

It was the summons that woke Hynd.

Chapter Twenty-Five

The room was dim, for the shutters were still drawn against the heat, though a wind that had begun to waft off the hills promised a cooler evening.

It took a moment or two, therefore, for Hynd's eyes to adjust from the brightness of the day outside, and, after he had greeted Ottavio sitting there behind his desk, to make out who it was in the low armchair beside the empty fireplace.

Guercio moved his head, but that was all. No one spoke. The room was full of menace, so that Hynd looked about him as if he had come onto a battlefield, to choose where he would place himself. His choice fell on a heavy wooden armchair against the wall on the other side of the room from Guercio and about ten feet from Ottavio.

There was a window beside the chair, and seizing the occasion to take an initiative from this shadowy tribunal Hynd with a sudden movement pushed open the shutters and let the light flood in. He put his elbows on the sill and leaned out.

The window looked over a terrace. Below the terrace was the swimming-pool. The girl was lying in the shade of an umbrella, wearing a bikini. Carmine sat near her and leaned down, talking to her. Hynd felt the sexual hit of her in the pit of his stomach. She was thirty feet away but even so he was aware of it. Whenever he met her he was conscious of it. He supposed it belonged to this moment of her youth, that everywhere she went she gave off that sexual aura, moving around in it as if she walked in a dream.

Something nudged the back of his thigh. It was the infatuated mastiff. He sat down on the tall-backed chair and the dog sat beside him, its head making a rest for his hand.

'Cesare,' Ottavio said. 'Come here.'

The dog went to him obediently, accepted his fondling of its ears and opened its mouth to let him grip its lower jaw, clearly a familiar caress; but when he had finished, it returned to sit beside Hynd, where it moved its head impatiently until he laid his hand on it.

'You see,' Ottavio said to Guercio. 'The dog tells itself that he is the master.'

'All the same,' Guercio said, 'it is folly. A dog is only a dog.'

Hynd looked at Ottavio and all at once saw how old he was, that age had begun to take the life out of him; not just age, he thought. The great Italian anti-corruption drive, the move against the Mafia, the arrests of politicians and mafiosi, the suicides in prison of businessmen who had been leaders in Italian life – all this meant that the ground on which the old man had been accustomed to stand was falling away under his feet.

Hynd thought too that something had gone wrong with the meeting from which Ottavio and Guercio had just come. It came to him that perhaps the menace which he felt in the room was not a hostility from these two men towards him, but that they had brought it with them from the meeting, that it was a threat which covered all three of them.

'This conference you've been to,' he said. 'Something went wrong there?'

'That is not your business,' Guercio said.

'Of course it is his business,' Ottavio said. 'He is of my household, and, also, I need to discuss it with him. I need to find out where he stands.'

'He is not of your household,' Guercio said. 'He is your prisoner, or rather he is our prisoner. You are his jailer. And if you find he stands in the wrong place, what then? You will kill him, eh? And if you think he can be useful, do you think you can trust him in a thing like this? Kill him and have done. We need clear heads and a clear field. Hynd does not belong in this.'

'I saved your damned life for you,' Hynd said. 'What kind of a shit are you?'

'Complete. What kind of a shit are you?'

'No,' Ottavio said. 'This is my house. I will not allow this throwing of insults. We are here to talk business.'

'Then ask him,' Guercio said. 'Ask him if you can trust him, this Englishman you have a fantasy about bringing into your Family.'

Ottavio sighed and bent over the desk and straightened up again. 'Bah,' he said. 'So, it was a fantasy or a whim. I have no sons, and you know him yourself, you know he is hard and strong and quick and ruthless and he has it up here.' He tapped the side of his head. 'He's intelligent and he has experience.'

'And he is not Sicilian.'

Ottavio gave a wonderfully expressive shrug of his whole upper body, defeated and aggressive at the same time, and cracked the flat of his hand down on the desk-top.

'No, he is not Sicilian. But he was here in my house,

328

under my eye, and I could see what he was, who he was. And living here in my house, you understand, as a son of mine might have done if one of them had lived. So I gave myself a little holiday, I gave my brains, my reason, a little holiday, and I tell you it made me feel good, even though all the time I knew it was a day-dream. So shut up, Guercio, hey? And let's get on.'

'Ask him if you can trust him,' Guercio said again.

'Don't be a fool, Guercio,' Hynd said. 'How could I answer a question like that? A minute ago the two of you were asking yourselves whether to kill me now or wait till later. The only reason I didn't kill you both then was that I haven't worked out how to get out of the house in one piece.'

'You could have killed us both?' Guercio said. 'You have a weapon?'

'No,' Hynd said, 'of course I don't have a weapon. I'm a prisoner here.'

'Then how would you have killed us?'

Guercio was not being sceptical; it was genuine curiosity, and Hynd was offended. To him it was an uncouth question to ask a professional, as bad as meeting a lawyer or a doctor at a party and asking them for advice. But he had a hold on his temper now, since he thought he might be about to learn something, so he gave Guercio the simple truth.

'Who knows? I would have decided to do it, and then done it.'

Ottavio said, 'You see, Guercio? I believe him, and you do too. You see what kind of man he is?' These professions of esteem from Ottavio had begun to irritate Hynd, they were too effusive and the source they came from left them valueless as soon as they were uttered, so that he received them as both seedy and untrustworthy.

'Why don't you get down to it?' he said. 'You've got something to say to me. Say it.'

Ottavio gave him a cold eye. It was one thing for Hynd to tell him he'd been ready to take his life back there, it was another to forget the courtesies, the respect.

'What's your deal with Mr Casson?' Ottavio said. 'You had a business relationship with him? You still have it? If you leave here, do you go back to working with him?'

So it was Casson. That could be something to work with, that could be the break. Hynd looked down at the mastiff's brindled scalp and moved his fingers on it. The dog turned its head and gave him a serious look, as if it knew what was going on in him; and as if to say when the hunt started, it would be at his side.

Guercio came in: 'Are you for him or against him? That's what we want to know.'

Hynd said, 'I need to know why you're asking. Give me more.'

Guercio had got one of his cigars going, and he waved it about, pointing it now at Ottavio and now at Hynd.

'Listen to him,' he said to Ottavio, and then to Hynd, 'And when you know why he asks you this, you will tell him either that you hate Casson or you love him, whichever is more politic.'

'No,' Hynd said. 'When I tell you what I feel about Casson, you'll believe me, Guercio. You'll believe me. But it is personal, and I won't give you that until I know why you need to know.'

'Let us have a drink,' Ottavio said, 'and keep our tempers.' He stood up and came out from behind his beautiful desk. He went to a cupboard beside the fire-place and took a bottle of brandy from one shelf and a glass from another, and half filled it and gave it to Guercio. The next one he brought over to Hynd, and the third he took back to the desk.

'I am an old-fashioned man, as well as an old man. Guercio is not so old as I am and not so old-fashioned either, but he is old-fashioned enough. This lad, this Parentucelli, is not like us. Yes, he has all the qualities, he is mafioso of mafiosi, but he does not respect the wisdom of experience. I do not mean only my experience, or Guercio's experience, I mean the experience of the Brotherhood, the history of the Brotherhood.'

He held up his glass to the light from the window beside Hynd and looked into the pale liquor as if to say the wisdom of experience lay there and look what that had come up with. Indeed, it was excellent Cognac, none of the local firewater. Hynd still held his own glass warming in his hand, and had not yet put it to his lips, but he had seen the name Delamain on the bottle.

'We are like the Church,' Ottavio said. 'The Church has known persecution. We are being persecuted now.'

Hynd's mind flew around, first recovering from the comparison between the Mafia and the Church and then asking what persecution was he talking about, the early martyrs? The catacombs in Rome? Yes, by God, he was.

'What does the Church do when persecution becomes extreme?' Ottavio said. 'It lies low – even, it goes under-ground. Parentucelli and the others, most of the others, are waging war against Italy. We have killed judges and prosecutors and politicians, and others. Here in Sicily we have done that. I have done that. At first it made sense, it was a deterrent. But it was not enough, it did not deter, and now there is a whole campaign, now there are arrests by the hundred, confessions from informers. Now politicians and the heads of great companies lie in prison. Some of them commit suicide.'

He emptied his glass at a gulp and shuddered and put it down.

'So,' he said. 'Guercio and I think it is time to lie low. That we should get on quietly with our business, make money. So long as no one is talking about money, no one is talking about anything. That's what I said to them. But they have no ears, they do not listen to me, or to Guercio, or the few who agree with us.

'They bring in this man Casson and this organization of his, and hire them to fight back. So Casson's people have blown up the Uffizi Gallery in Florence. They explode bombs in the streets of Rome and Milan. What will they do next? Will they blow up the Pope? Will they attack the Vatican with helicopter gunships as they did Guercio's villa in the mountains?' He flourished a hand towards the Alps, six hundred miles away.

They had hardly been helicopter gunships, but that did not disturb the sense of Ottavio's argument.

'And since we are talking about the north,' Ottavio said, 'consider how the Lombardy League is growing in strength. Up there is the wealth of Italy. They want an independent state, these people. They want a new state with what they call clean government, no corruption, a wall round it to keep us out. Well,' he shrugged, 'in the end they will find they can't keep us out, but it would be inconvenient, it would disturb business.'

He poured Cognac into his glass and then, remembering the obligation of the host, stood up and went

over to replenish Guercio's glass. Hynd was watching
Guercio as well as Ottavio, watching them both. Ottavio's colour was up, he was saying all this as if he
were a demagogue, boiling over with political passion,
warming himself up to go out and speak to the crowd.
And Guercio was with him all the way, full of unconscious movement, nodding, coming upright in his chair
and leaning forward at the orator, clenching his fist and
then opening it, staring at the palm of his hand, going
off into his own mind, and watching the Cognac now,
filling in his glass, with a wild and distracted eye.

'And that is what Parentucelli and the others want,'
Ottavio said, 'and it is their answer to everything. They
want to destabilize Italy, that is their word. They want it
to break up. So what does that give us? An independent
Sicily? An independent Lombardy, a separate Puglia, a
free Tuscany? Another war like Yugoslavia?'

He took in some Cognac. 'What will that do to us?
What will that do to business? Where will our money
come from then? It is what I said before: so long as no
one is talking about money, my friend, no one is talking
about anything.'

He was leaning over Hynd now. 'Drink.' His voice
was suddenly harsh as if Hynd was showing signs of
being indifferent to the Cause. Hynd drank, and held
out his glass to be filled again. He took no taste of the
brandy, only the fire of it.

Ottavio put the bottle back on the desk but stayed
on his feet. 'My heart is Sicily. My feet are on Sicily.'
He gave a ridiculous smile, half-maniac and half-child,
and actually stamped his way right across the room.
'Wherever I am my eyes see Sicily.' He flung open the
shutters of the window. Even the opera in Palermo

would offer no better melodrama than this.

Ottavio, Guercio, Hynd, and the dog looked out over Sicily and the sea, each of them yielding to the spell of that moment.

'Sicily,' Ottavio said, 'is our birthplace, but it is only our birthplace. We cannot come back only to Sicily, or we shrivel and die. We work, John Hynd, in the fabric of society, of the people, of the whole state, of all Italy, and that gives us a door to the whole world. Parentucelli and this man Casson will bring Italy into chaos if they have their way.'

He went over to the cupboard and put the brandy back on its shelf and shut the door on it, and returned to his place behind the desk, and grew calm.

'Enough of that. Guercio and I told them what we think. Parentucelli embraced me warmly as I left, like a brother, like a son to a father. Therefore it is war.' His eye on Hynd's had a dead and meaningless look, like the eye of a shark. 'I and Guercio must strike first, or we will go down.' His voice became very soft. 'So tell me,' he said. 'How is it between you and Casson?'

'There is blood between us,' Hynd said. 'He owes me blood.'

This was the ancient language of feud, and it went straight home to Ottavio, carrying the certain, atavistic sustenance of his mother's milk.

'Ah!' he said. 'Why is there blood?'

Hynd detested this, to have to speak about her, but he had known it was inevitable and his life hung on it.

'Because of a woman.'

Ottavio's head came forward expectantly, and Guercio said, 'What woman? What is the story?'

Ottavio waved a reproving hand at such impatience; such lack of decorum.

'Casson threatened to cut her throat.'

'She is your woman?' Guercio said.

'Mine? No, I would not say that.'

'Then whose is she?' Guercio said.

The project of trying to explain the idea of a woman's right to her own life to a man like Guercio made even Hynd smile a little.

'Your family?' Ottavio said.

'My tribe.' Hynd thought he could, with honesty, say that of her. There was a sense in which they belonged to the same tribe, a consanguinity not of the accident of birth, but of the spirit.

Guercio made a grimace and a sceptical sound with his lips round the fresh cigar he was lighting.

Hynd crossed the room in a breath and slapped him hard three times across the face. The mafioso's nose began to bleed and the shredded stub of the cigar sat fatuously in his mouth. Hynd reached into his jacket and took his pistol away from him, slipped the magazine out and threw the gun on the floor.

'Guercio,' he said to him. 'You are a vile and shallow man. If you do that again while we are talking of this I'll kill you on the same day I kill Casson, and throw you into his grave for him to lie on.'

Guercio was scarlet with rage. He spat the cigar away and from out of the blood on his face he began to make an extraordinary roaring noise. Hynd moved back from this wretched performance and then saw that the dog was with him. Cesare had planted himself in front of Guercio and was baying him; with the hair on his neck and along the ridge of his back standing up, and his teeth bared, he snarled and barked at Hynd's enemy, ready to tear his throat out.

Guercio was shocked into silence. Then he began saying, 'No,' over and over. 'No,' he said. 'No, no.'

The door opened and Leopetto came in with his gun ready. Ottavio said, 'Quiet, Cesare, quiet,' and the dog went down onto its haunches but stayed there, quivering with the wish to attack and its eyes staring at Guercio, telling him it was not finished yet.

'Thank you, Leopetto,' Ottavio said. 'But there is no problem.' He indicated the door with a smile and a movement of his head and the astonished Leopetto hung there for a moment taking in the scene before him, and then went out and closed the door behind him.

Hynd went to the window that opened on the hillside and the distant sea and leaned there against the wall. The sun laid shadows from the laurels on the heat-smitten grass, and in them, as if he was looking at a scene painted by his mind, he saw Caroline sitting. She sat with her head up, looking not at him but along the slope to some far mountain, or cloud, or bird high in the air. Her hair blew over her eyes and she put a hand up to move it back with that gesture of hers.

Hynd blinked and she was gone. He turned into the room and saw Ottavio watching him, watching him and Guercio and the dog alternately. Guercio was turned sideways in the chair with his eyes turned sideways on the mastiff, which lay now with its head on its paws but still, so far as it was concerned, holding the man at bay.

It was Ottavio who interested Hynd. The old man was showing every sign of pleasure and of what came across as a deep satisfaction.

'You have made your point,' he said to Hynd. 'Call your dog off.'

It was a rare man who would tolerate seeing his own dog give its loyalty to another, but Hynd knew where that came from: it came from Ottavio's investment in his idea of Hynd. And that, too, was where some of his manifest satisfaction came from. Hynd, apparently, had done it again.

'Padrone,' Hynd said, 'your word is my command.' He did not suppose that such levity about what was, after all, at the centre of Ottavio's life – absolute obedience from his following – was likely to succeed, but he had found the line irresistible.

It brought, however, an ironic smile to the old man's face, and for that instant, while Hynd smiled back, the two of them were in a rapport.

'Cesare,' Hynd said. 'Come here,' and then, absurdly, in English, 'Heel, boy, heel.'

The mastiff gave Guercio a last particular look as it rose and turned away, and came in two cheerful bounds, tremendously pleased with itself, to Hynd.

'Stout fella,' he said, and whacked it on the shoulder. 'Come on, then.'

He went back to his chair and sat down, with the dog at his side again.

Ottavio got up, lithe now as a young man. 'Here,' he said, giving Guercio the handkerchief from his breast pocket. 'Wipe the blood off your face. Pull yourself together.'

He stooped and picked up Guercio's pistol and put it in his pocket and, having dusted off, as it were, the aftermath of the late crisis, he resumed his place behind the desk.

Guercio wiped at his face and looked at the blood on the handkerchief and glanced at Hynd, then wadded the cloth with a clean patch uppermost and spat on it and wiped his face again. He threw the handkerchief into the hearth.

He looked at Ottavio, and at Hynd, and back at Ottavio, and his face was expressionless.

'That was too much,' he said to Ottavio. 'He has to die.'

'Don't be a fool,' Ottavio said. 'We know what we wanted to know. He has a grievance against Casson. He is Casson's mortal enemy, because of the threat Casson made against this woman, whoever she is, whatever she is to him. And we know this, Guercio, because you insulted his mention of her – you did not even insult her, only the mention of her, and you saw what he did to you. And you heard what he said. And Casson, Casson threatened to cut her throat.

'So tell me, do you believe it, that if there is one thing he longs to do it is to put Casson away? Or do you not believe it? And tell me, if you believe it, do you think it would be wise to have him on our side against Casson and Parentucelli, or not? This man who rescued you from Casson once before? This man who cleared the road to your house, driving the car you asked him to drive so that if there was an ambush or a bomb laid for you the danger of it would be his? This man who tells us to our faces that he was ready to kill us, here in this room?'

'He insulted me.'

'And you insulted him, by his lights, and I admit they are mysterious to me, but you insulted him. You are even, the two of you. Shall we recruit him for this or not?'

'He will not do it,' Guercio said. 'He is not of us. He is not here to help us. That is not why he came.'

'He will do it,' Ottavio said. 'He is Casson's enemy. Everyone in this house is Parentucelli's enemy, Hynd as well. It is in Hynd's interest, and in his heart,' and Hynd was astonished at the penetration of the look Ottavio cast at him, 'and in his soul, to do this.'

'He must apologize to me.'

'He will not apologize,' Ottavio said. 'Shall we make him one of us, for this little war with Casson and Parentucelli, or are you confident that you, and this old man here who talks to you, can deal with them on our own?'

'That dog is dangerous to me. You must shoot it.'

'No,' Ottavio said. 'The dog behaved as a dog should.'

Guercio said, 'I must think.'

He left his chair and stood in front of the fireplace and looked out of the window onto the sea, looked at Ottavio, at Hynd, at the dog, and out of the window again.

'It may be,' he said, 'that I will agree. But we must have safeguards. We must talk about that. Send him away, just now. Him and the dog. I am too angry to have them in the room with me just now. You and I will talk now, and, later, you will talk to him.'

'Good,' Ottavio said. 'Take the dog, my friend,' he said to Hynd. 'You will find Leopetto outside.'

Chapter Twenty-Six

'I have agreed.'

'What have you agreed?'

'I have agreed to Ottavio's proposal that you may be a help to us,' Guercio said, 'against Casson and Parentucelli.'

'Why have you agreed?' Hynd said.

'Because you are gifted. You are a man of your hands – well, that is common enough – but also you have a cool head and a quick mind. And I have talked with Leopetto and Silvestro and Carmine. They have made a judgement about you. They say that if Parentucelli is against us, we are probably doomed men whatever we do. But that we will fight, of course, and since we are to fight, we will fight better if you are one of us. They are right, and I know it.'

Guercio had come to Hynd where he sat with Leopetto at the table in the courtyard. He had said to Hynd, 'Tell the dog to make friends with me.'

'You wanted to kill him. You wanted to kill me.'

'That is all changed,' Guercio said. 'I had been humiliated. I was in a rage.'

'The humiliation has not been lifted,' Hynd said. 'So why this?'

Guercio gave one of his shrugs. 'Survival. Ottavio is right. We have common enemies, you and I and the dog. We can assist one another.'

Hynd had spoken to the dog, and Cesare had sniffed

Guercio's hand and withdrawn his hostility.

'Good,' Guercio said. 'Let us take a little walk.'

So now they were walking along the hill. Above them rose the mountains, far below them was the bay next to the village, a great sheet of white sand blinding in the sunlight, and beyond that the blue and glittering sea.

'Well then,' Hynd said, 'if we are to fight, where will it be?'

'Parentucelli is like a snake,' Leopetto said. 'He strikes fast. He will come here.'

'How many men do we have?'

'This minute,' Leopetto said, 'here at the house, about twelve. There are a hundred who would come to fight for Don Ottavio, but if it is to fight against Parentucelli we can only count on twenty. And they are good men enough, you understand, but not exceptional.'

'He means they do not have *élan*,' Guercio said. 'And *élan* is what we need if we are to have a chance against Parentucelli.'

'You,' Hynd said to him, 'did not come to Sicily alone?'

'No. I have two men with me, but I left them in Palermo, to spy on Parentucelli.'

'Then I am sorry,' Leopetto said, 'but they are lost men.'

Guercio looked up at him and lifted his chin, as if to say I know, I know. He wiped a handkerchief round the back of his neck. 'This heat,' he said. 'Let us sit under the tree.'

It was an oak tree, not mighty, but it cast a shade.

'What will Parentucelli do?' Hynd said.

'He will want to settle with Don Ottavio and me

before the ship . . . before Casson carries out this great operation of his.'

'That tells me nothing.'

'Very well,' Guercio said with a sigh. 'It gives him three days, no more.'

'His first men may be here tonight,' Leopetto said. 'He will send men into the village, to frighten the people. They will stand and look at the sea, have a drink at the bar. They will do nothing, but they will be there. Only to see his men will let the people know they will be best just to go about their business, and see nothing. They may not even know whose men they are, but they will understand why they are there.'

'If it were you, how many would you send for that?'

'Two cars,' Leopetto said. 'Eight or ten men. Then tomorrow, three or four cars, so he would have, say, thirty or more men. It should be enough.'

'Well,' Hynd said. 'We have the dog, after all.'

The mastiff, at this moment, became aware of an opportunity to display itself in action, and ran on the slant down the side of the hill, barking at the approach of a group of strangers.

The strangers were two men, one of the men respectably dressed in cotton trousers and white shirt, the other man and the woman in shorts. They were fifty or sixty yards off but the appearance of the first man woke a memory in Hynd.

'Talk of the Devil,' he said to himself, and aloud he bellowed to the dog.

Leopetto had put his hand inside his coat, but brought it empty away. 'It is the Frenchman from the Marinelli house,' he said. 'Sciandri said he had friends coming to join him.'

342

Seeing them sitting there under the tree, the Frenchman came on ahead of the others. Hynd did not smile at the sight of Seddall with that scrubby-looking fuzz on his face.

'It is a hot afternoon,' Seddall said. 'May we join you for a moment or two in the shade?' He inclined his head at Leopetto. 'I believe I have seen you in Agnello's,' he said.

'And I have seen you,' Leopetto said, 'although we have not spoken.'

The woman took off her wide-brimmed straw hat and gave her head a shake so that her golden curls tumbled about. She said something in French to Seddall, and Guercio said to her in her own language, 'You are from France also?'

'From Paris,' she said in French. 'We are having a sailing holiday.' She indicated the third man, a stocky man who made the appropriately courteous gestures with head and face. But Hynd watched his eyes, which were unceasingly busy, taking in the three sitting under the tree, the patch of country immediately about them, the terrain that sloped up to the mountains, and the lie of the land along to the shoulder of the hillside, beyond which lay Ottavio's house.

Seddall offered cigarettes, which were accepted by Leopetto and Hynd, and said they had been for a walk, as Madame Oseille wanted to stretch her legs after so many days lounging about on the yacht. Hynd, recognizing the French word for Sorrel, looked at the legs, which were long and tanned, and let that account for his smile.

He caught the gaze of the man with the scouting eyes, fixed on him intently as if the man was trying to read a secret out of him, and he raised an eyebrow, and the man moved and looked down at the sea.

Seddall said they were on their way back to the village, and he supposed that if they went on round the hill they would find a way down.

Leopetto said no, far better to head straight down there, see, using that small white house as marker, and they would find themselves on the road at no distance from the village at all.

Seddall thanked him and said they would be on their way, as he had promised his friends a drink in Agnello's before dinner: he hoped that perhaps he might have the pleasure of seeing the signori at Agnello's, and his eyes left Leopetto's and drifted over Hynd's on their way to say farewell to Guercio.

Then the strangers went down the hill towards the small white house, idlers on holiday, sublimely unaware that they had interrupted a discussion on how to wage a war to the death.

When they were on their way, Guercio said, 'It is time to go back to the house. Ottavio will want to see you.'

Ottavio was brief. His face was sombre now, the elations of the earlier meeting gone. He was the warlord in his age, he was Sforza contemplating the last stand.

'So,' he said. 'It is time to trust each other.' He pushed across his desk an automatic pistol and a box. The pistol was a Beretta. 'It holds twelve,' Ottavio said. Hynd took the lid off the box. Inside it were cartridges and a spare clip.

'And this,' Ottavio said.

He held out to Hynd a sheathed knife. It was very plain, a worn wooden hilt and a nine-inch blade. 'It was my grandfather's. The steel is Milanese. Try it, it is like a razor.'

Hynd felt a moment of fatigue from holding the revered object in his hand, at being endowed with this emblem of a myth that meant nothing to him and meant everything to the old man who gave it to him.

But he tried the blade, and, yes, it was sharp.

'I will go down to the village,' Hynd said. 'I want to see what's going on.'

'Carmine will drive you,' Ottavio said.

'No,' Hynd said. 'I will go alone, and I will walk. I want to get the feel of the place. Besides, Carmine must care for your grand-daughter.'

'I have sent the girl away. I have sent all the women away. If some of Parentucelli's men come tonight, there could be among them some of those who were at Lecce, and who will recognize you.'

'Let them. Parentucelli, will he come?'

'Perhaps not tonight,' Ottavio said, 'but he will come. To do what he means to do, to exterminate me and the men of my Family, he must come. He would dishonour both himself and me if he did not.'

Hynd turned to go.

Ottavio said, 'At the meeting in Palermo we discussed this business that Casson and his people are to do. Casson was there.'

Hynd did not move, but spoke to the window through which he had watched Carmine and the girl. 'Are you saying that Casson will be with Parentucelli?'

'I am saying only that he was in Palermo,' Ottavio said. 'He and a Russian called Murashov. Murashov sailed here on the ship they are going to use, all the way from the Baltic.'

'The ship?' Hynd said. 'You forget, Ottavio, I know nothing about a ship. I am trusted only to fight for you.'

'Why should I not tell you?' Ottavio said. 'Tomorrow, this week, everything ends for me. It is another of their grandiose ideas. By now the ship will be lying in the Gulf of Sirte. She is going to raid a prison island down to the south of Sicily to set free many men of the Mafia who are imprisoned there.'

'So,' Hynd said. 'Casson and a man called Murashov. Any others with them?'

'Two or three,' Ottavio said. 'They did not come into the meeting. Murashov was returning to the ship, I don't know about the others.'

'If he has men to back him,' Hynd said, 'I think Casson will come. To see for himself what happens here.'

Ottavio was about to comment on this but Hynd, still looking out of the window, spoke again.

'They are falling into my hand,' he said, 'like ripe pears.'

The Don looked at him, and wondered what he was looking at. He saw a man not of extraordinary size, and if anything slightly built rather than otherwise; a man who did not fill a room with any magnetism of his presence; a man, indeed, who where he went inhabited a quiet, yes, a man who moved in quiet, like a religious.

He saw a man armed only with a pistol and a knife, who spoke of an invasion by these Palermitans and their outlandish allies as if they were so many rows of wheat who would, since to him it was the natural order of things, fall to the edge of his scythe.

Either the man had gone mad, or he was always like

this. At this moment the man turned to him and, as if he saw what was in Ottavio's mind, smiled to himself, and went to the door and out.

An extraordinary lassitude came over Hynd on the way to the village, as if the moment of fatigue that had come over him when he was solemnly presented with the grandfather's knife had waited till now to demand fuller expression. It was a lassitude of the spirit, whatever it was about, but its effect was physical.

He thought he would be glad to be done with all this, and back in his house, just himself, his books, his music, his thought, the hills and the cold northern sea.

Just himself, in his chosen place. Just himself.

He stopped and looked around him, but he did not see far. He did not see the perpetual blue sky, the eternal sea, the loom of the mountains.

He saw only himself, content and alone.

Without thought he lay down on the grass at the roadside. In these pictures of himself back in his own life, he had conjured up no image of Caroline Swift.

Why was this? Was it that in coming out from his fastness and throwing himself again into the world that had once been his, the world of action and risk where he played his own hand, made the rules himself and relied only on himself, he had returned to reality and escaped – he flinched at the word but held to it – from a chimera of his own making: not of hers?

He felt cautiously in his spirit and in his heart, with a sense of nourishing a kind of tentative hope, a hope so delicately poised between being and not being that it must not be too richly fed by his attention, by his noticing of it.

He lay with his hand over his eyes against the glare

of the day and felt his body relax, and his spirit with it; felt the actual muscle of his heart relax, as if it had been freed of a burden.

Shakespeare came to him: 'Richard's himself again,' and with that a resilient surge of wellbeing that led to the bombast – he knew it was bombast but that was all right with him – of, 'Come the three corners of the world in arms, and we shall shock 'em.'

Why the three corners? Why three? He must find out when he got home.

He sat up suddenly and glanced about him alertly, and said aloud, 'Then why do it?'

He saw the white dust of the road, he looked back the way he had come, and then along the way he was going. He moved his head from side to side, hearing the tensions at the back of the neck come loose. He looked at the palm of his hand, and then peered, blinking, at the sky.

'Why?' he said. 'Why? Because I will do it, that's all. I will do it without cause, for my own hand.'

Chapter Twenty-Seven

At Agnello's in the early evening there were not so many of the old men there as usual. A few hours ago a black car had driven off the road at the edge of a field that belonged to Giulio Bisticci, and five men had got out of it and stamped around, stretching their legs.

Bisticci was busy in the next field, and went on being busy while he watched them. After a while he knew what kind of men they were, and he sent his son Guido, the twelve-year-old, down by the paths away from the road to let the village know.

At a table outside the bar Harry sat with Sciandri and with the young Adonis, taking their ease in the evening air. But Sciandri was less at ease than his companions.

When the fisherman went into the bar to get wine, Mark Sedgwick said, 'Something's up.'

'Yes,' Harry said. 'I wonder if this is it.'

Sedgwick looked where Seddall was looking and saw a car come to rest by the harbour's edge. Five men got out of it and stared about them, and then came towards the bar.

Sciandri, emerging with three glasses in his hands, did not see the men until he had placed the glasses on the table and sat down. When he did see them he jerked his head back as if to look at Heaven for a moment, and then put out his hand and drank half the wine in it at a gulp.

The men approached. 'You,' one of them said to Seddall, sitting there in his old shirt and trousers with his unkempt beard, 'where is the man Sciandri?'

'Sciandri?' Seddall said. 'I think he is still out in his boat.'

'You are not Sicilian,' the man said at Seddall's accent. He was a man of enormous size.

'No,' Seddall said.

'What are you?'

Seddall looked at him and said nothing.

Sciandri stood up and opened his mouth to speak.

The man with all the questions took Seddall's head in both hands and began to squeeze it. Seddall had never known anything like it. His head began to sing. He felt his skull being crushed in on his brain. He felt he was losing consciousness and scrabbled for his revolver.

The young Adonis was on his feet and the knife in his hand went an inch into the big man's side. The big man let go of Seddall's head and stepped away from him as he turned to see what was stinging his side.

'That's right,' Sedgwick said, and pushed the knife in all the way, and then as the man stood, tottering like a colossus in an earthquake, Sedgwick drew his pistol and at the same time gave the man a shove so that he fell over.

Seddall drew the Smith and Wesson but he could not see well and shook his head to clear his eyesight.

The next thing he heard shouts, gunfire, bullets whacking into the wall beside him, one spinning off forever whining like a giant mosquito; and through all this noise he saw before his bloodshot and tear-filled eyes a dance of dark figures in a glittering brightness.

Then silence, and the stink of cordite, and his eyes cleared, and the revolver was still unfired in his hand.

Five men lay dead on the stones.

Mark Sedgwick stood out there with his hair wild and gilded in the sunlight, shoving the spare clip into his pistol, looking at another man standing ten paces off with a gun in his hand.

The other man slowly let his gun arm fall, and Sedgwick did the same. The newcomer walked round the bodies of the vanquished, and gave something between a nod and a bow to Mark Sedgwick as he came.

'Hello, Seddall,' John Hynd said coolly. 'That's a good man you've got there.' Sedgwick was semaphoring reassuring signals to Kit Fraser and Sorrel on the deck of the ketch.

Harry saw that Fraser had binoculars focused on the bar and stood up and waved to show that he was in one piece, and then sat down again. He looked at Sciandri, who had an odd expression on his face; the cast of it was still grim from the killings, but there was a slight turn to the mouth and a glint in the eyes.

Men came out of the bar and regarded the corpses on the ground.

'Who's your friend?' Hynd said, picking up Sedgwick's chair, which had been overturned in the excitement, and settling into it.

'Paolo Sciandri,' Harry said, and presented them to one another.

'You are a man of Ottavio's,' Hynd said.

'And you are the man who has been staying at his house,' Sciandri said.

'There may be another car to come,' Hynd said. 'It

might be a good thing if all the bodies disappeared, and the car too.'

'Whose men were they?' Sciandri said.

'Parentucelli's.'

Sciandri shuddered, or shook himself.

'Sciandri,' Hynd said, 'it is done. Now tell me, does Parentucelli have anyone here, living here?'

'No.'

'If the bodies are removed, and the blood washed off the stones,' Hynd said, 'will anyone here tell the story when more of Parentucelli's men come?'

'No one,' Sciandri said. 'Not even the children. This is Ciascia, not Palermo. The bodies can be put in Agnello's cellar. The car can be hidden.'

Sciandri got up and went to the men gathered round the bodies, which had already been despoiled of their guns. Now the watches were taken from their wrists and the money from their pockets, and they were carried into Agnello's. A hose was run out from the bar to wash the dead men's blood away.

Hynd reported to Seddall what Ottavio had told him about the *Baikal*, and Seddall went into the bar to pass this news on to Fawcett on the telephone.

Hynd and Sedgwick sat in the evening sun and talked.

By the time Harry emerged, Kit Fraser had sculled ashore from the ketch and was in conclave with the other two.

'Got through,' Harry said, 'for a miracle. Now, will you please tell me, Hynd, what this is all about, and who these fellows were.'

Hynd told him about the state of war between the factions of mafiosi.

'They have a plan,' Fraser said.

'Tell me.'

They told him.

'But this is merely a plan that may, or may not, rescue Don Ottavio from his predicament,' Harry said. 'Why should we take part in a Mafia war?'

'Because,' Hynd said, 'it may give me Casson.'

'Give us Casson,' Seddall said.

'No,' Hynd said. 'I am at feud with Casson. And you want Casson dead, because there is nothing else that will remove the threat he represents, but you are unable to say so. I want to kill Casson, and I will kill him.'

Seddall thought. He remembered that young Dodo had wanted to be here, and came out with a laugh that made him feel ill with himself. He walked over to the edge of the water and looked northwards over the sea. It was wine-dark under the declining sun. Homer had been right about that.

Then he thought: this Hynd is a very Odysseus for ingenuity.

He went back to the group at the table.

'I want to go over to the ketch,' he said, 'and I want Kit with me.'

Hynd looked at him with a thought in his face.

'What is it?' Seddall said.

'The inner council,' Hynd said, 'you and Fraser going off to deliberate. The wiser heads.'

'Perhaps,' Seddall said. 'Be that as it may, I don't want to be out on the boat when the next lot of panzers come in from Palermo. Can we put a watch on the road?'

'There is a watch on the road,' Hynd said. 'There is a watch on the Palermo road from a house with a telephone about ten kilometres out, and there is a watch on the Cefalu road as well, because you never know, do you? Sciandri has taken the Mercedes to hide it in a barn along there, so I asked him to stay there and keep his eyes open.'

Sculling Seddall out to the ketch, Fraser said, 'He's bloody competent, that man Hynd.'

'Yes,' Seddall said, 'but right now I'm thinking that bloody is the operative word.'

They sat on the deck of the ketch under the deep blue of the sky that was the beginning of night.

'Those killings,' Seddall said. 'What do you think?'

'I don't know,' Fraser said. 'It was all over before I knew it was happening. Didn't see it.'

'Why, Harry?' Sorrel said. 'What are you thinking?'

'To tell you the truth,' Seddall said, 'I don't know what I think either. Yes, I do. I think Hynd and Sedgwick are too good at it. They like it too much. And now they're planning another, another two, in fact, if Casson does turn up.'

'You don't really have a complaint, you know,' Fraser said. 'It has to be done. They do it and then they stop.'

'I see that,' Seddall said. 'But there's another side too. What do you think of Sedgwick?'

'I think he's a bloodthirsty little tyke.'

'And Hynd?'

'We know about Hynd,' Fraser said. 'Hynd is driven.'

Seddall said, 'The effect is the same.'

'No,' Sorrel said. 'To say that is not to say enough. They're both sensitive and emotional men.'

'Well, yes,' Seddall said. 'We can say we know that about Hynd, though by God it's not what he's showing just now. But how can you say that about Sedgwick?'

'I came down on this boat with him,' Sorrel said, and was glad that the night had come for she felt the heat rise on her face. 'We talked quite a bit.'

'I don't get it, Harry,' Fraser said. 'If Casson does come on the scene tomorrow there's a fair chance that this weird operation will actually turn out a success, and you won't get a medal but the top chaps will be frightfully pleased.'

'It's such a disgusting idea,' Harry said. 'And I feel like an interloper, in fact laying all these bodies out again in the sun, it makes me feel like the Gestapo in World War Two.'

'Laying the bodies out in the sun?' Sorrel said.

'It's what Hynd wants to do tomorrow,' Fraser said. 'To get this Palermo mafioso's goat and intimidate his men, so that they wonder who on earth they're up against. There's more to it than that, but that's the centre of it.'

Sorrel shivered. 'No, it doesn't sound pretty,' she said.

'None of this is pretty,' Fraser said. 'These are absolutely unscrupulous men coming to kill people, and Hynd's plan could work for us. Anything that disconcerts the enemy is advantage to us. You know how finely these things balance, in war.'

Seddall looked up at the stars. It was that sudden notion of Odysseus that had got to him, and the fierce suddenness of the night down here, and the ferocity of the heat and glare of the sunlight, and the quick simplicity of the killing and the bodies lying there on the stones, and the easy acceptance of it all by these Mediterranean villagers.

And this too: the part Caroline Swift had played in

it, as if she were Helen of Troy, and as if she and the rest of them were driven by the Fates, and nothing had changed in two thousand years, or however long it had been.

'You're right,' he said. 'You're right. It's just another mission and with luck the mission statement is about to be fulfilled. I need a holiday, and this is not it. We'll do it. Let's get back on shore.'

They rowed ashore and found Hynd and Sedgwick still at the table, in the glow of light from the door of the bar.

'Yes,' Harry said. 'We'll do it.'

'Good,' Hynd said. 'Now we wait for the second car.'

'If it comes,' Fraser said.

'They are bound to send one,' Hynd said, 'not having heard from their advance party. You must deal with it as you think fit. I'll go now, and prepare Ottavio for tomorrow.'

When it was night, and the people of the village either watched, or dreamed, or slept, the second car came.

Hynd was up at Ottavio's lair, which was now armed at all points, and Fraser and Seddall and Sorrel Blake were below decks on the big ketch, but Mark Sedgwick, lurking in an alley, was there when the car drove in. He saw it run past the mouth of the alley and heard the rasp of the handbrake and the slamming of car doors.

Silent on bare feet he ran to the corner. He made out three men standing in conclave. One of them got back in the car beside the driver and it moved down to the harbour with its headlamps on full, presumably in the hope that they might reveal to the nocturnal visitors some hint as to why the men of theirs who had come here in the afternoon had not returned.

The two on foot walked before the car, one on either side, to take full advantage of the illumination thrown by the lights. They saw nothing but closed houses; a two-wheeled cart standing on its end with the shafts pointing to the sky; a startled cat, with something in its mouth, glaring then vanishing over a wall. The car turned and went along the edge of the harbour, its lights shining on Agnello's bar and the stones in front of it, from which all blood had been washed and all ejected cartridges removed.

It went down past Agnello's and turned up a lane there, and the fruitless search went on. Half a dozen times the men on foot beat a tattoo on the doors of houses. Each time they did this a shutter was thrown open and questions were shouted and answered, and each time the colloquy led nowhere. Sedgwick's Italian was slight and he could make little of the Sicilian dialect, but he could tell enough from tones of voice and the body language of the peripatetic inquisitors to know that they were learning nothing.

Sooner or later, it seemed to Sedgwick, the invaders would see that this way of proceeding was pointless, and take a man or woman to extract the truth by violence or torture.

It was at the seventh house that their patience broke. The two men shouted furiously up at the man at the open window, and the man sitting beside the driver got out of the car and joined them, gesticulating at the door.

Upstairs, the shutter was pulled in with a bang. They began hurling themselves at the door, first one and then another crashing a shoulder into it or kicking it.

Time to play, Sedgwick said to himself.

He ran up in the dark of the street and when he was thirty feet from them he took his pistol in his hand, went down on one knee, steadied his breathing and, ignoring the man who was taking his turn at battering the door, shot each of the other two in the leg. It took three shots but the light was imperfect and the targets had been making unpredictable movements of anger and frustration, their limbs passing back and forth against the rear lights of the car.

Good enough, he said, as the two men fell, one on the road and the other against the back of the car, where he sprawled briefly and slid to the ground.

Sedgwick ran like a hare for thirty yards, sheltered by the dark, and when he ducked in behind an abutting wall the sound of the shots was still echoing in his ears.

He looked down the street. The man who had been attacking the door was standing now pressed against it, looking up the street to where the muzzle flash had lit the night. He shouted to the driver of the car, and its lights went out.

Sedgwick waited, on the *qui vive* for them to come in search of the invisible marksman. Then he heard shuffling sounds and groans and curses, and soon the shutting of the car doors. The lights flared again and it went off in a racing start, tyres squealing.

He made his way in the other direction through the warren of lanes and alleys until he came out on the harbour and saw the car run out into the open space and turn away from him, into the street where it had entered the village. He watched its lights climb the road away from the village, and vanish into the night.

He went to the quayside and waited, since they

would have heard the shooting on the ketch, and at the same moment that he heard the careful plash of sculls saw the dinghy.

It was Kit Fraser. 'What's up?' Fraser said.

Sedgwick told him.

'You put the wind up them nicely, by the sound of it,' Fraser said. 'And they never saw hide or hair of you?'

'No.'

'That's not bad,' Fraser said. 'They might just think there are an awful lot of us lurking about the place. Here, I'll steady the ladder while you climb down.'

Sedgwick ignored this. 'What's happening about the *Baikal*?' he said. 'Are we going to sail out and board her with cutlasses in our teeth?'

'You can take this death or glory stuff too far,' Fraser said. 'The *Baikal*'s too rich for our blood. Fawcett's fixing something up from London. God knows what, though. Right, come aboard. I want to get my beauty sleep.'

'No,' Sedgwick said. 'I'll hole up here somewhere.'

'You're an odd fish,' Fraser said.

'Thanks,' Sedgwick said. 'It's always good to be acknowledged.'

He went out along the road to Seddall's empty cottage, and lay on the parched gras. A dog that Seddall would have recognized came out of nowhere and, after they had spoken together, settled down beside him, and there they slept.

Chapter Twenty-Eight

In London it was still hot, but thunder was in the offing. The air under the grey and weighted clouds was breathless and enervating, the humidity noxious to activity, both physical and mental.

They were an informal gathering at young Deborah's father's house in Kensington, a council of war in the garden: Fawcett and his Dodo, and Jane Kneller, whom Seddall had advised Fawcett to rope in as a woman of mature wisdom, influence, and a mind of her own – which meant, in fact, that when all about him had been losing their heads, she had seen and shared Seddall's point of view.

'Mature doesn't seem quite the right word,' Fawcett said to Dodo as he helped her dump the remains of their al fresco supper in the kitchen. 'She looks rather young to me for someone in her position, and she looks absolutely stunning in those white leggings. You'd look good in those.'

'And that vest thing from Whistles,' Dodo said, looking down from the window at the white figure sitting alone on the lawn. 'She does have lovely long legs, I must say. The leggings are probably Marks and Sparks. They're as good as anybody's and they do fit skin-tight. What I can't make out, though, is what she's wearing underneath them.'

'What on earth do you mean?' Fawcett said, much intrigued.

'Well, there's no panty line,' Dodo said, 'and there would be if she was wearing any.'

'Perhaps she's wearing nothing underneath,' Fawcett said.

'Darling, of course she is,' Dodo said, 'wearing something, I mean. These leggings are as thin as anything, and she's not an ash-blonde. It would show here.' And Dodo, who was wearing floppy yellow shorts, put her hand to her crotch.

Fawcett graduated from being much intrigued to being perfectly astonished. 'Is this how women always talk about each other?' he said.

'Of course,' Dodo said. 'Here, take this.' She handed him a tray with coffee things on it.

They heard the street door slam. 'That'll be Daddy,' Dodo said. 'Wait, take this.' She put another mug on the tray. 'He'll probably come and join us. We'll be out in a minute.'

She went through to the front of the house. Her father was a tall, ruddy, craggy-faced man with wild white hair – wild now that he was retired from the Diplomatic, as he called it.

He affected such archaic mannerisms to distance himself from what he regarded as the callow, timid, incompetent milksops who in these degenerate times administered the nation's fortunes. He was, however, an inveterately cheerful man (did not brood over the Government's weakness of nerve, the blandly executed decimation of the Armed Forces in the face of an increasingly naughty world, or the modern Foreign Office habit of rationalizing itself into impotence over any international crisis that cropped up, but relished every act of folly or pusillanimity that justified his scepticism) and a full-blooded hedonist.

He served much in the East, and gave himself impartially to those aspects which suited his nature of Sufism, Buddhism, and the gods and goddesses, and even the animism, of the sub-continent. At the age of sixty-three, he would describe himself to a woman over their first dinner-date as having an eclectic soul, and as being a spiritual sensualist. Since this made good hearing, and was in any case pretty much the truth, and since also he had both a charismatic and an animal magnetism, and kept himself as fit as a fiddle, he led a vivacious life.

His friendship with his daughter was close, and since he had chosen to retire early after the death of his wife eight years before, this had brought him much happiness.

Dodo relieved him of his jacket, and took his arm. 'We're having a conference in the garden,' she said. 'Come and help.'

'Top Secret?' he said.

'Classified to the teeth,' she said.

'Good,' he said.

At the door that opened to the garden she came to a stop.

'Daddy, darling,' she said. 'Where would I get a plain white G-string, very small and plain, you know, just a tiny triangle?'

'Well,' he said, 'not in a posh lingerie shop, they'd have them all gussied up with lace to justify the price. You might find one in Soho. What's it for? Fancy dress party?'

'Come into the garden and see,' she said. 'You'll

work it out when you meet Jane Kneller.'

Which he did, in no more than the space of time it took him to say, 'How d'you do?'

'And you remember Mick Fawcett?' Dodo said.

He was manifestly struck by Jane Kneller, but he was able to say that yes, he remembered Mick Fawcett.

His daughter too was struck by Jane, but from a different cause. If Dodo herself had been so visibly admired on a first meeting, she knew that, despite her best efforts, her behaviour would have shown it, and that at the least she would have felt the colour come up in her face. All that showed in Jane was an amused comment in the cerulean eyes.

She was already a little in awe of Ms Kneller, as a woman of some power in Whitehall, and as an example of complete and quietly owned confidence. To see her also as the seductive and (in the present case) coolly distanced woman was something else again. A role model, in short, was in the process of presenting herself to Deborah Meadowhay.

'Dodo kindly invited me to come and help,' her father said. 'Pray enlighten me, therefore, as to the subject of your conference, if, that is, you are willing to break your obligations of secrecy so far as to confide in me. Dodo is one thing, but you two might hold a different view.'

A gust of wind came out of nowhere and Jane put up a hand to brush the pale sandy hair off her face. It was a practical gesture, an efficient movement, with no input of charm, never mind flirtatiousness, in it. Dodo decided to practise this.

'I take it we are all friends here,' Jane said, 'so I shall say, Sir William, that I am acquainted with the outline of your career, and I would be happy to open to you the question we have to deal with.'

'Thank you,' he said, 'and let's not be ceremonious. Call me Will. Briefed yourself on me when you knew you were coming here, I take it?'

'In some things,' Jane said, 'I like to know where I'm going.'

'I also,' Sir William said. 'So who's going to fill me in?'

'I should do that,' Mick Fawcett said. 'It's my operation, or will be if it ever gets off the ground.'

'Give me coffee, Dodo,' Sir William said. 'Embark on the narrative, Mick.'

While it was told him he leaned back and looked up at the sky, where the thunderclouds were moving off to the east and a fresher sky began to offer promise of a real summer evening.

'I see your predicament,' he said, when Fawcett was done. 'It would take seventeen meetings before the Navy was allowed to act, if it was allowed to act, and it wouldn't be. The Italians would not be quite so pussyfooting as us, nobody could be, but it needs to be done, the *Baikal* needs to be sunk without trace and without survivors' – Dodo felt a little strange in her stomach at this cool estimate of the requirement – 'by dusk tomorrow. We can assume the *Baikal* would go in at night: dark lends confusion to the deed. And our lines of communication with Italy are one thing, but beyond these are the lines of communication within the Italian government and bureaucracy, and we do not know that they are cleansed of friends of the Mafia, and, to all intents and purposes, the *Baikal* is at the moment on charter to the Mafia. Let me think.'

He consulted the sky, he consulted the long Kneller legs, he consulted the roses on the wall, and again the white-sheathed legs. He drew in a breath, his bright blue eyes looked at each of them with the dawning of an idea, and he rose abruptly and went into the house.

'He likes you awfully,' Dodo said to Jane. 'I can tell.'

'Nothing of the sort,' Jane said with a laugh that Dodo could only think of as merry. 'He fancies me, that's all.'

'He'd be dashed slow in the wits if he didn't,' Fawcett said.

'Thanks,' Jane said. 'And that's enough of that, I think. We are here to discuss different matters than these. I wonder if he's come up with something, it rather looked as if he has, and if he has, I wonder if it's something I want to know about.'

'You won't know till you've heard it,' Fawcett said, 'and by then it'll be too late to worry about it.'

'Quite right. I suppose I'm being pompous because you made me feel a bit focused-on back there.'

What extraordinary candour, Dodo thought, and thought too that if she was to aspire to emulate this woman she'd have to make it a long-term project. Some qualities, it was plain, came only with maturity.

Her father came striding down the garden with a newspaper in his hand.

'Took me a moment or two to find it,' he said. 'Last week's *Daily Telegraph*.'

He gave it, folded, to Jane Kneller, and indicated a photograph on the top half of the page.

She studied the picture and read the caption underneath. Her face became grave and deeply thoughtful.

When she spoke at last it was to say, 'I don't know. I really don't know.'

'You don't think they'd do it?' Sir William said.

'It's not that. In fact, I think they might.'

'So do I,' he said. 'I know the Ruler was really pissed-off with the Mafia, only last year, over a hotel he was building in Milan.'

'You were never stationed there, am I right?'

'No, but Tommy Masterson was, his last posting and one of his most agreeable, he said. Got to like the Ruler awfully. Tommy went there for a holiday in November.'

'What are we talking about?' Fawcett said. 'May I please see that photograph?'

Dodo was quite impressed by his commanding tone, considering that he was addressing a retired ambassador and a Home Office luminary.

Jane handed it to him, and Dodo looked over his shoulder while he examined it. It showed four fast patrol boats belonging to a Middle Eastern state that had been completely overhauled at a Toulon shipyard, and whose crews had been working up there, preparatory to sailing for the Red Sea by way of the Suez Canal.

'Why was the Ruler pissed off?' Fawcett asked Dodo's father.

'Extortion,' Sir William said. 'He expected to have to pay something, of course, he knows his way around. He's been involved in a few building projects round the world, Europe, South America, United States, by way of investing his oil profits. He expects to pay his protection money and to grease the facilitating palm. In this case, though, the Mafia went over the top, by his way of it. When his construction agent haggled over price, they shot him dead. The Ruler was deeply offended. I'd think he would be extremely pleased to get back at them. It would redeem his honour, cleanse his escutcheon, so to speak.'

'If it got out, however,' Jane Kneller said, 'in the press, I mean.'

'My dear Jane,' he said. 'Why should it get out? The Ruler himself would prefer simply to do it, and keep quiet about it after. He'd not like it talked about. The Government needn't know about it, so it won't leak. You and Tommy Masterson between you could fix it up with him. In fact Tommy can do that, but the Ruler might want a more formal assurance than one of us retired johnnies can give that it would suit HMG's book and would not be working against our interest in any way, simply from someone still in post, as it were. I do promise you.'

'Both of you seem to know what you're talking about,' Dodo said, 'but I don't. What *are* you talking about?'

'What they're talking about,' Fawcett said, 'is getting these boats to the Gulf of Sirte on their way home and sinking the *Baikal* with all hands as they pass. Am I right?'

'Spot on,' Sir William said. 'They've got twin 30 millimetre Oerlikons, these boats, they'll sink the *Baikal* in no time at all, eliminate any survivors, and be on their way. No one will be any the wiser.'

'What about spy satellites?'

'Spy satellites, dear boy, are not owned by the media,' Sir William said. 'And the operators and crew of this vessel, consisting as I understand it of former intelligence agents who've gone into business for themselves, are by definition anathema to those who control spy satellites. So that if, which is in any case not likely, a spy satellite is passing over the Gulf of Sirte at the time and identifies a brief naval action, that will swiftly be correlated with the cursory report your Colonel Seddall will make for onward transmission to the intelligence agencies of concerned countries saying only, for example: "*Baikal* sunk with all hands, date and time." '

Her father was in his element, this was evident.

'Shall I call Masterson?' he asked, of Jane and Mick.

These two looked at each other, and reached agreement. 'I'll just get you the profile of the *Baikal*,' Mick said. 'It's in my briefcase in the drawing-room.'

'My telephone, I take it,' Sir William said, 'is not bugged? You will have checked that too,' this to Jane Kneller, 'since you like to know where you're going?'

'Second nature,' she said. 'No, it's not bugged. Take this,' and she handed him a card. 'It has my home telephone number on it. I'll be home in an hour, if Mr Masterson wants to talk to me.'

Some time after, in a royal palace in the Middle East, the Ruler went out onto a balcony and looked westward, and took the dagger from his scabbard and felt the edge of it, and put it away again, and went back within. And that night, he was wonderful to the woman in his bed.

Chapter Twenty-Nine

Ottavio sat alone at the table in front of Agnello's bar wearing a white suit and under a straw hat, with his hands clasped on an old-fashioned Malacca cane. A hundred feet away, Sedgwick sat on a bollard looking out over the bay.

Other than Ottavio and Mark Sedgwick, there was not a living soul to be seen. Hynd had told the Don what he planned, and Ottavio had succumbed to what was, to him, the elegance of the scenario Hynd had outlined to him.

'If I live,' the old man had said, 'then perhaps I have another few years. If I am killed, it will be a good way to die.'

Then he had studied Hynd in silence for almost a minute, with the cold dispassion of a professional gambler who has staked his all on the turn of a card. 'I was not mistaken in you,' he had said.

He sat now – the goat staked out to draw the tiger – with no more protection than an ancient umbrella that still bore on its rim some of the letters that spelled Cinzano, and fortified by nothing stronger than a bottle of Pellegrino water, and began to wait.

What young men like Hynd did not know was that there was a time in a man's age when death became a friend. He knew that Hynd had the courage, or perhaps the fatalism, not to fear death, and Ottavio too had known these, and knew them still. But whatever gifts

369

they might bring him now, the strength to meet death would not be one of them, since he needed no strength for that. If death held out to him its skeletal hand, he would grasp it with what warmth was left in him.

He looked at the hands resting on the silver top of the Malacca cane and smiled at them. What had they not done when they were young and vigorous? The women they had caressed; the men they had killed, and the women they had killed too, for they had held a machine-gun for Giuliano at the Portella della Ginestra when they slaughtered those Communists picnicking on that mountain meadow in 1947; and the part they had played when he was little more than a boy in the *mattanza* – the great killing of the tunny fish – at Scopello, close by along the coast from here.

They had closed his mother's eyes, these hands. They had held his father's hand while he died. They had clasped his wife to his heart when she had died of grief after the deaths of her three sons; died even though he had avenged their deaths, blood for blood.

Most of all, they had strangled the monk from that abbey at Mazzarino far to the east, where the monks were both mafiosi and sex maniacs, and yes, how magnificently those strong hands of his had killed that foul creature, killed him so slowly that in his eyes nothing showed but the fear in the corrupt soul who had kidnapped, and who in front of his fellows had raped, the girl from Butera that Ottavio was going to marry.

He had married her anyway, so great was his love for her, his Angelina; married her in defiance of everything he had been brought up to believe about his own honour or his family's, and he had let no one live who so much as looked at him sideways.

A chicken came scratching in the dust at his feet and he kicked it away but it squawked and came back, so he reversed the Malacca cane and hit it on the head with the heavy silver knob. It fell down, struggled up again, wandered round in a circle, and stood for a moment while the eye turned his way and gave him a dirty look, then staggered off making a small indignant sound.

Ottavio laughed at the comedy of this little triumph, and called to Agnello for coffee and a newspaper.

'And take a bottle of Pellegrino to that lad over there,' he said, indicating Sedgwick, who sat in the annihilating heat with all the insouciance of a man who had been born and bred in a furnace, 'and this cigar.' He took one for himself from his worn leather cigar case, and laid one for Sedgwick on the table. 'And I shall want lunch in an hour.'

'Lunch?' Agnello said.

'Agnello,' Ottavio said, 'I may be a dead man tonight, but I shall not go hungry while I live.'

'What will you have for lunch?' Agnello said.

'I shall have that chicken,' Ottavio said, and he laughed uproariously and waved a merry hand at the fowl whose progress consisted of tottering a few steps along beside the wall, pausing to rest, and tottering another few steps. 'And you can eat its heart to give you courage.'

He laughed, not only because of the witty notion of eating the unhappy chicken, which was indeed less scrawny than most of its kind in this village, but because he knew Agnello was scared stiff to have his bar play so visible a part in what was being done here today. He understood Agnello's fear and knew it to be justified, because whatever happened there would be an afterwards, a reckoning, and simply because Ottavio had chosen Agnello's as the stage for what might be the last big event in his life, Agnello might figure on that reckoning.

Ottavio, however, was indifferent to Agnello's fear. Men of fear were to him men of another race, too far removed for him to bother with, except as they afforded him amusement.

Give me men like Hynd, he said to himself, and looked across to the car that Parentucelli's men had come in yesterday, which was stationed halfway between Agnello's bar and the wretched stone houses that stood on the other side of this open space that was too shapeless to call a piazza, and in which the corpses that these men had become now sat. For Hynd had improved on his original design to lay their bodies out on the cobbles, and had put the car out there instead with the dead men in it.

On an impulse Ottavio stood up and tilted his hat to the angle he held to be fashionable for a man of his power and distinction, and walked over to the car swinging his cane with the assurance of a boulevardier, for he was not yet decrepit and carried the cane for show, not for use.

The men in the car had been there since sunrise and now it was noon, with the sun at such a heat that the sky was white. Although the car's windows were shut the flies had found their way in to feast on the blood, and because the corpses had been in their oven for hours, a foul miasma had begun to smear the glass.

What a man this John Hynd, this Englishman, was. 'Even I,' Ottavio said to the men in the car, 'would not have thought of doing such a thing to you.' And then, in case they might suppose he was apologizing to them, he tapped the glass of a window mockingly with his cane. He peered more closely through that window, for he had recognized the man inside, who sat with his head leaning against the glass. It was no less a personage than Parentucelli's right-hand man, who bore the good Palermitan name of Smiriglio.

'Smiriglio,' he said. 'How glad I am to see you here.'

He strolled back to his table outside Agnello's, and on the way he raised the hand with the cane in it to the young blond devil (Hynd had told him about this youth) sitting on the quayside, who in his turn saluted him with a right hand which held the bottle of Pellegrino delivered to him by Agnello, and a left that held the cigar Ottavio had picked out for him.

The boy was like a Greek god to look at, and yet it was he who had begun the war against Parentucelli's men, he who had set his knife in Smiriglio's side, reckless of the others who had come with Smiriglio, and not knowing that Hynd would arrive at the opportune moment to shorten the odds.

It warmed Ottavio's spirit to know that such men as young Mark – for he had got neither his tongue nor his memory round the lad's last name – as well as his own John Hynd, who waited on events in the darkness of Agnello's bar just as he waited on them out here, were with him on this profoundly . . . this profoundly, well, perhaps the word would do by itself: on this profound day.

Profound and fatiguing. Although he was a Sicilian and the endurance with which he bore the heat was part of his patrimony, now he was tired, and perhaps he might let himself fall into the sleep that was opening itself to him within.

Parentucelli and his men might not come before midnight, after all, or even not before tomorrow, so he could sleep just for an hour, a little hour, until Agnello, if he had not run away before then, brought his lunch out to him. He smiled, thinking of the blow he had dealt the chicken, and of its deranged and stupefied departure, and of the idea of eating it for lunch.

So smiling, he slouched down in his chair, put his feet up on its neighbour, laid his cane on the table, tilted his hat over his eyes, and fell asleep.

Comfortable in the shadowy recesses of Agnello's taproom, Hynd sat with the dog Cesare lying at his feet. He had watched the Don's promenade to the tomb of his enemies, the greeting he had given them, and the greeting he had exchanged with Sedgwick on his way back.

Hynd could only marvel at the young Adonis sitting there in the full assault of the sun's heat. Even had the village not been hiding in its houses with doors locked and shutters barred, at this time of day no one would have been fool enough to challenge the furious heat in that way.

'I don't want you to collapse with heatstroke,' Hynd had said to him.

'Tactically it's the place to be for fast, close-in action,' Mark Sedgwick had said. 'You in the bar and me on the outside. And for the next phase Fraser and Sorrel with the machine gun on that roof, and Seddall with his sub-machine gun lurking across the way. That's all we've got, and we have to be placed right. The heat is nothing to me, I don't know why. I've been in the Gobi, and worked up and down the Red Sea once on a drug lark, and rode the Gila Desert in Arizona, and the heat leaves me cold, you might say.'

It was Sedgwick who had proposed, in this way, the disposition of their limited forces, and Hynd and Seddall and Fraser had looked at it from every critical angle, and could find nothing to better it. Sedgwick was not just death on wheels and a pretty face. He had a head on his shoulders. A head that could take this temperature of somewhere between 110° and 120° Fahrenheit and not have its brains addled.

Hynd went closer to the door to make sure the golden youth had not been exaggerating. He saw no signs of weakness in the set of his body. He looked across to the little stone house with the pig-shed stuck onto it, where Fraser and Sorrel waited inside its stone walls with the trap door open, and where their heavy machine gun waited on the roof tented under a cloth to keep it cool. Seddall waited in another house up to Hynd's left. Sciandri had commandeered these places in Ottavio's name, and their owners had been, or so it seemed, honoured to have been chosen to be of service to the Don, and taken themselves elsewhere. Hynd supposed that since Ottavio had always been there, he must seem to them to be invincible.

Well, so far he had been. But time had moved on, and neither Ottavio nor the village had moved with it. Except that there were one or two telephones and an electrical supply, the place sat exhausted in the sun as it must have done for hundreds of years. The stone houses were low and primitive and without charm, some empty and gone to ruin, and those that were lived in were crumbling almost perceptibly, as if the people

of the place lived only in the present and the past: as if
the weight of the past was too much for them to bear,
and had left them with no sense that either they or their
village could do anything but survive until time wore
them out.

Hynd shook himself away from this reverie and
asked Agnello for some coffee, and went back to his
place. The dog, which knew it was siesta time and had
not moved while he walked about the room, gave a low
acknowledging sigh when he sat down, and the vigil
resumed.

Ottavio, in his sleep, was a boy again. He was taking
part in the great killing of the tunny fish at a younger
age than he ever had in fact, hacking and clubbing at
the great fish in the blood-red sea. Then, somehow,
all the men about him were not there any more, and he
was alone in the big broad boat, and the fish coming at
him along the bottom of the boat was not a tunnyfish
but a huge black shark.

Although he was full of fear, he went slowly to meet
it as it struggled towards him with cumbersome heav-
ings of its body, a hateful and hating creature inexorable
in its progress from a dark tunnel that led into the sea
– that came from the sea.

It reached him, a yawning cave of dreadful teeth, and
they fought. It tore great chunks out of his body. He
could no longer see the teeth that savaged him and was
attacking it with his own, biting great holes in its black
hide and finding it black within, until it had had enough
and turned and shrieked at him, the worst sound he
had ever heard, and fled down the boat, swimming now
for the boat was full of water, until it vanished into that

tunnel from which it had first emerged, back into the sea.

And when it was gone there were no wounds on the boy Ottavio, no great gouges in his flesh, no blood on him, no mark, no taste of that evil thing in his mouth. There was no blemish on him from the combat with that thing from the deep, that thing which he had driven back to the deep.

He sat alone in the boat, which was dry again and empty save for him, and looked out over the sea until it was nothing but sea, sea throwing back the blue of the sky and the glitter of the sun.

He woke and his eyes were dark and saw nothing of the scene before him, but there was a thought in his head the instant he awoke, and he spoke it aloud.

'What a man I was when I was a boy,' he said.

And he felt, which he had not felt as long as he could remember, alone.

He wished Leopetto was here, his henchman, or even Andrea Guercio, his brother in the Brotherhood, touchy and over-sensitive though Guercio was. But their place in today's scheme of things was to defend his home, and his place was to sit on here alone.

He had a mind even to call for Hynd to give him the dog Cesare for company, but, for one thing, Hynd had a use for the dog, and for another, he would not show such weakness to himself, never mind to any other man.

So he sat on, alone, with the darkness of the dream in his soul, and waited for the day to bring what it would.

The day brought nothing. No stranger, friend or foe, came to the village, and at nightfall Leopetto came with the car and Ottavio, wearied with that long day of waiting, slept the sleep of the dead.

Chapter Thirty

It was the next day at noon that Parentucelli came. His motorcade drove slowly down the winding road to the little fishing village with all the dignity of a head of state visiting a foreign capital.

Ottavio was glad the waiting was at an end. He had not wanted to sit here the whole of another day. For one thing his sense of the ridiculous would not have allowed it, and, besides that, all was not quite as it had been the day before.

Certainly, Hynd and the hound were behind him in Agnello's bar, that young Greek god was basking in the sun as if he had been used to live in it and had flown down here by way of a change, and the other foreigners were in their places. But the people of the village were suddenly dismayed. It was as if the charade of yesterday, in which nothing at all had happened, had told them that his power was not infallible.

The fishermen, who yesterday had been interested enough to stay with their families, awaiting the outcome, had today sent spokesmen to say they must take their boats out, for a living had to be earned. Which was to say that their little daily affairs were of more importance to them than the great affairs of such as he. Ottavio had nodded courteously, for indeed he understood them, whereupon one of the spokesmen had said boldly that they could not abide another day of that car standing there with the dead bodies rotting in it.

They were men with families, and it was a bad thing for families to see.

At this, Ottavio's countenance had turned cold against them, and he had said that what happened to that car and those within it was nothing to do with them.

The boats had gone to sea, some of them with womenfolk and the older children on board. Other families had gone up to spend the day in the mountains. So that today the village not only appeared deserted – it was, but for those too old or infirm to move, deserted in fact.

When they went off, he smiled ironically to himself, thinking that this must be how the old dukes and princes of Sicily had felt when they learned that in the resentment of the humble lay the seeds of democracy.

Well, for him it was only one more day, and if he lived they would soon remember how the world was ordered, and if he died it would no longer matter to him what happened here.

Now, the cars were down off the cliff road and out of sight. They must be on the edge of the village.

'They are on their way,' Ottavio said to the door behind him, and, 'Agnello, bring me a glass of brandy, now, at once.'

When this came, he lifted it in a toast like his salutation of yesterday to the young man who sat alone on the bollard by the harbour. Sedgwick, who had this morning decided to improve on the part he was playing, was acting the town drunk, and waved the wine bottle in his hand by way of reply.

The first car glided warily round the corner and stopped where the narrow street gave place to the open

ground beside the harbour. The first thing they saw –
since there was little else to see – was the big Fiat parked
on the quay with their men sitting in it, and reassured
perhaps by this, though still puzzled to know who had
shot at the men who had come in search of it two nights
ago, they moved forward a little way and came to a
halt.

Two other cars followed, and it was as the men in
them were getting out and taking in the fact that the
place appeared to be abandoned, as if plague had struck
down all the inhabitants in the night, that the men from
the first car saw that the men in the Fiat were corpses.

At first they stared at them, then they walked towards
them with great care, then they saw who they were,
and one of them ran back to the white BMW from
which their chief had now emerged.

The whole common mind of the punitive expedition
went to pieces as its members tried to grasp both the
enormity and the strangeness of what confronted them.
They went this way and that way and then came to a
halt, and called out to each other, and then drew
together defensively and looked all about them as if
they feared that the whole village was an ambush that
had been waiting for them to fall into it.

Only Parentucelli broke out from this chaos, stalking
in his pale blue silk suit with three men in his wake
over the empty, sun-smitten expanse, throwing no more
than a glance at the turmoil round the Fiat, to where
the bodies were.

He stared at them, from his height; his big head did
not bend to acknowledge them, he acknowledged
merely the fact. Then he saw the young man sitting on
the bollard and went to him.

'What has happened here?' he demanded.

The youth looked up from a beautiful and debauched countenance and shrugged and made a mouth that said he knew nothing, and put the bottle to his lips. But with his other hand he waved in the direction of the man sitting outside the bar.

Parentucelli pointed to the boy and to the water and two of his men lifted Sedgwick and threw him out into the harbour.

Sedgwick went down to the sand and swam back to the harbour wall and up the rickety ladder that hung there.

Parentucelli marched on to Agnello's with his three men behind him, almost running to keep pace with their leader.

The golden-haired youth followed slowly after with the curiosity of the drunkard, the water dripping from him as he went.

'You,' Parentucelli said to the man at the table, who was nodding in the noonday heat. 'What happened? Who killed these men?'

'Who can say?' the figure said, and lifted its head and Parentucelli saw that it was Ottavio.

Hynd, standing with his hand on the scruff of the mastiff in the dark cave that the light without made of Agnello's bar, saw Parentucelli's black eyes lose, for once, their intelligence, the radiant power he owned diffuse itself from his face, and his whole body stand fixed as if every limb had lost the gift of movement.

'What are you doing here?' he demanded.

'I? I live here,' Ottavio said. 'It is I who am surprised to see you here, surprised and honoured. Will you not sit, drink with me. Eat with me.'

'The men in that car are my men, were my men. They have been killed. Now they are set there in that car like puppets in a show. For how long? They have been gone forty-eight hours. Has the car been there all that time?'

Ottavio squinted up at him and threw a hand in the air to demonstrate how baffled he himself was by current events. 'I wish you would sit down,' he said. 'I can't look up at you against the sun. I know nothing of all this. There were shots here the other night. I don't know who is doing it, except that there are foreigners about.' With his head he indicated the bay. 'Those yachts out there, I don't know who these people are. Perhaps they had something to do with it.'

'Ah, foreigners,' Parentucelli said. 'You speak to me of foreigners, and what of that man Hynd you have taken into your household? I mistrusted him from the first. Well, he will get his come-uppance before the day is out.'

'You go too fast,' Ottavio said. 'Agnello,' he called out, 'another brandy, two more brandies. Sit down, my friend.' He gestured at the chair beside him, which like his own was in the shade of the umbrella. 'Let us be calm. Now, listen. You are right about Hynd, and you are wrong about him. First, I did not take him into my household, I took him as hostage, and that was agreed among us, that he should be held prisoner until all of us decided what to do with him. But you were right not to trust him: he has escaped.'

Parentucelli inspected the chair before he risked putting his blue silk trousers on it, and sat down. He sniffed at the glass Agnelli had brought him and made a face, but he swallowed a mouthful.

'When did he escape?'

'Three days ago, before all this trouble started.'

'He hoodwinked you,' Parentucelli said.

'I fear it is so,' Ottavio said. 'I am growing old. He was as mild as milk all the time he was at my house. Then three days ago, the man who took his food was found dead with his own knife in his heart, and Hynd was gone.'

Hynd, eavesdropping on this, was astonished by Ottavio's capacity for lying invention, and the persuasive deceitfulness of his voice.

He would have been more impressed if he had understood at how many levels this conversation was taking place; if he had known that neither of these Sicilians trusted anything the other said; that neither of them expected to hear the truth from the other; that they heard what was said with other senses than hearing; that each knew one of them would kill the other before very long; and that each accepted amiability and politeness as offering the appropriate currency in which to play out this game of deceit, which both knew they were playing.

Parentucelli wiped his hand across his face and regarded Don Ottavio for a long minute. He waved his arm to send the three men who attended him further away. 'Well,' he said. 'I have been hoodwinked too. This man Casson and his great promises – dust in the wind, nothing but dust in the wind.'

'Why do you say that?'

'You, bring me the Frenchman!' Parentucelli shouted, pointing at one of his men.

The man went towards the men standing around the cars and repeated this instruction, and a tall stumbling figure was brought from the white BMW and sent to meet him. He brought the man to Parentucelli.

'Take a seat,' Parentucelli said to the tall man, and waved his own man away again.

'This man, whose name is ... What is your name again?'

'Rénouvin,' the Frenchman said. He had a naturally thin, even gaunt face, and just now it looked to be in shock.

'Rénouvin was on the *Baikal*,' Parentucelli said. 'Tell your story, be brief, tell it simply.'

'Yesterday evening,' Rénouvin said, with an accent Ottavio found hard to follow, 'just before sunset, three fast naval boats, flying no flag, came at us out of the sun and the first we knew of it was that they were firing into us from the port side at three kilometres. They began hitting us almost at once, and came on firing without cessation.

'They were firing 30 millimetres, at something like six hundred rounds a minute, two guns from each boat, so thousands of rounds hit us in the first minute. The upperworks were destroyed, the ship on fire, half the crew dead or wounded. I dived overboard with a lifejacket under my arm and went as deep as I could and stayed down as long as I could. When I came up the *Baikal* was half a kilometre off and still moving away at about ten knots.

'The enemy had overshot her by this time, and they regrouped and went back again attacking from starboard. This time they aimed their fire at the waterline, and by the time they had finished their run she was listing to starboard and had begun to sink.'

Rénouvin stopped and looked at Ottavio's glass.

Ottavio pushed it at him, and he drank what was left in it.

'Thank you. There were some still alive on the *Baikal* and they got one life-raft over the side, quite possibly the only one not shot to pieces. I have never known a hail of fire like that in my life. The enemy lay off while the *Baikal* went on listing and those who had survived the attack, and were able, got themselves onto the raft; not many of them.'

He turned his head and looked at the ground for so long it was as if he had forgotten where he was. 'They waited till the raft was clear of the ship, and moved in on it. Then they waited till the *Baikal* went down, which she did at the end quite suddenly, in a sort of sideways dive. When she was sunk, they opened fire on the raft and shot it and the men on it into pieces.'

Rénouvin lifted his head again. 'It was all over in no time at all,' he said. 'The sun was about to touch the sea when they attacked, and the last of it was still resting on the rim of the horizon when they sailed off eastward.'

His voice changed and became dreamy. 'It was very strange. They came from the west, they destroyed the *Baikal* and her crew as if doing that was no more than an incident to liven up their voyage, and sailed on eastward.'

'How were you rescued from the sea?' Ottavio asked him.

'The noise and flash of the firing,' Rénouvin said. 'It attracted a fishing boat from the island of Lampedusa. They are impoverished people, and I paid them to carry me to Agrigento and hired a car from there to Palermo. It did not take a lot of money, but it was more than they earn in a week's fishing. And these people, they are primitives, they had no interest but to drop me off and sail back to their island.'

'You understood all that?' Parentucelli said.

'I understood it,' Ottavio said.

Hynd had understood it too. What it meant to him was that the official mission was more or less accomplished. So far as he was concerned, all that was left on the agenda was Casson.

'Take him back,' Parentucelli yelled indiscriminately at his followers. Rénouvin gave Ottavio a hopeless, perhaps pleading, look, but Ottavio had no further interest in him. Rénouvin was taken away again. Even if Ottavio had been interested to know, there would have been no point in asking what was to become of the Frenchman. He was of no value, and he knew things it would be better he did not know. In any case, it would not have been proper to ask.

'So,' Ottavio said, 'what, then, of Casson? Have we paid him yet? He has not fulfilled his bargain.' This was the proper way to ask if Casson still lived.

'Ah,' Parentucelli said. 'To us this is a misfortune, to Casson it is a disaster. He blames it on the man Hynd.'

'That is difficult to follow,' Ottavio said.

'He believes that Hynd is a member of the British secret intelligence.'

'What do they care about us?' Ottavio said.

Parentucelli shrugged. 'Not more than usual, I suppose. I think perhaps I could understand it if they were after Casson.'

'It is not a question that matters to me,' Ottavio said. 'You did not trust Hynd. I, in my turn, did not trust Casson. Where is Casson now?'

That old evil exuberance was back in Parentucelli now. Hynd, though lurking in the dimness of the bar and unable to see the man's face, could hear it in his voice.

'Well, Casson wanted to go to your house, Ottavio, to put paid to Hynd, and I let him.'

'You let him?'

'I let him.'

'My house?'

'Your house. I told him where it was. I had no need to offer him any men, he has some of his own.'

Hynd wanted this to be done with. He wanted to get out of there and after Casson. But he was held by the contrast in the two voices. Parentucelli springing his little surprise and gloating with that wild half-madness of his, and against that Ottavio, who sounded perfectly matter-of-fact, and only the slightest bit perplexed.

Hynd could not believe this of the old man, that he would, without the least hint of anger, listen to the other man say he had assisted Casson's desire to make an armed attack on his own home.

When Don Ottavio spoke again it was in the same matter-of-fact tone, but the words he used brought Hynd forward to stand just inside the doorway.

He saw Ottavio leaning back comfortably in his chair, watching the effect of the words he had just spoken. 'I come,' he had said, 'in the mouth of the mother-fucker who gave you birth.'

Parentucelli's face was congested and he began to mouth invective at Ottavio, but since none of it could come up to what had provoked it, frustration was added to his rage. It seemed to Hynd that at any moment he would fall on the ancient with his bare hands.

It was time.

He touched the dog's neck lightly and said, 'Kill.'

The mastiff hurled itself through the doorway and took Parentucelli by the throat and went to the ground on top of him.

Of the three men who had accompanied Parentucelli, one stared in horror and the other two went for their guns, but behind them Sedgwick's voice said, 'Don't. In any case, it's too late.'

The dog had torn his victim's throat out and the man was already dying. It was Ottavio who called Cesare off, lashing his rump with the cane until he came away, shaking his bloodied muzzle. The dog sat whining and shaking beside Don Ottavio with its eyes wide on the man still twitching in his death throes; with its head and shoulders thrusting forward and pulling back as if it was going to attack again; but not, in fact, with intent, simply living again what it had just done.

The mass of the dying man's followers now began to move upon the scene of this sudden drama, but a burst of heavy automatic fire laid across their path stopped them.

Parentucelli died, and under Ottavio's hand the dog began to grow calm.

'Very well,' one of the three henchmen said. 'What now?'

'Take up your dead,' Ottavio said, 'and go. And tell them in Palermo, this is my country.'

As the bodies were being loaded into the cars, and Agnello's hose was washing blood away yet again, a little Peugeot came running over the wet stones, right up to the table where Ottavio sat.

It was Leopetto.

'Guercio is dead,' he said, still sitting in the car, and his face was pale. 'And Carmine and Silvestro are wounded. We have three dead altogether. The house is burning. They had bombs and rockets and machine-guns, like the army.'

'Casson,' Hynd said. 'How many were they?'

'Only four,' Leopetto said, 'but their weapons were too much for us. Two we killed and two wounded, but their leader only a little. He ran off up the hill. We shot up their vehicle.'

'Then he will have to come down again,' Hynd said, 'to find his transport. The hills are Don Ottavio's. By tomorrow Casson would not be able to move in them, and he knows it.'

'Why are you alive?' Ottavio said to Leopetto.

'I am not sure that I am,' Leopetto said.

Hynd took a step closer to the Peugeot and saw that the man's stomach and thighs were all blood.

'Padrone,' he said formally. 'I need your car.'

'Take it,' Ottavio said. 'Do you want the dog?'

Hynd was on his way, and gave him no more than a glance. 'No,' he said. 'This one I can do alone.'

'This one you want to do alone,' Ottavio said. Then he set himself to look into Leopetto's eyes which clung to his, as if between the two of them they could conquer the mystery of death.

Chapter Thirty-One

Hynd threw the big Mercedes along the road to Cefalu. He rounded a corner and had a glimpse of a sheet of white sand that was the next bay, with a man walking on it. In the next moment the view was obscured by the rise of land between the road and the sea, and Hynd left the car there.

He moved secretly over the hummocks of parched grass and down the edge of the bay towards the sea, and found, as if the gods had put them there, a jumble of rocks where he could sit hidden and watch the man come to him.

He knew in his bones that it was Casson, since Casson was obliged to come to him to meet his destiny, though at this distance he could not yet make him out.

He knew that it was Casson making his way to Ciascia, expecting to find there Parentucelli, since here in Don Ottavio's fiefdom Parentucelli was the only hope he had, after attacking the people in Ottavio's house and burning it down. Casson reckoning on aid and comfort, a drink and a piece of sticking-plaster for the wound Leopetto had spoken of, and a celebratory dinner in Palermo tonight. Casson wondering where on God's green earth – well, on Sicily's parched earth – Hynd had got to.

Then the figure was near enough to see, and it was Casson.

His enemy came closer.

Hynd sat in his chair of rock and felt the ancient weight of the mountains that rose above him, and the weight of the heat that the sun from its zenith thrust down upon him. He looked out over the blue sea glittering with light.

Along the white beach Casson came, leaving a blemish of blood at every third or fourth step, a cursed but indomitable creature coming ignorantly to his end.

It came to Hynd for a moment, that since he now knew that he had begun to win free of that beautiful woman with the radiant but damaged spirit; that since she had taken her thrall away to spin the thread of her fate round the hearts of other men; then there was no longer any need to kill Casson.

He thought for that moment that he might sit there and watch his enemy pass and, after he had passed, sit on until the sun went down.

The thought did not hold him: watching the man come to him across the white sand, he knew that within him was another master than himself, that in the darkness of his own soul he had made a vow.

He stood up and looked into the hard grey eyes. They showed a moment of surprise and then perhaps disillusionment, but of this he did not wait to be made sure. He shot Casson in the heart. Then he jumped down onto the sand and fired the *coup de grâce* into the back of the head; for he did not hide from himself that it was an execution.

He sat on the beach a few yards from the body of his antagonist with his arms round his knees and looked north over the sea, over mountains and plains and forests, over broad rivers and fertile fields, to that small and simple house where he lived in Scotland.

There were no broad rivers there, only the small streams that came rushing off the hills. Few trees, only grass and rock swept by the wind and rain, sometimes the sun, where sheep and cattle lived off the rough grazing. These, and the perpetual sound of the sea.

He began to wonder if it was his place any more. If it was wilderness enough for him. There were wilder places in other countries where a man could be more alone with what was in him; places where the animals were wild, not tame; places where a man knew that all he could trust was what was in nature, in the unpeopled world about him, and to trust what was in himself, for they were the same; and where a man could learn to trust that, and that only.

He thought that this was what his living was for, and that this was the way he would like to live before he died.

He saw – they had been in his eye for some time, but only now did he see them – half a dozen fishing boats passing across the bay, the Ciascia fleet heading back to harbour.

At the same moment he was given a strong nudge between the shoulders, and here was the dog Cesare, panting from the long run in which he had followed the car from the village: followed by God knew what instinct, for Hynd had driven ten miles before he found the beach where Casson walked to his end.

The dog saw and sniffed at the body on the sand and grew quiet, and sat across from Hynd and regarded him.

Hynd stood up. 'Come on, then,' he said. 'We're going travelling, you and I. We're going a long way from here, to my country, and then I think we'll go a long way from there.'

He saw that the gun was still in his hand and put it away, and, leaving the dead Casson to whatever fate might befall him now, he let the dog lead him back to the car.

Chapter Thirty-Two

At the village it was as if no blood had been shed there since Gianucci had last slaughtered a horse. The hose had done its work again.

The boats were coming in from the day's fishing, people were in the streets, children rolled in the dust, dogs fought over scraps.

He found Seddall in Agnello's reading the *Giornale di Sicilia*.

'Where the hell have you been?' Seddall said. 'Have a drink. I gather from your Mafia friend that a certain ship which shall be nameless sank in the Gulf of Sirte yesterday with the loss of all hands.'

'These things happen at sea,' Hynd said, and took his glass from Agnello, but spilled some of it as he received a strong nudge behind his knee.

It was the mastiff. He got a bucket of water from Agnello, and the dog stood beside them, making appalling noises as it lapped from the bucket with its enormous tongue.

'You find Casson?' Seddall said.

'Yes,' Hynd said. 'Where's the old man?'

'Agnello's boy has driven him up to see the ruin of his house,' Harry said. 'He left the dog here for you, if you want it.'

'I don't believe I have much choice in that,' Hynd said. 'No, I do want it. We understand each other,' Hynd said.

'I had a thought,' Harry said.

'What was that?'

'Well, I doubt if you'll get that piano out of Raleigh,' Harry said, 'not the way things have gone.'

'I don't want it,' Hynd said. 'I couldn't play it. I'm not clean.'

'Good God,' Harry said, startled at this breaking of the tone.

'Get on,' Hynd said, and pushed his glass across the bar.

'I wondered if you'd like that little cutter I came here in,' Harry said. 'She's not worth much. She's old, she's wooden, but the hull's solid and she's in good nick. The bloke I borrowed her from wants to sell her, and I can get my Department to OK the funds for it. In fact at the moment I am my Department, I'll do it myself. I mean, you ought to have something out of this.'

'Ought?' Hynd said. 'What does that mean?'

Seddall looked at him. The man was somewhere else. 'It means,' he said, 'that you have earned a considerable fee.'

Hynd showed no sign of having heard this explanation.

'Do you want the boat or not?' Seddall said. 'Fraser's sailing for Corsica within the hour, he's on board now getting his boat ready for sea, and I can sail with him. My dunnage is on the cutter but I can shift it to Fraser's boat in a brace of shakes. We think it not wise to hang around here too long. We're hellish popular with the locals all of a sudden, but who knows what our friends from Palermo may be thinking right now.'

Hynd looked out through the doorway at the cutter sitting small, close, quiet, self-contained, but free always, at the least whim, to run for the open sea.

'I could sail her home,' he said.

'To Scotland?' Harry said. 'Rather a cockleshell for that, I'd have thought. I'd imagined you keeping her on the Med somewhere, and having sailing holidays.'

Hynd, for the first time, smiled. 'I think she'd be all right,' he said. 'It's not a bad time of year for it. There are three safe harbours in the western Mediterranean: June, July, August, and Port Mahon.'

'Who said that?'

'Andrea Doria,' Hynd said.

'Well, he ought to know,' Harry said. 'But then there's the Atlantic.'

'I could take the dog,' Hynd said, making nothing of the Atlantic.

'You're saying yes,' Harry said.

'I'm saying yes,' Hynd said. 'It'll help me get my health back, to sail her home.'

'Right, I'll move my belongings out of her,' Harry said, 'and she's yours.'

Two people drifted into view on the edge of the quay, and began to kiss each other freely, the two golden heads moving around each other.

'I didn't know about them,' Harry said. 'It's a bit odd. Sorrel's almost old enough to be his mother.'

'What's that to say to anything?' Hynd said. 'And be your age; any woman will always be old enough to be that lad's mother. Not that that's a crack against him. Women are unaccountable creatures. Come on. Let's get moving. I want to sail today.'

Harry wondered what had become of the devout Hynd, worshipper of Aphrodite, or Venus, or whatever you chose to call her, who had been reassembled to touch against Hynd's fate in the name of Caroline Swift. There had been a change in the man, as if Paris had dropped Helen off on the way to Troy to take up – well, to take up what? And here his eye fell on the fearsome dog, which had drunk its fill and was lying at Hynd's feet – yes, that was clearly the kind of thing – to take up wolf-hunting.

'You do realize you'll have to quarantine that dog when you get home,' Harry said.

'Quarantine?' Hynd said. 'I'm not going to put a creature like that in a kennel for six months.'

He summoned the mastiff with no more than a wave of the hand, and the creature sprang up and followed at his heel.

Seddall looked at them as they went, these two spirits who moved in their own atavistic world; looked at the golden couple on the edge of the harbour, the youthful killer and the gorgeous woman; looked down at the stones washed clear of the life-blood which had bled on them, and shone pristine and innocent in the perpetual sun.

Then he drained his glass and went out, back into the day.

Chapter Thirty-Three

Jane Kneller arrived for lunch at Rules clad in a pale green frock woven of silk and linen with the skirt to the top of the kneecap, and a plain jacket.

'I must say,' Harry said, 'you look absolutely A1 at Lloyd's. I hope that's not too forward.'

'It's not too forward,' she said, 'but it's not much of a compliment these days.'

'Pray sit yourself down,' he said, 'and drink some of that sherry, and I shall study to do better.'

'Let us eschew the sexual skirmishing,' she said. 'I should be delighted if you will dine with me next week.'

'Terrific,' Harry said, and the most wonderful, confused, self-mocking, rueful, and pleased smile worked its way over that lazily expressive mouth of his.

She looked at him with amusement. 'As for you,' she said. 'What is your sartorial secret?'

'My secret?'

'How do you get your suits to look so distrait?'

'Search me,' he said. 'My suits are perfectly good suits. This one's fresh off the cleaner's hanger this morning. It just happens, somehow.' He made a deliberate scrutiny of her face, a rewarding act at the best of times, but he went at it like a doctor looking for symptoms. 'I take it that you are well equipped with brothers,' he said.

'I have three brothers,' she said. 'Why do you ask?'

'Observe that I did not ask, I knew it. All this playing hard right up at the net. It's a sure sign.'

'I shall cast my eyes down and be demure.'

'I bet you could do it too,' he said. 'But if you do I shall be sick on the tablecloth.'

'What, here, in public?'

'Why not? I don't do anything anywhere that I wouldn't do anywhere else, if you follow me.'

'I think I follow you all right,' she said, 'but you put it ambiguously. Do you mean that you restrict your behaviour or that you do what you feel like wherever you happen to be?'

'The latter.'

'That's the impression I formed at our first meeting. A cat among pigeons wasn't in it.'

He made a grimace. 'Yeah, that conference, so-called. Let's get some food.'

'What are you having?'

'Whitebait and steak and kidney pie.'

'My dear Harry, how can you eat a meal like that when it's eighty-four in the shade?'

'I have been too much abroad. I only flew home yesterday and it's been nothing but office paperwork ever since. So I want to celebrate by having some solid English nosh, good old-fashioned London food with Stilton afterwards. That's why we're eating here.'

'Then you will certainly be sick on the tablecloth,' she said. 'I should like sole, please.'

He offered her one of his Gauloises and she took it. 'Your stock is rather high, around and about,' she said. 'Did you know that?'

'It won't last. I've trod on too many toes. My face never fits for long in the corridors of power.'

'I've heard it said. The buzzy word to use about you just now is rebarbative.' He saw her head lift, and an enquiring expression on her face; her excellent, good-looking, alert and intelligent face.

He turned and saw the big black man in the million-dollar suit. 'Doffene,' he said, 'and don't tell me this is a coincidence.'

'Hi, Harry. No, not a coincidence.' He looked across the table. 'So you are Jane Kneller?'

She had heard a note in Seddall's voice, and she spoke with reserve. 'And I assume that you are Mr Doffene of the NSA. How did you know who I was?'

'I wanted to talk to Harry fast. I'm only in London for twenty-four hours, so I found out what he was doing and where and who with. Sit here?' He pulled out the chair beside Harry.

'Sit for five minutes, Doffene, but you're not joining us for luncheon. I have a code about who I eat with.'

'Yeah,' was all Doffene said to that, but he had gone from diffident to cold and angry. 'Damn it, Harry, I have to do what's best for my own government.'

'That's the difference between you and me. I act for my country, not for its government.'

'That's not a distinction for you to make, Harry. It's why your name has a bad smell where it counts. Tell him, Ms Kneller.'

'What's this about?' Jane said.

'I was at a UN conference in the States and Doffene agreed to be my message post for Hynd, when Hynd was undercover in Italy. Hynd told Doffene to tell me he wanted Caroline Swift looked after, he thought there was danger to her. Doffene didn't tell me. He sent the CIA instead to take her in.'

'You were behind that,' she said to Doffene. 'Well, well.'

He heard the Home Office in her quiet comment. 'It was for her own good,' he said, 'to keep her safe.'

'I don't quite believe that, Mr Doffene.'

'You did it,' Harry said, 'because you wanted a hold over John Hynd, to be sure he didn't quit the job, and I don't like you for that. But what puts you on my shitlist is that you cheated me and lied to me. You can't make that good, so there's no point in trying.'

The whitebait arrived.

'Anything else?' Harry said.

'Why I wanted to see you while I'm here. I got this letter in Washington.'

He laid it on the tablecloth, and Harry read it.

Doffene,
Look behind you when you walk the streets at night.
John Hynd

'What does he mean?' the American asked.

Harry turned the note round so that Jane could read it.

'He means that he's going to kill you, I should think,' Harry said with utter indifference.

'Why, for God's sake?'

'Because he was in love with Caroline Swift.'

'Was? You mean he isn't now?'

'It was what they call an obsession, I suppose,' Harry said. 'I think it ran out on him, in Sicily.'

'Then why this, now?'

'It's impossible to understand Hynd. It's as if he felt himself ruled by fate, no, not ruled by, under an obligation to fate, something like that. It makes him implacable.'

'So what am I to make of this?' Doffene said.

'I should do it,' Harry said.

'Do what?'

'Look behind you when you walk the streets at night.'

'That's all you have to say?'

'Absolutely all. So long, Doffene.'

Doffene got up, and you could have grated cheese on the frown that lined his brow. He looked at Jane, as if a woman might have a more humane message for him.

'Take lots of care, Mr Doffene,' she said, and he gave her an absent-minded nod, and went away.

'What I like about this place,' Harry said, 'is that they give you lots of lemon,' and stabbed a fork into the yellow flesh.

'I can't think why you're not the most popular man in London,' Jane said. 'You have such a way with people.'

'You didn't exactly fall on his neck yourself.'

With the sole, she said, 'There's a woman in Mongolia called Olivia, riding camels, I believe.'

'Olivia has now found her way to Hong Kong, and has reason to remain there, apparently.'

'How do you feel about that?'

'That's my business.'

'*D'accord.*'

'I'm not a philanderer.'

'I know that, you extremely nice fool. And neither am I.'

Lunch went pleasantly on its way.

When it was time to order coffee, he said, 'Do you

see a woman with yellow curls and a boy like a Greek god in the corner on my starboard quarter?'

'Yes,' she said, laughing. 'Am I to have a surprise?'

'If you'd like it. That's Sorrel Blake and Mark Sedgwick. I thought to ask them to join us for coffee.'

'You planned this, Harry Seddall. Why didn't we all lunch together?'

'Because I wanted you to myself, thank you very much. And I wanted you to meet them. Kit Fraser's working today, and Hynd's up in Scotland, and Dodo and Mick Fawcett are off having a holiday in the sun somewhere, now that the war's over. Sorrel's helping me hold down the office.'

'Lord, I don't know about Master Sedgwick. He sounds frightfully brutal.'

'He's good at what he does, it's just that he's completely ruthless about doing it.'

He ordered coffee for four, and waved them over.

Jane Kneller's meeting with Sorrel Blake was easy and natural, since they recognized at once that they had things in common. She braced herself to meet the young man who had been described to her as the next thing to a psychopath.

The young Adonis took her hand and looked at her as if she had been given all the gifts the gods could give a woman, and then for no more than the merest flash of a moment his eyes bared to a complete and knowing intimacy, as if when the gods chose her for this munificence he had been among them.

She broke the gaze between them and looked at Seddall, and saw sardonic amusement all over that experienced and ironical face. She didn't flirt with a man often, but she would damn well flirt with Seddall now.

'Sit beside me,' she said to Mark Sedgwick.

'That was Doffene, wasn't it?' Sorrel said, looking flushed and lovely and full of excitement, her eyes going back and back to Mark Sedgwick, as she sat down beside Harry. 'He didn't even notice me. He went out walking very oddly, as if he was trying to break through a spider's web.'

'He is, but he won't manage it,' Harry said. 'He had received a message from John Hynd.'

'I can imagine,' Sedgwick said cheerfully. 'Dead meat, that's what he is now.'

Jane recoiled slightly at this, and was amazed at the look of passion – call it by its name, the look of pure lust – that the young man's remark fetched from Sorrel.

'There's a message for John Hynd,' Sorrel said. 'From Caroline Swift by way of Tony Carver. Tony has her address in Spain, if Hynd would like to go and see her.'

'Why doesn't she just phone Hynd herself?'

'You don't know a lot about women, do you, Harry?' This from Mark Sedgwick, to Seddall's surprise.

'Don't I?' he said.

Jane and Sorrel looked at each other. 'No,' Jane said, 'it seems that you don't. Perhaps it's part of your charm.'

But Harry barely heard this. His thought was of John Hynd and Caroline Swift, two beings who seemed fated, each of them in a different way, to live their lives according to a rule he knew nothing of. Each of them lived as if they were the expression of a mystery that ran in their blood, with a kind of instancy and freedom that could hardly be separated from chaos, that was even perhaps an acceptance of chaos. Surely only the gods could do that? Was it hubris, or did it take a courage he did not have?

He came to himself to find Jane Kneller's hand on his. 'Come back to earth,' she said.

'It's awfully dull,' he said, 'but I'm afraid that earth's where I live.'

That evening John Hynd had been busy, and was about ready to leave. He had loaded the cutter, lying in the rocky bay below the house, with his library of books and his small arsenal of weapons, and was just attending to the last detail of his departure when the phone rang. He put down the can and went inside. The house stank of petrol, but the phone was by an open window and he was able to breathe some clear air while he spoke.

The dog, who was now a complete sailor after the long voyage from the Mediterranean, was standing his watch on the boat, waiting trustfully for Hynd. As he went into the house Hynd looked down and gave him a wave, and got a bark in return.

It was Harry Seddall. They exchanged greetings, and Seddall gave him the message that had been conveyed by Tony Carver.

'Did he give you a number to call him on?' Hynd said.

'Yes, he did.'

'Then tell her luck from me,' Hynd said, 'and say the world is her oyster again.'

When he had put the phone down he went outside and poured the last of the petrol onto the log house. He looked round him once, at the hills and the sky and the sea, then he struck a bundle of matches which he had tied together with thread, and tossed it through an open window, and ran down the hillside.

He heard the house explode in a rush of flame but did not look back till he was on the shore, and then only for a moment before he plunged into the sea and swam out to the cutter.

Once on deck he made much of the dog, but briefly, hoisted mainsail and jib, pulled up the anchor, and used the engine to get out of the bay.

Then he cut the engine, and with the sails flapping and the boat heaving on the swell, watched the great bonfire that the house made, the flames and the smoke and the sparks flying upward, and something moved in his heart and his spirit, but he knew not what.

Then he turned the boat to the wind and settled down at the tiller with the dog beside him, and put himself upon the sea.